Praise for Diane Kelly's
DEATH, TAXES, AND A FRENCH MANICURE

"*Death, Taxes, and a French Manicure* is a hilarious, sexy, heart-pounding ride that will keep you on the edge of your seat. Tara Holloway is the IRS's answer to Stephanie Plum—smart, sassy, and so much fun. Kelly's debut has definitely earned her a spot on my keeper shelf!"
    —Gemma Halliday, National Readers Choice Award Winner
                            and three-time Rita nominee

"The subject of taxation usually makes people cry, but prepare to laugh your assets off with Diane Kelly's hilarious debut *Death, Taxes, and a French Manicure*."
                            —Jana DeLeon

"Quirky, sexy, and downright fabulous. Zany characters you can't help but love, and a plot that will knock your socks off. This is the most fun I've had reading in forever!"   —Christie Craig, award-winning author of the
                            Hotter In Texas series

"Tara Holloway is Gin Bombay's BFF, or would be if they knew each other. Kelly's novel is smart, sexy and funny enough to make little girls want to be IRS agents when they grow up!"   —Leslie Langtry, author of the
                            Bombay Assassins mystery series

"With a quirky cast of characters, snappy dialogue, and a Bernie Madoff–style pyramid scheme—hunting down tax cheats has never added up to so much fun!"
                            —Robin Kaye, award-winning author of
                            The Domestic Gods series

Death, Taxes, *and a French Manicure*

DIANE KELLY

St. Martin's Paperbacks

This is a work of fiction. All of the characters, organizations, and events portrayed in this novel are either products of the author's imagination or are used fictitiously.

DEATH, TAXES, AND A FRENCH MANICURE

Copyright © 2011 by Diane Kelly.
Excerpt from *Death, Taxes, and a Skinny No-Whip Latte* copyright © 2011 by Diane Kelly.

For information address St. Martin's Press, 175 Fifth Avenue, New York, NY 10010.

ISBN: 978-0-312-55126-1

Printed in the United States of America

St. Martin's Paperbacks edition / November 2011

St. Martin's Paperbacks are published by St. Martin's Press, 175 Fifth Avenue, New York, NY 10010.

10 9 8 7 6 5 4 3

To C—who somehow manages to love me, despite me

$\mathscr{A}$cknowledgments

Many people played a role in helping me take a little idea and develop it into my debut novel. I couldn't have done it without them and I'll be forever grateful.

First, to the great people at the IRS. What an intelligent, talented, and driven bunch! Thanks for answering my questions and providing details about the fascinating world of special agents. And thanks for all you do on behalf of honest taxpayers!

To Trinity Blake, Celya Bowers, Angela Cavener, Vannetta Chapman, Michella Chappell, Angela Hicks, and Kennedy Shaw. Your valuable input, never-ending support, and, above all, your friendship have made all the difference. It's a blessing to have you in my life.

To the Arlington Kick-Ass Writers Group: Gay Downs, Urania Fung, Charles McMillen, and Simon Rex-Lear. You truly are kick-ass.

To the wonderful writers who judged my manuscripts in contests: Jerol Anderson, Christie Craig, Cynthia D'Alba, Mary Dickerson, Terri Dulong, Tina Ferraro, Candace Havens, Ellen Henderson, Kristan Higgins, Virginia McCullough, Denise Belinda McDonald, Tara Seplowin, A.Y. Stratton, Jo Vandewall, and Heidi Vanlandingham. I can't thank you enough for your feedback and encouragement. You helped me believe in my work and myself. What an incredible gift! It would be impossible to fully pay you back, but I'll do my best to pay it forward.

To the many members of Romance Writers of America who've shared their talents and wisdom over the years. It's a privilege to be part of such a professional, supportive organization.

To my wonderful team at St. Martin's Paperbacks. To my very smart and always upbeat editor, Holly Blanck. Working with you has been an absolute pleasure! Thanks to Danielle Fiorella for designing such a perfect and irresistible cover! To Eileen Rothschild for her efforts in marketing my books. I appreciate your hard work! And to everyone else who had a hand in bringing my books to readers, thank you!

And lastly, to my readers. I hope this book brings laughter to your day. I wrote this for you.

CHAPTER ONE

*S*ome People Just Need Shooting

When I was nine, I formed a Silly Putty pecker for my Ken doll, knowing he'd have no chance of fulfilling Barbie's needs given the permanent state of erectile dysfunction with which the toy designers at Mattel had cursed him. I knew a little more about sex than most girls, what with growing up in the country and all. The first time I saw our neighbor's Black Angus bull mount an unsuspecting heifer, my two older brothers explained it all to me.

"He's getting him some," they'd said.

"Some what?" I'd asked.

"Nooky."

We watched through the barbed-wire fence until the strange ordeal was over. Frankly, the process looked somewhat uncomfortable for the cow, who continued to chew her cud throughout the entire encounter. But when the bull dismounted, nuzzled her chin, and wandered away, I swore

I saw a smile on that cow's face and a look of quiet contentment in her eyes. She was in love.

I'd been in search of that same feeling for myself ever since.

My partner and I had spent the afternoon huddled at a cluttered desk in the back office of an auto parts store perusing the owner's financial records, searching for evidence of tax fraud. Yeah, you got me. I work for the IRS. Not exactly the kind of career that makes a person popular at cocktail parties. But those brave enough to get to know me learn I'm actually a nice person, fun even, and they have nothing to fear. I have better things to do than nickel-and-dime taxpayers whose worst crime was inflating the value of the Glen Campbell albums they donated to Goodwill.

"I'll be right back, Tara." My partner smoothed the front of his starched white button-down as he stood from the folding chair. Eddie Bardin was tall, lean, and African-American, but having been raised in the upper-middle-class, predominately white Dallas suburbs, he had a hard time connecting to his roots. He'd had nothing to overcome, unless you counted his affinity for Phil Collins's music, Heineken beer, and khaki chinos, tastes that he had yet to conquer. Eddie was more L.L. Bean than LL Cool J.

I nodded to Eddie and tucked an errant strand of my chestnut hair behind my ear. Turning back to the spreadsheet in front of me, I flicked aside the greasy burger and onion ring wrappers the store's owner, Jack Battaglia, had left on the desk after lunch. I couldn't make heads or tails out of the numbers on the page. Battaglia didn't know jack about keeping books and, judging from his puny salaries account, he'd been too cheap to hire a professional.

A few seconds after Eddie left the room, the door to the office banged open. Battaglia loomed in the doorway, his husky body filling the narrow space. He wore a look of purpose and his store's trademark bright green jumpsuit, the cheerful color at odds with the open box cutter clutched in his furry-knuckled fist.

"Hey!" Instinctively, I leaped from my seat, the metal chair falling over behind me and clanging to the floor.

Battaglia lunged at me. My heart whirled in my chest. There was no time to pull my gun. The best I could do was throw out my right arm to deflect his attempt to plunge the blade into my jugular. The sharp blade slid across my forearm, just above my wrist, but with so much adrenaline rocketing through my system, I felt no immediate pain. If not for the blood seeping through the sleeve of my navy nylon raid jacket, I wouldn't have even known I'd been cut. Underneath was my favorite pink silk blouse, a coup of a find on the clearance rack at Neiman Marcus Last Call, now sliced open, the blood-soaked material gaping to reveal a short but deep gash.

My jaw clamped tighter than a chastity belt on a pubescent princess. This jerk was going down.

My block had knocked him to the side. Taking advantage of our relative positioning, I threw a roundhouse kick to Battaglia's stomach, my steel-toed cherry-red Dr. Martens sinking into his soft paunch. The shoes were the perfect combination of utility and style, another great find at a two-for-one sale at the Galleria.

The kick didn't take the beer-bellied bastard out of commission, but at least it sent him backward a few feet, putting a little more distance between us. A look of surprise flashed across Battaglia's face as he stumbled backward. He clearly hadn't expected a skinny, five-foot-two-inch bookish woman to put up such a fierce fight.

Neener-neener.

He regained his footing just as I yanked my Glock from my hip holster. I pointed the gun at his face, a couple drops of blood running down my arm and dropping to the scuffed gray tile floor. "Put the box cutter down."

He stiffened, his face turning purple with fury. "Shit. IRS agents carry guns now?"

Although people were familiar with tax auditors, the concept of a special agent—a tax cop—eluded most. But we'd been busting tax cheats for decades. Heck, when no other law enforcement agency could get a charge to stick, we were the ones to finally bring down Al Capone. And if we could nab a tough guy like Capone, this pudgy twerp didn't stand a chance.

By our best estimate, Battaglia had cheated the federal government and honest Americans out of at least eighty grand and didn't seem too happy when Eddie and I'd shown up to collect. Now, with my partner on a potty break, Battaglia was treating me like I was a shrimp and he was a chef at Benihana.

The madman sneered at me, revealing teeth yellowed by age and excessive soda consumption. He waved the blade in the air. "If you shoot me, you better shoot to kill. 'Cause if you don't, I'm gonna carve you like a pumpkin."

My gunmetal-gray-blue eyes bored into Battaglia's. "Daddy had a strict rule about firearms. Anything we killed we had to eat. No amount of barbecue sauce would make a hairy guy like you palatable."

He raised the box cutter higher. Now that just burned me up. He didn't think I'd do it. He was wrong. Still, I'd only shoot as a last resort. Not because I was some kind of bleeding heart. There was just too much paperwork involved. Besides, gunplay was hell on a manicure and I'd just had my fingers freshly French-tipped yesterday.

Since threats hadn't worked, I decided to try persuasion.

"Look. If I shoot you, I'll have to fill out a form. I hate filling out forms."

He snorted and rolled his eyes. "You hate filling out forms and you took a job with the IRS? What are you, some kind of idiot?"

So much for my powers of persuasion. Now I was beyond burned up. Now I was hot and bothered. "Drop the box cutter, you sorry son of a bitch."

There I went again, exposing my country roots. Growing up in the rural east Texas town of Nacogdoches, I was taught how to curse a blue streak by my brothers. But now I was a sophisticated city girl living in Dallas, a member of the Junior League, and I needed to act like it. Problem was, this jerk was making it hard to remember my manners.

Battaglia lunged again, a green blubbery blur coming right at me. I ducked aside just in time to avoid being slashed again and hollered for my partner. Eddie appeared in the doorway, spotted the box cutter, and took a running leap onto Battaglia's back. Battaglia outweighed Eddie by a good hundred pounds. He managed to stay on his feet, but with Eddie riding him his focus shifted from slicing me to shreds to shedding the tall guy playing horsey with him. It was just the opportunity I needed. I took aim.

Blam!

The bullet hit the blade of the box cutter, sending it flying out of Battaglia's hand. Battaglia let out a throat-searing scream, barely audible over the ringing in my ears from the gun blast. Eddie screamed too, but I wouldn't embarrass him later by pointing it out. Eddie slid off the man's back and I slid my gun back into the holster. A foot hooked behind the ankles, an elbow jammed into the solar plexus, and the guy fell on his butt with a *fwump*. Ta-da!

Eddie yanked Battaglia's arms behind him and slapped cuffs onto his wrists. *Click-click*. After rolling Battaglia onto his side, he stood over him, his gun pointed at Battaglia's head.

I took a deep, calming breath. With Battaglia now immobilized, the adrenaline waned and the hurt kicked in full force. *Yee-ow!* The cut pulsed with a raw, prickly pain. I gritted my teeth and checked my manicure. My index fingernail was chipped. Damn. Should've killed the asshole when I had the chance.

Eddie must've seen me wince, because he trotted back to the tiny bathroom across the hall and returned with a stack of white paper towels from the dispenser, pressing them firmly to my forearm. A few seconds later, he lifted the towels and peeked under them. "Looks like you'll live. Besides, experiences like this build character."

As if. "Right."

Sure, Eddie talked tough, but I'd seen his face when he noticed the blood on my arm, that flash of alarm and concern. He wasn't fooling me.

Eddie jerked his head at Battaglia. "You want the honors?"

"Hell, yeah." I reached into the pocket of my raid jacket and pulled out the black wallet that held my creds. I finagled a laminated card out of the wallet—my rookie cheat sheet. Stepping directly in front of Battaglia, I read from it, making a conscious effort to control my natural Southern twang. "You have the right to remain silent."

Battaglia glared up at me from the floor. "Screw you, bitch."

"I said you have the right to remain *silent*." I waved the card at him. "Nowhere on here does it say you have the right to be an obnoxious dipshit."

Not only are steel-toed shoes great for kicking, they also serve as effective gag devices. When Battaglia opened his foul mouth again, I shoved the toe of my shoe into it. The Treasury's special agent manual didn't exactly recommend this technique as standard operating procedure, but when you're in the field sometimes you have to improvise. Battaglia struggled on the floor, gagging and whipping his head from side to side in a futile attempt to dislodge the shoe wedged between his lips. I rattled off the remaining Miranda warnings, slid the card back into the wallet, and removed my shoe from Battaglia's mouth.

"Let's get him out of here." Eddie jerked the man to his feet and pushed him out the door of his office and onto the sales floor of the auto parts store. I followed, stopping briefly to wipe the saliva from the toe of my shoe with a chamois displayed at the end of aisle three. Eddie pushed Battaglia forward, his gun shoved into the man's right kidney.

We squeezed past a teenage boy wearing saggy jeans, a Nickelback concert T-shirt, and a metal hoop through his left eyebrow. He turned to us and held up a package. "This the right spark plug for a '72 El Camino?"

"Nah, kid," Battaglia said as Eddie forced him past. "You want the one on the top shelf."

A bewildered female clerk looked on as I called the U.S. Marshal's office from my cell phone and Eddie kept a gun trained on her boss, sitting against the front wall like a naughty schoolboy. After I finished the call, I stole a look under the paper towels to see if the cut on my arm had stopped bleeding. Almost.

When the marshals arrived, Eddie gave them the rundown. One of the men eyed me with something akin to hero worship. "You shot a box cutter out of his hand? Really?"

"Yep." I forced a smile. True, I was a great shot. But what wasn't great was that I'd occasion to prove it. Just because we special agents were trained to handle weapons didn't mean we could use them willy-nilly. Any use of force deemed excessive or unnecessary could lead to dire consequences. Reprimands. Desk jobs. Dismissal.

After the marshals hauled Battaglia away, Eddie gathered up the store's records, stuffed them into two cardboard boxes we found in the storeroom, and carried them out to my BMW. He dropped the boxes into the trunk and slammed it closed.

I put a hand on Eddie's arm. "Eddie?"

My partner glanced down at my hand, then up at me. My concerns must have been written on my face because Eddie said, "You had to use your gun, Tara. There's no way we could've wrestled the weapon out of Battaglia's hand. Not with the way he was carrying on."

"Really?"

He nodded. "Really."

I released my grip on his arm. "Thanks."

"Anytime."

It was comforting to know Eddie was on my side, sure, but his words failed to totally reassure me.

Eddie and I climbed into my car. From my purse I retrieved my sunglasses, a stylish tortoiseshell pair with silver-plated scrollwork earpieces, Brighton knockoffs. I slid them on, glancing over at Eddie. "Want to go topless?"

"Sure. We could use the fresh air." He pushed up the sleeves on his raid jacket. "Besides, I gotta work on my tan."

"Yeah, right." The guy was already the color of hot chocolate and, when he wasn't being a smart-ass, could be just as sweet.

I pushed the button to lower the Beamer's black vinyl top. The motor whirred as the top folded back, letting in the already warm early March air. In north Texas, spring starts around Valentine's Day and wraps up by Easter. Then we have eight months of summer, maybe a month each of fall and winter, and head right back into warmer weather. Not that I was complaining. The warm weather gave me plenty of opportunity to drive with the top down on my convertible Electric Red 325Ci.

On a government salary, I'd never be able to afford one of these babies brand-new. This particular car had been seized by the Treasury Department to satisfy delinquent taxes owed by some deadbeat who thought the feds wouldn't catch up with him. Surprise! His loss was my gain. I'd bought the car for a song last month when the government auctioned it off.

Eddie glanced over at me, our little moment now over, his smart-ass side back in business. "Who would have gotten this cherry car if Battaglia had managed to kill you today?"

"Shut up, Eddie."

"I'm just asking. Any chance your partner is mentioned in your will?" He cocked his head and flashed a toothy, hopeful smile.

My grip involuntarily tightened on the steering wheel. "What part of 'shut up' did you not understand?"

I knew Eddie was only trying to make light of the situation in his own goofy way, but the truth was Battaglia could have put an end to our lives today.

And it scared the hell out of me.

Sure, I could pull off the tough-chick routine, but when it really came down to it I enjoyed being alive and preferred to stay that way. A little danger kept the blood pumping, but getting killed was something I could live without. Especially when everything in my closet was so last season, nothing I wanted to be buried and spend eternity in.

I reached down to turn on the stereo, tuned it to my favorite country station, and cranked up the volume to drown out that voice in my head telling me that maybe I should prepare a will, just in case I wasn't so lucky next

time. The voice was also warning me I'd be in big trouble
once I got back to the office. I revved the engine, exited
the parking lot, and headed back to headquarters.

When my boss found out I'd fired my gun, she'd kick my
ass. But what can I say? Some people just need shooting.

CHAPTER TWO

A Case of
My Own

Viola, the longtime secretary for Criminal Investigations, shook her gray curls and reached across her cheap metal desk to take the form from me. She glanced at the paper, her brow furrowing when she noted the caption. "A firearm discharge?"

"Sorry. Believe me, I hate paperwork as much as you do."

Viola shot me a skeptical look over the top of her bifocals.

Treasury Department procedures require special agents to file a report any time they discharge a firearm. My superiors would have to investigate the incident, make sure the shooting was justified. I wasn't looking forward to my interrogation. There was no telling how things would turn out when the director of field operations and internal affairs reviewed the facts. My instinctive reactions, decisions made in the heat of the moment and driven by fear and adrenaline, would be examined under a microscope, second-guessed, analyzed to death. Hell, the nightly news ran stories all the time about cops raked over the coals for using their Tasers or shooting criminals who'd resisted arrest or pulled a weapon. Some of the officers faced criminal charges themselves for the shootings. If their defense attorneys could whip out a loaded handgun and aim it at the jurors, no doubt fewer cops would be indicted. Maybe I should bring a box cutter to my hearing, rush at the men who'd decide my fate, give them a small taste of what I'd just gone through. Then again, I'd never get a box cutter through building security. Only officially issued weapons were allowed inside.

Viola stamped the form with today's date, added it to a stack of documents to be copied and routed, and turned her eyes back on me. "So? What happened?"

Eddie perched on the edge of Viola's desk, his long legs stretching all the way to the floor. He turned to Viola. "The dude who owned the store came at her with a box cutter. Tara had no choice but to shoot."

This time Viola shot Eddie her skeptical look.

"It's true." I removed my raid jacket and pulled back the sleeve on my blouse to show Viola the oozing two-inch gash on my forearm, a bloody souvenir from the bust. "The guy was freaked, but he walked away without a scratch." Which was more than I could say for myself. I was both scratched and freaked. But I was trying hard to hide the latter. In my line of work, any sign of wimpiness put you on the fast track to a desk job. No way could I sit behind a desk all day. I'd ridden a desk for the past four years at a stuffy downtown accounting firm and it had just about done me in.

Working at Martin and McGee had been excruciating. Day after day crunching numbers in a cramped cubicle surrounded by other accountants crunching numbers in their cramped cubicles, the only sound the *clickety-click* of dozens of drones inputting information into spread-sheets and tax forms. By the end of the day, my ass would be numb from sitting for ten hours straight. If I'd stayed at that mind-numbing, ass-numbing job a day longer, the cleaning crew would have found me dead at my desk from a self-inflicted pencil shoved through my eye.

Viola took hold of my wrist and inspected the cut, her maternal instincts overcoming her usual I-don't-get-paid-enough-to-put-up-with-this-crap demeanor. "You better get that looked at."

"I will." I hoped I wouldn't need a tetanus shot. I had enough holes in my arm for the moment.

Eddie and I headed out of Viola's office and down the hall, cutting out of work early. One bust was enough for one day. Besides, it was Friday and I had plans to attend a black-tie charity event at the Dallas Arboretum tonight. I'd need a little extra time to stop by the nail salon to have my manicure repaired.

Eddie slung his jacket over his arm as we walked down the narrow hallway, which glowed a faint, eerie green from the shiny industrial paint and fluorescent lighting. "I loved the way you shut that guy up today."

"A lady like me doesn't appreciate foul language."

He snickered. "Lady?"

I shot him a shut-up glare. "You're lucky my arm's hurt or I'd punch you right about now."

Eddie eyed me intently, the humor now gone from his face. "What is it with you, girl? I've been a special agent for eight years and haven't once had to fire my gun."

I shrugged. "Just lucky, I guess." I didn't tell Eddie what I was really thinking. That scumbags like Battaglia didn't take a petite woman like me seriously. If the only way I could earn respect was by drawing my gun, what future did I have in this job?

Probably none.

I'd come to work at the Dallas IRS office just six weeks ago after completing extensive training at the Federal Law Enforcement facility in Glynco, Georgia, where I'd earned the distinction of being the best marksman in the group of trainees. Although the hard-core agents who trained us seemed surprised to see a woman hit every paper target square in the heart, I knew I'd shine on the firing course. Having a gun nut for a father and two brothers who lived for deer season, I'd learned how to handle a gun before I was fully potty trained. Daddy'd bought me my first Daisy BB gun as a present for my third birthday. Every day I'd practice shooting empty root beer cans off the old picnic table in our backyard.

When I was a little older, my father took me to the skeet range, where I quickly learned to hit a moving target. With a sharp eye and a fast finger, I rarely missed, though I'd limited my shots to nonliving targets. I'd never seen the sport in hunting, especially when timed feeders and deer blinds were involved, and I sure as heck wasn't going to douse myself with animal urine to mask my scent. Chanel No. 5 was more my style, thank you very much. The only hunting I did was bargain hunting.

Eddie and I tiptoed as we neared the open office door of our boss, Lu Lobozinski, aka "the Lobo." We heard the Lobo speaking with Ross O'Donnell, an attorney from the Justice Department who represented the Treasury on a regular basis. We ducked and darted past, hoping we wouldn't be noticed sneaking out early.

"Tara!" barked Lu's raspy, two-packs-a-day voice. "Get your butt back here."

So much for sneaking. I sighed and performed a quick about-face.

Eddie followed me back down the hall, putting his thumbs in his ears and wiggling his fingers at me. "Tara's in trouble, Tara's in trouble."

I rolled my eyes at him. "Grow up, would ya?"

I stuck my head in the door and eyed the pear-shaped older woman, sitting in her cushy high-back leather chair behind her expansive, paper-covered desk. Lu had been with the IRS since the late sixties and appeared to have time-traveled from that decade. Today she sported a lime-green polyester pantsuit with shiny black vinyl go-go boots. The box of hair color may have said "strawberry blond," but the Lobo's eight-inch beehive was really more pink than red, like a cotton-candy wig. Take forty years and forty pounds off her and she could star in an Austin Powers movie.

When I'd interviewed for a special agent position several months ago, Lu had leaned forward across her desk, her eyes—fringed with sixties-style false eyelashes—narrowed and fixed on mine. "I didn't get to be director of criminal investigations because I've got a vagina, and I didn't sleep my way to the top."

"I believe you." What man would have the balls to approach such a tough broad? Besides, the polyester pantsuits did nothing for her sex appeal.

She'd pointed her lit cigarette at me, her smoking a blatant violation of office policy but one nobody apparently dared to challenge. "I'm director because me and my people have collected over ninety-seven million dollars in past-due taxes for this agency."

"Impressive."

She took a deep drag on her cigarette and blew the smoke out through her nose. "Don't suck up."

"Yes, ma'am."

She flicked ashes into a Styrofoam cup containing the dregs of her morning coffee. "As soon as I reach a hundred mil, I'm retiring."

My gaze locked on hers through the swirling smoke. "Hire me and before you know it you'll be sitting around in your bathrobe watching soap operas and sucking down bonbons."

She stared at me for a few seconds, her cigarette poised just inches from her lips. I didn't look away. And I didn't blink.

She took another drag on her cigarette, then shot a poof of smoke out the side of her mouth. "You're hired."

"Hot damn."

But that was then and this is now, and now I was in the Lobo's office trying to defend myself while Eddie and Ross looked on. "I'm sorry, ma'am, but there was nothing else I could do."

The Lobo frowned, her thin, drawn-on brows pulled together in a single line. "What the hell're you talking about, Holloway?"

So she didn't know I'd fired my gun. *Yet.* "Um . . . nothing?"

Lu held out a business card between two fingers that might be wrinkled if they weren't so meaty. She waved it impatiently, cigarette ashes dropping onto her desk. I stepped forward and took the card from her, careful to avoid the lit cigarette. The card read "Christina Marquez, Drug Enforcement Agency."

"Who's this?"

"A rookie at the DEA. Some granny reported that an ice-cream man named Joe Cullen sold her fourteen-year-old grandson a joint right along with his Fudgsicle. You and Marquez are going to put the ice-cream man out of business and get our piece of the pie."

Ironically, the IRS doesn't discriminate against dirty money, demanding its share of the profits whether earned legally or not. Since most illegal income goes unreported, the Treasury's special agents are often pulled into other agencies' investigations to locate and seize the government's share of the revenue.

Lu flicked ashes into an orange plastic ashtray. "I ran a check on Cullen. An electronics store filed a cash transaction report on him last year. He bought thirteen grand in stereo and television equipment with cash, but he's only reported fifteen thousand in income on his tax returns for the past few years."

Those numbers didn't add up. The guy definitely had some "splainin" to do.

I turned to Ross, a squat guy in his early thirties wearing a basic brown suit, his skin pale from long hours spent in windowless courtrooms, his dark hair beginning to give way to male-pattern baldness. Ross was blessed with the unflappable demeanor of Mr. Rogers, his ability to remain calm under pressure an obvious asset in a field where constant conflict was the name of the game.

"Do we have a search warrant?"

Ross shook his head. "No go. Judge Trumbull said she needs more than the statement of some quote-unquote snot-nosed bed wetter before she'll let y'all go barging into the guy's home and ransack his panty drawer."

Appointed by John F. Kennedy during the heyday of the civil rights movement, Magistrate Judge Alice Trumbull had been on the bench as long as the Lobo'd been with the Treasury. The two had a long history of butting beehived heads. How a liberal judge like Trumbull had survived in the tight-assed, conservative political climate of Dallas was beyond me.

The Lobo stubbed out her cigarette and set the ashtray aside. "You'll need to go undercover, Tara, get some more evidence on this guy before we can proceed."

Eddie, who'd been eavesdropping outside the door, stepped into the Lobo's office. "You're cutting our baby girl loose on her own?"

At twenty-seven I was hardly a baby, though I was the newest, youngest, and smallest special agent in the office.

Lu leaned back in her padded chair and put her hands behind her head. "This guy's small-time stuff, Eddie. Too pissant for any of our experienced agents to bother with."

But not too pissant for me, the newbie. I probably should've been insulted by the exchange, but I was too excited to finally have my own case to care. "Woo-hoo!" I threw my fists in the air. Big mistake. The pain in my arm kicked back in with a vengeance.

Lu shot me her cut-the-crap look. "Give Marquez a call."

"Will do. See ya', Ross."

I slipped the business card into my wallet and Eddie and I stepped back out into the hall.

"I remember my first solo case," Eddie said, holding the glass door open for me as we headed out of the building. "Busted a middle-aged mom who volunteered to serve as treasurer for the PTA at her kid's school. Stole twenty grand before they caught on to her."

"Shoot, that's low. What did she do with the money?"

"Lotto scratch-offs. The irony is she actually won, doubled the money. The school used the extra funds for asbestos removal and a field trip to the planetarium."

We rounded the building, making our way into the adjacent parking lot.

"Any big plans for the weekend?" I asked Eddie.

"Just the usual. Soccer games and birthday parties." Eddie and his wife, Sandra, had twin six-year-old girls who were not only demons on the soccer field but also very popular judging from the number of birthday parties they were invited to. "I'm going broke buying Barbie dolls for all those little girls."

"Remind me to buy stock in Toys 'R' Us."

Eddie and I reached our cars, parked side by side in our usual spots at the far end of the lot. "See ya."

Eddie gave me a two-finger salute and climbed into his

maroon minivan, ready to return to his role as husband and father.

I lowered the top on my Beamer, slid my sunglasses on, and left the lot. Carrie Underwood blared from my speakers as I drove to a minor emergency clinic a few blocks from the office. I parked in the back lot so my precious car wouldn't be dinged by the doors of a lesser vehicle. Two spots down sat a gleaming blue Dodge Viper, pimped out with shiny spinner hubcaps and a personalized license plate that read DR AJAY. I walked around to the front of the building and opened the door.

The redheaded receptionist glanced up as I came in, and had a clipboard ready for me by the time I reached the counter. Her nametag said KELSEY and her yawn said her day had been a long one. "What's your medical issue?"

I pulled back my sleeve for the second time to show off my battle wound.

Kelsey's freckled nose scrunched. "Ouch. What happened?"

I took the clipboard from her. "I was attacked by a nut with a box cutter. Had to shoot it out of his hand." Okay, so that last part was bragging. But not many people had my gun skills and I was proud of them.

She looked me up and down, taking in my conservative business attire and diminutive stature, clearly dubious. "You a police officer?"

"IRS. Special agent." When she still looked confused, I added, "Tax cop."

"Oh." She handed me a pen. "Sounds dangerous."

I shrugged. "Your job seems scarier to me. You could be exposed to the Ebola virus or flesh-eating bacteria."

"We don't see too much of those around here. The worst thing I've seen was a guy who came in here with a light bulb stuck up his—"

"Stop!" I held up a palm. "I'm getting a visual."

Kelsey shuddered. "You're right. It's too horrifying to talk about." She gestured toward a row of chairs. "Take a seat. Dr. Maju will be with you shortly."

I sat in the closest chair and filled out the forms. I checked the boxes to indicate no, I'd never suffered from asthma, heart palpitations, hemorrhoids, or an STD, and no, I wasn't pregnant. Can't get pregnant when you're not getting any.

Sigh.

When I'd completed the forms, I returned to the counter. Dr. Ajay Maju walked up behind Kelsey and placed a file on her desk. Dr. Maju was Indian, on the short side, with shaggy-stylish shiny black hair and thick brows. His white lab coat hung open to reveal fashionably torn blue jeans and a green Abercrombie & Fitch T-shirt. Dr. Maju appeared to be only a year or two out of medical school, not much older than me. But hopefully he'd be competent enough to handle my minor medical problem. He was attractive in an oddly boyish, slightly exotic kind of way.

"You were slashed with a box cutter?" Despite his all-American attire, his staccato words were tinged with a Hindi accent. The guy was a poster child for culture clash.

"Yep." I stuck out my arm.

Dr. Maju held my wrist and took a quick peek, then waved for me to follow him.

"Here's Ms. Holloway's file." Kelsey handed the doctor a thin manila folder as he left the reception area.

Once we were in the examination room, I hopped onto the table, the stiff white paper crinkling under me. The doctor set my file on the counter. He grabbed a stethoscope and a blood pressure monitor from a drawer and checked my pulse and blood pressure. When he was done, he pulled a tiny black flashlight out of the pocket of his lab coat and shined it in my right eye.

I tried not to blink. "What's that for?"

"Mostly just to irritate my patients." He shined the light in my other eye and called for a nurse.

The doc cleaned my wound with antiseptic, the acrid smell burning my nostrils. Once the blood was gone, he inspected the cut more closely. "You're going to need a few stitches."

Shoot. "Will I need a tetanus shot, too?"

Dr. Maju consulted my computer file. "No. You are good for another three years."

Thank heaven for small favors.

I turned my head away and contemplated the illustrated breast exam poster on the side wall, my eyes focused on the cartoon nipple while Dr. Maju injected a local anesthetic, sewed me up, then affixed a square bandage over the wound. When he finished, he turned my inner arm upward, thumped on a vein with his index finger, and drew some blood. He handed his nurse the vial. "Full workup." He pressed a cotton ball to the inside of my arm for a couple seconds, fixing it in place with a piece of gauze tape. "In six months we'll need to run the blood tests again."

"Why?"

"To determine if you have contracted a horrible disease that will cause you a long and agonizing death."

I rolled my sleeve back down. "You might want to work on your bedside manner."

Dr. Maju shrugged. "This is not the Mayo Clinic. You get what you pay for."

On my way home, I stopped by the nail salon. Rather than simply repair the damage Battaglia had caused, I opted for a complete mani-pedi instead. After what I'd been through today, I'd earned it. Besides, the nail technician's new bottle of sparkling candy-apple polish would go perfect with the dress I planned to wear that night.

While the tech massaged my feet—*aaaah*—I read

through the business pages of the *Dallas Morning News*. As one of the government's financial experts, I was expected to stay on top of developments in the business world, especially those in my region. Not much in the paper today. Two area wineries had joined forces in hopes of gaining market share. A local charter bus company had filed for Chapter 11 bankruptcy. First Dallas Bank had been forced to revise and reissue its financial statements after banking regulators discovered its reserves had been significantly overstated. Of course, the bank's management blamed its outside auditors for failing to discover the "inadvertent error." Ever since the Enron debacle brought down not only the energy company but also its CPA firm, accountants had become convenient scapegoats for unscrupulous corporate officers who intentionally misstated their financials.

The report could indicate the management of First Dallas Bank played fast and loose with the law. Then again, it could mean nothing. Accounting wasn't nearly as simple and straightforward as it might seem. Heck, there were half a dozen acceptable methods for computing depreciation and valuing inventory. Honest mistakes could easily go unnoticed. At this point, however, any problems fell under the purview of the Office of the Comptroller of the Currency. Reserves didn't affect taxable income. In other words, not the Treasury Department's problem.

I moved on to the comics.

A half hour and fifty dollars later, I emerged from the salon with twenty freshly French-tipped nails and a fresh attitude. Tara Holloway wasn't about to let the jackasses—or the Jack Battaglias—of the world get her down.

CHAPTER THREE

Hottie in the Hothouse

Long ago, my mother's grandparents had owned land in east Texas near the site of Spindletop, the most famous oil strike in Texas history. My great-grandparents made a fortune when they sold their land to oil speculators, and they'd developed a taste for things opulent and luxurious. I'd inherited their taste but none of the money, all of which was lost during the subsequent 1929 stock market crash. Go figure.

My female ancestors learned to fake it, living a Dom Pérignon champagne lifestyle on a Lone Star beer budget. Mom taught me everything she knew about living large on a shoestring. I'd adopted her strategies. My town house sat just north of downtown, in a trendy neighborhood of young professionals known as Uptown. I'd snatched the place for a song during the recent real estate crash, purchasing it in a short sale from a couple who'd decided the

suburbs would be a better place to raise the child they were
expecting.

The living and dining rooms of my brown brick home
were adorned with tastefully carved cherrywood and tap-
estry furniture, a top-of-the-line Ethan Allen ensemble I'd
scored at a huge secondhand discount via an estate sale.
Not that I'd ever reveal that dirty little secret to anyone.

After tossing my purse and briefcase on the couch, I
checked on Henry the Eighth and Anne Boleyn. Henry was
an enormous, furry cat, part Maine coon, with a haughty
attitude, assuming air, and brown hair just a shade darker
than my own. He lay atop the massive armoire that housed
my television and stereo, his furry paws curled over the
front edge, passing judgment on the world from his high
post. I gave him a quick pat on the head, which he tolerated
but clearly did not appreciate. Snob.

"Anna Banana," I called. "Where's my girl?" Anne was
a thin, creamy-white, nervous cat. But at least she wouldn't
have to worry about providing a male heir for Henry. Both
had been fixed just after I'd adopted them from the shelter.
Anne crawled out from her hiding place under the couch
and ran over to me. I scooped her up and cradled her in my
arms, where she purred affectionately.

"Want to help me get ready?" I asked Anne as I carried
her up the stairs to my bedroom.

She responded with a meow.

Unlike my elegant first floor, the private upstairs rooms
of my town house contained an eclectic but comfortable
mix of garage-sale bargains and hand-me-down pieces
from my parents and older brothers.

I walked into my bedroom and set the cat down on my
rumpled bed. She curled up on the faded patchwork quilt
and napped as I stripped out of my work clothes, showered, shaved, and shampooed. Once I'd dried and styled
my hair and reapplied my makeup, I slipped into my beau-

tiful gown. The dress was red, strapless, and sequined, with
a slit running up to my lower thigh, two inches shy of slutty.

I admired myself in the mirror. I looked feminine.
Glamorous. Sexy.

Nailed it.

I climbed into my car, switching my radio from the country station to a classical setting and mentally switching
from Tara Holloway, butt-kicking tax cop, to Tara Holloway, sophisticated city girl. Fifteen minutes later, I pulled
to the curb in front of a building downtown that housed a
dozen trendy loft apartments. Typing with my red-tipped
thumbs, I texted my best friend, Alicia Shenkman, letting
her know I'd arrived.

In a few moments, Alicia stepped outside, looking su-
premely chic, as usual. Her platinum-blond bob ended in
asymmetrical points on either side of her face, one edge
stopping midway down her left cheek, the other tapering
to an end along her right jawline—like one of those cubist
Picasso paintings except less twisted. Though the look bor-
dered on severe, it went well with her pointy facial features
and her even sharper mind and wit. She wore a fitted black
satin evening gown with three thick straps that ran up from
the bust and over one shoulder, her only jewelry a tiny pair
of onyx earrings.

Her doorman opened the passenger door of my car.
Alicia thanked him and slid into the seat.

"You look fabulous," I told her.

"Thanks," she said, looking me over. "So do you. Love
the nails."

I splayed my glittery fingers across the steering wheel.
"They're not too much?"

Alicia slid me a knowing look. "If they weren't too
much, Tara, they wouldn't be *you*."

She knew me well. As well she should. We'd been best

friends for over eight years. We'd met at the University of
Texas, in our Accounting 101 class. We'd been assigned by
the professor to work with four other students on a group
project. Two minutes into our first team meeting, it was
clear Alicia and I would be both the brains and the work-
horses of the operation. The other students rode our ambi-
tious coattails to an easy A.

Alicia and I moved in together the next semester, renting
a teeny two-bedroom apartment within walking distance
of the university. After completing our studies, we both
graduated with honors and had our pick of job offers.
Martin and McGee, one of the larger regional CPA firms,
had offered us both a lucrative compensation package for
positions in their Dallas office. We accepted and moved to
a much larger, much nicer apartment in the yuppie Dallas
enclave known as the Village.

A couple years later, our manager at Martin and McGee
assigned the two of us to work on a consulting project for
one of the big downtown law firms. Soon thereafter, I
walked into the law firm's copy room and discovered Alicia detained in the arms of a junior associate. She assured
me there was no need for a writ of habeas corpus. Daniel
Blowitz had stolen Alicia's heart and, soon thereafter,
stole my roommate. She moved into his pricey downtown
loft, while I bought my priced-for-quick-sale town house
and adopted the cats from the animal shelter for company.
As much as I missed living with Alicia, it had been time
for us to move on to the next phase of our lives. Besides,
the tax deductions on the town house saved me a chunk of
change every year come April fifteenth.

Alicia gestured to the bandage on my wrist, her brow
furrowed in concern. "What happened there?"

"On-the-job injury." I told her all about Jack Battaglia
and the box cutter, how I'd shot the blade out of his hand.

"Thank God you know how to handle a gun." She stared

at me a moment longer, her expression perplexed. "You're either really brave or totally crazy."

"There's a fine line between the two, isn't there?"

"Yes," she said. "And you're straddling it."

"Speaking of straddling things, what's Daniel doing tonight?" I asked.

Alicia sighed. "Working late. He's got a trial that starts next week."

Daniel's absence explained why I hadn't had to twist Alicia's arm to convince her to come with me alone tonight. She and Daniel were joined at the hip, figuratively when not literally. Alicia routinely arranged double dates and had set me up with a series of Daniel's friends and co-workers. Unfortunately, though they'd all been nice enough guys, none had sparked my interest.

I eased away from the curb, made the block, and headed east, to the Dallas Arboretum. Once we'd arrived, a valet helped Alicia and me out of my car. I handed the young man my keys, cringing seconds later when the sound of gears grinding erupted behind me.

The outdoor gardens, which were bright and vibrant in spring and summer, were dead and dull tonight, the flower beds empty, the crape myrtle trees bare of leaves. An enormous temporary greenhouse had been erected on an open lawn area near the bronze spouting toad statues. Ahead of us, men in classic tuxedos and women in cocktail dresses and gowns streamed into the glass structure. I was the only woman not wearing a traditional black dress. I tended to be a bit of a rebel. It was part of my charm.

Alicia and I took our places in line. The evening air was cooling down but still bearable. A murmur of chitchat blended with the sounds of car engines and doors slamming as more guests arrived.

As we neared the door of the greenhouse, I handed Alicia the ticket I'd bought for her. She glanced down, noting the price. "Whoa. You dropped a hundred bucks each on these tickets?"

I nodded. Good thing part of the cost would be tax deductible. I could ill afford the tickets, but I couldn't wait to see the new exhibit and, besides, it was for a good cause—expansion of the children's garden.

Gardening with my mother had been one of the highlights of my childhood. There was something almost spiritual about digging in the dirt together, turning an empty flower bed into a beautiful, colorful display. While my dad and brothers bonded on hunting trips, freezing their asses off huddled together in a deer blind at the crack of dawn, Mom and I had bonded on warm afternoons over petunias, pansies, and composted cow manure. I couldn't drive past a feedlot without the stench reminding me of home.

Alicia and I inched forward and eventually reached the front of the line. A banner stretched over the entryway, welcoming us to "A Sneak Preview of Spring—Sponsored by Wakefield Designs."

The couple in front of me handed their tickets to the attendant and stepped aside.

And that's when I saw him.

The guy taking tickets wore a standard black tux, but rather than the typical black bow tie and cummerbund, his sported gray-and-black stripes. A subtle nonconformity, but one that told me he, too, stretched the rules. He had the same sandy hair and masculine bone structure as Aaron Eckhart, but sans the chin dimple. Though he was broad shouldered, he wasn't tall, only five foot nine or so. But that still gave him seven inches on me. It also meant that, with benefit of heels, I could look him in the eye rather than up his nose. A perfect fit. And speaking of eyes, his were the same shade of green as Texas sagebrush. *Nice.*

Our gazes locked and an instant attraction was almost

visible between us, drawing us to each other like a bee to a flower. I found myself wondering about the size of his stinger.

Giving him a smile, I held out my ticket. He smiled back, revealing straight, white teeth only an adolescence spent in braces could produce.

When he looked down to take my ticket, his eyes ran up from my exposed ankle to where the slit stopped above my knee. Not lecherous, merely the natural response of a man with a healthy libido. And how could he not look when I'd purposely struck a bent-knee pose that would give him a peep of my lower thigh? Still, the heat in his gaze nearly melted my panties.

He gestured to the bandage on my forearm. "Give blood today?" His voice was deep, with a sexy timbre and just a hint of a Southern accent.

"Not intentionally."

"Sounds like there's a story there."

"There is," I said. "And it's not pretty."

His focus shifted to the line of people waiting behind me, then returned to my face. He cocked his head. "Maybe you'll share it with me later?"

Hell, yeah! I thought. But I shrugged, feigning nonchalance. "A glass of wine might loosen my lips." *Two glasses might loosen some other body parts. Three glasses and I'm all yours, buddy.*

His smile became a sly grin as he took Alicia's ticket and handed each of us a program. "I'll look for you at the bar."

We stepped past him into the greenhouse.

Alicia glanced back.

"Is he checking out my ass?" I asked in a whisper.

"No. He's taking someone else's ticket."

Dang.

Consulting the map in the program, Alicia and I strolled

through the winding walkways of the exhibit. The air was moist thanks to the simulated brook flowing throughout the exhibit, the rush of water creating a pleasant auditory backdrop augmented by the soft buzz of standing heaters spaced along the path. We passed brightly colored plants displayed on multiple levels, with yellow daffodils at our feet and flowering vines twisting up wooden trellises towering over us. Further on, colorful orchids and bromeliads in shades of pink, purple, and red bloomed among an assortment of exotic trees and variegated foliage.

After a half hour meandering through the conservatory, I stopped in front of a colorful bulb garden containing fringed flowers in a wide variety of hues. "Aren't these parrot tulips pretty?"

"I don't want to hear any more about tulips," Alicia said, "until I put some cabernet between *my two lips*." She took my arm and all but dragged me to the bar.

The guy from earlier stood nearby. I'd enjoyed the flora, but he made for some pretty hunky fauna. A hottie in the hothouse.

He was engaged in conversation with a fit older man with thick salt-and-pepper hair, close-set dark eyes, and a long, thin nose, giving him a possumlike appearance. A young woman hung on the man's shoulder. The girl was nipped, tucked, and augmented to within an inch of her life. With the two cantaloupes protruding from her tiny black cocktail dress, it was a miracle she didn't topple over in her four-inch strappy black heels. I had nearly a decade lead on her, the man at least three. The girl's hair was frosted blond, her eyes an unnatural turquoise courtesy of colored contacts, her skin the Oompa-Loompa orange of self-tanning cream.

When my sexy ticket taker noticed Alicia and me stepping into line at the bar, he excused himself and joined us. "Enjoying the exhibit?"

"It's beautiful," I said. "I love the parrot tulips. I never realized they came in so many colors."

"Over a hundred varieties." He extended his hand. "I'm Brett Ellington."

I took his hand in mine, surprised to find his skin somewhat rough and callused. Not that I minded a little friction. But his hands felt more like a workingman's hands than I'd expected given that he looked so at ease in his tux. "I'm Tara Holloway." I hiked a thumb at my friend. "That's Alicia."

"Hey," she said.

"Hey," he said back.

We turned to the bartender and placed our orders. A cabernet for Alicia, merlot with a cherry for me. Brett also ordered the merlot. Hmm. I wondered what else we might have in common. Unsatisfied lust, perhaps?

Brett handed the bartender a twenty to cover our drinks, slipping a couple of extra bucks into the tip jar. We took our drinks and stepped aside, finding an open spot near a display of yellow hibiscus.

I sipped my merlot. "Do you work here at the Arboretum?"

"Not exactly. Our firm was hired to do some projects here this spring. I'm a landscape architect for Wakefield Designs."

That explained the calluses.

"Wakefield Designs?" Alicia repeated. "The sponsor?"

He nodded.

"How generous," I said.

"Yeah, not really. Mr. Wakefield knows these events attract a wealthy crowd. He figured tonight would be a chance to drum up business for the firm. I'm supposed to be schmoozing. By chance, do either of you manage a hotel that needs new landscaping? Maybe own a shopping mall or an airport?" He put his wineglass to his mouth.

"Sorry, no," I said. "All I've got is a ten-foot-square patch of grass."

"And a bush," Alicia added, "in dire need of pruning."

Brett choked on his wine, coughing to clear his throat.

I shot my friend a pointed look. "Are you referring to the evergreen shrub in my front yard?"

"Of course." Alicia raised a palm, all sweetness and innocence. "What else would I be talking about?"

Brett watched me, a grin playing about his mouth, amusement in his eyes. Not only was he good-looking and nicely built, but he also had a sense of humor. Maybe I should let him prune my bush. I suspected he'd have just the tool to get the job done.

"Are we keeping you?" I asked.

"No." He waved a hand dismissively. "I'm all schmoozed out. Besides, I've already landed a new client." Brett angled his head discreetly to indicate the couple he'd been speaking to earlier. "That's Stan Shelton, the president of First Dallas Bank."

First Dallas? Wasn't that the bank I'd read about in the paper earlier? I cut my eyes to Shelton. He looked perfectly respectable. Then again, it was hard not to look respectable in a tuxedo.

"Stan and his wife asked me to design the landscaping for a property they acquired on Cedar Creek Lake."

Ever notice how rich people don't buy things? They *acquire* them.

"Sounds great."

"The best part about it," Brett said, "is that they're giving me free rein. They didn't specify the style or anything, just a budget."

"So you get to surprise them?"

"Essentially. Of course, they'll want to approve the plans before we put in anything permanent, but I'll get a lot of creative freedom."

My job offers a lot of creative freedom, too. For instance, when restraining an unruly suspect, I get to decide whether to use a full or half nelson.

Alicia glanced around, waving her cocktail napkin in the general direction of the bulb garden. "I'm going to take another look at those pink things."

I knew she had no interest in the "pink things," she just wanted to give me the chance to hook up with a nice guy. It had been a while.

She wandered away, leaving me and Brett alone. He gestured toward the double doors leading out to a patio, raising an eyebrow in question. I nodded, gladly surrendering to the sweet destiny that brought the two of us to that same spot, on the same night, at the same time.

Brett led me outside onto a flagstone terrace where we spent a few minutes in quiet conversation among the magnolias, enjoying our wine, lingering in the fresh winter chill. When he noticed me shiver, he slipped out of his tux jacket and draped it over my shoulders. The fabric was still warm from his body heat, the collar bearing his crisp, clean deodorant-soap scent. I shrugged deeper into it. *Mmm.*

Brett was just as intoxicating as the merlot. As a gardening buff and a single female, I was impressed not only by his extensive knowledge of trees and plants, but also by the way his well-formed bicep flexed each time he raised his wineglass for a drink. And the way he looked at me made me feel more beautiful than the colorful blooms inside the greenhouse.

"I still haven't heard the story," he said. "How did you 'not intentionally' give blood today?"

I tossed back the remaining wine in my glass, fished out the wine-soaked cherry, and set the empty glass on the tray of a passing waiter. "I had a little run-in with an unco-operative taxpayer today." Okay, so calling the exchange "a little run-in" was an understatement. But that sounded better than telling him a hairy, deranged criminal had tried to send me to the Eternal Revenue Service in the sky. I popped the wine-soaked fruit into my mouth, noticing Brett's gaze follow my fingers to my lips.

I told him about my day, about reviewing the financial records for the auto parts store, Battaglia attacking me with the box cutter, Eddie jumping on the guy's back. I left out the part where I shot the blade out of Battaglia's hand. I wasn't ashamed of my ass-kicking side. It's just that right then, as I stood there in my beautiful sequined dress, with my perfect nails and carefully coiffed hair, I felt soft, sensuous, feminine. That's how I wanted Brett to see me, at least for now. If this went anywhere, there'd be plenty of time to introduce him to my other side later.

As I told Brett the story, his expression morphed from intrigued to shocked. "Does that kind of thing happen often?"

"Thankfully, no."

"I hope the judge throws the book at him."

"Me, too." And I hoped the book was the tax code. All five volumes of it.

He took a sip of his wine. "So a special agent is like an investigator?"

"You got it." My job was to kick ass and take Social Security numbers.

"Been with the IRS long?"

"Only a few weeks." I'd been thrilled to land the job. After years sitting in a cubicle at the accounting firm, I'd grown soft and hadn't been certain I'd make the cut. I'd all but killed myself during my special agent training, losing six pounds and achieving six-pack abs in the process. I'd returned briefly to Martin and McGee to wrap up some projects, clean out my desk, and give two weeks' notice to the managing partner, Scott Klein.

Brett's eyes roamed over me, sizing me up. "So if I don't get my taxes filed on time, would you come after me?"

"Yep." My gaze locked on his for a moment, then I let my eyes roam up and down his body in return. "I might even seize your assets."

His eyes flashed as his pupils dilated. "That could be fun."

A classy guy with a naughty side. I knew right then I had to have him.

"What about you?" I asked. "How long have you worked for Wakefield Designs?"

Brett told me he'd worked for Wakefield for six years, since he'd earned his degree in landscape architecture from Texas A&M, a rival university. "I'd like to see you again," he said.

"I don't know," I teased. "I'm not sure I can date an aggie."

He crossed his arms over his broad chest in mock exasperation. "Should've known better than to ask out a snooty *tea sip*," he said, tossing out the antiquated, but still used, slur for UT students and alum. He shot me a wink and my body temperature soared. He reached into his pocket and pulled out his cell phone, asking for my phone number and programming it into the device as I rattled it off.

Alicia wandered outside then, teetering slightly on her heels. She'd apparently forgone the flowers and instead returned to the bar for another glass of wine or two. As much as I would've liked to stay and talk more with Brett, I could tell Alicia was as bored as I'd been when she'd dragged me to the modern art museum. No sense testing the limits of friendship any further. Besides, it couldn't hurt to leave him wanting more, right?

Brett and I bade each other good-bye, and Alicia and I
headed out.

She glanced back. "He's checking out your ass now."

"And?"

"He's smiling."

CHAPTER FOUR

The Men of My Dreams

When I returned home, I slipped out of my jewelry, dress, and heels, and walked into my bathroom. The white tile floor was covered with cat litter, Henry having kicked most of it out of the box as usual. After sweeping up Henry's mess with a whisk broom, washing my face, and brushing my teeth, I donned my standard not-the-least-bit-sexy sleepwear—old gray gym shorts with an unraveling hem and an oversized burnt-orange T-shirt with the head of a longhorn steer, my college mascot, emblazoned across the front.

My days at UT had been hard work, but they'd also been a blast. I'd shocked my fellow accounting majors by joining the campus chapter of the NRA. While the other students relieved their stress with shots of tequila at local bars, I'd head over to an indoor firing range near campus to take some shots of a different variety. Nothing like squeezing off a few rounds to take the edge off prefinals jitters. I still hit the firing range on a regular basis, partly to keep my aim accurate, partly to relieve the stress of my job.

I climbed into bed, snuggling under the soft quilt with Anne curled up under the covers beside me. As I settled in, the cut on my arm began to throb again and my mind replayed the day's events over and over like ESPN after a ninety-yard touchdown.

I could've been killed today. As in dead. As in my ghost forever roaming among the bargain racks at Neiman's with unfinished business, still searching for that perfect pair of red stilettos.

Grabbing a novel from my night table, I read for a few minutes in a vain attempt to take my mind off Jack Battaglia and his box cutter. Eventually I turned out the light and stared up at my ceiling fan through the dim moonlight coming through the window, hoping to bore myself to sleep. I finally drifted off, only to spend a fitful night in dark, frantic dreams, fumbling to free my gun from its holster while fighting off dozens of huge, hairy men wearing green jumpsuits and wielding box cutters.

Sunday afternoon, when Mom and Dad would have returned home from church, eaten lunch, and finished cleaning up the dishes, I called home. Annie climbed onto my lap as I sat down on the couch with the phone. I scratched her under the chin and she thanked me with a soft purr.

After the usual preliminaries, Mom said, "You met someone, didn't you?" Mom was a regular Madame Cleo.

"How can you tell?"

"You sound happy, honey."

"Don't I usually sound happy?"

"Okay. *Happier,* then."

I told her all about Brett. Well, I told her everything I

knew about Brett, which really wasn't much. He was a landscape architect. Grew up in Dallas. Had gorgeous green eyes that could cause a girl's panties to burst into flame. Of course that's not precisely how I put it. *Nice eyes,* I said.

"How's work?"

I snorted. "You'll get a kick out of this." I told my mother about Battaglia, the box cutter, my perfect shot.

Mom was quiet a moment. When she finally spoke again, equal parts worry and sarcasm tainted her words. "What part of that story was I supposed to get a kick out of?"

Annie rolled over onto her back so I could scratch her chest now. "Come on, Mom. No need to get yourself worked up. The attack was a fluke thing."

"Lord, I hope so."

"Put Dad on the phone." He'd understand.

As expected, Dad was far more impressed than Mom, probably because he was the one who'd taught me how to handle a gun and figured my unerring aim was the direct result of his skilled instruction. "You shot the box cutter out of his hand? You shitting me?"

"I shit you not."

"Atta girl."

I beamed. An "atta girl" was the highest compliment a father could bestow on a daughter.

As we ended the call, Mom made me promise to keep my doors locked at night and to let her know how things progressed with Brett. Dad made me promise to shoot the next guy who pulled a weapon on me. I made the two of them promise to cut back on fried foods.

Monday morning, along with what seemed to be millions of other commuters, I slowly eased my way through the rush-hour gridlock on the one-way streets of downtown

Dallas. The bright and blinding morning sun lit the streets
running east-west, while those running north-south were
shaded by the towering skyscrapers that formed the impressive skyline. I yawned, as much from the auto exhaust that
was slowly asphyxiating me as from sleepiness. I turned
onto Commerce Street and continued on to the Earle Cabell
Federal Building that housed the Treasury Department's
main office and various other federal government agencies. I pulled into the parking lot at 8:45, zipping into my
usual spot at the back next to Eddie's minivan.

Once inside, I headed straight to the break room for coffee. I desperately needed a caffeine boost and I'd downed
the last of my breakfast blend at home the previous morning. I suppose I could've made a run to the supermarket
last night, but I'd been too busy daydreaming about Brett
to think about groceries. Unfortunately, when I'd gone
to bed, the happy daydreams left and the terrifying night-
mares returned.

When I'd taken the job with Criminal Investigations, I'd
known it posed some risks. Though rare, attacks on special
agents had occurred before. A small number had even been
killed in the line of duty. Not long ago, a man who'd accu-
mulated a large tax bill had intentionally crashed his
single-engine plane into the IRS building in Austin, killing
himself and an IRS employee. People could be unpredictable and dangerous. All the more reason to make sure my
blood supply contained an ample amount of caffeine for
maximum performance.

Eddie and two other male agents stood in the kitchen,
sipping coffee and discussing basketball, lamenting the
Mavericks' loss to the Utah Jazz over the weekend. Eddie
declared the Mav's performance "downright shameful."

Lu swept into the room with a cigarette dangling from
her bright-orange mouth, the smells of smoke and
industrial-strength hairspray sweeping in with her. With all

the shellac on her beehive and a lit cigarette mere inches away, it was a miracle her hair didn't go up in flames. She'd outdone herself today, wearing a bright yellow crocheted vest over a purple turtleneck and purple-and-white striped flares. She held a roll of tape in one hand, a piece of paper in the other. She spoke from the side of her mouth to prevent her cigarette from falling. "Outta the way, boys."

The men stepped aside while Lu taped the paper to the fridge. The sheet featured a crudely drawn thermometer, like those used at telethons to indicate the progress of fund-raising. The current level showed ninety-seven million dollars. The thermometer topped out at a hundred mil.

"What's that?" I asked as I poured coffee into my stainless steel travel mug.

One hand now free, Lu plucked the cigarette from her lips. "An incentive. The agent who gets me to retirement will be paid a ten-grand bonus."

Ten grand, huh? I could do a lot with ten grand. Pay off my student loans. Take my mother on a cruise to Mexico. Buy lots of treats for my cats. Heck, ten grand would cover a lifetime of manicures.

Better get to work then, huh?

Thus incentivized, I took my coffee and headed to my office. Once I'd settled at my desk, I dialed the number on the business card the Lobo had given me the previous Friday.

After a few rings, a woman answered the phone in a singsong voice that sounded more like a sorority girl's than a DEA agent's. "Agent Marquez."

"Hi, Christina. It's Tara Holloway, from the Treasury Department."

"Tara! I'm so glad you called."

I took a sip of my coffee and gagged on the bitter brew. I remembered now why I'd stopped drinking the office's cheap swill. "Tell me what you know about our ice cream man."

"Well, his name's Joseph Cullen, but he goes by 'Joe Cool.'"

"Like Snoopy?"

"Uh-huh." She giggled. "We got a tip from an elderly woman who claims Joe sold her grandson a joint."

"Any priors?"

"Two. One misdemeanor for stealing an *American Pie* DVD from Blockbuster—how tacky is that?—and one felony DUI he's on probation for. Nothing violent."

"Good to know." I'd dealt with enough violent men lately. "What part of town is he working?"

"Southside, near the Cotton Bowl."

Not the best part of town. "Let's meet, formulate a game plan."

"My office or yours?" she asked.

"Does yours have decent coffee?"

"God, no. It's sludge."

I suggested a bagel shop downtown. The DEA office was only a few blocks from the IRS, so the shop would be convenient for both of us. Plus, the place served high-quality coffee, the kind that slid easily down your throat and into your veins.

"How will I know you?" Christina asked.

"If you see a tall blonde with big hair and big boobs," I said, "that won't be me. I'll be the flat-chested brunette who looks like a librarian." Or so I'd been told, more than once. But better bookish than bimbo.

"You're so funny!" she squealed.

"And you're so . . . lively."

On my way out, I passed Eddie in the hall. "I'm meeting the DEA agent at Benny's. Want me to bring you something back?"

"How about a cheese and jalapeño bagel?"

"No problemo."

Eddie put his arm around me and gave me a sideways hug. "You take such good care of me."

I elbowed him playfully in the ribs. "I owe you. You've always got my back."

Josh, another special agent who was both a technical wizard and a total weenie, breezed past us, his spongy blond curls still damp from his morning shower, leaving a wet mark on the collar of his light blue dress shirt. "If Eddie's got your back, Holloway, that means he's putting you on the front lines, making you take the risks." Josh pretended to take aim with a machine gun and emitted a *bam-bam-bam* before continuing on his way.

Despite the melodrama and cheesy sound effects, Josh had a point. I crossed my arms over my chest and shot Eddie a pointed look.

Eddie threw his hands in the air. "You're in training! How are you going to learn if I don't let you get in there and mix it up? Besides, adversity builds character."

"Yeah, right."

"Well, if that's how you feel," Eddie said, "I'll tell the Lobo to reassign you to work with Josh."

He had me again. "Oh, hell no."

Josh was a perpetual thorn in the side of the other special agents in the office. Whiny, wimpy, yet fiercely competitive, Josh did not work well with others. The twerp had the sniveling attitude of an overzealous hall monitor. The men claimed he threw his weight around to compensate for a pitifully small penis. I hoped never to verify that claim.

Then again, the other agents hadn't exactly welcomed me with open arms, either. When Lu first introduced me to the team, she'd requested a volunteer to train me. There'd been no immediate takers. Nobody wanted to babysit a rookie who might slow them down. Besides, I could tell from their assessing glances that they weren't impressed by what they saw.

As the agents sat there stone-faced, I felt the heat of an angry blush on my cheeks, a flashback to gym class where nobody wanted the short, scrawny girl on their team. Until I spiked a volleyball down their throats, that is. I turned to the Lobo. "They must have heard about my incredible marksmanship." I'd tossed my head defiantly. "They're afraid I'll show them up." I peered back at the agents with a determined glare.

From the back row, Eddie'd snickered and stood. "The girl's got game. What the hell, I'll take her on."

He'd never regretted his decision. Okay, maybe once or twice he had, like last Friday when he'd had to rescue me from that hairy blade-wielding ape, but he'd been nice enough not to tell me so.

As I walked to the bagel shop, my cell phone chirped from inside my purse. I pulled it out and checked the caller ID. The readout indicated the call came from Scott Klein, the managing partner of Martin and McGee.

I flipped the phone open and held it to my ear. "Hi, Mr. Klein."

"Hello, Tara. How are things at the Treasury Department?"

Tough question to answer, at this point in particular. "Let's just say there's never a dull moment."

"Uh-huh." Klein paused a moment, as if weighing my response. "Alicia Shenkman tells me you were attacked last week. That you had to shoot someone."

"Alicia has a big mouth."

Klein chuckled. "She misses working with you."

I missed working with Alicia, too. Goofing around with her was the one thing that had made my former job bearable. Tossing a rubber band ball back and forth over the top of our cubicles, watching funny videos on You-

Tube during our coffee breaks, lunchtime shopping excursions.

"You planning on staying on?" Klein asked.

"Yes, sir," I responded without hesitation. "I am." I carefully stepped over the legs of a scruffy-bearded homeless man sleeping on the sidewalk. The man wore a faded green sweat suit two sizes too small and reeked of alcohol, perspiration, and desperation.

"Okay, then. Just know that if you ever want to come back to Martin and McGee, we've got an office waiting for you."

I stopped in my tracks, one leg on each side of the hobo. "Did you say 'office'?"

"I'm offering you a management position, Tara. You have unique talents. Nobody has a nose for corporate fraud like you."

I did have an uncanny ability to sniff out accounting irregularities. For some reason, thinking like a criminal came naturally to me. Apparently, skipping school and underage drinking had taught me some valuable skills.

"We're prepared to offer you six figures."

Whoa. "Does that include the numbers after the decimal point?"

Klein chuckled. "Nope. All six figures come before the decimal."

For a brief moment, I wavered. A cushy management job at a prestigious CPA firm. A big salary, 401(k) matching, four weeks' paid vacation. No crazy men with box cutters.

But, no. I couldn't do it.

Even if I'd be ditching the cubicle, I'd still be riding a desk all day and that just wasn't for me. I loved the action as a special agent, the snooping around, that *Bingo!* feeling when I finally found the smoking gun that would nail a tax cheat. I'd been bored stiff at the accounting firm and no amount of money could change that. "Thanks, Mr. Klein. I appreciate the offer. But I love being a special agent."

The homeless man lying between my legs stirred and opened his bloodshot eyes.

"All righty, then. But if you change your mind," Klein said, "give me a call."

"Will do." I snapped my phone shut. "Excuse me," I said to the man and continued on my way to the bagel shop.

CHAPTER FIVE

*U*ndercover Angels

I'd just ordered the bagels and a caramel latte with whipped cream when someone tapped me on the shoulder. I turned around to find myself face-to-face with a life-sized Latina Barbie.

Christina was tall, thin, and busty, with big brown eyes and full lips. Her lustrous black hair hung halfway down her back. She performed a curtsy in her fitted black-and-white polka-dot minidress, then waggled her fingers at me in a cutesy wave. "Hi!" she gushed. "You have to be Tara, right? 'Cause you look like a librarian, just like you said."

I took in her painted acrylic nails, her perfectly arched brows, and her four-inch heels. She should be wearing a tiara and tossing Tootsie Rolls from a parade float, not hunting down drug dealers. My thoughts spilled out of my mouth before I could stop them. "You've got to be kidding me."

Her brown eyes flashed with fury and before I knew what was happening, Christina had wrapped her arm around my neck and pulled me into a headlock. "No," she hissed in my ear, her voice now low and tinged with a sharp Spanish accent. "I'm not kidding you at all."

So Barbie had spunk.

Agent Marquez and I had received the same training, so within seconds I'd performed the evasive maneuvers needed to slip out of her grip, skipping the stomp on the instep so as not to mar her adorable patent leather pumps with polka dot bows on the toe. I faced her and held out my hand. "I'm sorry. That was inexcusably rude of me. It's just that you don't look at all like a DEA agent."

She took in my delicate facial features, my tastefully drab olive-green linen pantsuit, my hair pulled back with a tortoiseshell barrette. "Well, you look *exactly* like an IRS agent."

"Touché."

We traded smiles. She took my hand and gave it a firm shake, all forgiven.

After we received our orders, we slipped into a booth at the back of the shop. Christina handed me a manila envelope. Inside was an enlarged driver's-license photo of Joseph Cullen, aka Joe Cool. Joe had a goofy smile, an acne-pocked face, and the worst haircut I'd ever seen. "The guy wears a mullet?"

Christina nodded. "We may have to kill him."

I smiled. The girl might be annoyingly bubbly, but at least she had a sense of humor. This bust could be fun.

The printout indicated Joe was only five foot six and a hundred and forty-five pounds. Two female agents should be able to take him down easily. Of course I'd never expected a porker like Jack Battaglia to move as fast as he did, either.

"HUD foreclosed on a crack house in the middle of

Joe's ice-cream route," Christina said. "I had keys made for us." She pulled a key out of the envelope and slid it across the table to me. "We can use the house as our base of operations."

"Good idea." I handed the file back to Christina and tucked the key into my purse.

"If we're going to run a successful stakeout in that neighborhood, we'll have to make some adjustments to our appearance. If we go in dressed like this"—she gestured at our clothes—"Joe and everyone else will be on to us in a heartbeat."

Looked like it was time to get back in touch with my blue-collar roots.

We left the bagel shop, ready to get started. "I just need to run these by my office." I held up the white paper bag containing Eddie's bagels. "They're for my partner."

Christina and I walked to my office, her heels click-clacking on the sidewalk as she all but skipped along next to me. When we reached the homeless man, asleep again on the sidewalk, I tucked a second bag containing a nutritious whole wheat bagel and a bottle of orange juice under his arm.

We arrived at the Treasury building and made our way down the hall. Viola assessed Christina with a sharp eye as we approached her desk. Like me, Christina was deceptively benign looking. She'd already proven that when she'd taken me down at the bagel shop. When we drew near, Viola turned her pointed look from Christina to me. "Lu's looking for you."

Dang. She must've received her copy of my firearm discharge report. I'd known this was coming. I'd just hoped for a longer reprieve.

Christina waited in my office while I went to see the Lobo. I took a deep breath and rapped tentatively on the door frame.

Lu looked up from the stack of paperwork on her desk. And she didn't look happy. "Well, well," she said, picking up the cigarette from her ashtray and taking a deep drag. "If it ain't the Annie Oakley of the IRS."

I stepped into her office. "Didn't Eddie tell you what happened? That Battaglia attacked me with a box cutter?" I knew my partner would back me up. Eddie and I hadn't worked together long, but we'd gelled instantly. His loyalty was one of the few things I could count on these days.

Lu blew smoke out her nose, like a dragon with a bee-hive. "'Course he did. But rules are rules. You're officially on administrative leave until we can hold a hearing and get this mess straightened out."

Dang.

"But we can't spare you," she said, "so don't stop working."

Sheez. "Some leave."

She waved her hand. "Get out of here and get back to work."

"Yes, ma'am."

I retrieved Eddie's bagels and Christina from my office, and we headed down the hall to Eddie's digs. Eddie glanced up from his desk where he sat virtually buried in Battaglia's records. His CPA license hung on the wall behind him next to a Dallas Cowboys cheerleader calendar featuring a woman with a pair of large pom-poms in her hands and another pair nearly bursting out of her tiny halter top. I tossed the bag to him.

He caught it in midair. "Thanks." He set the bag on his desk, then stood as Christina stepped forward with her hand out. I introduced the two.

"Nice to meet you, Christina." Eddie shook her hand, then turned it over and raised her wrist to his nose. "Wow, you smell nice."

Christina giggled. "Thanks. I went to one of those places

that make personalized fragrances. I call this one 'Christina in Bloom.'"

Eddie grinned. Although he was happily married, Eddie was also a hopeless flirt. "It suits you perfectly."

I picked Eddie's framed family photo off his desk and held it up to Christina. "These would be Eddie's wife and kids."

"She's pretty," Christina said, taking the frame out of my hand, "and your girls are adorable."

"Thanks. I'm a lucky guy." Eddie sat back in his rolling chair and pulled a bagel out of his bag. He fished around in the bag with his hand and, coming up empty, pulled it toward him and peeked inside. "What? No cream cheese?"

"Oops." I shrugged sheepishly. "I forgot."

Eddie shook his head. "It was only a matter of time before the love died."

Christina returned the photo to Eddie's desk and we headed out the door.

"Take pictures of the takedown," Eddie called after us. "Two-on-one action, I don't want to miss that."

Urk. Men.

CHAPTER SIX

*P*laying the
Part

We headed out to the parking lot and climbed into my BMW, putting the top down to enjoy the pleasant spring day. As we left downtown, I changed lanes on Elm Street just past the historic book depository. Something about driving over the big *X* painted on the street, marking the spot where President Kennedy had been shot, gave me the creeps. A handful of tourists stood on the infamous grassy knoll, looking over at the road then up at the old building, no doubt wondering if there was any credence to the second-shooter notion advanced by conspiracy theorists.

An hour later at a trendy store at the Galleria, Christina and I searched through racks in the juniors section for appropriately inappropriate attire to wear on our upcoming undercover gig. Though it was only March, daytime temperatures already reached the low eighties and the summer stock was out and primed for purchase.

Christina sorted through a rack of colorful tops, sliding the hangers aside as she looked over the offerings. "See anything that'll make us look like slackers?"

I held up a skimpy black T-shirt that read DIVA in glittery silver lettering across the front. "How about this?"

She scrunched up her nose. "It's totally tacky, so it's totally perfect. What do you think of this?" She held a pair of hot-pink hot pants up to her waist.

The tiny shorts looked to be a size three. They also looked like they'd fit her perfectly. I fought the urge to bitch-slap her. "Trashy. Get them."

She added them to the stack accumulating on her arm.

"How far do we have to take this whole undercover thing?" I asked. "I want to look the part, but I'd draw the line at a tramp stamp or belly button ring."

"So I should cancel the appointment for the nipple piercing?"

The mere thought had me hunching my shoulders in phantom agony.

"Listen up." Christina put one finger in the air and waved it in a zigzag pattern in front of my face. "This undercover thang ain't jus' about wearing the right gear," she said in a sassy voice. "It's about puttin' on the right attitude."

"And the 'right attitude' would be what, precisely?"

"That everyone can kiss our sweet little asses." She kissed her fingertips, cocked her hip, and gave her right butt cheek a resounding slap.

Hmm. I kissed my fingers, stuck out a hip, and slapped my ass. "How's that?"

She frowned. "Needs work."

We snatched several pairs of seamless no-line underwear from the lingerie display. Didn't want our sweet little asses to have panty lines in these tight clothes.

We headed into the dressing rooms with our selections,

choosing the largest room to share so we could swap the selections we'd squabbled over. Inside the room, I slipped out of my loafers, then removed my jacket and hung it on a hook.

Christina glanced over at me, gesturing at the bandage on my arm. "What happened?"

I explained the injury, giving her the basic details of Battaglia's bust.

"He didn't know you carried a gun?" She slipped into a pair of skintight jeans and zipped them up. "What part of 'IRS Criminal Investigations' did he not understand?"

Maybe if the word got out that IRS agents were armed, we'd have fewer problems. "Yeah. It was pretty stupid. He would've spent only a month or two in jail for the tax fraud. But assault on a federal officer will put him away for years." I slipped the black top over my head, tugging it down into place. I didn't know Christina well enough to openly discuss my concerns about my job, but I was curious to know if she'd been through the same experience, suffered the same doubts. "You ever been attacked?"

"Not yet."

"Not yet? You expect to, then?"

Christina turned to look at her butt in the mirror, performing a series of squats to test the flexibility of the fabric. Satisfied, she stood and looked at me. "If you don't expect an attack, you won't be ready for it."

"True." I hadn't expected Jack Battaglia to do what he did. And I hadn't been ready for him. I'd never make that mistake again.

After trying the clothes on and finding the right shoes to complete our outfits, we paid for our purchases with our government-issued credit cards and headed back to the dressing rooms to change into our new panties and outfits. We emerged from our separate rooms and gave each other the once-over. Christina appeared all of eighteen in the teeny pink shorts and tank top.

"It needs one final touch." I reached over to her shoulder, pulled her black bra strap out from under the tank top, and let it hang off her shoulder. "There."

Christina took in my tight black T-shirt, the hip-hugging Capri pants that showed my belly button and very nearly revealed my coin slot, and the over-the-top flip-flops embellished with sparkling silver sequins. "You've got the clothes right, and your manicure is cute, but we've got to do something about your hair and makeup. Too conservative." She pushed me through the lavender curtain back into the dressing room.

While Christina had glitzy, striking cover-girl qualities, I was more like the attractive but less showy sort of woman on page sixty-two of a magazine, in an ad for floor polish or tampons. I decided to let Christina have her way with me, makeup wise, that is.

She whipped lipstick, blush, and eye shadow out of her enormous purse and set to work, pausing occasionally to evaluate her progress. After emboldening my features with a metallic rose lipstick and thick black liquid eyeliner, she put one last dab of powder on my nose and declared my face "Done." Putting her hands on my shoulders, she turned me around to face the mirror.

I took one look and gasped. "I look like a—"

"Ho." Christina dropped the makeup back in her bag. "You'll fit right in where we're going."

I turned back to the mirror and took another peek. I squinted but could still hardly recognize myself. She'd made my thin lips appear pouty and sexy. Very Angelina Jolie. Or John Madden.

"Now for your hair." Christina scavenged a hairbrush and a small spray can out of her purse. She removed my barrette and brushed through my hair. "Face me," she ordered.

I turned around and she used her fingers and hairbrush to tease my hair into a wild mane. She stepped back to admire her handiwork. "Just right." Grabbing the spray, she shook the can and aimed. *Psshh.*

The spray seared my eyes and nose, and my skin felt like it was on fire. I screamed, my hands flying to my face. "It burns!" I choked out between coughs. "It burns!" My eyes watered like never before, gushing tears like a geyser. I dug the heels of my hands into my eyes, desperately and vainly trying to ease the pain.

"Oh, poop," Christina muttered through the blistering haze. "This isn't my hair spray. This is my pepper spray."

"Pepper spray?" I shrieked. "What the hell!" Temporarily blinded, I reached out to throttle her, but she managed to evade my grabbing hands, probably by jumping onto the bench. "If I catch you, Christina, I'm going to kill you!"

My fingers found an empty plastic hanger on one of the hooks and grabbed it. I swung the thing like a machete, but never made contact, unable to find my target. "Shit!" I tripped over something on the floor, probably my purse, and fell into the wall, shaking the flimsy structure.

"Watch it!" hollered a girl in the adjacent dressing room.

Two loud raps sounded at the doorway to the fitting room. "Everything okay in there?" a clerk asked. "There's a weird smell and I heard screaming."

"We're fine," Christina called, materializing again and pushing a wad of tissue into my hand. "You'd scream, too, if you saw the way Tara looked in those pants."

Now I was *really* going to kill her.

Ten minutes later, I could finally breathe normally again and make out blurry images. My tears had smeared most of the eye makeup Christina had so carefully applied, but no way would I let her touch me again.

People stared at me as we walked through the mall, averting their eyes when I caught them gawking. Christina treated me to a garlic-butter pretzel by way of apology.

I swallowed a huge, yummy bite. "You're lucky I can be bought off so easily."

"I am," she agreed. "If you'd held out, I would've upped the offer to include a raspberry lemonade."

"Damn."

We took the elevator down to the parking garage and climbed out on the second level. Christina took a few steps forward, then stopped, her head rotating as she tried to locate the car. "Didn't we park in section 2B?"

I shook my head. "No. I would've remembered that. I would've thought Shakespeare. You know, '2B or not 2B.'"

Christina grunted. "You must've been really popular with the guys in college."

"Don't forget I've got a gun in my purse."

She arched a brow at me. "So do I."

"Oh. Right." Shoot. "Was it 3C?"

After fifteen minutes of walking in circles, we finally found my car in row 8D. I hoped we'd be more adept at nailing Joe Cool than we were at locating our parking space. We tossed our bags in the trunk and climbed in. I turned to Christina. "I'm not so sure this car will fit in with the south Dallas crowd. What do you drive?"

Christina frowned. "Two thousand eight Volvo C70."

"Sweet. Convertible?"

"Of course."

Pretty pricey for a rookie agent. "DEA auction?" I guessed.

"You know it."

We sat there for a minute, considering our dilemma. "You gave me an idea." Christina snapped her fingers in the air. "Let's go."

Following Christina's directions, I drove to the DEA's impound lot, leaving the top up this time so the wind couldn't further irritate my eyes. The noisy, crowded lot, situated under a freeway overpass, smelled of dust and gasoline. We headed through the metal gate on foot and walked up and down the rows of seized vehicles, searching for one that would fit our cover. The bright sunlight glinting off an occasional windshield or chrome bumper burned my already sensitive retinas, but luckily most of the cars were too dirty to generate much of a glare.

Christina stopped in front of an old baby-blue Volkswagen Beetle. "This is cute."

I pulled open the door. It came off in my hand, clunking to the ground. "I thought drug dealers drove nice cars."

"The smart dealers do," Christina said. "But the smart ones don't usually get caught, either."

"Whoa!" I jumped back as something furry darted out of the car and under the rusty horse trailer parked next to it. We hurried farther down the row.

I stopped in front of an ancient Oldsmobile that was brown all over except for a green passenger door. "How about this one?"

Christina stepped up to the window and peeked inside. "Nuh-uh. Vinyl seats. Our thighs will stick to them."

"What's this I hear about sticky thighs?" We turned around to find the attendant, a pudgy man sporting oil-stained gray coveralls and an equally oily grin. His lecherous gaze traveled up and down our bodies, taking in our revealing clothing and the things it revealed. Urk. The rat had been less offensive.

Christina reached into her purse, pulled out a small black leather holder, and flashed her badge. "We're special agents going undercover. We need something reliable but not flashy."

The man looked up in thought, then gestured for us to

follow him. He led us a few rows over, then stopped and pointed. My gaze followed his finger, stopping on a powder-pink '86 Cadillac Coupe de Ville.

"A Mary Kay car?" My face turned from the car to Christina.

She shrugged.

The car had a rip in the vinyl top and was missing three hubcaps, but other than that it appeared complete. Fortunately, the registration and inspection were still in date, too. We wouldn't have to worry about getting pulled over. "How does it run?"

"Great," the attendant said. "The engine's huge. Lots of power under the hood. And just look at the size of that back-seat. You could have a party back there."

If we did, this guy certainly wouldn't be on our guest list.

Christina stuck out her hand. "Keys, please."

CHAPTER SEVEN

Warming Up to the Ice Cream Man

On our way to south Dallas, Christina and I made a brief detour by Sam Moon's, the bargain accessory store run by a Korean entrepreneur and a harem of pretty Korean women. Sam Moon offered a competitive shopping experience far too intense for the mere recreational shopper. I headed straight to the jewelry section and forced my way in between two other women, their efforts to elbow me back unsuccessful. When they noticed my bloodshot eyes and splotchy face, they turned tail and headed for another display. Looking like a crazed drug addict has its benefits. With elbow room to spare, I picked out three pairs of dangly earrings and dropped them into my plastic shopping basket.

A few aisles over, Christina fought with another woman over a striped silk scarf. "I had it first." Christina yanked the scarf out of the woman's hand.

"No you didn't," the other woman spat, grabbing an end and tugging.

Christina slapped at the woman's hand but the woman refused to let go, her eyes narrowing. Christina scored a coup when she looked over at the next table, let go of the scarf, and squealed, "Ooh! I see a cuter one over there."

The woman dropped the scarf on the floor and dashed to the other table. Christina did a quick one-eighty, snatched the striped scarf from the floor, and bolted for the checkout stand.

"My eyes are still burning," I said once we were back in the car. "We need to make a stop at the doc-in-a-box."

Following my directions, Christina drove to the medical clinic, the two of us belting out as much of Bruce Springsteen's "Pink Cadillac" as we could remember, filling in the blanks with the standard "na-na-nas." She parked in front. No need to worry about this car's doors getting dinged. The thing was built like a friggin' tank.

Kelsey glanced up from behind the counter as we came in. "Back again?" Her eyes moved from my face to the pink Cadillac visible through the glass front of the clinic. "What is it this time? Makeover gone horribly awry?"

Christina stepped up beside me. "I accidentally shot her with my pepper spray."

Kelsey raised her eyebrows. "That's a new one."

A few minutes later, Dr. Maju summoned me from the waiting area. Today, under his open lab coat, he wore a SpongeBob SquarePants T-shirt with his jeans, just the thing to inspire a patient's confidence. He glanced at Christina. "To hell with the Privacy Act," he said to me. "Bring your gorgeous friend with you."

Christina giggled and followed me back to the exam room.

Once I was seated on the exam table, Dr. Maju slid a stethoscope up my shirt and gestured with his free hand at Christina. "What's your friend's situation? Is she available?"

"Do you really think you should be hitting on other women while you've got your hand up my blouse?"

He rolled his eyes, focused on his watch, and counted my heartbeats. Finished, he pulled the stethoscope back out. "Is she free for dinner tonight?"

My head oscillated to Christina. "You free for dinner tonight?"

She gave him a flirtatious smile. "Sure."

I turned back to Dr. Maju. "She said no."

"Smart-ass."

Christina jotted her phone number down on Dr. Maju's prescription pad and handed it to him. "I'm Christina."

"Ajay," Dr. Maju said, taking the paper from her hand. "Now please take off all your clothes."

"Me? Why? I'm not the patient."

"Why else?" he said, raising his palms. "I want to see you naked."

Christina giggled again. Now I was really starting to feel sick.

"Um, hello?" I waved at the doctor from the exam table. "I've got third-degree burns here. You've scored your date already. Can I get some attention now?"

"Oh, all right, you big baby." Dr. Maju shined his tiny flashlight up my nose and in my eyes, though this time it probably wasn't just to annoy me. He reached over to a cabinet and pulled out a bottle of clear liquid. "Lie back on the table. This may sting."

"Can't get any worse than it already is." Or so I'd thought. "Dang!" My eyes burned for the second time that day as Dr. Maju flushed them out with the solution. He took the pad and wrote a prescription for a skin cream while I blotted my eyes with a tissue.

* * *

As we rounded a bend on the interstate, the enormous Cotton Bowl stadium and the towering Ferris wheel on the adjacent state fairgrounds came into view. Christina exited the freeway into a part of town I'd never been to before, but one she seemed familiar with, probably from earlier busts. On the frontage road sat a small used-car lot, a red and white banner strung between two poles promising NO CREDIT CHECK. We turned the corner and passed a brick strip mall containing a pawn shop, a liquor store, and a dollar store. Heavy iron burglar bars covered every window in the center.

The shopping center gave way to a neighborhood for which the term "blighted" would be a compliment. An overturned shopping cart served as a lawn ornament on the dusty, grassless square plot in front of the first house, a faded wood-frame model missing most of its trim. Broken-down cars rested on blocks in gravel driveways or yards, one at a curb bearing a bright orange sticker posted on the windshield by the Dallas PD, warning the vehicle would be towed if not moved soon. At various houses along the route people sat on the sagging stoops with sagging faces, as if waiting for someone or something they never really expected to come.

"This is depressing."

"This is the 'hood," Christina shot back. "What did you expect?"

I was used to a higher class of criminal, if there was such a thing. In order for someone to evade their taxes, the person first had to have income. Most of the income in this neighborhood probably came in the form of food stamps and housing assistance.

Christina took a few more turns before pulling into the dirt driveway of a single-story wood house surrounded by a chain-link fence, the steel wires bent in several places. The gate had been torn off its hinges and lay next to the drive. What little paint remained on the house was the yellow-brown color of mustard jar crust. I hoped it wasn't lead based. A slumped porch spanned the front of the house as if too lazy to sit up straight. Miniblinds missing several slats hung crookedly in the few windows not covered with plywood. The yard was mostly bare, with a dozen or so dandelions serving as a lawn. Behind the house sat a detached garage that leaned precariously to the right against an oak, having given up the will to live.

Christina cut the engine. "Here we are. Home sweet home."

I stared at the dump. "The 'Condemned' sign must have fallen off."

We climbed out of the car and headed to the porch, stepping on it tentatively lest it collapse under our weight. Christina unlocked the door and we stepped inside. A foul stench greeted us.

I pinched my nose shut. "It smells like something died in here."

"Or *someone*." Christina waved her hand in front of her face. "I'll get the windows. You find out what that smell is."

"Wimp."

The den was small and dusty, containing only a filthy rust-colored corduroy couch with duct tape holding the cushions together. A few cigarette butts and an old tattered phone book lay on the floor. Christina stepped over to open the windows, while I continued into the kitchen. The countertops and linoleum were a hopelessly outdated avocado green, the countertops nicked and dull, the flooring splitting at the seams and curling up at the edges. A white fridge with a Rent-2-Own sticker on it stood next to the stove. No doubt the rent was past due. Against the back wall sat two large black trash bags oozing moldy, rotten garbage. Flies swarmed through the air above the bags while their maggot spawn wriggled among the debris. I suppose I should have been glad it was only garbage and not a decaying corpse.

Bile came up in my throat but I forced it back down. "I'm a big girl," I told myself. "I'm a federal agent. I'm tough. I can do this." I pulled my skimpy T-shirt up over my nose, grabbed the bags, and yanked them out the back door, sending the roaches that had been hiding under them scurrying under the cabinets and refrigerator. The screen door slammed shut behind me with a loud *thwack*.

I let my shirt down and gulped in a breath of the fresher outside air, then pulled the bags around the side of the house and out to the curb as fast as my legs would go. So much for being a diva. When I went back inside the house, Christina had all but the plywood-covered windows open and the odor had begun to clear out.

The two of us looked around. The house had two bedrooms with horribly marred walls, one bearing three fist-sized holes. The small bath sported a cracked mirror, a tub with a three-inch scum ring, and a toilet with no seat.

"This is disgusting." I yanked the mildew-covered plastic shower curtain off its rings. "How can people live like this?"

Christina shrugged. "I've seen worse." She opened the cabinet under the sink and bent down to look inside. She shrieked and scrambled backward, knocking me into the tub. Leaping in after me, she yanked her gun from her purse, shoved a clip into it, and aimed it at the cabinet. "Something's in there!"

"What do you mean something's in there?"

"I don't know what it was. But it was furry and had claws and pointy teeth."

"Another rat?" I pulled my gun out, too.

"No. Too big for a rat. It looked, I don't know, like a small bear or something."

Despite the lax laws in Texas regarding exotic pets, I

sincerely doubted a bear had made its way into the neighborhood.

There was no way to get out of the bathroom without
passing the open cabinet. I'm not sure what Christina had
seen inside, but I wasn't sure I wanted to find out.

A moment later, a furry brown foot with long black
claws appeared under the open cabinet door. Whatever was
in there was climbing out. A few seconds later, another foot
appeared. Then another, and another. A face peeked around
the door, a cute face with brown fur and black circles
around the eyes.

I rolled my eyes. "For God's sake, it's just a raccoon."
Having been raised in the country, I'd had plenty of oppor-
tunities to interact with these creatures, once engaging in
hand-to-paw combat with a coon who'd tried to steal a bag
of hot dog buns off the picnic table in the backyard. Raccoons were bold, sure, but they were no match for a couple
of armed women. I stepped out of the tub and waved my
hands at the creature. "Shoo."

But the beast didn't shoo. Instead, it bared its teeth and
charged me. "Holy shit!" I fell back into the tub, scram-
bling to get to my feet.

"Just a raccoon, huh?" Christina held her gun aimed at
the creature's face.

The raccoon stood on its hind legs two feet away, glar-
ing up at us, lips curled back to show its fangs.

"I've never seen one act like this before," I said.
"Maybe it has rabies."

"Rabies? Great. You better shoot it before it bites us."

I would already face an inquiry for shooting at Jack
Battaglia. If I fired my gun again, my superiors would
think I was a loose cannon, a liability to the department.
I'd probably lose my job. "Why don't you shoot it?"

The raccoon wasn't baring its teeth anymore. Without
its fangs showing, it was actually kind of cute.

"I can't," Christina said. "I couldn't live with the guilt. And it wouldn't be good for my karma."

"Screw your karma. I've heard that a person exposed to rabies has to get fourteen shots with a ten-inch needle."

"Then shoot the damn thing already."

I looked at the raccoon again. It blinked its big brown eyes at me. "Aw, hell. I can't do it, either."

We tried again to shoo the critter out the door. Again it charged us, ramming into the tub. Not looking so cute anymore. We had to do something quick or the darn thing would climb into the tub with us. I shifted my Glock to my left hand and grabbed Christina's gun from her. *Bam!* I put a hole in the floor only two inches from the varmint. Exactly where I'd aimed.

The raccoon hightailed it out of the bathroom. Three much smaller raccoons scurried out of the cabinet and ran after it.

Ears ringing from the blast, I climbed out of the tub, stepped to the door, and took a look. The mother raccoon lumbered into the living room and climbed over a windowsill, her babies trailing after. Thank goodness we'd opened the window.

"What the hell!" Christina stepped out of the tub. "What do you think you're doing, grabbing my weapon?"

I handed her gun back to her. "If I'd shot my gun, I'd have to file a report. And if you'd shot your gun, you'd have to file a report. But since *I* shot *your* gun, neither one of us has to file a report."

She frowned. "You sure about that?"

"I work for the IRS," I said. "I know loopholes." Actually, I wasn't at all sure whether a report was required. But my logic sounded plausible on some level.

She removed the clip from her gun and shoved them both back into her purse. I did likewise. Then I checked my manicure. The sparkly red polish was intact. Good.

With the vermin vacated and our tour complete, we headed back outside, sitting down on the stoop.

"How does this whole undercover thing work?"

Christina stretched her long legs out in front of her. "Basically, we pretend to be users, try to gain the dealer's trust, then make a buy."

Not too complicated. "How long does it take?"

She lifted one shoulder, noncommittal. "It varies. Some of the bigger stings take months, years even. A small operator like this guy? Three, maybe four weeks, tops."

Reaching into my purse, I pulled out a pencil and a notepad. "If we're going to be stuck in this dump for weeks, we'll have to do some shopping." I began to make a list, starting with air freshener and roach spray.

"Don't forget the disinfectant," Christina added. "Antibacterial soap, too. And a toilet seat."

When I finished adding her suggestions to the list, I slipped the notepad back into my purse.

A police cruiser rolled slowly up the street, windows down, a tall, black officer at the wheel. He pulled to a stop in front of our house. "Got a report of a gunshot in the area," he called. "You girls hear anything?"

"Nope," I said. "Not a thing."

Christina shook her head.

The cruiser rolled on.

"Lying to cops," Christina muttered. "Our karma is so screwed."

We were about to climb into the pink Caddie again when we heard the warbling bars of ice-cream truck music in the distance.

My gaze met Christina's. "Joe Cool?"

She bobbed her head affirmatively.

I opened my purse and pulled out my wallet. No bills. Shoot. Given that cash was virtually obsolete these days, I rarely bothered to carry any. "Got any singles?"

Christina rummaged through her purse and checked her wallet. "¡Ay caramba! I've only got sixteen cents." She held up a Visa card. "You think he takes plastic?"

Some undercover agents we were.

We searched the Cadillac's ashtray and floorboards. Nothing. The attendant at the impound lot had likely cleared out anything of value in the car.

The music grew louder and several blocks down an ice-cream truck came around the corner, its once-red paint now oxidized to a flat, rusty orange in the Texas sun. The truck headed slowly up the street toward us. At two o'clock in the afternoon on a school day, only a handful of customers presented themselves. A thin black woman in a flowered housedress came out of a house five doors down and waved at the van. A toddler wearing only a diaper followed her to the truck, wobbling on his chubby legs. A few seconds later, the woman backed away holding two ice-cream bars and handed one to the kid.

Christina hopped onto the trunk of the Cadillac, putting her feet on the bumper and leaning back suggestively. I didn't have time to strike such a seductive pose, and even if I had, with my short build and flat chest I could never achieve quite the same effect. I chose to simply lean back against the fender.

The ice-cream truck started up again, rolling toward us at the whopping rate of three miles per hour. A pair of black speakers mounted on top of the truck continued to blare the silly children's tune.

I snapped my fingers as recognition kicked in. "I know that song. My kindergarten teacher taught it to the class."

"Mine, too."

Christina and I launched into song. " 'Do your ears hang low? Do they wobble to and fro?' " We added the motions we'd learned years ago, pretending to tie knots and bows.

Finally, the truck rolled up to our house. The driver

glanced over at me and Christina and slowed, the truck's engine sputtering, its brakes giving off an earsplitting screech as it came to a stop.

The driver turned his face to us. Sure enough, it was Joseph "Joe Cool" Cullen, complete with the zit-pocked face and greasy mullet he'd sported in the photo we'd seen earlier. He flashed a sleazy grin as his gaze locked on Christina's breasts.

I leaned her way and whispered, "Bet his ears aren't the only thing he's got that hangs low and wobbles to and fro."

She groaned softly at me and waggled her fingers at Joe.

"Hey, there," Joe called from his truck.

Christina gave him a "hey" back, drawing the word out into three syllables as only true Texans can.

Joe stood up and came to the window. "Ice cream?"

"Don't got no money," Christina said.

I mentally cringed at her abuse of the English language, but her butchered grammar made her sound as trashy as she looked.

Joe gestured for the two of us to come over. Christina slowly slid down the trunk of the car, stretching her long legs out in front of her. She sauntered over to the truck with me tagging along behind like a pesky puppy.

Joe was even more repulsive up close. Across his nose was a sprinkling of what at first appeared to be freckles but on closer inspection turned out to be blackheads. Nasty.

"Haven't seen the two of you before," Joe said.

"Just moved in today." Christina leaned sideways against the truck, running a finger along the plunging neckline of her tank top, pulling it down slightly to give Joe more cleavage to ogle. The guy practically drooled.

A few seconds later, he turned to me, taking in my still-red face and puffy eyes. "What happened to you? Piss off your boyfriend?"

My blood instantly turned to molten lava. It wasn't just

his words that enraged me, it was the nonchalant way he referred to domestic violence. I fought an ironic urge to yank him out of the truck and shove his face in the festering garbage at the curb. I took a calming breath. "Nah. Just allergies."

Joe leaned out of the window, putting himself as close as he could to Christina without getting out of the truck. "Today's ice cream is on the house. Consider it a welcome gift."

Christina shot Joe a coy smile, then stepped back to scope out the choices pictured on the side of the van. "Hmm. I can't decide." She bent over unnecessarily, pretending to take a closer look. She stuck her ass out, making sure Joe got a nice view, proving just what she'd do for a Klondike bar.

His mouth hung open in a gaping grin, revealing a collection of silver-filled teeth and a lifetime of substandard dental hygiene. If he didn't close his lips soon, he'd start collecting flies.

After a few seconds, Christina stood back up. "I'll have a Fudgsicle."

Joe handed her an ice-cream bar, then glanced over at me. "How about you?"

"Bomb Pop."

He rummaged through the waist-high freezer, then handed the popsicle to me.

"Thanks."

"No problem."

I unwrapped my Bomb Pop and took a big bite off the top. Yee-ow! Brain freeze.

Christina turned and walked back to the Cadillac, swinging her hips just enough to give Joe a show. I followed her. After Christina resumed her position on the trunk of the car, Joe flopped back into the driver's seat and started the truck. He took one last look at Christina

before easing the van into gear. Poor, stupid guy. Here he
was welcoming us to the 'hood with free ice cream when
the whole reason we were here was to bust his sorry ass.
I almost felt sorry for him.

    Almost.

CHAPTER EIGHT

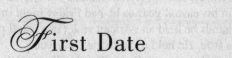

First Date

Brett phoned as I arrived home from work and asked me out to dinner. Initially, I was tempted to decline. As much as I wanted to see him again, the dating advice in *Cosmo* said a girl shouldn't make herself available on short notice. But the frozen pizza in my freezer was coated with frost and the only things in my pantry were a box of Fruity Pebbles and a bag of kitty kibble. The kibble was fresh, but a quick taste test indicated the cereal had grown stale.

"You're in luck," I told Brett. "George Clooney had to cancel. He caught the flu."

"What a coincidence," Brett replied. "Megan Fox canceled on me for the same reason."

He could give as good as he took. That was promising.

I agonized for half an hour over what to wear and changed outfits five times, finally settling on a light blue cowl-necked sweater, skinny jeans, and mules. Cute without looking like I was trying too hard to impress him. I sat on the couch with Annie, watching the early news and waiting for Brett to arrive. At the sound of a car pulling into the driveway, my pulse quickened and Annie's ears pricked up. When Brett knocked on the door, the cat leaped off my lap and darted under the sofa.

I took a deep breath and opened my front door. Brett stood on the porch, dressed in jeans, a long-sleeved green Henley, and sporty tan loafers. He looked just as yummy in his casual gear as he had Friday night in his tux. In his hands he held an African violet in a small pot shaped like a frog. He held it out to me. "For you."

"How sweet, Brett. Thanks. I've got the perfect place for it." I took the plant from him, carried it to the kitchen, and situated it next to the sink, where it would receive indirect sunlight.

He leaned back against the counter. "What sounds good for dinner?"

I'd been raised on a strict Southern diet of chicken-fried steak and mashed potatoes and had been thrilled to discover the variety of ethnic cuisine available in Dallas. Still, I knew some people were squeamish about certain foods. "You eat sushi?"

"Love the stuff."

Not a wuss about food. Another point in his favor.

We climbed into Brett's black Lincoln Navigator and drove to a hole-in-the-wall sushi bar a few blocks from my place. The pretty Asian waitress led us to two seats near the far end of the bar. Once we were seated, Brett tore the paper off his wooden chopsticks, pulled them apart, and drummed a quick version of the "Wipeout" drum solo on the edge of his plate.

"Impressive," I said.

"Played percussion in my high school marching band."

"A band geek, huh?"

He chuckled. "Yeah. You?"

"Nah. I have no musical talent whatsoever," I said. "I was more the type to hang out under the bleachers and drink beer."

He emitted a teasing tsk-tsk and shook his head. "My mother warned me about girls like you."

I smiled. "Yep, we're nothing but trouble."

He cocked his head and narrowed his eyes, assessing me. "Sometimes a little trouble can be a lot of fun."

Oh, yeah.

I chased the California roll with a glass of sweet plum wine, while Brett braved a cup of hot sake. Over dinner, we learned more about each other. Like me, he was the youngest in his family, though he had only one older sibling to my two. He'd grown up in Highland Park, an exclusive area of Dallas, and had attended a top-notch private school. I'd grown up in a dilapidated farmhouse in east Texas and attended public schools. Clearly we'd been raised in very different environments. Still, we'd ended up here together, sharing our stories, a platter of sushi, and a pleasant evening.

Fate, perhaps?

The two of us overdosed on wasabi, using our chopsticks to load the green blobs onto our sushi, grimacing when the lethal stuff kicked in, then doing it all over again.

Brett finagled more wasabi onto his avocado roll. "This stuff is addictive."

I fanned my hand in front of my face in a vain attempt to relieve the stinging sensation in my sinuses. "Total masochism." I took a long drink of water. Now that I knew a little about Brett's upbringing, I was curious how he'd chosen a career in landscape design. "When did you decide you wanted to be a landscape architect?"

He gave me a sheepish grin. "After I wrecked my father's golf cart." Brett explained that, at the age of fifteen, he and some buddies sneaked their fathers' golf carts out in the middle of the night and took them out on the course at the nearby country club to race. Brett was winning when he swerved to avoid a sand trap, lost control, and drove straight into a water hazard. "The engine was ruined."

I laughed. "Were you punished?"

"Grounded for an entire month. To pay for a new cart, my father canceled the lawn service and made me take care of the yard. Ironically, that's when I discovered how much I enjoyed landscaping work. I added some bushes out front, expanded the patio, built an archway into the backyard. I did such a good job on my parents' yard that several of our neighbors hired me to do their lawns, too. I made a small fortune."

I shook a finger at him. "I hope you paid taxes on that income."

"Of course. Wouldn't want the mean old IRS coming after me." He shot me a wink.

As we each snagged a final piece of sushi, we found we shared a fondness for British television.

Brett dipped his sushi in soy sauce. "You watch *MI-5*?"

"Own the complete set on DVD." The suspenseful show featured a team of British counterterrorism agents who had to spy, scheme, and kick major ass to achieve their missions. Naturally, I loved it.

Brett eyed me, his expression hopeful, his lip curled up in a mischievous grin. "The only polite thing would be to invite me back to your place to watch an episode."

I held my *kappamaki* aloft and gave him a coy smile in return. "Is that so?"

After dinner, we returned to my town house. Let it never be said that Tara Holloway failed to follow proper etiquette. As we came in the door, Annie peeked out from under the couch. When she noticed Brett she jerked her head back out of sight. *Stranger danger.*

"Who's the fraidy cat?" Brett asked.

"That's Annie," I said. "She has trust issues." She'd been dumped at a shelter with a half-dozen littermates. Who could blame her? I gestured to Henry, lying on his side atop the armoire, napping in his roost. "The overfed, narcissistic lump of fur up there is Henry."

Henry partially opened one eye, glanced our way, and, seeing nothing of any interest, twitched his whiskers and went back to his nap.

While Brett loaded the first of the season one DVDs into the player, I went to the kitchen. The African violet that had been so pretty and perfect only two hours ago now bore jagged-edged leaves, a telltale sign my cats had been happily chomping on the plant while we'd been out to dinner. Bad kitties. Good thing it wasn't toxic.

I uncorked a bottle of my best merlot, a $5.99 bottle I'd picked up on sale at the grocery store. As much as I enjoyed the stuff, I could tell little difference between the cheap brands and more expensive varieties. A buzz is a buzz. I poured two glasses, plunking a maraschino cherry into mine.

When I returned to the living room, I found Brett sitting on the couch with Henry draped across one leg. Brett appeared intact, no bites or claw marks.

"How'd you manage to get him down without losing an eye?"

Brett smiled. "Trade secret." He scratched the cat behind the ears and Henry closed his eyes in kitty bliss.

"I'm jealous." The rotten cat rarely let me touch him. Never mind that I fed, brushed, and spoiled him. Maybe it was a guy thing and the two were engaged in some sort of interspecies male-bonding ritual.

I settled on the sofa, leaving two feet between me and

Brett. Far enough away not to seem eager, but close enough
to be conveniently accessible should a romantic mood develop. Five minutes into the show, Brett shifted closer and
settled his arm on the back of the couch behind me.
Henry gave me an eat-litter-and-die look, hopped down
from the couch, and trotted off. Ten minutes into the show,
Brett's arm slid down around my shoulders. Twenty minutes into the first episode, he whispered, "The suspense is
killing me."

I turned to him. "You mean the show?"

He shook his head and gave me a seductive grin. "No.
Not the show." He put a finger under my chin, lifted my
face to his, and pressed his lips to mine.

Mmm. His mouth was soft, warm, and wonderful. My
God, the guy knew how to kiss a woman. I could only guess
at his other talents—it was far too soon for things to get
physical—but if he was as skilled with the rest of his body
as he was with his mouth, I'd be in for a real treat if this
relationship continued.

The episode ended. I came up for breath and checked
the clock. Ten. Dang.

"I think we better call it a night." Tomorrow was a
workday, after all.

Brett sighed but acquiesced. He left me with another
warm kiss. I would've killed for a dozen more.

CHAPTER NINE

Girlz in the 'Hood

The next morning, I dressed in a pair of the no-line panties and a scandalously short denim miniskirt I'd bought for nightclubbing back in college. The fabric barely covered my butt. I topped the skirt off with a bright yellow T-shirt knotted tightly above my belly button, revealing several inches of bare stomach. I may not have much to offer in the way of cleavage, but thanks to my frequent workouts with Eddie, at least my stomach was flat and rock hard. So long as I was going for the Daisy Mae look, I figured I'd wear my red leather ropers. I applied a heavy coating of eye shadow and mascara on my eyes and put on twice as much blush and lipstick as usual, carefully applying the cosmetics to my still-sensitive face.

After trying in vain to fluff out my hair like Christina had done in the mall's dressing room, I bent over at the waist and sprayed my hair as I shook my head. When I stood back up, my hair stuck out wildly in all directions like I'd just climbed off a roller coaster. An enormous pair of silver hoop earrings completed my tacky ensemble. If Brett saw me now, he wouldn't even recognize me.

Anne sat on the bathroom countertop watching me, her pupils large. I bent over and looked her in the face. "What do you think, Annie girl?"

She hissed, jumped off the cabinet, and darted under the bed. I took a glimpse at myself in the mirror. "You're right, cat. Take me to the curb, I am white trash."

At the office I filled out my expense report and handed the form to the secretary in the accounting department along with an envelope containing the receipts for my new trashy clothing, the cleaning supplies, and the toilet seat. I crossed my fingers the expenses would be approved. Accountants were generally known for being tight-asses, and the internal accountants at the IRS were the tightest asses of all. They pinched pennies until Abe Lincoln screamed for mercy.

Josh, wearing his standard khaki pants, blue button-down shirt, and malicious scowl, stood at the water fountain as I came down the hall. He looked me up and down. "My, my, if it isn't Larry the Cable Girl." He held an imaginary spittoon to his lips, making a *puh-ting* sound as he pretended to spit tobacco juice into it.

I put a hand on my hip. "Not that it's any of your business, but I'm on an undercover assignment."

Josh's blue eyes flashed envy and he bolted by me, taking off in the direction of Lu's office, probably to complain. He'd never been assigned an undercover operation, but it was his own fault. He was a whiz with computers, but his people skills stank. Rumor had it he was a cyborg.

I'd brought along a suitcase full of clothes, as well as

some things to make the stakeout more enjoyable—a small cooler full of food and drinks, some magazines, my laptop. I carried my things outside and sat on my plastic cooler on the sidewalk in front of the office building, waiting for Christina to pick me up. A few minutes later, Eddie walked up with Ross O'Donnell, the attorney from the Justice Department.

Eddie took me in from the top of my teased hair to the bottom of my scuffed cowboy boots. "You can take the girl out of the country, but you can't take the country out of the girl."

Back in Nacogdoches, I'd been known to curse a time or two, but I was trying to change my uncultured ways. Still, I couldn't let Eddie's blatant affront go unchecked. "Kiss my derrière."

"Classy comeback," Ross said. "What with the French and all."

Eddie wore his double-breasted gray power suit and shiny silk black and gray checkered tie, clearly attired for a major bust.

I shielded my eyes from the sun as I looked up at him. "Who's going down today?"

"The owner of Chisholm's Steakhouse."

Chisholm's was a popular high-end restaurant downtown, near the financial district, the kind of place where expensive wines were uncorked and slaughtered cattle found their way into the arteries of the rich and famous while million-dollar deals were sealed.

Eddie slid his sunglasses into the breast pocket of his suit. "The owner and his wife are in the middle of a nasty divorce and she ratted out her husband for cheating on his taxes. Of course, she claims she knew nothing about it until just recently."

"How convenient."

In the restaurant business, cash transactions were common, which made it easy to fudge the profits. That type of garden-variety tax fraud offered little intrigue. I was glad I had my own case to work on instead.

Christina rounded the corner in the pink Cadillac, the back tire riding up on the curb as she cut the wheel a little too close. Driving that long car was like steering a cruise ship. She rolled to a stop at the curb and leaned over in the front seat to peek up at me through the passenger window. She wore a skintight cap-sleeved pink top along with black imitation-leather pants and high-heeled black boots. Her hair was floofed within an inch of its life and her boobs were hiked up so high in a push-up bra they'd virtually become shoulder pads. "Your face looks much better today. Ready to head to the Taj Ma-hurl?"

"Yep." I picked up the cooler, my suitcase, and my backpack and put them in the trunk next to a small television set Christina had brought with her. I slammed the trunk closed and climbed into the front seat.

Christina had just put the car in gear when the Lobo stepped up to my window and rapped on it, ashes falling from the cigarette in her hand. Today Lu wore a clingy knee-length dress in a swirled pattern of turquoise and pink, the bottom trimmed with balled fringe. At first glance she appeared to be wearing coordinating blue tights, then I realized the blue swirls on her legs were varicose veins. Instead of go-go boots, today she sported cork platform shoes. Talk about a fashion victim. This outfit should be a felony.

"Where the hell do you think you're going?" she demanded through the glass.

I unrolled the window. "We're heading out to stalk the ice-cream man."

"Didn't you get Viola's message?" Lu took a deep drag

on her cigarette, letting the smoke waft back out through her nose. "She left one on your cell."

I opened my purse and pulled out my mobile phone. The battery was dead. Oops. "What was she calling about?"

"Your hearing on Battaglia's shooting is at nine." Lu jerked her head toward the building. "Get your butt in there."

I glanced at my watch. Eight fifty-three. Dang. No time to change my clothes. I'd have to defend myself in this skanky outfit.

I showed Christina where to park and we went into the building, Christina's leather pants making that odd crunching sound, her heels again click-clacking as she followed me inside.

"Good luck," Viola called as I passed her desk.

"Thanks." I was going to need it.

Josh eyed Christina and me as we walked by his office, stepping into the hall and following us as we made our way to Internal Affairs. "Tara's going down," he called after me, following his comment with a "Boop . . . boop . . . boop," like the sound of a submarine diving.

Christina glanced back at Josh. "Who's the dork?"

"That's Josh," I said. "He's a cyborg. His dad was human, his mom was a Pentium III."

When I arrived at the conference room, Eddie was waiting outside. He'd just received word of the hearing, too.

I stepped closer to my partner. "Eddie," I whispered. "I'm scared. What if I get fired?" No way could I go back to desk work. I'd sooner die. Maybe I'd have to shoot myself next time.

Eddie squeezed my shoulder. "You'll do fine. Besides, this type of experience builds character."

I punched him in the arm.

He rubbed his bicep, then held the door open for me

and Christina. When Josh tried to come in, Eddie put one hand on each doorjamb, blocking the doorway. "This doesn't involve you."

"It doesn't involve her, either." Josh pointed to Christina.

"No," Eddie said. "But she smells pretty so she's allowed to stay." He stepped inside and slammed the door in Josh's face.

The Lobo stood at the window, a crumpled green pack of cigarettes in hand, ready to take another smoke break as soon as my hearing was over.

Eddie gestured to the pack in the Lobo's hand as he walked past her. "That's not your usual brand."

"I switched to menthols," she said. "They freshen your breath."

Yeah, right.

On the far side of the long rectangular conference table sat two older men, one white-haired, one gray—the director of field operations, or DFO for short, and a seasoned investigator from Internal Affairs. Both wore navy blue suits and condemning expressions. They took one look at my outfit, exchanged glances, and frowned.

"Please excuse my attire." I unknotted my T-shirt so it would at least cover my belly button and attempted to smooth my untamed hair. "I'm working undercover and only got word about this hearing five minutes ago."

I slid into a seat across from the men, folded my hands on the table, and tried to appear as calm and professional as possible under the circumstances. Not easy when you've broken out in a cold sweat and every muscle in your body was so tense it hurt.

"Hi, y'all," Christina chirped. She hiked her thumb at me. "This is one smart, tough chick you've got working for you." She smiled and put her hand out across the table, leaning forward, her boobs likely to pop out of her shirt any second. "I'm Christina Marquez from the DEA, by the way. I'm working with Tara on the undercover case she mentioned."

The men looked at each other as if unsure how to respond to the big-haired bimbo before them. Finally, the DFO slowly extended his hand across the table to shake hers. The investigator followed suit. Christina plunked down into the chair next to me.

My first reaction was annoyance that Christina didn't seem to realize the critical nature of this meeting, but when the men kept sneaking glances at her as I related the events of last Friday's bust, I realized *her* bust served as an effective distraction.

I explained I'd been innocently perusing documents in the office of the auto parts store when Battaglia entered, wielding the box cutter. I pulled back the fresh bandage on my arm and showed them my stitches, hoping to earn some pity points in my favor.

Christina gasped. She sat bolt upright, slapping her palms on the table, opening her big brown eyes wide, and poking out her breasts in indignation. "My God! He cut you?" She turned to the men across the table. "Clearly Tara did what she had to do." She crossed her arms under her cleavage, pushing her breasts up even further. "Case closed."

"I agree," said the DFO. The investigator murmured his assent.

I signed the record of their findings to be placed in my permanent Internal Affairs file. The Lobo signed off, too, and handed the form back to them. They slipped the form into a file and opened the door to leave. Josh fell forward into the room, obviously having been listening at the door, the nosy twerp. He turned and quickly scurried away like the little rodent he was.

Once the higher-ups had gone, Lu shook a cigarette from the pack in her hand. "That went much better'n I expected." She stuck the cigarette between her lips and shooed us out the door. "Everyone back to work now."

Eddie walked me and Christina out to the Cadillac. "I can't believe I didn't have to testify," he said to me. "I figured we'd be begging them not to transfer you to the audit department."

"Oh, please," Christina said. "Men are so easy. Just show them some boob and you can get whatever you want."

Aha. I'd had my suspicions she'd been playing a part back there. Under all that poofy hair was a nimble brain.

"I owe you one," I told her.

The two of us climbed into the Caddie and waved good-bye to Eddie. Standing alone in the parking lot, he looked wistful, as if he wished he were going undercover on a stakeout. Beats the heck out of reviewing accounting ledgers all day.

On the way to the crack shack, I quizzed Christina about her date with Dr. Maju. "Fess up. How was your date with Ajay last night? Did he rock your Casbah?"

"We had a great time. I'm hoping to see him again." She honked the Caddie's loud horn as a silver Mustang sailed across three lanes in front of us, nearly taking off our front bumper. That's Dallas traffic for you.

"Well, I hope I *never* have to see Ajay again." I scratched at the itchy tape holding the bandage to my forearm.

"He's a great kisser, you know."

"No, I didn't know. He's never slipped me any tongue. Just a tongue depressor."

"He was all over me last night," Christina said. "Like that Hindu god with all the hands. What's his name?" She twirled a finger in the air as she tried to remember.

"Vishnu?"

She snapped her fingers. "That's the one."

Twenty minutes later, we pulled into the gravel driveway of our shack-away-from-home. Across the street, two young Latino men wearing jeans and white wife-beater shirts leaned over a primer-gray seventies-era Nova, tinkering under the hood. The portable stereo at their feet blasted Tejano music. A huge, muscular black dog was chained to a tree in the yard, eyeing me and Christina and drooling, as if wondering what we might taste like. Chicken, perhaps? He hadn't been neutered, sporting a pendulous pair of egg-shaped testicles. He appeared to be part pit bull, part Rottweiler. What would that make him? A pitweiler? A rottbull? Either way, it didn't sound nearly as cute and friendly as a labradoodle.

Next door, a heavyset frizzy-blond woman stepped out onto her porch, a cigarette in one hand, a can of beer in the other, and a scowl on her face. "Turn that goddamn wet-back music down!" she bellowed.

The young men pretended to ignore her, though one of them nudged the volume button with the toe of his work boot, turning the music down a few decibels from earsplitting to simply irritating. The other muttered something about "white trash."

"Shouldn't these people be at work?" I asked.

Christina just snorted in reply.

I grabbed the roach bombs we'd bought the day before out of the plastic bag. "First things first."

After we triggered the bombs, we had to stay outside for two hours, giving the fog time to work its deadly magic. I retrieved my cooler and backpack from the car, sat down next to Christina on the front steps, and unzipped the bag. I'd brought my tax return—filing single yet again—but I really wasn't in the mood to work on it.

"I've got some magazines. Want one?" I pulled out the most recent issue of *Reader's Digest* and held it out to her.

Christina slapped my hand and hissed, "You get caught

'improving your word power' around here and you'll
blow our cover."

"Oh. Right." I wasn't very good at this undercover thing
yet. "How about this?"

Christina accepted my second offering. "*Cosmo*. That's
more like it."

I handed her a Diet Coke from the cooler and the two
of us spent some time checking out the latest fashions,
sniffing perfume samples, discussing the ridiculous crap
written up in the Agony Column.

" 'My boyfriend says I'm too loud when we make
love,' " Christina read aloud. " 'But I can't help expressing
my pleasure. What should I do?' "

I rolled my eyes. "The answer's obvious. Get a new
boyfriend who knows a good thing when he's got it."

One of the guys across the street glanced over at us,
called out in Spanish—something about a *puta*, was it?—
and the other laughed. Christina glared at them and raised
her middle finger.

"What did he say?" I asked.

"He asked if we were prostitutes. He won ten bucks on
the Lotto and wanted to know how much that would get
him."

When I'd first moved into my town house, my neighbors
had brought me homemade oatmeal cookies in a cute little
basket. Things apparently worked differently here. I looked
across the street and raised my middle finger, too, treating
him to a French-tipped bird. Turning back to Christina, I
said, "That's great you can speak a foreign language."
Though Spanish hardly qualified as such in Texas. Since
I grew up near the Louisiana border, French was standard
high school fare. But I'd long since forgotten everything I'd
learned, which wasn't much to begin with. "Are your parents from Mexico?"

She shook her head. "My family emigrated from Uruguay three generations ago. My parents only speak English. I learned Spanish from the live-in maid."

Christina certainly wasn't the stereotypical Latina woman. "You had a full-time housekeeper?"

Christina nodded. "Daddy's loaded. Coffee imports. But he's very controlling. Typical Latino machismo bullshit. I originally joined the DEA to piss him off, but then I discovered I actually liked the job. Who other than the federal government would pay me to read *Cosmo* all morning?" She fanned the pages of the magazine and handed it back to me.

I checked the time on my silver bangle-style watch. "It's been over two hours since we set off the roach bombs. Should be safe to go back in now."

Christina stood and led the way up the rickety steps and into the house. I slammed into her back when she stopped unexpectedly, emitting a cry of disgust. I peered around her to see hundreds of dead or dying cockroaches littering the scuffed wood floor, a few on their backs, their legs dopily bicycling in the air. Nasty.

After we cleaned the place up and aired out the smell of insecticide, we unpacked the cooler, spread a clean sheet over the filthy sofa, and plugged in the television. We spent the afternoon being couch potatoes, waiting for Joe and watching trashy talk shows. Squinting at the small TV screen, I scrutinized Maury's guest, who paraded back and forth across the stage in leopard-print spandex pants, gold sequined tube top, and black stilettos, her—or his—bleach-blond hair bobbing in long spiral curls.

Christina leaned toward the television for closer inspection. "That's gotta be a guy."

"No way." I gestured at the screen. "Check out the crotch. No bulge."

"Ever heard of duct tape?"

Sounded like a challenge to me. "Want to make it interesting?"

"Sure," she said. "Loser buys the ice cream today."

We leaned forward in our seats as Maury stepped up next to his guest. "Georgina is . . . a man!" The live audience whooped it up.

"Shoot." The ice cream would be on me.

My freshly charged cell phone chirped and I went to the kitchen to get it. It was Viola.

"I heard from accounting," she said. "They denied all your expenses."

"On what grounds?"

"Unnecessary."

Those tight-asses in accounting would have me sitting around this roach-infested house in my Donna Karan suit, crouching over a seatless toilet. Sheez. Martin and McGee never balked at reimbursing my expenses. Heck, they even paid for our parking and gave us a generous per diem for meals during tax season. There had been some benefits in working there. Not enough to make me want to go back, but still.

We tuned in to a soap opera as we ate a late lunch. By then it was about time for Joe to make his appearance. I'd brought along a blue nylon fanny pack to hide my gun and cuffs in, and I set about clipping the bag to my waist in preparation for the ice-cream man. The gun and cuffs probably wouldn't be necessary, but if I'd learned anything in the last few days, it was to never underestimate anyone. Jack Battaglia had seemed harmless until he was coming at me with that box cutter.

Christina scrunched up her nose. "A fanny pack? That's so nineties."

"I'm not trying to be stylish here. I'm trying to conceal

my weapons. There's nowhere to hide a gun in this short
skirt."

"Sure there is. I worked on this at home last night.
Watch." Christina slid her gun into the waistband of her
cheap pleather pants, tied the striped scarf she'd scored at
Sam Moon around her waist as a belt, then clipped her
iPod to the scarf to hold it in place and conceal her gun.
She raised her palms. "Voilà."

"Creative."

The faint tones of tinny ice-cream truck music drifted
in through the open windows.

"There's our man." I dug through my purse and retrieved my wallet. Never one to welsh on a bet, I dropped
a couple of singles into Christina's outstretched palm.

We stepped onto the porch to wait. The guys across the
street had disappeared, the hood now closed on the car,
the dog nowhere to be seen. After a few minutes, the ice-
cream truck music grew louder and Joe's rusty van rounded
the corner down the street. He slowly made his way toward us, stopping several times for young children clam-
oring to buy a cold treat.

As he approached our house, Christina waved and he
stopped the truck. She sauntered to the van, doing that
sexy hip-sway thing while I trotted along like a pathetic
sidekick.

"Hey." Joe's gaze ran up and down Christina's body
and his lips spread in a sleazy grin.

"We got money today." Christina allowed a sexy Spanish accent to ease into her voice as the words rolled slowly
off her tongue. She waved the bills at him.

Joe leaned through the window, his eyes darting around
as he tried unsuccessfully to hide the fact he was peeking
down Christina's tight, low-cut shirt. "Uh . . . Fudgsicle?"

Christina tossed her head, her dark locks swaying.

"Nah. I want to try something different." She peeked up at Joe with bedroom eyes. She put a pink manicured nail to her lips, drawing Joe's attention to her mouth. "What else you got that tastes good?"

Joe about came unglued, his Adam's apple bobbing as he swallowed hard. "Bomb Pop?" His voice cracked.

"Okay."

Joe reached down into the freezer and fumbled around. He found a Bomb Pop and handed it to Christina. She gave him the bills and he returned her change.

"See ya tomorrow." Christina waggled her fingertips at Joe and turned back toward the house.

Joe's eyes locked on Christina's ass as she sashayed her way back through the yard and disappeared into the house. Joe continued to stare after the screen door had swung closed.

I waved a hand in front of his face. "Hello?"

His head jerked in my direction. "Oh, yeah. What can I getcha?"

"I'll have a Bomb Pop, too."

I paid for my purchase and headed back to the house, noting that the two guys from across the street had come out of their house now and were headed to Joe's truck. I stepped into the living room and walked to the window, looking through the dusty slats of the miniblinds. Christina stepped up beside me, sticking a finger between the slats to expand our view. Outside, Joe was bent down at his service window, talking closely with our neighbors. Joe stepped away from the window, then returned a few seconds later and handed the guys a small brown paper bag.

"Granny got it right," Christina said, taking a lick at her Bomb Pop. "He's dealing."

CHAPTER TEN

*I*ntuition

The next week and a half was basically a repeat of our first day undercover, minus the pepper spray and pretzel. Christina and I dressed trashy, hung out in the 'hood, and did our best to suck up to Joe. It wasn't easy. Not only did he make our skin crawl, but the Latino guys who lived across the street made a habit of stepping into line behind us each day, disabling us from engaging in private conversation with Joe and rushing us through our exchange.

We'd rented a U-Haul and moved a few pieces of furniture into the house to make ourselves look legit. The spare dresser from my guest room. A whitewashed bookcase from Christina's apartment. A wobbly dinette set with three mismatched chairs that we'd picked up for fifty bucks at Goodwill.

Sleeping on an air mattress on the floor left a lot to be desired, and left me with a sore back, but if we didn't spend some of our nights at the house the neighbors might become suspicious. As if the accommodations weren't bad enough, nights in the 'hood offered a cacophony of police sirens, car horns, and barking dogs. The mama raccoon and her offspring had taken up residence in the attic, banging around up there like they owned the place. Yet, as much as we missed a good night's sleep, our tired, droopy eyes enhanced our pretense, giving us the strung-out look of drug users.

The usual spring drizzle had set in, forcing us to remain inside the house most of the day. At first it was fun to hang out, surf the Net, and watch television, but after a few days I developed a raging case of cabin fever. It didn't seem to me we were making much progress, but Christina assured me that prolonged periods of downtime were normal on a stakeout, that things were moving along as expected, and that, unlike a tax investigation, the progress of a drug case couldn't be measured in stacks of paperwork.

I checked in at the office several times, performing tri-age on my in-box and taking care of the items that couldn't wait. I noted the thermometer in the break room now read ninety-eight million. One of my fellow agents had scored big in a case involving a chain of discount furniture stores, taking the Lobo that much closer to retirement. But there was two million left to go and the ten-grand bonus was still up for grabs.

After work on Friday, Christina dropped me at my town house. I changed out of my trashy clothes and into a pretty skirt and blouse. I drove into the parking lot of my favorite French restaurant, the chichi Chez Michel, pulled down the visor, and quickly checked my hair and makeup in the mirror. My lips definitely needed attention. I applied a coat of plum-hued gloss, rendering them soft, luscious, and kissable. I handed my keys to the waiting valet.

Stepping through the frosted-glass doors of the restaurant, I spotted Brett sitting at a secluded table in the back, next to a window. When he saw me walk in, his handsome face lit up.

My stomach gave an excited flutter. We'd attended a play at the Majestic Theater the previous Saturday, spent Sunday afternoon at a home-and-garden show at the convention center, and had dinner at a Mexican restaurant earlier in the week, but the new-car smell still hadn't worn off our relationship.

I weaved my way past other diners to our table. Brett stood and walked around the table to greet me. I looked up at him, admiring the way his tailored charcoal suit draped across his broad shoulders, the way his soft green tie perfectly matched his eyes. He gave me a hug, his body lean and firm, a byproduct of time spent on landscaping projects and golf courses.

"Hey, Tara."

"Hey."

He kissed me gently, his hand sliding from my shoulder to the nape of my neck. His touch sent shock waves down my spine, making me want to rip off his jacket and tie and have my way with him right there on the crisp, white tablecloth, salad forks be damned.

I returned the kiss, melting into his arms. When I realized I'd been clutching him too close and too long for proper decorum, I released him from my grasp and stepped back.

He grinned slyly, his voice low and husky. "That was quite a greeting."

Brett pushed the chair under me as I sat down. On the table was a glass of my favorite merlot, ready and waiting for me, complete with a cherry. Just how I liked it. This guy paid attention.

He reclaimed his seat on the other side of the table.

"I take it from the suit you weren't planting trees today."

"Nope." He explained that he and one of the commercial architects from his firm had met with a potential client today to pitch designs for a medical complex.

"How'd it go?"

"We got the job."

I raised my glass. "Congratulations."

He clinked his glass against mine. "Thanks."

The waiter arrived to take our order. I quickly perused the menu, deciding on a relatively simple mixed greens and goat cheese salad since I'd be having the calorie-laden crème brûlée for dessert.

"Oui, madame," the waiter said, taking my menu.

Over dinner, we discussed the turbulent world of Dallas politics, debated the possible causes for the reduction in the bee population and the effect it might have on gardening, and discussed the previous night's episodes of our favorite British comedies. After spending the day on a stakeout in a former crack house, I needed to be able to let my guard down, experience this normality. Brett's presence was calming, reassuring. I felt safe with him.

"Working on any interesting cases?" Brett asked.

Given the secretive nature of my current undercover operation, there wasn't much I could tell Brett. "Kind of," was all I said.

He waited for more. He didn't get it.

"I'm sorry, Brett. I wish I could tell you more, but a lot of what I do is highly confidential."

He chuckled. "Covert ops?"

His comment was closer to the truth than he realized.

"Not exactly Navy SEAL stuff," I said, "but yeah."

He raised his palms. "Okay. I got it. No shoptalk." He reached across the table and took my hand in his. "I just hope you're not working on anything dangerous."

"You're sweet to worry." His concern warmed my heart. He'd begun to care about me. Woo-hoo! Still, I wondered if my inability to share the details of my job would become a problem. I wasn't sure how I'd feel if the shoe were on the other foot. But I couldn't reveal anything that might jeopardize the case. You never knew what might be overheard or innocently shared with a coworker or family member and inadvertently become public.

"Are you?" Brett asked. "Are you working on a dangerous case?"

I wasn't sure what to say because I wasn't entirely sure myself how dangerous the case was. I certainly hadn't expected Jack Battaglia to go after me like he had. Was Joe a true threat? Hard to tell. He was scrawny, not too smart. Then again, he was a drug dealer. Still, the biggest danger was probably that the decrepit house would collapse on us.

"I'm not sure," I said finally. I suppose I could've told him then that I carried a Glock, handcuffs, and pepper spray, but mentioning the weapons might only serve to underscore the danger of my job. Better to ease him in, feed him details over time as we came to know each other better.

Brett exhaled, released my hand, and sat back in his chair.

The concern that had warmed my heart only a moment ago now had me hot and bothered. Jack Battaglia hadn't realized how tough I could be, and now it seemed as if Brett, too, were questioning my ability to take care of myself. Of course, the reason it bothered me so much was that I harbored the same doubts. Still, it was my ability and my right to question it, not his. Time to turn the tables. "What about your job?" I demanded. "You work with nail guns, chain saws, heavy equipment. You could be run over by a tractor or fall into a wood chipper, end up like Steve Buscemi in *Fargo*."

Brett shuddered, then raised his white cloth napkin and waved it. "Okay, okay. I surrender." He put the napkin down. "I'm sorry if I offended you, Tara. I know you can take care of yourself. I just don't want to see you hurt. It's only natural for a guy to feel protective of his woman."

His woman? Oddly, the statement got both my ire and hopes up. "You consider me *your woman?*" I looked across the table at him, noting the playful smile on his face. He hadn't truly gone caveman on me. He was only teasing, flirting, testing the waters. Maybe I needed to lighten up.

"You're not like anyone I've ever met, Tara."

"How so?" Okay, so now I was blatantly fishing for compliments. But I was also curious how Brett saw me, what qualities he found attractive.

"You're . . ." He looked up as if searching for the right word. Finally, he found it. "Feisty."

Yeah, "feisty" pretty much summed me up.

"I don't want another guy getting his hands on you until we've had a chance to see where this goes. What do you say?"

I looked into his gorgeous green eyes, noted the sincere smile on his soft lips, and damn if I didn't forgive him on the spot. Now, what to say to his offer? It had been a while since I'd dated anyone exclusively. But it had also been a while since I'd met anyone as attractive, fun, and interesting as Brett. We seemed to be a good match so far, and the idea of him going out with another woman made me feel, well, *icky.* I shrugged. "What the heck."

Brett chuckled, shook his head, and took my hand again. "What the heck it is."

After the waiter brought the dessert, Brett leaned toward me over the table, gazing into my eyes, his expression seductive now. Instantly, my body temperature kicked up ten degrees. I hoped my antiperspirant could handle it. It had already been through a lot today. The foreclosure didn't have central AC and the window units had either been removed by the former owners or stolen.

"Remember that client I told you about?" he said. "The one with the lake house?"

"The banker, right?"

He nodded. "The construction is complete now and I'm heading out to the lake tomorrow to survey the property. It'll be an overnight trip." Brett watched my face as if trying to gauge my reaction. "Come with me, Tara."

Oh, I'd like to come with him, all right. Still, we'd only known each other two weeks. It was awfully soon to spend the night together, wasn't it? Even if we had just agreed to date exclusively?

Brett seemed to sense my hesitation. "There's a nice resort on the lake. I reserved a suite with two bedrooms."

A suite? Sweet. And separate beds would take some of the pressure off.

Brett ran his thumb down the back of my hand, triggering a tingle that raced up my arm, made a sharp turn, and headed south, stopping for an extended vacation at my equator. "How about it?"

I mentally ran through my schedule for the weekend. I'd planned to mow my tiny lawn, but for ten bucks the boy who lived next door would take care of it. I'd planned to see the latest chick flick with Alicia, but she'd understand if I rescheduled. I was also going to work on my tax return. But the return wasn't due for a few more weeks. It could wait.

I raised a finger. "One sec." Pulling my phone from my purse, I sent a quick text message to Christina, asking if she'd mind covering the house alone this weekend so I could go out of town with Brett.

OK, came the reply a few seconds later. *But U will O me.*

Not a problem. She'd bought me off with a pretzel and she was probably just as easy. A bottle of vanilla-scented bath oil should cover it. "Let's do it."

Brett smiled and gave my hand a quick squeeze before releasing it. "Great."

My heart somersaulted at the thought of spending so much one-on-one time with Brett. Going away together for the weekend would certainly crank our relationship up a notch. I wondered if it would end with at least one notch on the bedpost, too.

Brett saved the last few bites of his steak for his Scottish terrier mix, asking the waiter for a doggie bag. We split the crème brûlée for dessert, engaging in a round of rock-paper-scissors to see who would get the last bite. Brett won, rock over scissors, but while his hands were raised in victory, I scooped the last spoonful off the plate and into my mouth before he could protest. He watched me lick my spoon clean, a hungry look on his face despite having just enjoyed a sizable filet mignon. I can be such a tease sometimes. It's part of my charm.

We decided to call it a night at that point since we needed to get an early start the next morning to make the hour-long drive to the lake. Brett tipped the valet when the young man brought my car around, then turned to me. "See you at eight." He gave me a soft good-night kiss, then pulled back, putting his tongue to his lips. "Tastes like stolen crème brûlée." He grinned, then quickly stole another kiss from me. "There. Now we're even."

I made a quick stop by the nail salon on my way home from the restaurant. The nail tech removed the sparkly red polish, replacing it with traditional white French tips.

When I returned home, I headed straight upstairs to pack. I stepped into my walk-in closet, wrangled my black soft-sided suitcase down from the shelf, and opened it on the bed. Annie promptly climbed into it and curled up in the corner, watching me.

I returned to the closet and looked around. If another

woman searched through my clothing, she would assume two very different women lived here rather than just one. My wardrobe comprised two extremes—feminine heels, sophisticated cocktail dresses, and conservative business suits on one side of the closet, with T-shirts, faded jeans, and scuffed boots on the other. I guess I'm unofficially bipolar. The rough-and-tumble tomboy I'd been while growing up in Nacogdoches still lived in me, but part of her had been replaced by a young woman who enjoyed the more sophisticated things in life.

I shooed my cat out of the suitcase and she settled on my pillow instead. Along with a pair of cream Bermuda shorts and a sporty short-sleeved knit shirt, I decided to pack a deep purple calf-length fitted skirt and a coordinated short-sleeved sweater. I dug in my panty drawer and retrieved my red lace bra and the matching itchy, uncomfortable red lace thong I'd recently bought but had yet to put to use. I wasn't sure I understood thongs. When I was young, my brothers had yanked my underwear up my crack, giving me a wedgie as punishment for eating the last Twinkie or telling Dad they'd been dipping snuff behind the barn. Weren't wedgies supposed to be a bad thing? Now, all of the sudden, women were intentionally wearing wedgies. Made no sense to me. But, not to be left out of the fashion trend, I'd bought one of the torture devices.

I slingshot the thong into the suitcase and added my oh-so-sexy red silk nightgown. I wasn't sure whether the panties or nightie would actually be used this weekend, but best to be prepared for all eventualities, right? I zipped the bag shut.

I woke early the next morning to get ready for the trip. I dressed in sandals, jeans, and a ruffled red cotton blouse that accentuated the auburn highlights I'd paid my stylist two hundred bucks to carefully and strategically streak into my brown hair. You know, for that natural look.

Dr. Maju had removed my stitches a couple days ago, but a raised pink line remained on my forearm, marring my skin. He'd told me to take it easy and recommended an over-the-counter antiscarring cream to reduce the visual effects of the injury. I slathered a healthy coating over the area. At least my nails were perfect.

I grabbed my suitcase and makeup bag and headed downstairs to my living room.

Brett arrived promptly at eight, wearing neatly pressed navy chinos and a navy-and-tan striped golf shirt that were slightly at odds with his scuffed, ankle-high work boots. Annie hid, as usual, but when Henry saw Brett he trotted into the foyer and began winding around Brett's ankles. Brett picked up the furry, demanding beast and cradled him in his arms, scratching him under the chin. Henry launched into a loud, rumbling purr.

I glared at my cat. "Ungrateful brat."

Brett chuckled, set Henry down gently on the parquet floor, and relieved me of my luggage.

"Thanks."

Henry shot me a go-to-hell look and wandered off, his fluffy brown tail twitching.

After double-checking to make sure the cats had plenty of food and water, I locked up the condo and followed Brett out to his SUV. He lifted the back door to put my bags in the cargo bay, pushing aside a large cardboard box bearing the logo of a local printing business. He slid my luggage in next to his golf clubs. His was an extensive, top-of-the line set, the heads of the woods covered with cloth protectors that matched the black-and-white bag.

Brett closed the hatch and we stepped around to the passenger side. On the door was a small round dent that might be easily overlooked if not for the circle of white paint drawing attention to it.

"What happened here?" I asked, pointing at the recently acquired ding.

Brett cringed. "That's what happens when you park too close to the green during a junior tournament."

"Ah." I could relate. Once, when we'd been doing target practice back home, my oldest brother accidentally put a bullet through my mother's ornamental windmill. Boy, had she been pissed.

Brett leaned in to give me a warm kiss once I was settled. *Mmm.* This trip was starting off great.

After climbing in the driver's side, he turned to me and smiled. "You're mine for the whole weekend. I must be the luckiest guy on earth."

"You might not feel so lucky when the weekend's over." Though I was joking, I knew this trip represented a benchmark for our relationship. Traveling, spending extended periods of time together, was a proving ground for a relationship. If a couple could not only tolerate, but take pleasure in, each other's company for two days straight, their relationship had a real chance of succeeding.

He backed out of my driveway, commenting on the sad state of the single, malformed evergreen bush that constituted my front yard landscaping. I'd tried to trim the darn thing, even given it some plant food, but nothing seemed to help. I probably should've dug up the ugly shrub and replaced it with something more attractive, but between the long hours I'd worked at the CPA firm and the demands of my training at the IRS, I simply hadn't had the time.

We wound our way out of my neighborhood, noting the new buds developing on the trees. A couple more weeks and north Texas would be in full bloom. Pollen counts would reach critical mass, creating a beautiful hell for allergy sufferers.

"The bluebonnets will be out before long," Brett said, referring to the bluish-purple flower that carpeted the state late each spring. "We'll have to take a drive down to the hill country soon, check out the wildflowers."

"Sounds great."

We headed east out of the city on Interstate 20, the same interstate I'd traveled many a time with my mother on shopping excursions into Dallas, the pinnacle of our mother-daughter bonding experiences. Twice each year when I was a teenager, Mom and I would make the three-hour drive to Dallas from our home in Nacogdoches, our destination the Neiman Marcus flagship store, dishing up designer delights since 1908, looming like a high-fashion Mecca on the western horizon. Years later, passing the CPA exam had given me confidence, but it paled in comparison to the day Neiman's issued me a credit card with a thousand-dollar limit.

Brett and I continued on until we were a dozen miles past the extensive suburban sprawl of Dallas. He turned off the interstate onto a two-lane highway. Half an hour later, we headed along a narrow, tree-lined county road running around the perimeter of Cedar Creek Lake. Brett punched a button to turn on his car's GPS system and a map appeared on the screen.

We drove for another mile, passing Lakeside Lane, Lakeshore Lane, and Lakefront Lane before the GPS directed us to turn right onto Lakeview Lane. Someone with a real creative mind had named the roads out there. Bet it was hell on the mailman keeping it all straight.

Brett turned onto the street and we entered a neighborhood of massive mansions, each with its own unique style. A sprawling, tile-roofed Mediterranean flanked with imported palms sat next to a stately English Tudor with topiary horses rearing up on each side of the gated driveway. I wondered if the horses dropped leafy piles of topiary poop for the owners to muck.

Halfway down the street, Brett rolled to a stop in front of a two-story lodge-style house built atop a small rise overlooking the lake. "Here we are. The Sheltons' place."

Although the house was newly built, it was designed to appear aged and rustic, in the traditional understated style of Texas luxury. The exterior was light-colored Austin stone accented here and there with natural wood trim. A black iron rooster-shaped weather vane perched atop the pinnacle of the roof, pointing east in the light wind. Rough, unfinished shutters framed the plate-glass windows.

Near the main road were wide tire tracks, probably from trucks used to haul materials to the construction site. The ground immediately surrounding the house had been cleared to build the house, but several stray pieces of lumber and a number of large dirt clods were scattered farther out. A stand of small, scrubby mesquite trees remained along the edges of the large lot.

Brett pulled onto the shoulder of the road and parked the SUV. We climbed out, greeted by a cool breeze carrying the refreshing scents of cedar trees and lake water. I stood behind the car while he retrieved his camera equipment from the back. As Brett pulled out his camera bag, the black nylon strap caught on the top of the printer's box and pulled it off, the lid falling to the ground at my feet.

"I'll get it."

Brett slung the camera case over his shoulder. "Thanks."

I knelt down to pick up the cardboard lid before the wind could catch it and carry it off. When I stood to put the top back on the box, the stack of colorful glossy brochures inside caught my eye. I took one out and skimmed over the paper.

The pamphlets advertised an investment seminar

sponsored by a firm called XChange Investments. Normally an investment seminar wouldn't catch my attention. I was still paying off those pesky student loans from college and had little money to invest. But this seminar involved foreign currency exchange, or "Forex," a hot topic at the Treasury Department given the large number of scams that had surfaced in recent years. Con artists had duped investors out of hundreds of millions of dollars with promises of high returns with little to no risk. Many of the investors ended up destitute, losing their life savings to these swindlers. The Commodity Futures Trading Commission, or CFTC for short, was charged with regulating the Forex market. Unfortunately, with so many investors falling for the too-good-to-be-true promises of unscrupulous promoters, the CFTC simply couldn't keep up.

Though profits could be made by taking advantage of the price differentials among foreign currencies, Forex posed high risks relative to other types of investments. With the stock market, the price of one stock didn't depend on the price of the others. In theory, in a bull market, all stocks could increase in value and everyone could be a winner. But Forex investment was what insiders called a "zero-sum" game. Currency investment functioned like a seesaw—when one currency went up in relative value, another went down by an equal amount. If one Forex trader gained, another lost. No wealth was created overall. What's more, the legitimate Forex investment programs were generally offered by the larger brokerage houses, which carefully screened investors to ensure those putting their money in foreign currency could afford to lose it. Legal Forex futures were traded on established exchanges or boards of trade approved by the CFTC.

The flyer noted the investment seminar was scheduled for early May at a hotel in Shreveport, Louisiana, a two-hour drive east of where we now stood. The fact that the presentation would be held at a hotel wasn't necessarily unusual, but the brochure gave no permanent address or phone number for XChange Investments, only a Web site address. Seemed as if the company, and its officers, preferred to remain untraceable, raising a huge red flag.

Why would Brett have a box of these brochures in his trunk?

I held the flyer up. "What's this?"

Brett glanced over at me and shrugged. "Stan asked me to drop those off here."

Hmm. An odd prickle ran up my neck. The IRS had provided me with a Kevlar vest, a Glock, and a laptop when I'd joined the agency, but the best tool a special agent had was intuition. My intuition said I should look further into this XChange Investments. When Brett turned away, I quickly folded the flyer and slid it into the back pocket of my shorts. Surely they wouldn't miss one copy, right?

CHAPTER ELEVEN

Suspicion

After closing the trunk, I stepped around the car to stand next to Brett. He stared at the house for a moment, concentrating, his face intent as he tried to visualize the house with different types of landscaping.

"You know what would be perfect here?" I asked.

"What's that?"

"Pink plastic flamingos."

Laughing, Brett put an arm around me and pulled me to his side. "I don't think plastic flamingos are exactly the style my client is going for."

Being pressed up against him felt nice. His body felt warm and firm through the fabric of his shirt, which had me wondering how much warmer and firmer he'd feel without the shirt, chest to chest, skin to skin. Would I soon find out?

He dropped his arm from around me and raised his

digital camera to take photographs of the house. He snapped several shots from the road, then several more as we made our way across the dirt to the front porch. He'd been smart to wear the boots. Before I realized what he was doing, Brett turned around and snapped a photo of me.

"Hey!" I put my hands on my hips. "You're supposed to give a lady some warning."

"It's more fun to catch you off guard. Keep you guessing." He shot me a wink. He stopped before the oversized front door and fumbled through his pocket. "The Sheltons gave me a key and the security code so I could go inside, get a feel for the place, and check out the views. They've got houseguests staying here, but they're out for the day." Finding the key, Brett unlocked the heavy front door and stepped into the house, punching numbers on an electronic keypad mounted on the wall inside to deactivate the alarm.

"Whoa." I stepped into the foyer, which extended thirty feet up to an enormous deer-antler chandelier suspended from the second-floor ceiling. The air inside the house was cool. The walls were lined with the same rough, natural stone as the outside, giving the house the indomitable feel of a fortress and giving me flashbacks to my fifth-grade field trip to the Alamo. I'd bought a velvet sombrero and a pair of hand-painted maracas as a souvenir. So did most of my classmates, to the chagrin of the chaperones, teachers, and bus drivers. We'd cha-cha-chaed the entire three-hundred-and-fifty-mile trip home.

To the right of the door sat a small white cardboard box bearing the name STAN SHELTON and PERSONAL written in large block letters with thick red marker. The entire box appeared to be wrapped in clear tape. Whoever packed it had made damn sure the thing couldn't be opened without a lot of effort. It would take a machete to hack into that box.

The flooring under the box was composed of thick

planks of honey-colored pine. Brett and I walked forward, descending three wide steps into an expansive living room with a vaulted ceiling, our footsteps echoing in the empty expanse. I glanced around, noting that other than a folding table and chairs in the kitchen, the downstairs was not yet furnished. I walked over to the fireplace and stepped inside, having to duck only slightly to fit.

"This fireplace is bigger than my cubicle at my last job." Only managers and partners had offices at Martin and McGee, and only partners had offices with windows. We peons had been crammed into tiny cubicles and saw natural light only before eight A.M. and after six P.M. I got out and about much more in my new job with the Treasury, one of the many things I loved about being a special agent.

Brett stood in the center of the room, scanning the surroundings, too, though he seemed less impressed. Of course, given that he worked for one of the most prestigious architecture firms in Dallas, he was likely used to this type of luxury. He walked over to the plate glass that made up the back wall of the living room, offering an unobstructed view of the lake a mere fifty yards beyond the house. "Nice view."

What an understatement. The view of the blue-green water, adorned here and there with small whitecaps, was nothing short of spectacular. The triangular sails of sailboats rose off the water in the distance. A few grayish birds skittered along the water's edge while several more hung over the water, floating in the breeze.

Brett snapped several photos of the view from the living room, then made his way past the portable card table in the breakfast nook. I followed him into the kitchen. The extensive maple cabinets housed a glass-front wine cooler large enough to hold at least fifty bottles of wine. The countertops were pink granite, native Texas stone like that used at the state capitol building in Austin. The faucets and fixtures appeared to be made of copper. Brett took a small pad of paper and a pen out of his pants pocket and jotted down a few notes.

The rest of the house was equally impressive, from the ten-by-ten walk-in closets to the enormous whirlpool tub in the master bathroom, big enough for two. Daydreaming, I imagined Brett and me naked in the huge tub, bubbles up to our chins, the white froth obscuring the fun going on underneath, a tickle here, a caress there, enough to make a rubber ducky blush.

When I looked up, I found Brett watching me. He gave me that sly smile of his. Was he thinking what I was thinking? I think so. And I think I liked it.

A guest bedroom upstairs contained only a king-sized brass bed covered with a crumpled black satin comforter and a distressed-wood dresser on top of which sat half-empty bottles of Bacardi and Jack Daniel's.

Next to the bed stood two large blue hard-sided suitcases, no doubt belonging to the Sheltons' houseguests. The suitcases were horribly scratched and battered, as if they'd endured lots of use by their owners and abuse by airport baggage handlers. From the handles hung white paper tags with "DFW" printed on them, evidence of a recent flight into the Dallas-Fort Worth airport. There was also a customs sticker on each suitcase showing an inspection had taken place at the departure point, designated as "SJO." What did SJO stand for? San Juan? St. John's? San Jose?

"Let's go out back," Brett suggested. We'd finished touring the inside. Time to check out the backyard. We made our way down the wide staircase and into the living room. French doors led from the living room onto a wide rectangular patio that was made of the same stone as the house and spanned the width of the structure. The bare

backyard sloped gently down to the lake. Without the
house to block the wind, the breeze was stronger out back,
tossing my hair about my face, making short work of the
effort I'd put into styling my locks. Once we'd reached the
water's edge, Brett turned and spent a few minutes considering the back of the house. He took several more photos,
then packed his camera equipment back into the bag and
zipped it closed.

"Decks," he said finally, thinking aloud. "This house
needs a series of wooden decks and walkways leading
down to the water. A rustic gazebo with an outdoor kitchen
for entertaining. Colorful ground cover for the slope, to
prevent erosion. Live oak trees, mature ones along the
sides to provide shade without disrupting the view of the
water."

I looked at the house, trying to visualize the design
Brett had described. "Sounds beautiful." His plans had
me thinking again about my yard. Hopefully I'd find time
for gardening this spring now that I'd no longer spend day
and night cranking out tax returns. As a girl I'd loved gardening with my mother, and I missed the simple pleasure
of digging in the dirt, nurturing a plant until it rewarded
me with beautiful blooms, transforming raw earth into a
small paradise. I could definitely see why Brett found
landscape architecture so gratifying, knowing his concepts, sketches, and plans could turn a yard full of dirt
clods and scrubby trees into a gorgeous backyard haven.

Brett pulled the notepad out of his back pocket again
and jotted more notes. "The crew will need an excavator.
A rototiller. A backhoe to dig the holes for the trees."

While Brett wandered around the yard with his measuring tape, obtaining the dimensions of the property, I
stood at the water's edge and watched two sailboats racing
across the lake in the distance. Looked like fun.

When Brett finished his measuring and note-taking,

he walked over to me. "I'll have to come back again later this afternoon to see how the sunlight hits at different times of the day."

"Why's that important?"

"Knowing how much sun a space gets helps me determine which types of plants will grow best."

"Oh." Made sense.

He checked his watch. "We should be able to check into the hotel now. I just need to do one more thing before we go."

He led me back to the front of the house. Stowing his camera equipment in the back of his Navigator, he grabbed the box of pamphlets and carried it to the front door. I waited by the car as Brett opened the door, set the box on the floor in the entryway, then punched in the code on the wall keypad to reset the alarm. He grabbed the small taped box I'd noticed earlier and tucked it under his arm before closing the door. When he returned to the car, he shifted the box to his other arm to help me in.

I tried to sound nonchalant, but first the brochures and now the box had me buzzing with curiosity. I gestured at the package. "What's in the box?"

Brett shrugged. "No idea. Just playing courier for Stan and his houseguest." He closed the door on me.

Hmm . . . So Stan Shelton was somehow involved with the foreign currency exchange deal. Not necessarily unusual for a banker. But I hadn't noticed the name of First Dallas Bank—the bank Stan Shelton was president of—anywhere on the brochures. My recent training in financial scams probably made me overly suspicious, but something had my senses buzzing.

Brett climbed into the car, sliding the small box into the glove compartment in front of me, the word PERSONAL in bright red letters mere inches from my face, taunting me. Was I just being nosy? Or was there something going

on? And did I really want to spend my first weekend away
with Brett thinking about tax fraud?

The only one of those questions I could answer defini-
tively was the last one, and the answer was a big, resounding, "Heck no!"

CHAPTER TWELVE

A Con Man and a Gentleman

We drove a few miles farther along the lake and turned into the resort, passing a threesome of middle-aged men standing on the golf course, one of them bending over to push a tee into the close-cropped grass.

Brett slowed down to watch. The man stepped into place, swung, and sent the ball sailing in a long arc down the fairway. "Nice shot."

I made nice shots, too. Of a totally different variety, of course. I could handle a steel Glock with ease, but my skills with a titanium driver were limited.

The resort was two-story ivory stucco, boasting balconies trimmed with black iron railings and a lighthouse façade at the far end. My pulse raced as we pulled into the breezeway. Soon Brett and I would be led to our room, the room in which we might possibly make love for the first time.

I wondered what kind of lover he would be. Brett was a gentleman, sure, but he had his naughty, rebellious side, too. That dichotomy was one of the things I found so intriguing about him. Would he be a slow and gentle lover, tenderly bringing me to climax? Or would he ravage me, treating me to a passionate experience that would leave me sweetly sore the next day? Was it too much to hope for both?

After removing the white box from the glove compartment, Brett handed the uniformed valet his keys. The man helped me out of the car before loading our luggage and Brett's golf clubs onto a rolling cart. A bellhop followed Brett and me through the automated glass doors and into the foyer, which was decorated in a combined nautical-fisherman theme, the hanging light fixtures shaped like the wheels of sailboats, the walls adorned with plaster casts of fish made to resemble award-winning specimens caught in the lake.

Brett set the white box on top of his suitcase on the cart and obtained the room key while I waited with the bellhop. Brett stood facing the registration desk, his pants drawing tight across his firm backside as he reached into his pocket for his wallet. *Nice.*

Not to brag on myself, but I was in pretty good shape, too. You can't hurdle filing cabinets to chase down tax evaders without exercising regularly. Eddie and I worked out together at the downtown YMCA for an hour or so after work most days. The elliptical machines were my favorite, though Eddie refused to use them, saying men looked like prancing sissies on them.

Brett turned around with a key card in hand. "Room 206," he informed the waiting bellhop. We made our way to the elevator and climbed in.

The elevator dinged as it reached our floor, and Brett and I stepped out into the hallway. Behind us, the bellhop attempted to push the baggage cart forward, but one of the wheels caught in the groove at the bottom of the threshold and became stuck, causing the luggage and golf clubs to shift. The cart tilted precariously. The man gave it a forceful shove in an attempt to set it back on course. The box Brett had picked up at the lake house toppled off the front of the heavily laden trolley just as it careened forward. The front wheel rolled over the box, hopelessly crushing it, one end splitting open as luggage avalanched off the side of the cart, the golf bag tilting and spilling the clanking clubs onto the floor.

The bellhop apologized profusely as Brett helped him straighten the baggage cart and gather the luggage and golf clubs. "So sorry, sir."

"No problem," Brett said, unfazed. A lesser man would have lamented the mistreatment of his clubs. "These things happen."

I bent to pick up the smashed box, inadvertently releasing a small cascade of checks, which flowed out onto the carpet. As I knelt to scoop them up, I noted the checks were drawn on personal accounts in varying amounts, most ranging between ten and twenty thousand dollars. All were made out to XChange Investments. I took a quick glimpse behind me to see if Brett was looking, but he was still busy helping to gather up our luggage. I squeezed the box so that the end gaped open and peeked inside. The box contained several more checks and a large stack of bills held together with a red rubber band. I poked a finger inside to riffle through the bills. Most appeared to be fifties and hundreds. By my quick calculation, there was several thousand dollars cash in the stash.

Whoa.

Something odd was definitely going on here. Nobody carried that much cash around, especially in these days of electronic banking when cash was virtually obsolete. Nobody but pimps, drug dealers, or money launderers, that is. But Brett was none of those things. So what was he doing with this box?

I glanced back at Brett again. He was loading my suitcase onto the cart and hadn't seemed to notice what I was doing. Quickly, I shoved everything back into the box and cradled it in the crook of my arm so the contents wouldn't spill out again.

When we reached the suite, the bellhop rolled the cart into the main room to unload our luggage. Brett and I followed him inside. The suite was decorated in heavy oak furniture, the blue and gold tones of the fabric that covered the love seat and armchair reflected in the seascape paintings on the walls. The base of the tableside lamp was a white ceramic heron with long gray legs and a pointy gold bill. The decorator had certainly played up the water theme. Open doors situated on either side of the living area led to the two bedrooms, which were similarly decorated.

Brett tipped the bellhop when he finished unloading our luggage, then saw him to the door. When Brett returned to the room, I held the smashed box out to him, watching him closely to gauge his response. Did he know what was in the box?

He took the box from me and turned it in his hands, carefully holding the torn end closed so the contents wouldn't spill out. "That cart really did a number on this, huh?"

"Yeah."

He stepped over to the narrow closet next to the entry door, opened the small wall safe situated inside, and slid the mangled box into it. After shutting the safe, he turned the key and stuck it in his pocket, then closed the door to the closet.

What now? My gut told me something was up. But guts didn't matter. Evidence did. And that evidence was now locked securely away in the room's safe. I wasn't exactly an ace safecracker and, even if I were, I couldn't tell my boss I'd opened a locked safe without permission. The agents who trained us in Glynco hammered the rules of criminal evidence into our heads and we'd been tested extensively on them. Our attorneys would have a fit if they knew I'd collected evidence without a search warrant. Besides, Judge Trumbull would throw the evidence out of court and me into jail. A bright orange jumpsuit would clash horribly with my auburn highlights and the wardens probably didn't allow manicure scissors in the cells.

Looked like I'd have to figure out for myself if Stan Shelton or his houseguest were involved in illegal activity. But if Shelton or his visitors were involved in fraud, did that mean Brett was involved, too? After all, someone wouldn't just hand a box full of cash over to a casual acquaintance, would they? It was highly unlikely.

Damn.

I looked over at Brett, taking in his honest green eyes, his genuine smile, his strong jawline that spoke of strong character.

No. No way. Brett came from an affluent family and made a good living on his own. He didn't need to supplement his wealth by getting involved in a scam. But wasn't it usually the rich who were involved in financial scandals? Once people tasted the good life, they always wanted more. It often seemed the more a person had, the greedier he or she became. Like Michael Milken. Leona Helmsley. Bernie Madoff.

But surely not Brett. I refused to believe he'd take part in anything illegal. In fact, I was ashamed of myself for even thinking he could be involved. He'd simply been asked to do a client a favor by playing mailman, delivering a couple of boxes, nothing more.

Right?

Hell, rather than drive myself crazy wondering, why

not just ask him? "What's with all the checks and cash in the box?"

Brett glanced over at the closed closet. "Must be a deposit or something."

He seemed nonchalant. Maybe too nonchalant. Then again, Brett had been raised in a bubble of propriety and didn't deal with criminals on a daily basis like I did. Besides, he didn't work in the financial world. Maybe he didn't realize how fishy the situation seemed. Was he being honest with me? There was no way to tell for sure, but either way it was clear I'd get nothing useful out of him.

Forcing the negative thoughts from my mind, I stepped to the window and pulled back the lightweight curtains. The room overlooked an amorphously shaped pool and patio area where a few guests relaxed on padded lounge chairs or at umbrella tables. Two small boys were the only ones willing to brave the pool's still-cool water, splashing in the shallow end while their mother sat on the steps nearby, a martini glass in her hand, ruining all chances of that mother-of-the-year award. *Here's to you, boys!*

Brett walked up beside me, putting his hand on my back as he took in the view. His touch was gentle yet firm, reassuring and right. I'd been an idiot to question his integrity. A warm flush raced through my veins. Being alone with him in a hotel felt a little strange. And a lot exciting.

"Ready for lunch?" he asked.

"Give me a minute to freshen up?"

"Sure."

I grabbed my makeup case and stepped into the bedroom on the right, closing the door softly behind me. In the large, luxurious bath, I hurriedly touched up my hair and makeup, trying to force my windblown hair into a style that didn't look like it belonged on a troll doll. When I was finished, I walked back to the living area.

Brett was nowhere to be seen, and the other bedroom

door was closed. A voice on the other side caught my attention. I could hear only Brett speaking, so he must have been on the phone. The door muffled some of his words, but it was clear he was not pleased. I eased closer to the door, my ears perked.

"The agreement was fifty grand, cash up front."

There was a short pause as Brett apparently listened to the person on the other end of the line.

"Unacceptable. Either you get me what you promised by Wednesday or the deal is off."

What was that all about? What deal?

I'd never heard Brett sound so forceful. It was kind of sexy, revealing a tough, aggressive side of him I hadn't seen before. We were still in the honeymoon phase of our relationship, comfortable with each other but with lots more to learn. Clearly, we both had aspects of our personalities that had yet to fully surface.

I didn't let myself entertain the thought that the phone call might have something to do with the cash he'd stashed in the safe. Brett was a Rotarian, for goodness' sake. And surely if he were involved in a financial scam he would have dumped me the second he learned I worked for the IRS. The mere idea that he could be involved in something illegal was absurd.

But fifty grand? Cash?

When Brett ended the call, I stepped back over to the window so he wouldn't know I'd been listening.

He opened the door, seeming surprised to find me there. "That was quick."

I gave him a smile. "A woman motivated by food can move really fast."

Ten minutes later, we were seated on a patio, enjoying the fresh warm air, the view of the water, and a couple of mimosas while we waited for our meal.

Brett reached into his pocket, pulled out a case, and slid on a pair of sporty aviator-style sunglasses. He turned his chair to face me. "The resort rents Jet Skis. Want to take a run around the lake after lunch?"

I'd never been on a Jet Ski before, though I'd ridden the Guadalupe River in an inner tube several times with college buddies, a Styrofoam cooler of beer floating along with us. But what the heck, I was an adventurous girl. "Sure. Sounds like fun."

We dined on overstuffed paninis. Although Brett's posture was relaxed, his jaw worked several times, revealing pent-up tension, probably due to the heated phone call I'd overheard earlier. Brett hadn't mentioned the call, and I didn't want him to know I'd been eavesdropping, so I didn't ask about it. No guy wants a meddlesome girlfriend, especially this early in the relationship. Besides, who was I to demand explanations when I hadn't told him about my new case with the DEA?

After lunch, we changed into our swimsuits and made our way to the resort's marina. A row of brightly colored Jet Skis bobbed alongside the dock, as well as a number of paddle boats for the less daring. After we'd been given brief instructions and signed the requisite waivers, releasing the resort from liability for any boneheaded maneuvers on our part, the attendant showed us to our Jet Ski, a larger model made to seat two. The man handed each of us a thin neon-yellow life jacket from a wooden bin on the dock. Brett helped me into my vest, his hands mere inches from my breasts as he cinched the nylon belts across my front. I gazed up at him. He, too, seemed to sense the sexual tension. He tugged playfully on the end of the straps, pulling me to him for a warm kiss that promised much more to come.

Brett climbed aboard first, reaching out to help me across the narrow gap between the wooden dock and the wet bike. The vessel bobbed slightly as I settled on the seat behind him. I wrapped my arms loosely around his waist, acutely aware of every point of contact between our bodies.

Brett started the motor and the water churned behind us. He eased slowly away from the dock, picking up speed once we'd cleared the buoys marking the no-wake zone.

"Want to see how fast this thing can go?" he called back over the engine noise.

"Heck, yeah!" I wrapped my arms tighter around Brett's waist, pressing my chest to his back, only the thin life vests separating us. It felt natural, right.

We picked up speed, zooming across the lake. The spray was cool, but bearable now that the sun had made its way higher in the sky. Brett glanced back at me. The smile on my face said it all. I hadn't had this much fun in a long time. I needed this diversion. Between my training and new job, I'd focused on nothing but work the past few months.

Brett slowed as we approached a trio of bass boats clustered together in a shallow cove, each vessel containing a single angler atop an elevated seat. Large coolers sat on each deck, the beer inside sure to disappear over the course of the day, to be replaced by dead, dull-eyed fish.

"Your turn to drive," he said.

We carefully changed places. Brett wrapped his hands around my waist now, rubbing his right thumb across my abdomen, a gesture of intimacy that caused certain parts of me to tingle.

I turned my head to look back at him. "This is nice."

He pulled off his sunglasses and our gazes locked. He leaned forward to kiss me, soft and warm and long. I felt as if I were floating, and not just because we were on the water. The kiss deepened and grew increasingly hot and heavy. The Jet Ski rocked up on a small swell, and I pushed back against him to regain my balance. He pressed back, the hardened flesh at my lower back letting me know he wanted me as much as I wanted him.

Brett lifted the hair at the nape of my neck, applying his warm, wet mouth to that sensitive spot. He kissed his way up to my ear. *Mmm.*

Our embrace was shattered when a red and silver ski boat loaded with young men—who were also loaded—buzzed past us at top speed, its engine giving off a deafening roar and creating a rollicking wake.

I glared at the speedboat driver racing away from us. Where's a harpoon when you need one? I grabbed the handle grips. "This might get a little bumpy," I told Brett. "Hold on tight."

"Wow. That's just what a guy likes to hear." He scooted closer to me and wrapped his arms tightly around my waist, nuzzling my ear.

I gunned the engine and we zipped after the speedboat, bouncing over its wake, the Jet Ski becoming momentarily airborne. Behind me, Brett whooped. I laughed and turned the wheel to the left as far as it would go, causing the Jet Ski to bank precariously as I executed a series of tight donuts. Boy howdy, was this fun.

After an hour of tooling around the lake, we pulled back to the dock and climbed off the Jet Ski, handing the attendant the key.

"That was a blast." I unbuckled my life vest and stowed it back in the bin.

Brett followed suit. "Maybe I should splurge on a wet bike. I've had some luck with my investments recently."

I wondered if the investments he referred to were foreign currency investments, like those promoted on the brochures he'd left at the Sheltons' lake house. But I didn't ask. I wasn't sure I wanted to know. Then again, if he had invested with the outfit advertised on the brochure, that would mean he was innocent, wouldn't it? No one would knowingly invest in a scam. And, of course, there might not even be a scam.

I had so many questions.

What I needed were some answers.

We returned to the suite, where each of us showered in our separate bathrooms. As I lathered up, I couldn't help but think of Brett doing the same in his shower, mere yards away. I wondered if he, too, was thinking of me. I hoped so.

When we were both cleaned up and dressed, we returned to the Sheltons' house. I'd hoped to do some snooping around now that I knew about the checks and cash, but Brett didn't venture inside on this visit. Instead, he meandered around the perimeter of the house, stopping every dozen feet or so, looking up at the sky and making notes.

"Any chance you could let me into the house?" I called from the front porch, where I sat waiting on the steps. "I need to use the bathroom." It was the only excuse I could think of to get inside.

He came over to unlock the front door and again disarmed the security system.

"Thanks," I said, hoping he'd go back out to finish his work.

Fortunately, he did.

I sneaked upstairs and made my way into the bedroom containing the furniture and suitcases. Through the window, I saw Brett bending down to take soil samples from various spots around the property, scooping trowels of dirt into plastic containers. Good thing he was busy with his mud pies so I could take a look around.

I checked the closet. Three men's business suits in transparent dry cleaner bags hung on one rod, a couple of frilly dresses on another. A shiny pair of men's dress shoes stood neatly under the suits, while a pair of silver stilettos lay strewn under the dresses, as if they'd been kicked off in haste. The dresser drawers were empty. I found nothing incriminating in the night table other than a prescription bottle of Viagra and a leather codpiece. Ew. On the bathroom counter I discovered a shaving kit and a makeup case, both packed.

For the most part, the guests appeared to be living out of their suitcases. Either they hadn't been here long or they wanted to keep their belongings corralled to enable a quick exit.

A quick check of the suitcases indicated they were locked. Why would someone lock their suitcases inside a private residence? Habit? Or did the locked suitcases indicate an innate lack of trust? In my experience, people who didn't trust others were usually not trustworthy themselves.

"Tara?" Brett's voice came from downstairs.

Sheez! I hadn't heard him come inside. Thank goodness he didn't catch me trying to open the suitcases. How would I have explained that?

I tiptoed out of the room. "Coming!"

CHAPTER THIRTEEN

Will We or
Won't We?

That evening, Brett and I feasted on an elegant, excessively rich, and decidedly delicious dinner at the resort's restaurant, beginning with a goat cheese and sun-dried tomato salad, followed by fish smothered in lemon-butter sauce, nothing like the fried baloney and mayonnaise sandwiches I'd grown up on. We topped off the meal with a bottle of merlot. Brett made sure my wineglass contained a cherry, undaunted by the waiter's raised eyebrow.

"I haven't seen you in purple before," Brett commented. "It's pretty on you."

I gave him a smile. Seems the skirt and sweater set had been a good choice. The fitted skirt emphasized my lean legs, while the sleeveless sweater exposed my tightly toned arms. Heck, I worked hard at the Y. Might as well show off a little.

Several times during the meal, I caught Brett watching

me across the candlelit table. Our eyes met and held for several seconds, communicating what we weren't quite ready to put into words. We wanted each other. Bad.

After the waiter recited the dessert options, Brett asked if it might be possible to have the chocolate fondue served in our room, along with a bottle of champagne.

"Certainly, sir."

Brett arranged to have room service deliver our dessert a half hour later to allow time for our dinner to settle. After signing the credit card slip and returning it to the waiter, Brett stretched a hand across the table to take mine, the warmth of his skin sending yummy signals to other parts of my body with hungers yet to be satisfied. "Want to take a walk along the shore?"

"A walk sounds wonderful." Might as well get our blood pumping and our bodies warmed up. Wouldn't want to pull a muscle during our upcoming bedroom romp. Two weeks of dating was long enough for sex, right? I'd been unsure before, but things felt different now, felt right.

Brett and I wound our way down a curved flagstone path to the lake. The evening had grown dark by then, and the amber lights from the hotel's patio reflected off the water, turning the whitecaps gold under the starry sky. The water surged onto the shore and receded with a soft *shush-shush* sound. A brisk, cool breeze blew off the water, refreshing and energizing.

I took off my sandals and carried them as we made our way down the moist, sandy ground of the lakeshore. Brett took off his loafers, tucking his socks inside and rolling up the legs of his pants. We walked along the edge of the lake, letting the water lap at our feet. Every nerve ending in my body was on high alert, especially those on my backside where the red lace thong was now creeping up.

I looked up at Brett. "This was a great idea."

"I've got another one." Brett took my hand and pulled me to a stop. He stepped in front of me, dropped his shoes to the ground, and cupped his hands under my chin, turning my face up to his. This kiss was just as warm as his earlier kisses, but far more passionate, demanding even. After a few seconds, he opened his mouth and our tongues began to tango.

This was good stuff. I tossed my sandals aside. *Splash*. Oops. My shoes had landed in the lake, but at that moment I didn't give a rat's patootie. All I cared about was Brett, being close to him. I wrapped my arms around his neck and stepped closer, my chest pressed to his. The heat between our bodies grew, making the night air feel even cooler in contrast, the opposing sensations making my body feel incredibly alive. I could feel my heart racing, the blood pulsing through my veins, desire fueling a fire inside me that only Brett could extinguish. He'd better make it quick. We'd reached a four-alarm level.

Eventually, Brett backed off, taking his mouth off mine. I kept my eyes closed, feeling weightless, as if the breeze could just blow me away.

After a few seconds, I opened my eyes and found myself meeting Brett's gaze. His eyes were hooded, his pupils dark. Clearly he was a man with longings, needs, wants. And I wanted nothing more than to fulfill each and every one of them.

Two squealing kids came running up the shore ahead of their parents, throwing rocks into the water, invading our privacy. Brett retrieved my wet sandals from the lake, laughing as he shook the water from them. Arm in arm, we meandered back to the hotel. I would've been up for an all-out sprint back to the room, but the slow pace only gave more time for the anticipation to build.

We took the elevator up to our room, my breaths coming shorter and faster as the doors opened onto our floor.

We headed down the hall, my waterlogged shoes emitting a soggy *sklurch* with each step.

Brett opened the door and we entered the room. My heart spun with expectation and my skin felt as if it were tap-dancing on my bones. This was it. The night we'd seal the deal.

Brett dropped the key card onto the coffee table. He gestured to the room-service cart, laden with a fondue pot full of delicious-smelling melted chocolate, an assortment of fruit for dipping, and a bottle of champagne in a crystal ice bucket. "How does champagne sound?"

"Like this." I put a finger inside my cheek and made a "pop" sound.

Brett shook his head but grinned, amused, as he pulled the chilled bottle from the bucket.

Sure, I had a goofy side, and it often reared its head at inopportune moments. But just as I was attracted to Brett for the normality he brought to my otherwise crazy world, I suspected my occasional eccentricities, my somewhat wild and unruly nature, were part of the reason Brett was attracted to me.

While Brett poured us each a glass of bubbly, I took my soggy shoes into the bathroom and freshened up. When I finished, I looked at myself in the mirror, trying to psych myself up. Instead, the uncertainties kicked back in. Images of the colorful Forex brochure flashed in my mind and a tiny voice in the back of my head whispered to me to think twice before doing something stupid, before entangling myself—emotionally and physically—with a potential criminal. But other voices in my head screamed, "Don't listen, you idiot! He's a great guy! Go for it!" and soon the tiny naysayer was drowned out.

We sat side by side on the couch, Brett's arm draped around my shoulders as we enjoyed the champagne and chocolate-dipped strawberries, cherries, and raspberries.

"Mmm." I closed my eyes as I swallowed another delectable bite of chocolate-covered fruit. "This is *sooo* good."

Brett took my hand and lifted it to his lips. His voice was husky and low. "Some chocolate dripped on your finger."

Before I knew what he was doing, he'd slipped my pinky into his mouth, gently sucking the sweet chocolate from the tip.

"Mmm," I said again, my eyes on his mouth now. "This is even better."

When the champagne bottle was empty, Brett gently took the crystal stem glass from my hand and set it on the table. He took both of my hands in his, pulling me up from the sofa. He looked deep into my eyes and found the answer he'd been looking for.

Yes. Yes-yes-yes-yes-yes, hell, yes!

He glanced down into the fondue pot. "There's a little warm chocolate left." His lips spread in a naughty grin. "Should we bring it with us?"

"Heck, yeah. Can't let anything that yummy go to waste." Sweetly sore it is.

Brett handed me the pot, then scooped me up in his arms and carried me into his dark bedroom. I rested my head against his shoulder, inhaling the musky, manly scent of him. He laid me gently on the bed, kicking off his shoes and sliding onto the spread beside me. He kissed me, sweet, soft champagne-and-chocolate-flavored kisses. I hoped he'd never stop.

He took the still-warm fondue pot from my hands and set it on the night table. I turned to him and we lay on our sides, kissing some more, pressed together in a warm, full-body embrace. His fingers tangled in my hair as he tasted my mouth, the flesh under my jaw, the sensitive spot on my neck just below my ear. My nipples tightened, and I began to throb with want. I slid my foot slowly up his leg, past the crook of his knee and over his taut thigh, my skirt bunching around me as I wrapped my leg around his lower back. Using the leverage to pull his body hard against mine, I angled my knee outward, opening myself up to him, only his clothing and a thin strip of red lace separating us. Perhaps I shouldn't have been so assertive our first time, should have let him take the lead, call the shots. But I wanted him so badly I simply couldn't help myself.

Brett responded with a groan that could only mean my maneuver had pleased him. He put his hand on my thigh, grasping the fabric of my skirt and drawing it up to expose my bare flesh. He spread his warm fingers over my skin, cupping my ass. He rocked against me then, his full, firm ridge pushing against my inner thigh, telling me he was ready for more and creating a raw, carnal ache inside me. I wanted him—now!—but something this sensual, this delicious, should be savored, not rushed.

His lips moved down my neck, kissing, sucking, biting. His hand worked its way under my sweater. His fingers brushed my rib cage, then the side of my breast, then his thumb worked its way back and forth over my lace-covered breast in an arc that crossed my swollen, sensitized nipple and made me gasp with pleasure. In one smooth movement, he pulled me to a sitting position, removing my top. He tossed the sweater onto the armchair in the corner. His eyes flashed with dark desire as he took in my red lace bra. "I should've known you'd be wearing your signature color somewhere."

He traced the outline of the lace with a lazy fingertip, watching my face, gauging my reaction. His finger left a warm trail along the edge of the fabric and it was all I could do not to scream, *Touch me now!*

I tilted my head and grabbed his hand, putting a stop

to this sweet agony. "There's a fine line between pleasure and torture, Brett."

A soft, seductive chuckle escaped him. With both hands, he reached for the clasp between my breasts, unfastened it, and freed my breasts from their cages of lace. He pushed the straps off my shoulders and removed my bra, tossing it onto the chair on top of my sweater.

"My turn." I knelt on the bed, nuzzling his neck and leaving steamy kisses along his collarbone as I tugged the hem of his shirt out of his pants. I pulled it over his head, and soon his shirt joined the stack of clothing accumulating on the chair.

Brett's shoulders were round, muscular. His chest was covered with coarse, sandy hair, enough to be masculine without being overly brawny. As I kissed his neck and chest, I ran my index finger in a zigzag down the cleft between his well-defined pecs, trailing it down to circle his navel, then working my way back up again.

Brett exhaled sharply and echoed my earlier words. "There's a fine line between pleasure and torture, Tara." He wrapped his arms around me then, turning to lower me back down to the bed, his chest just close enough to mine that I could feel the soft friction of his hairs on my skin. I could only imagine how good it would feel to be completely skin to skin with him.

I was on my back and he lay on his side next to me, one leg stretched over my thighs now, his weight pinning me to the bed. He touched my breasts, his caresses alternating between slow and soft and firm and insistent, but each of them effective, generating sensations I'd never experienced in quite the same way with any other man. Reaching over to the night table, Brett dipped his finger in the warm fondue chocolate, flashing a mischievous smile as he spread the sweet, sticky substance in circles around my rigid nipples. As he bent his head down to lick the chocolate from my body, I arched my back, raising up to meet his wet, warm mouth, emitting an involuntary cry of pleasure as his tongue circled my breast.

Brett may appear conservative and refined, but looks could be deceiving, couldn't they? Clearly, underneath that reserved, respectable exterior, Brett was a bad, bad boy.

When Brett had expertly removed all trace of the chocolate, he moved his lips to my ear, his breath warm on my skin. "You like that, don't you?"

All I could do at that point was whimper. I'd never wanted—*needed*—a man so badly.

He reached down and slid his fingers under the waistband of my skirt. He began to slide the skirt down. My body screamed, "Take me now!" But my mouth screamed, "Wait!" A knot of worry had formed in my gut, and I couldn't let this go any further.

Was Brett a bad boy? Was he involved in a con game?

I sat up, putting a hand on Brett's chest and pushing him backward on the bed.

He took my wrist in his hand and pressed me back down. "Don't worry. I brought protection."

I squirmed out from under him and sat up again, turning away from him, my legs now hanging over the side of the bed. I looked down at the floor, unable to look at him. "That's . . . not the issue, Brett."

He reached out from behind me to put a hand on my bare shoulder, forcing me to turn to look at him. His chest heaved with labored breaths and his voice was strained. "Then what is it, Tara?" He looked into my eyes, searching for answers.

My heart whirled in my chest like an off-balance washing machine. I could barely breathe. "I . . . I just can't do this." I gasped for air. "Not . . . yet."

He stared at me for a moment, his expression confused, disappointed, and frustrated, maybe even a little hurt. But thankfully not angry.

Hell, I felt confused, disappointed, and frustrated, too. What was wrong with me? Wasn't this what I wanted, what I'd been waiting for?

But something didn't feel right. That damn suspicion had reared its head again, refusing to let me make an irreversible mistake. There'd be plenty of time for lovemaking once I'd eliminated all my doubts, convinced myself Brett had nothing to do with any type of scam, that Brett might be a bad boy in bed but that he wasn't a bad boy elsewhere.

I forced a smile at him. "I'm sorry, Brett. I really thought I was ready for this. I want this. I want you. I do. But . . . this is a big step. I need—" *To know you are innocent.* "A little more time."

Brett's shoulders sagged. He watched me for a few moments, quiet, taking deep breaths to calm himself. "I understand," he said finally, running a hand through his hair. "You're nothing but a tease." He grabbed a pillow and whopped me softly upside the head with it.

"Hey!" I grabbed my pillow and whopped him right back.

We fought with the pillows for a few moments, laughing and wrestling on the bed until I could feel the scar on my forearm straining with the exertion.

Self-conscious now, I stood and picked my clothing up off the chair, holding my sweater and bra in front of my naked chest. Unable to face him, I looked down and mumbled, "I really am sorry, Brett."

"Me, too." Brett climbed off the bed and stood in front of me, putting a finger under my chin to raise my eyes to him. "But I'd rather you be sorry you didn't make love to me than sorry you did."

*   *   *

Sleeping in Brett's warm, strong arms did wonders for me. With him next to me in bed, I felt physically safe and secure. Try as they might, Jack Battaglia and his sharp box cutter couldn't invade my dreams that night. Instead, I dreamed of Brett, what it would have been like to make love to him.

In the morning, while Brett continued to doze, I slipped out of bed and took a long, hot shower. My breasts were still tender, my entire body aching with unfulfilled want the water couldn't wash away.

Brett woke as I stepped into the doorway, wrapped in one of the hotel's thick, luxurious blue towels.

"'Mornin,'" he drawled from the bed, his voice deep and gravelly from sleep. He somehow managed to look both adorable and sexy in his rumpled state.

I bent over to give him a kiss on the cheek and he playfully grabbed at my towel.

"Up and at 'em, mister," I commanded. "I'm starved."

A grin pulled at Brett's lips. "I did enjoy more than my fair share of the fondue last night, didn't I?"

While he showered, I used the mirror in my room to apply my makeup and fix my hair. I dressed in my Bermuda shorts and knit top, sliding my feet into a pair of tennis shoes. Brett emerged from the bathroom in khaki shorts paired with a colorful golf shirt sporting a palm tree motif.

After a nice breakfast on the poolside terrace, Brett retrieved his bag of clubs from the room and changed into his spiked, saddle oxford-style golf shoes. We headed out to the resort's driving range so he could hit some balls.

I knew the basics of golf. Martin and McGee hosted a tournament every year, and its staff was expected to have at least a passing knowledge of the game. I'd taken a few lessons when I'd worked there and eventually my skills had improved from laughable to simply embarrassing. I much preferred to take shots on a firing range than a driving range.

Brett purchased a large bucket of balls in the clubhouse and we walked across the close-cropped grass to the range.

"Did your father teach you how to golf?" I asked.

Brett nodded. "Got my first set of clubs for Christmas the year I turned five. My father and I played every weekend until I left for college. We still play as often as we can."

Father-child bonding over a golf game, the more sophisticated equivalent of me and my brothers hunting with my dad. "That sounds nice."

"Want to hit a few?" he asked, lifting the bucket of balls higher.

"Nah. I'd make a fool of myself. I'll just watch."

I took a seat nearby on the covered patio of the clubhouse. Brett selected a spot between two other golfers and pulled out the legs on his bag's built-in stand. After retrieving a wooden tee from a zippered pocket, he looked over his clubs, carefully choosing an iron. He bent over to stick the tee in the ground, grabbed a ball from the bucket, and positioned it on the tee. To loosen up, he took a few practice swings, the well-formed muscles in his broad shoulders flexing and shifting as he swung the club. *Nice.* I could watch this all day.

Ready now, he stepped into place and swung. *Ping!* He sent the ball in a long, perfect arc over the grass.

The man at the spot next to Brett watched the ball sail through the air and gave a long whistle, impressed. "What's the secret to hitting like that?"

Brett pointed the handle of his club at me and smiled. "Showing off for a beautiful woman."

Corny, sure, but sweet. I felt myself blush as the man glanced my way.

As Brett made his way through the bucket of balls, I watched him closely. Was he what he appeared to be on the surface, a nice guy with traditional values? Or was he something else underneath? When would I know for sure? How long would I have to live with this ache of unsatisfied desire?

The first thing I did when Brett dropped me back at my house on Sunday was fix myself a heaping bowl of Fruity Pebbles. I'd enjoyed the rich food at the resort, but after all the fancy meals—the morning's breakfast was a fluffy spinach quiche—I was craving some real food.

The second thing I did was dump my laundry into the washing machine. Anne stared at me from her perch atop the dryer, her head cocked. That cat knew all my dirty secrets, like the fact that I hated doing laundry and usually put it off until I had absolutely nothing clean to wear. My weekend with Brett had me feeling invigorated, though, and I decided to put that energy to good use. I poured a scoop of detergent into the washer and pulled the knob to start the water.

The next thing I decided to do was run an Internet search on that foreign exchange outfit. What was the name of it again? Investment Exchange? I'd need to check the flyer to be sure.

The flyer had been in the pocket of my jeans, which I'd put in my laundry bag, which—oh crap!—I'd dumped in the wash. I ran to the laundry room and yanked on the knob to stop the machine. By the time I found the paper among the wet, heavy clothes, the agitator had shredded it to tiny, damp, illegible bits. Maybe this was a sign that I shouldn't look further into the matter. Then again, maybe I was just a moron.

I flopped down on the couch with my laptop. Since I couldn't recall the specific name of the Forex program, I simply searched "foreign currency exchange." The search brought up an overwhelming number of sites, some of them in other languages, not surprising given the subject matter. I tried to narrow the search by adding the words "First Dallas Bank" and "Shreveport" but none of the links seemed right. Without the name, I could waste hours hunting through the sites trying to find out more about this particular investment program. Dang. I'd have to figure out some other way to get information.

CHAPTER FOURTEEN

$\mathcal{B}$ringing Out the Big Guns

Monday morning, Christina picked me up at my town house. I patted Henry the Eighth on the head and gave Anne a quick kiss on the cheek, her white whiskers tickling my face, before heading out to the pink Cadillac.

"How was your weekend?" she asked once I'd climbed in. "Did you and Brett cross-pollinate? Did he fertilize your garden?"

I put my nose in the air and harrumphed in mock indignation. "I'm not one to kiss and tell."

She giggled. "That means you didn't get any."

She had me there. Now, in the bright light of day and with some distance between us, it seemed incredibly stupid that I'd put a stop to things with Brett Saturday night. No way could he be involved in some type of financial scam. Heck, I wasn't even sure there was a scam to begin with. I'd panicked for no good reason and missed out on the perfect opportunity to be close to him. What an idiot.

Christina had some things to take care of at her office that morning, so she dropped me at the IRS. I spent a couple of hours helping Eddie comb through the records for Chisholm's Steakhouse. There was a significant amount of cash run through various bank accounts that wasn't accounted for on the restaurant's tax returns, clear evidence of tax fraud. "These cheats didn't even have the courtesy to challenge us."

Eddie sighed. "Yeah. This case is a snoozer."

The most interesting cases involved offshore accounts, hidden assets, multilevel conglomerates with falsified audit reports. Enron-type stuff that required us to dig for clues, play financial detective. Chisholm's Steakhouse was a no-brainer in comparison.

Later that morning, I went to the break room to snag a Diet Coke from the vending machine. Lu's thermometer had edged up a bit more, showing an additional hundred grand had been collected, and none of it by me. Chisholm's would likely bring in a sizable amount, but not enough to get the Lobo to the hundred million mark. I needed a big case of my own to have any chance of winning the bonus.

Could the foreign exchange outfit be that case?

I reviewed what little I knew. Whoever operated the Forex plan was staying at Stan Shelton's lake house, which meant the two had some type of close relationship, either personal or business. Shelton had arranged for Brett to deliver the flyers to the guests at his lake house so, presumably, he knew about the investment program. Sheltons' guests had transferred significant amounts of cash and checks to Shelton, through the box Brett had been asked to deliver. Shelton was the president of First Dallas Bank, which had recently been penalized by banking regulators for misstatements on its financial reports.

It wasn't much. But was it enough to persuade Lu to let me open a new case and do more digging?

I headed to Lu's office and rapped on the open door. "Got a minute?"

"Got good news for me on the ice-cream man?"

"Not yet," I said, slipping into one of her wing chairs, "but we're working on it."

"Well, work a little harder," she said. "I've got big plans for my retirement. Taking a trip to Maui. And I'm not going to get there any time soon if you don't bring some money in."

"Then you might be interested to hear this." I told her what I'd learned.

When I finished, she tapped her fingers on the desk for a moment, thinking. "It could be something," she said, "or it could be nothing. Give the OCC a call, see what they'll share from their investigation into First Dallas. If it looks promising, I'll let you open a case."

It wasn't exactly a yes, but it was close enough. Woo doggie!

"Tara?" Lu said as I stood to leave. She shot me a pointed look from under her penciled brows. "Don't you go falling for this Brett fella. Not until we know which side he's on. Hear me?"

My gut seized up. "Yes, ma'am."

I went to my office and called the Office of the Comptroller of the Currency, the federal agency charged with regulating the nation's banks. After several transfers, during which I was treated to a Muzak version of Aerosmith's "Walk This Way"—pure sacrilege!—I finally reached the agent who'd led the First Dallas Bank investigation.

"I suspect the bank's management may have known the financials were incorrect," the agent said, "but we couldn't prove they'd intentionally done anything wrong."

Not surprising. Any incriminating evidence had likely been deleted or shredded.

"How did the bank become a target?" I asked.

"We received a tip from an employee."

An informant. It doesn't get much better than that. "Any chance you'll share his name and number?"

The agent gave me a name—Dave Edwards—and a phone number. No time like the present, right? As soon I ended the call with the OCC, I tried the number.

Edwards answered on the third ring. After I identified myself, he hesitated a moment. "Let's meet up," he said in an overly cheerful, overly familiar voice, as if he were speaking to a buddy. Other ears in the vicinity, no doubt.

"When's good for you?"

We arranged to meet Friday evening at six o'clock at a coffeehouse near his home in the suburban town of Mesquite. It was unlikely we'd run into anybody from the bank there but, just in case, I'd dress in civvies and leave my gun at home.

"I'm particularly interested in foreign currency transactions the bank president might be involved in," I told Edwards.

"Got it," he said.

I was curious to see what, if anything, Edwards might find for me on the Forex scheme. If it turned out to be something big, maybe I could involve Eddie, give him something more interesting to do. Then again, if it looked like big bucks were involved, maybe I'd keep the case all to myself. Selfish, sure, but if I were the one to get Lu to the hundred-million mark, I wouldn't have to listen to any more ribbing about being the office rookie. Then again, Edwards might find nothing. It was entirely possible that all of my suspicions were simply the result of an overactive imagination.

Christina returned for me at noon and we took off for

Roachingham Palace, driving to a deli for takeout salads on the way. As we waited in the drive-thru lane, Christina removed a small plastic case from her oversized purse as she dug for her wallet.

"What's that?" I asked.

Christina found her wallet and shoved the kit back down into her purse, where it wouldn't be visible. "Field test kit. After Joe sells us the drugs, I'll have to test them and make sure they really are illegal drugs before we can arrest him."

The Dallas Police Department had been rocked several years ago by a fake drug scandal in which a number of people were swept up in alleged drug raids. The apprehensions boosted the department's arrest statistics and the approval rating of the police chief. But when a clever defense attorney later demanded the drugs be retested by an independent lab, it was discovered that the white, powdery substance purportedly seized from many of those arrested was not cocaine but, in fact, nothing more than ground-up drywall. The FBI investigated the "Sheetrock Scandal," heads rolled, and the police chief was fired as a result of the trumped-up charges. No doubt all branches of law enforcement were sure to dot their *i*'s, cross their *t*'s, and test their drugs as a result.

Today, I'd worn skintight jeans and a periwinkle-blue top. Christina had dressed in a black tank top and yoga pants. After lunch, she rolled out a thin mat on the living room floor. I'd brought some work with me and, while I reviewed copies of Chisholm's bank statements, circling all of the cash deposits in red pen, she slid a DVD into her laptop and ran through a series of stretches and poses, her position matching that of an impressively limber woman on the screen.

"Planning to moonlight as a contortionist?" I asked, circling yet another unreported deposit.

"It's yoga, you moron. This is called the 'One-Legged King Pigeon Pose.' "

"I thought maybe you'd had enough of chasing down drug dealers and decided to join the circus."

"Don't make me have to kick your ass," Christina said, looking up at me from under her dark bangs.

I set the papers aside, stood, and put my hands on my hips. "I'd like to see you try."

You'd think I would've been taught a lesson after the incident at the coffeehouse, but unfortunately I'm sometimes a slow learner. Before I knew what was happening, Christina grabbed my ankles and yanked my feet out from under me. I landed with a *whump* on my butt. Luckily, I landed on the mat so the only thing bruised was my ego.

I ignored her chuckle and positioned myself on the mat like the woman in the video. During our afternoons at the Y, Eddie and I typically spent a half hour on the cardio equipment and another half hour pumping iron. Yoga seemed wimpy in comparison.

I shifted as the woman on the screen repositioned herself, my jeans riding up on my rear. "I don't see how posing like a Gumby doll can be much of a workout."

"You'll see," Christina said.

We shifted positions again, bending over so our heads were between our legs. "What's this position called?" I asked. " 'Kissing Your Own Ass'?"

The woman instructed us to hold the pose for thirty seconds. After fifteen, my thighs were shaking and I was rethinking my earlier assessment.

"Quit grunting," Christina said. "It's distracting."

"This is harder than it looks."

"Told ya!"

I bailed out and flopped back onto the sofa.

An hour later, we heard the faint notes of ice-cream truck music.

Joe.

Christina and I dug dollar bills out of our purses and walked to the door.

Christina stopped just before stepping out onto the porch. "I can tell Joe's interested, wanting to make a move on me. That could work to our advantage. Today, I'm bringing out the big guns."

"Our Glocks?"

She rolled her eyes. "You're such a rookie." She reached her hands up the back of her tank top and unhooked her black bra, pulling it out through the armhole and tossing it aside. She quickly ran her hands down hard over her bare breasts, perking her nipples up to a fully erect position clearly visible through the fabric. She pointed to her breasts. "These are the big guns I was talking about." She marched out the door and down the steps, her pointy breasts leading the way.

I followed her out the door. "Nice to see you'll do anything for the agency."

"You have to work with the tools you've got."

"Maybe you can get a professional nipple tweaker. I heard J-Lo has one."

Joe turned the corner and headed toward us. Through the front window, we saw him smile when he spotted Christina. The smile grew wider when he spotted her barely covered chest.

Christina smiled back but whispered through unmoving lips, "Is it just me or does this guy get more disgusting every time we see him?"

"They teach ventriloquism at the DEA?"

When Joe had rolled to a stop, we stepped up to the truck. Christina placed her hands wide apart on the window ledge, leaning forward to give Joe a clear view of her cleavage. "Push-Up," she said.

Joe handed her the ice cream and she slid him a buck. I

ordered a Drumstick. The guys from across the street wandered over then, just as they had most other days. Dang. So much for our plan to try to make a buy today.

Joe and the guys watched as Christina used her teeth to pull the paper wrapper off the top of the Push-Up. With the plastic stick, she slowly eased the circular treat up out of its cardboard sheath. Bringing the ice cream to her lips, she ran her tongue slowly in a full circle around the edge. She looked up at Joe and, when their gazes locked, gave the ice cream a hard flick with the tip of her tongue.

Thud. Joe hit the dirt face-first, having fallen out of the truck's window and into the yard. Christina and I looked down at him, a few stray pieces of dried grass now stuck in his greasy mullet.

Christina reached down, grabbed an arm, and pulled Joe to his feet. "You okay?"

"Uh, yeah," he mumbled, a blush spreading on his acne-pocked cheeks. "Just lost my balance."

Our neighbors snickered.

Joe climbed back into his truck, tried, unsuccessfully, to regain his cool, and turned to the guys, his gaze flicking to me and Christina, who suddenly seemed unwelcome despite the nipples. "Can I getcha?"

We stood aside as they placed their order and paid for their ice cream. The taller of the two glanced back at me. Was that a hint of impatience on his face? The two lingered, as if also hoping for some one-on-one time with Joe.

When the situation grew awkward, we aborted our mission, crossing the yard to the house. Christina yanked the door open, almost pulling it off the hinges. The door slammed shut behind us. Once inside, she kicked her bra across the floor. "We could move faster if those jerks from across the street didn't keep getting in the way."

We settled on the couch and I peeled the wrapper from my ice cream. "You sure sent Joe for a loop. But, you know, if you're going to perform sexual favors on that ice cream bar, you should at least make it buy you dinner first."

Christina ignored me. "I checked Joe's arm for tracks when I helped him up. He looks clean."

"Is that good or bad?"

She shrugged. "You never know. Sometimes users are easier to manipulate. Sometimes they're more unpredictable, more violent."

I'd rather not deal with any more unpredictable, violent people. My experience with Jack Battaglia had been more than enough for me. Sure, it was fun to carry a gun, to feel tough and in control, but I only truly like *playing* cop. Shooting at a human-shaped paper target and shooting at a real person were two different things entirely. Actually having to use my gun to defend myself hadn't been fun at all.

I hoped I'd never have to do it again.

CHAPTER FIFTEEN

No Sale

Alicia e-mailed me that afternoon. Daniel's case was dragging on and she wanted some company. Christina and I arranged to meet her for dinner at an Italian place in Lakewood.

Although I hadn't shared the full details of Joe's case with Brett, Alicia, as my longtime best friend, had been privy to the full scoop after pinky-swearing to keep mum. She seemed as surprised as I had been to see a woman like Christina working for the DEA. Yet, despite the fact that Alicia was chic and sophisticated and Christina was giggly and girlie, the two hit it off, chocolate martinis being their common denominator.

With Alicia's financial savvy and Christina's street smarts, I realized the two could provide some much-needed insight into the situation with Brett. Over dessert,

I spilled my guts, hoping for some reassurance. "It's probably nothing, right?"

Alicia frowned. "I don't know, Tara. The whole thing seems odd."

"I'm with Alicia," Christina said. "Whether he knows it or not, looks like Brett's their cash mule."

Damn. I stabbed my fork into my tiramisu.

My cell phone chirped later that evening, after Christina and I had returned to the crack house. It was Brett.

"How was your day?" he asked.

How did one describe a day of hanging out in the 'hood, waiting for a drug dealer, being forced to abort a buy? At least I hadn't been forced to shoot anyone today. "Today was . . . fine. How about you?"

"Good." He paused a moment, and when he spoke again, his voice was soft. "I've been thinking about you all day, Tara."

My heart pogoed in my chest. "Me, too." Of course I didn't tell him my thoughts were equally split between swooning and suspicion. Now, though, as I heard his deep, sexy voice, the pendulum had swung back to swooning.

Brett went on to tell me that Stan Shelton had invited Brett and a guest to sit in the bank's skybox at Thursday night's Texas Rangers game and he'd like me to come along.

"Sounds like fun." It also sounded like the perfect opportunity to ply Stan Shelton for more information about that foreign currency exchange program. But I'd have to be careful. If I came on too strong, he might wonder about my motivations.

I'd been flattered the Lobo had trusted me to handle Joe's case without a more senior Treasury agent supervising me. Still, Joe's case was chump change relative to some of the high-dollar cases in the office. If I brought in a new big-dollar case myself, I'd be a hero, the little rookie who could. There was no telling how much money could be involved in the Forex deal. But I bet it was a lot. If I were the agent to get Lu to her hundred-million goal, my career would have no limits.

But what would it mean for my relationship with Brett? If he were involved, our relationship would be over, of course. I didn't date crooks, no matter how good-looking and sexy they might be. Even if he wasn't involved, he'd likely be upset that I'd kept information from him, used him to get to a target. But this was my job. He'd understand, right?

After we chatted a few minutes more, I hung up the phone. I'd planned to work on my tax return tonight, but now I was too distracted by my upcoming date with Brett and interrogating Shelton to focus on numbers. Instead, I decided to wax my upper lip. Nothing turns a guy off more than a woman with beer foam in her mustache.

Tuesday morning, I dressed in my scuffed boots, my old jeans with the worn-out knees, and my faded 1993 Billy Ray Cyrus concert tee.

Christina eyed my shirt. "Tell me he's not that 'Achy Breaky Heart' guy."

"One and the same. My older brothers drove over two hundred miles to Houston to see him in concert." I'd begged them to take me along but they'd refused. They had dates to impress, and showing up with their kid sister in tow wouldn't have gotten them to second base. Back then, I'd been too young to travel so far from home, but heck, so were they. My oldest brother had turned sixteen only a week before, the ink hardly dry on his driver's license. Knowing they'd never get permission to go, they'd told my parents they were spending the night with a friend. To appease me—and to buy my silence—they'd promised to bring me a shirt from the concert.

"You've come a long way, girl."

I had. And I hadn't. Sure, I generally wore designer labels to work and on dates, and I felt classy, stylish, and *me* in them. But I had to admit these old clothes felt very broken in, very comfortable, very *me*, too. I'd had this particular pair of jeans since I was a teenager and they'd been with me through some mighty good times. They fit like a second skin.

I thought more about the upcoming baseball game. It was generous of Stan Shelton to invite us to the bank's skybox, and I'd like to think he'd extended the invitation simply because he was impressed by the plans Brett had come up with for the lake house. But was there more to the story than that?

Then again, maybe I was being overly distrustful again. Was it really so odd for a banker to trust a guy like Brett with a deposit, even a large one? Maybe not. Brett was clean-cut and responsible, and since bankers dealt with huge sums of money every day, maybe the deposit hadn't seemed like a big deal to Shelton. Still, if the two knew each other only as landscape architect and client, it would be odd for Stan to entrust the funds to Brett. Right?

Ugh. I didn't know what to think. But I planned to keep a close, discreet eye on their interactions at the baseball game. Maybe I could discern something from the way the two interacted. My gut told me Brett was one of the good guys. But my head wasn't so sure.

An hour later at the house Christina launched into full yoga mode, on her back in a lavender geometric print crop top, her ankles behind her ears, her hip-hugging Lycra yoga shorts riding up, revealing the bottom curve of her butt cheeks.

"You should do that for Joe," I said. "He'd confess all to you in ten seconds flat."

Christina ignored me, pulled her shorts out of her crack, and shifted on her mat.

At my suggestion, Christina and I had driven to a nearby nursery that morning and bought a flat of pink and white petunias, a large bag of potting soil, and two terra-cotta pots. We spent the late morning planting the flowers, setting the pots on either side of the front door when we were finished. After watering the flowers, I used a whisk broom to clean the spiderwebs and dirt off the windows and porch. When I finished sweeping, I checked my manicure. No damage. Good.

The two guys across the street were under the hood of their Nova again. No stereo today. I couldn't blame them. The woman who'd hollered at them before looked downright scary. Their enormous dog lay in the shade, panting and watching us.

When Christina and I were done, we stood back and admired our handiwork. The shack would never be attractive, but at least now it looked like we'd made some effort.

Christina and I made do with sloppy peanut butter and jelly sandwiches for lunch. I went over more of Chisholm's Steakhouse records as we watched Maury. His guests for the day were women unsure which of a dozen or so men had fathered their babies. Ew.

Christina shook her head and clicked off the television. "If this is the kind of crap that's on TV during the day, I'm glad I've got a job."

I consulted my watch. "About time for Joe to make his appearance."

Christina pulled herself up off her yoga mat. "Let's go a few blocks over so the guys from across the street won't get in our way."

We left the house and headed north up the sidewalk in the direction from which Joe always came.

The Latino guys across the street sat upright on the

hood of the Nova. "Where you going?" one of them called after us.

"For a walk," I snapped. Our destination was none of their business.

Three blocks down we heard the tinkle of Joe's music. We waited in the shade of a pecan tree, standing among a scattering of hard broken shells.

Joe pulled to a stop a few houses down when a trio of dark-haired, freckle-faced girls ran out of a garage waving dollar bills. When Joe spotted Christina and me stepping in line behind the girls, a horny grin spread across his face. Once he'd served the girls, he leaned forward on the window ledge and flashed a smile that was probably intended to be seductive but, with his tongue protruding through his front teeth, was more along the lines of repulsive. The stained T-shirt and too-tight jeans he wore did nothing to add to his appeal. "What're y'all doing here?"

Christina shrugged. "Nothin' better to do. Decided to take a walk."

Joe glanced over at me, taking in my torn jeans. "Gotta say, there's something real attractive 'bout a girl with the knees worn out on her jeans."

Urk.

"What can I get you today?" Joe asked.

Christina put a hand on the window ledge and stepped closer, her face only inches from Joe's. "I'm not in the mood for ice cream today," she said, her voice low but firm. "What else you got?"

The two locked eyes for a few moments. Finally, Joe looked away down the street. "All I got is ice cream."

Christina continued her laserlike stare. "That's not what we hear."

Joe turned back to her and paused for a moment, considering. Then he broke eye contact again, gazing down at the floor of his van, scratching at a zit on the side of his face with his index finger. "Can't always believe what people say."

Christina tossed her long, dark hair. "Too bad." She turned and walked off down the sidewalk, Joe's disappointed gaze locked on her butt as she went.

I wasn't sure what to do, so I just trotted after Christina, catching her at the corner. "Looks like we struck out."

"No," she whispered. "He's just going to make us wait. Any dealer with half a brain won't jump on a sale to someone they don't know."

"You think he's got half a brain?" Seemed generous to me.

Joe's truck rumbled as he eased it away from the curb behind us. A few seconds later he drove slowly past, glancing wistfully at Christina through the open window.

On Wednesday and Thursday, we purposefully stayed inside the house when Joe's truck came by. Christina thought it would make us seem less eager, that Joe might begin to wonder whether he'd passed up a lucrative new customer who'd since found a source elsewhere.

The extra free time gave me a chance to run by the nail salon for a manicure. I opted for blue French tips this time, with a baseball on each pinky and a *T* on each thumb for the Texas Rangers. If that showing of support wouldn't give the team a competitive edge, I didn't know what would.

Christina dropped me back at my town house Thursday afternoon. Anne crawled out from under the couch and met me at the front door as I came in. "How's my girlie-girl?" I picked her up and scratched her under the chin. "Hey, Henry." I walked under the nose of my snobby Persian, as usual perched up high on the entertainment center. He yawned and stretched a furry paw out toward me. A small gesture, but one that let me know he'd missed me. I gave his chin a good scratching, too.

After giving the cats some attention, I decided to check in with my parents. I hadn't spoken with them in a few days. My father answered the phone. After the usual preliminaries, he asked if I'd be interested in coming home for the weekend and attending a gun show at the Nacogdoches County expo center. Not only would I enjoy seeing my parents, but the weekend could also provide an opportunity for me to get some distance from Brett, objectively evaluate the situation.

"Gun show sounds like fun."

"It's a date, then."

We chatted for a few minutes, then my mother got on the line. I assured Mom I was fine, work was fine, the cats were fine. I knew what question was coming next, and even mouthed the words as she spoke.

"How are things with Brett?"

"Hard to say, Mom."

"What's that mean?"

"It means I want to talk to you about it this weekend. In person." In case I needed a shoulder to cry on.

"Okay, then," she said. "I'll make pralines."

Pecan pralines, the Southern antidepressant.

We concluded the call and I went upstairs, Anne trotting up the steps behind me. After showering, I dressed in a Rangers jersey and jeans and applied fresh makeup, doing a little trick Christina had shown me with the eyeliner, accentuating my gray-blue eyes. The doorbell rang as I was putting on my earrings. "Kiss-kiss," I told Anne, who lay on my pillow, assuring me a face full of fur next time I slept on it.

When I entered the foyer, I could see a burst of red and yellow through the beveled glass on my front door. Flowers! I yanked opened the door.

Brett wore a short-sleeved royal-blue button-down,

jeans, and loafers. In one hand he held a colorful bouquet of parrot tulips wrapped in green tissue paper, in the other a white cardboard cylinder sealed at both ends with plastic caps.

"Brett! They're beautiful." I took the bouquet and gave him a kiss on his freshly shaved cheek, catching an enticing whiff of his spicy aftershave.

"The night we met you mentioned that you liked the parrot tulips."

Liked them? I'd gone gaga over them. The size and variety of the specimens had been breathtaking. How sweet of him to remember.

Brett followed me to the kitchen. Retrieving a glass vase from the cabinet for the tulips, I filled it with cold water and carefully arranged the flowers. Perfect. I set them on the middle of my butcher block island, then turned and gestured to the cylinder in his hand. "What's that?"

He grinned. "A surprise." He waved me over to my kitchen table. Once we were there, he uncapped the tube and shook a set of blueprints out of it. He spread the thin paper out, using my cat-shaped salt and pepper shakers to anchor the top corners, grabbing two soup spoons from a drawer to hold down the bottom edges.

I glanced down at the blueprint. The structure diagrammed was unmistakably my town house, complete with the chimney on the left, the twin dormer windows upstairs, the front door with the glass oval. But in the blueprint, the awkward evergreen was gone, replaced by a row of beautiful pink rosebushes standing in a perky line, English ivy forming a lush bed underneath them. A black wrought-iron trellis stood between the front windows, covered in Carolina jessamine bursting out in yellow blooms. A small redbud tree was staked in the center of the yard, alternating red and white geraniums encircling its trunk, natural round river stones outlining the bed. On either side of the front walk, just before the porch, were two shepherd's hooks supporting hanging baskets of multicolored moss rose.

"Wow," I said. "What a transformation."

Brett smiled. "You like it?"

"I love it!" I stood on tiptoe and gave him a warm, sweet kiss.

"I'll be back with a crew in the next few days."

The plants and materials alone would cost several hundred dollars. With a crew to install them, the job would run well over a thousand. This was the most generous, most thoughtful gift anyone had ever given me. What's more, it must've taken Brett hours to sketch the plans. He'd captured my home in perfect, painstaking detail, even drawn Annie sitting in the upstairs window, licking her paw.

The guy was willing to do all of this for me, and I hadn't even been willing to give him a hand job last weekend. I should be ashamed of myself.

"It'll be nice to have a garden to tend to," I said. "I've missed that. The only gardening I've done in months was planting a few petunias." The second the words left my mouth I wished I were a vacuum cleaner so I could suck them back in.

Brett cocked his head, puzzled. "I didn't see any petunias outside."

Of course he didn't. The petunias were at the crack house. Damn. Oh, well. It was too late now to take my words back. Besides, he had a right to know about my undercover assignment, didn't he? If we were going to have a relationship, one with any chance of a future, I had to let him know what I was up to, at least the basics. It was only fair.

"I planted them at a house we're using as a base for an investigation I'm working near the Cotton Bowl—"

"The Cotton Bowl?" Brett frowned. "That's a rough part of town."

"No need to worry," I said. "I've got my partner with me at all times." Not to mention my gun and pepper spray.

"Good," Brett said. "I feel better knowing Eddie's out there with you."

"It's not Eddie." I told Brett the primary details about the case, including my new partner, the tacky clothing, the pink Cadillac. I left out the cockroaches, the fact that the neighbors thought I was a *puta*, the fact that I carried weapons.

"You've been hanging out in a former crack house, waiting to bust a drug dealer?" He stared at me for a moment in disbelief. "I know you're smart and well trained, Tara, but that still scares me."

"It's not like TV, Brett. Most criminals surrender willingly."

His expression changed from disbelieving to perplexed as he tried to process everything I'd thrown at him. "Is it normal for an IRS agent to do this kind of thing? Going undercover? Working with the DEA?"

Not normal for an auditor, but normal for a special agent. We were criminal law enforcement, after all. "Yep. All part of the job."

"The DEA agent has a gun, right?" he asked. "Just in case something goes wrong?"

"Yes. *And so do I.*

Our gazes met and held for a long moment, and I noted the genuine care and concern in his eyes. Heck, I'd feel the same way if our roles were reversed.

"It's sweet that you're worried about me, Brett. But there's two of us and only one of him. Besides, the guy we're after doesn't have a violent record. I'll be fine." At least I hoped so.

I stepped toward Brett and put a hand on his cheek, hoping to melt his defenses. Lucky for me, it seemed to work. He pulled me to him, held me tight, and kissed the top of my head.

CHAPTER SIXTEEN

$\mathscr{B}$lips on My Radar

We made small talk as we drove to the ballpark, discussing normal topics like the new seafood restaurant that recently opened downtown, the never-ending road construction on the Dallas freeways, the beautiful azaleas beginning to bloom here and there around town.

I glanced over at Brett. "How are your plans for the Sheltons' lake house coming?"

He signaled to change lanes. "Moving along. We've got the decks and pathways mapped out and partly completed. We're still waiting on the oak trees to be delivered. The nursery's late with the order."

The mention of deliveries reminded me of the boxes from Stan Shelton. With any luck, I'd get a chance tonight to question Shelton about the foreign currency exchange program. But if he knew I was a Treasury agent, there would be no way he'd divulge anything to me. "Have you mentioned to Stan that I work for the IRS?"

"No," Brett said. "He's a busy guy. We've only had time to talk business."

Perfect. "If the subject of my career comes up tonight, would you mind just telling people I'm a CPA?" It wouldn't be a lie, after all. I was certified. Possibly certifiable, too.

Brett shot me a puzzled look. "Why?"

"Telling people you work for the IRS is like telling them you have herpes. Instant social death."

He raised a brow. "That bad, huh?"

"People are intimidated by IRS agents. I don't want anyone to feel uncomfortable. I just want to have a good time." Liar, liar, pants on fire.

"Okay," he said. "CPA it is."

The stadium loomed ahead and we pulled into the VIP parking lot. Brett rolled to a stop next to an attendant decked out head to toe in blue and red Rangers gear. He rolled down the window and handed the attendant a parking pass.

We found an open space a few lanes over. As we climbed out of the car, a couple walked by. Brett called after them.

The man and woman stopped and we caught up to them. I recognized the two as the couple Brett had been speaking with at the Arboretum's charity fund-raiser. Stan Shelton was dressed in creased navy slacks and a gray knit shirt, his young wife in a skintight black miniskirt, black heels, and a sheer white blouse over a black bra.

Brett introduced me to Stan and we shook hands. When Stan turned to introduce his wife, I noticed a port-wine birthmark in the rough shape of a turtle on the back of his neck. He put a hand on his wife's back. "This is Britney."

I extended my hand to Britney then, noting the enormous diamond on her left hand, the gem the size of a thirty-eight-caliber bullet. "Nice to meet you, Britney."

She took my hand, but instead of shaking it she turned my hand up and examined my nails. "Cute manicure. Love the baseballs."

"Thanks."

The four of us wove our way through incoming traffic and tailgate parties, Britney bringing up the rear since she could take only baby steps in her tight skirt and heels. Not that I had any room to call her trashy after the getup I'd worn most of the day.

I debated trying to wheedle information about the currency exchange seminar out of Stan on our way in, but decided it was too soon. I'd wait until he'd had a drink or two and was more relaxed, then I'd catch him with his guard down and grill him for information.

I glanced back at Britney. "Your lake house is beautiful. The stone and granite are a wonderful combination."

Britney shrugged. "I'm not going out there until the wet bar and hot tub are up and running."

We handed our tickets to the usher and proceeded through the turnstile. Inside, Brett purchased two programs, handing one to Stan, rolling up the other and tucking it under his arm. We made our way to the escalator to ride up to the box.

Teetering on her heels, Britney took hold of the escalator's handrail and glanced at Stan. "You made sure they're going to have Cuervo tequila, right? That cheap crap they served last time gave me a hell of a headache."

"Sure it wasn't the fact that you downed eight shots of it?" Stan skewered Britney with a look that said he was having second thoughts about his second wife.

We followed Stan and Britney through the special entrance to the skyboxes. First Dallas Bank's box sat in a prime location behind home plate, next to the announcer's booth, affording us a spectacular view of the field. At the back of the box was a bar, its surface covered with bottles in all shapes, sizes, and colors. A dark-haired woman dressed in a blue and red uniform stood at a buffet table, laying out a dainty spread of cocktail shrimp and crab-stuffed mushrooms, along with a heavier selection of bratwurst and sauerkraut. Something for everyone.

"This looks delicious," I said to the attendant. She looked up and smiled.

Stan, Brett, and I loaded plates with food. Britney turned up her nose at the offerings. "Cuervo shots," she barked at the server before wobbling her way down the steps to look out on the field.

Brett took my hand and helped me down the rows of padded seats. The box provided a much better view than the nosebleed section in which I usually sat. We were so close I could easily read the names on the backs of the players' shirts. I took a seat, while Brett stood on the steps, talking with Stan. Britney flopped into the seat next to me, crossing her legs and swinging the top one impatiently.

I attempted conversation. "Do you work, Britney?"

Britney snorted. "Stan works me hard enough in the bedroom every night. That's all the work I intend to do."

Too much information. I choked down the bite of brat-wurst lodged in my throat. "How did you and Stan meet?"

Britney flipped a lock of hair over her shoulder with a coral-tipped fingernail. "I used to do his first wife's hair." Then Britney started doing her client's husband, apparently.

Britney glanced up at Brett and Stan, then leaned toward me. "You should dump your boyfriend and find an older man. They've got lots of money, their kids are grown, and the best part about it is their parents will either be dead or too embarrassed to acknowledge you. Either way, no in-laws to deal with."

"I'll take that under advisement."

Small talk with this small-minded woman had proved pointless. I turned my attention to the field below.

"Gawd, I hate sports," Britney muttered. "The only way I can get through these games is by getting plastered." She proceeded to do just that as quickly as possible, downing in rapid succession the three tequila shots handed to her by the server. Britney returned the empty shot glasses to the tray and snapped her fingers at the woman. "Keep them coming."

The waitress glanced at me. I discreetly crossed my eyes and she discreetly smiled back.

By that time, a few other couples had entered the box. I wondered if any of them were involved in the Forex investment program. I also wondered if any of the men were Dave Edwards, the informant who'd been working with the OCC, the man I was scheduled to meet with the following night.

Stan introduced Brett and me to those in the box. Many were high-ranking bank employees and their spouses. A few others were clients, no doubt invited due to the substantial balances in their accounts judging from the Rolex and Piaget watches on their wrists. Edwards wasn't here. Either he wasn't high enough on the bank's food chain to warrant an invitation or he was otherwise occupied.

We resumed our seats, standing when the national anthem began to play. Britney swayed, her bare shoulder bumping mine. At the rate she was putting away the liquor, Stan would be dragging her back to the car by her ankles at the end of the night.

When the anthem ended, we settled in for the game. From his seat on the other side of me, Brett draped an arm lightly around the back of my chair. He ran his thumb down my upper arm, leaned toward me, and stole a cheese-topped nacho from my plate. A devilish grin tugged at his lips as he whispered, "Too bad they're not serving fondue."

His touch and innuendo ignited a spark of desire in me,

resurrecting that unsatisfied lust. I wanted Brett. I wanted
to connect physically with him, enjoy the more primal side
of the male-female relationship. With any luck, I'd be able
to get the information I needed soon, free myself of my
suspicions, and satisfy this sweet ache within me.

Halfway through the first inning, another couple walked
in. The man was middle-aged with a double-breasted suit
and the sleaziest shit-eating grin this side of the Red
River. So much gel slicked back his hair it appeared to be
made of plastic. The guy had salesman written all over
him. Hanging on his shoulder was another young blonde,
this one in skintight low-slung black jeans, a low-cut
V-neck top in a zebra print, and high-heeled black leather
ankle boots, her skank quotient rivaling that of Britney.

"Brit!" the woman squealed, clattering down the steps
in her spike heels.

"Chelsea!" Britney shrieked, leaping from her seat.
"Look at you!"

"Look at *you*!" Chelsea shrieked back.

Chelsea's skin was even more tanned than Britney's,
though Chelsea's tan appeared natural.

The two women hugged. "I've missed you," Britney
said, hanging on Chelsea's shoulder, probably as much to
maintain her balance as a gesture of friendship.

"Me, too," Chelsea said. "I'm so glad to be back. San
Jose is a total drag. Nothing to do but hang around by the
pool and drink all day."

Such torture. Sheez. I stuck out my hand. "Hi, I'm Tara
Holloway."

"Chelsea Gryder." Chelsea's fingers barely touched
mine before she released my hand. Guess she didn't find
me all that interesting.

"Did you say you've been in San Jose?" I asked. "I love
California." My family had driven to Disneyland once
when I was six and I had fond memories of the costumed

characters, the Dumbo ride, my oldest brother puking up funnel cake after riding the teacups.

"Not San Jose, California," she said. "San Jose, *Costa Rica*." She rolled her eyes. "Big difference."

Costa Rica? Funny, I had never given much thought to Costa Rica until recently. For years, Switzerland and the Caribbean islands had been known as places where banks could be trusted to hide funds for customers all over the world. The IRS had caught many a tax evader who'd wired funds to Swiss or offshore banks and failed to disclose the income and transfers. The developing Third World countries in Latin America were joining the game now, wanting a piece of the action, and the profits, too. Costa Rica was a new blip on the IRS radar.

That odd tingle started up again, my instincts kicking in, telling me something was up. Then again, Costa Rica was a popular tourist destination. The country's beautiful beaches, lush rain forests, and low cost of living attracted quite a few travelers. Maybe Chelsea and her husband had been in Costa Rica on vacation. Just because I hadn't had an urge to travel there didn't mean that something was up. Maybe my instincts were wrong. Maybe that tingle was for naught.

Before I could inquire further, Chelsea Gryder summarily dismissed me. She and Britney launched into a mutual admiration session, complimenting each other's clothing choices, jewelry, perfumes. There was no way I could ask Chelsea more questions now without seeming intrusive.

Brett and I gave up our front-row seats so the women could sit together. As we headed up the steps, I noticed Shelton standing by the bar at the back of the room with Chelsea's husband. The two stood so close they could have been in a football huddle.

I looked up at Brett. "Do you know the guy who's speaking with Stan? Chelsea's husband?"

Brett glanced over at the men. "Yeah. That's Michael Gryder. Let's get another drink and I'll introduce you."

So Brett knew Chelsea's husband. That didn't necessarily mean anything, did it? I wondered if Chelsea and her husband were Shelton's guests at the lake house, the ones who had sent the box of checks and cash back to Shelton. The ones with the luggage marked SJO.

Fresh drinks in hand, Brett led me over to Stan and Michael. They stopped speaking immediately. Brett put a hand on my back. "Michael, this is my girlfriend, Tara Holloway. Tara, this is Michael Gryder."

I shook Gryder's hand. "Pleasure to meet you. Are you a banker, also?"

Gryder shook his head, offering no further information, instead taking a huge bite of bratwurst.

As if that were going to stop me. "What line of work are you in?"

He glanced away, spent several moments carefully and thoroughly chewing the meat, then finally swallowed. My eyes were still on him, my expression expectant, when he turned back. Was it my imagination or did he seem to stiffen?

He wiped his mouth with his napkin. "Investments," he said softly.

"Oh?" I tilted my head in a gesture of mock innocence. "What kind of investments?" Foreign currency, perhaps?

Gryder and Shelton exchanged glances, then Gryder forced a smile at me. "I focus on specialized investments designed exclusively for qualified, high-net-worth individuals."

A vague answer with undertones of "butt out," but, hey, I was always up for a challenge. "Sounds interesting. What investment firm are you with?"

"I have my own private firm."

"Really? How fascinating." I took a sip of my wine.

"What's the name of your company?" No way could he avoid such a direct question.

He tossed back his scotch on the rocks, ice and all. He eyed me as he crunched down hard on an ice cube. "XChange Investments."

I ducked my chin. "Exchange? As in foreign currency exchange?"

Gryder gave a small nod.

"Foreign currency seems to be a popular investment trend. I'd love to hear more. Do you have a business card?"

"No," Gryder said, much too quickly. As if realizing he'd sounded short he mumbled, "Sorry."

What legitimate businessman doesn't carry cards and jump at the chance to land a new client? Now my suspicions felt like more than a hunch. Something fishy was going on and it wasn't just the cocktail shrimp. But my behavior was already bordering on pushy and rude. If I asked any more questions, the men might realize I was up to something. I'd have to find another way to obtain more information. A forced smile spread across my lips. "It was nice meeting you, Michael. I'll leave you men to your guy talk." I gave them a wink and left them at the bar, returning to my seat.

As the three men huddled, talking privately, I again had to wonder if Brett was somehow involved in a scam. But how could such a charming guy be a con artist? Then I remembered most successful con artists are charming. Acting like a boor didn't exactly entice people to open their wallets.

I glanced back at them. Brett said something and Stan chuckled, giving Brett a friendly slap on the back, a gesture that seemed oddly comfortable and familiar for two men who shared only a business acquaintance. Was there more to their relationship than that of landscape architect and client?

A sick feeling invaded my stomach when I thought about Brett possibly being involved in something illegal. I felt even sicker when I realized I'd likely be the one to bust him if he were. I'd been looking forward to slapping my handcuffs on Brett, but not for an arrest. But if he were up to something, he'd be an idiot to date an IRS agent, and Brett was no idiot. Then again, he could be like Jack Battaglia. Underestimating me. And what was that old saying about keeping your friends close and your enemies closer? My head began to spin. It was too much to wrap my mind around.

I watched them as discreetly as I could. The three stood close, their expressions intent now. Whatever they were discussing, it seemed serious. After a few moments, their little powwow broke up. Brett took a seat next to me, while Shelton and Gryder settled on his other side. I tried to eavesdrop on their conversation without being obvious. The two had turned their topic to their wives.

"Chelsea's insisting I buy her a Hummer," Gryder said. "Damn thing's more tank than car. I asked her what the hell she needed one for and she said it would be useful for hauling things. The only thing she ever hauls is ass. She's cost me over two grand in speeding tickets this year alone." Gryder took a sip of his drink and glanced down at Chelsea as if mentally comparing her value to the sticker price of a Hummer. His frown said things weren't looking good for her.

Everyone turned their attention to the game as Derek Jeter came up to bat. The Rangers' pitcher threw a fastball that Jeter sent screaming toward the outfield. It was nothing short of a miracle when the second baseman somehow yanked the ball out of the air. Jeter was out. Without thinking, I jumped out of my seat and threw a fist in the air. "Boo-yah!"

Uh-oh. My inner redneck had reared its head.

Brett looked up at me, a grin tugging at his lips. A blush crept up my cheeks as Shelton, Gryder, and a few others in the room eyed me, too.

"Sorry," I whispered to Brett as I sat down. "Don't know what got into me."

Brett chuckled, unfazed, an amused glint in his eye. He seemed to find my wild, uninhibited side attractive. Thank goodness. It wasn't always easy keeping myself in check.

CHAPTER SEVENTEEN

A Case of Bad Bratwurst

During the seventh inning stretch when Gryder excused himself to visit the men's room and Brett returned to the bar to get us fresh drinks, I slipped back down to the front row and slid into the seat next to Chelsea. Gryder'd been evasive, but I'd been keeping an eye on his wife. A half-dozen drinks had made their way past Chelsea's glossy lips and they were likely to be loose.

Chelsea and Britney wore equally vacuous expressions, droopy red-rimmed eyes, and inebriated flushes. I made small talk for a few seconds to put them at ease before getting down to the nitty-gritty.

"Michael seems like a great guy. How long have you two been married?"

She glanced up, as if mentally calculating. " 'Bout six months."

Not long. Not surprising. "How'd you meet?"

"I used to work the front desk in a hotel. The La Paloma in Tucson. Michael stayed there for a few nights. Said I was the most beautiful girl he'd ever seen. You know, love at first sight."

Love. Right. What in the world could Chelsea and Michael have in common?

"Three weeks later, he gave me this." She held up her hand. The rock on her ring finger was even larger than Britney's.

"Wow," I said. "Who could say no to that?" A woman looking for something more than a sugar daddy, perhaps? I forced a smile. "Did you two have a big wedding?"

"No." Chelsea shook her head. "We eloped a few days later. Got married in Cancún."

"How romantic." How *interesting*. A convenient meeting. A short courtship. A quickie Mexican wedding ceremony, their marital status not on record in the U.S. Still, this could all mean nothing. I could simply have an overactive imagination. Then again, I'd be a fool to ignore my instincts, right? And what could it hurt for me to dig a little deeper? I leaned closer to Chelsea. "I've got some funds to invest and I'd love to make us both some money. Your husband's foreign currency program sounds great. How does it work?"

Chelsea's face contorted in confusion, as if I'd just spoken Swahili. "Hell-if-I-know." It came out as one word. She tossed back the remaining white wine in her glass. Her head lolled slightly, like a bobblehead doll's.

"Does he have an office here in Dallas?"

She shook her head.

"Somewhere else, then?"

"Look," she said, an ironic choice of words since she was having trouble focusing on my face. "All I know is

that he spends all day at the bank or on his cell phone."
She shrugged, telling me that was all she knew about his
business. Somehow that didn't surprise me.

Neither did the Rangers' twelve-to-two loss.

As Brett and I were on our way home in his car, I decided
as long as I was fishing for information, I might as well
figure out what Brett knew. Or at least what he was willing to tell me.

"Gryder's investment program sounds like a potential
moneymaker." I watched his face. His expression didn't
change. "I don't know much about foreign currency exchange, though. How are the transfers handled?"

"I have no idea."

Hard to tell if he was being sincere since his eyes were
locked on the road in front of us.

"You've never asked him about it?"

"No. I'm not interested in that kind of thing." Brett
made a quick check of the outside mirror as he took the
exit for my neighborhood. "I stick to traditional investments. Blue-chip stocks. An occasional bond. Besides,
Stan made it clear he doesn't want Michael soliciting any
of his contacts."

Hmm. That was a juicy tidbit of info. "Why not?"

Brett shrugged. "I guess because it would compete with
the investments the bank offers."

Or because Shelton was trying to fly under the radar,
keep his involvement to a minimum in case the shit ever
hit the fan.

Was Brett telling me the truth? Or was he feigning ignorance? I couldn't tell. The only thing I knew for sure
was that I wanted to believe him. "What were you talking
to Stan and Michael about by the bar?"

Brett shot me a pointed look. "Nothing you'd want to
hear. Trust me."

Trust him? Could I?

Brett changed the radio station when a commercial came on, changing the subject, too. "Britney and Chelsea sure can put away the liquor."

As the former high priestess of beer-chugging, I could put away the liquor, too, but at least I could handle it without falling all over myself. Britney had tripped on the steps on her way to the ladies' room during the eighth inning, falling back on her ass, flashing her crotch to everyone in the seats. No wonder she didn't have panty lines in that tight skirt. No panties. Not a natural blonde, either.

"Want to try that new Thai fusion restaurant in the West End this weekend?" Brett asked. "It's gotten rave reviews."

"No can do. I promised my parents I'd come home for a visit this weekend." I didn't mention that Dad and I planned to go to a gun show. I hadn't yet told Brett I carried a gun on the job. If he knew I had a personal collection, too, who knows how he'd feel. No sense adding fuel to the fire, right? Not at this point anyway. Once I was absolutely certain he was innocent, I'd come clean about the guns, my suspicions about Shelton and Gryder.

"Darn." He sighed, glancing over at me. "I'll miss you."

"Me, too." It was both the truth and a lie. I would miss him, but frankly I was glad to have an excuse to put things off a bit. I needed more time to investigate, to think things through, to figure out what was going on with the Forex program and if Brett was involved in it.

As we neared my house, Brett reached over and put a warm hand on my thigh, casting me a dark, steamy glance that let me know what was on his mind. My heart began to whirl in my chest. We'd come close to making love at the resort, and we'd be even less inhibited with each other now. Tonight could be a chance to become closer to Brett, to take this last big step toward solidifying our relationship.

If only I could set aside my doubts.

Brett eased his Navigator around the curve onto my street and pulled into the driveway, cutting the engine. He turned to me and our gazes locked. "Can I come in?"

I saw nothing in his eyes but a man wanting to be close to a woman. Nothing suspicious, nothing deceitful. I'd been wrong to doubt him. Right?

Of course.

Sure.

Probably.

Maybe.

Ugh. Maybe wasn't good enough. I put a hand on my stomach. "I'm not feeling too well, Brett. I think that bratwurst may have been bad."

Icky, I know. But a digestive issue was the best excuse I could think of on short notice, and one he wasn't likely to argue with. Besides, it wasn't a total lie. With the fears and doubts gnawing at my stomach, I really did feel a little sick.

Brett groaned in frustration. "Sure it's the bratwurst?" he asked, cocking his head as his eyes searched mine. "Not something else?"

Uh-oh. Was he on to me? "What else would it be?"

He didn't answer, just eyed me skeptically for a moment before shrugging his shoulders. He climbed out of the car and walked me to the door.

CHAPTER EIGHTEEN

*N*umbers Don't Lie

Friday morning, I stopped by Eddie's office to drop off the paperwork I'd reviewed for the steakhouse. I set my briefcase on his credenza and unsnapped the locks. "Any new developments?" I hadn't been by the office in a few days and was feeling a little out of the loop.

He turned around in his swivel chair. "The Lobo's been riding me all week, wanting to know how much I can seize from Chisholm's."

"How's it looking?"

"Real good. Yesterday I found two hundred grand in cash in a safe-deposit box." Eddie leaned back in his chair, put his hands behind his head, and grinned. "I just may be Lu's golden boy."

I narrowed my eyes at him. "Maybe *I'm* going to be her golden *girl*."

Eddie snorted. "Yeah, right. You'll be lucky to collect five bucks from that ice-cream man."

Eddie was probably right. If Joe had any money he'd get a better haircut and visit a dermatologist. Still, if I couldn't be the one to get the Lobo to her hundred mil, I just hoped it wasn't that sniveling weenie Josh.

I removed the paperwork from my briefcase and held it out to Eddie.

"Thanks, Tara." Eddie stood to take the stack of documents from me. "Let me know when I can return the favor."

"How about now?" I jotted the name Stan Shelton on a yellow sticky note, tore the page off the pad, and handed it to Eddie.

Eddie glanced down at the note. "Who's this?"

"One of Brett's clients." I told Eddie about the Forex flyers I'd seen, about Gryder and his evasiveness at the ballgame, that Gryder and Shelton could be in cahoots. I didn't mention that Brett had shuttled a sizable deposit between the two. No sense further implicating Brett when he might very well be innocent. Or maybe I was just refusing to face facts.

Eddie raised a brow. "You may be on to something."

"Mind running a search on Shelton? I'll look into Gryder."

He cocked his head. "You'll cut me in?"

"Only if you cut me in on Chisholm's." I drive a hard bargain.

He narrowed his eyes for a moment, considering. "What the hell. If either of these cases takes Lu to a hundred mil, we'll split the bonus."

"Deal." Five grand would still buy a lot of manicures.

"I'll see what I can dig up," Eddie said.

I returned to my office and settled at my desk with a mug of coffee. First, I ran a search on the IRS database, pulling up Brett's tax filings. He hadn't yet filed his return due this year, but I couldn't fault him for procrastinating when I hadn't filed yet, either. His tax records for the previous year showed an impressive salary, but no reported gain or loss from international currency exchanges. He'd indicated that he owned no foreign bank accounts. He'd also claimed no foreign tax credits.

Was that the truth? Or was it a bunch of lies?

Then again, if Brett had only recently become involved, there would have been no transactions to report yet anyway. I didn't know what to think. But my heart felt warm and full when I noted his charitable contributions amounted to more than many people earn in a year. He'd given substantial amounts to a local homeless shelter, the Humane Society, an assortment of environmental groups, and, not surprisingly, the Arbor Day Foundation. Surely a generous guy like him wouldn't be involved in an investment scam or tax fraud. Then again, the contributions could be falsified. According to the records, he'd never been audited. Ugh.

The data showed Brett had filed a Schedule C last year, the form for taxpayers who operated a business as a sole proprietorship. Strange, given that the architecture firm he worked for paid him as an employee and issued a W-2 at the end of the year. What's more, he'd reported no revenue, claiming only a few thousand in business expenses, including real estate taxes.

What was that about? Odd he'd never mentioned that he ran a business on the side, especially since my job involved financial matters, and the only property he'd ever mentioned owning was his house. Brett was keeping secrets. But what was he holding back? And why?

Next, I ran a full-scale search on Michael and Chelsea Gryder. They hadn't yet filed a return for the preceding year, either. Seemed everyone was putting off filing until the last minute. Because they'd been married only six months, they wouldn't have filed together in earlier years. I pulled up Michael's transcripts for the last decade. He'd reported income in the low six figures each year, enough to support a high-class lifestyle without raising red flags. Still, I bet there was a lot of income going unreported. Chelsea may be cheap, but that rock on her finger wasn't.

Gryder had reported a different address for each tax year, never remaining in one place for long, almost as if he were hoping that by keeping on the move nobody would catch up to him. The notations in the filing status column also caught my eye. Gryder's status had cycled from married joint, to married separate, then back to single three times during the last decade, chronicling a series of short, unsuccessful marriages. Before Chelsea, there'd been a Matilda Gryder, an Amber Gryder, and a Lindsey Gryder. Given the birth dates of his latter two wives, Gryder had a history of shacking up with barely legal young women. Matilda Gryder, on the other hand, was fifteen years older than Michael, presumably either a sugar mama or a trailblazing cougar. My money was on sugar mama.

No returns had been filed in the name of XChange Investments. It took quite a bit of digging to confirm the company wasn't incorporated in the U.S., nor was it registered as a foreign corporation in any state.

Josh walked past my open office door then, backtracking when he realized I was at my desk. He stood in my doorway, a smug look on his face as he waited for me to acknowledge him. After ten seconds of being ignored, he couldn't take it anymore. "Guess who I've been assigned to investigate?"

Should've known he'd only stop by to gloat. I crossed my arms over my chest and leaned back in my chair. "Hmm. Could it be the tooth fairy? After all, she passes out all that money to children and has never reported any income."

Josh rolled his eyes.

"Santa, then? He's got all those elves working for him but never once filed a W-2."

Another eye roll.

"The Easter Bun—"

"No! It's Nathan Broadhurst." Josh did a little victory dance in my doorway, including some pelvic thrusts. I could've gone my entire life without seeing that.

The name Nathan Broadhurst meant nothing to me. I raised my palms.

The eye roll was now replaced by a derisive snort. "He's on TV all the time? Plays for the Mavericks?"

A sports figure, sure to be a high-profile, high-dollar case. Still, I wasn't jealous. A wealthy athlete was sure to have a team of attorneys on retainer, ready and willing to make the investigation as painful as possible for the special agent assigned to work it.

"Broadhurst was paid like a gazillion yen for endorsing some type of Japanese washing machine," Josh continued. "Didn't report a dime of it."

I swung my fist in an upward motion. "Go get 'em, tiger." Or just *go*. Fortunately, Josh left, though I heard him stop at the office next door to brag to another special agent.

I turned back to my computer. I hadn't had the forethought to ask for Chelsea's maiden name at the game last night, but I was able to track it down by accessing the W-2s filed by the La Paloma hotel, where Chelsea had been working when she'd met Michael. The only employee by that name was a Chelsea Nicole Reynolds who'd earned a whopping eighteen grand last year. I jotted down the address listed on the W-2 and ran a search of the Tucson real property records. The home at the given address was a tiny three-bedroom model owned by a Fred and Patricia Reynolds. The house had been built in the 1960s and had a current market value of only $52,000. Chelsea'd had a modest upbringing and still lived with her parents when she'd met Michael. No wonder she'd been swept off her feet so easily.

I took a sip of the now-lukewarm coffee I'd picked up on my way in and logged in to NCIC, the National Crime Information Center, the federal law enforcement database of criminal records. My search showed no weapons registered in Michael's or Chelsea's names. That fact provided only small assurance. Not all states required that guns be registered, and firearms could be purchased through various means that left no record. Though Chelsea had a public intoxication charge in her files, neither she nor Michael had a violent criminal record. Good. I'd seen enough violence to last me a lifetime. Jack Battaglia and his box cutter had been more than enough for me.

I continued my investigation into Gryder, running a simple Internet search next. Gryder'd been a busy guy. The Net first turned up a negotiated settlement with the Louisiana State Securities Board relating to a horizontal drilling venture that hadn't been on the up-and-up. According to the report, Gryder paid some restitution but served no jail time, instead turning state's witness and fingering two other men involved in the scam while himself enjoying immunity. A trust company he'd founded in Boise had ended up in receivership, bailed out by the Idaho banking department and, indirectly, Idaho taxpayers. Gryder'd been charged with criminal fraud in the state of Florida in relation to a questionable real estate venture. Thanks to a plea deal his attorney had negotiated, Gryder avoided jail time on that charge, too, though he'd served a year's probation. A newspaper account noted the swindled investors were outraged by the plea deal, but the prosecutor cited a lack of hard evidence needed to nail Gryder in court.

Yep, sleazeballs like Gryder were masters at hiding evidence. They played financial shell games, destroyed documents, transferred money around and commingled it with legitimate or laundered income, making it difficult if not impossible for prosecutors to track funds. The heavy caseloads imposed on local prosecutors and the state attorney general offices also discouraged them from pursuing con artists. Overwhelming numbers of man-hours were involved in researching these scams, hunting for proof, preparing for trial. What's more, given the complexity of the scams, the scarcity of hard evidence, and the technical intricacy of applicable laws, explaining a convoluted scam to a jury and convincing them to convict proved a daunting task for government attorneys.

As a result, white-collar criminals like Gryder had a tendency to resurface, like buoyant turds, undeterred by the government's slap on the wrist and the fines they paid with other people's money. These penalties did little to dissuade them from setting up shop again once the regulators were distracted by some other creep running a scam.

Still, the tides were beginning to change. With so many people affected by the Enron, WorldCom, and Adelphia scandals, the public was beginning to pay attention. Bernie Madoff had received a 150-year sentence for his crimes. Even Martha Stewart, with her infinite resources, hadn't been able to avoid a short stint in prison for her financial crimes.

At any rate, learning Gryder had been involved in financial shenanigans several times before only strengthened my resolve to bring him down. For good.

Per the property records, Gryder'd registered both a new Lexus and a Camaro with the Arizona DMV several months ago. He had yet to transfer the registrations to Texas, a sign that he didn't intend to stick around the Lone Star State for long. No real property was held in his or

Chelsea's name. Not surprising, since real estate was one of the easiest assets for the government to seize. Con artists normally sent their funds to offshore accounts beyond the reach of the American government.

Despite an extensive search, no phone numbers turned up in either Michael's or Chelsea's name. Probably the two used prepaid cell phones, which were difficult, if not impossible, for law enforcement to trace and tap.

Gryder's credit report indicated he'd filed bankruptcy twice—once in the nineties, the other just before the recent change in bankruptcy law made it more difficult to get debts discharged. I took personal offense when I noted that an accrued tax debt of over three hundred grand had been discharged in the bankruptcy.

He'd screwed his creditors, the IRS, and honest taxpayers.

Time to screw him back.

I printed out the information and stuck it in my briefcase. It would come in handy later when we'd ask Judge Trumbull to issue a search warrant.

I'd just finished looking at Gryder's records when Eddie rapped on my door frame. He stepped into my office bearing a small stack of documents. "Far as I can tell, this Stan Shelton is squeaky clean. No arrests, not involved in any lawsuits. Registered Republican. Serves as a deacon in a Methodist church." He handed me the computer printouts. "One divorce two years ago. Remarried now."

I looked over the papers. Copies of car registrations. Stan's voter registration information. His divorce decree, citing irreconcilable differences. Property tax information on his house in the city. Nothing particularly unusual or useful. "Has he filed all of his tax returns?"

Eddie nodded. "He's current. Nothing looked out of the ordinary."

I stuck the papers in my briefcase. "Thanks, buddy."

"Anytime."

After Eddie left, I ran a search on XChange Investments. A Web site popped up. After logging on to the site, I played around for a few minutes, going through the various pages. The site detailed Gryder's investment scheme for "qualified high-net-worth individuals interested in a complex yet risk-free investment program in foreign currency promising a guaranteed annual thirty percent return."

As if. No legitimate investment guaranteed a return that high.

Yep, I'd seen it before. This alleged investment was nothing more than an elaborate pyramid scheme, the stated qualifications and complimentary language used to stroke the egos of the financially unsophisticated. Unfortunately, there were plenty of people naïve enough to fall for this type of scam.

I knew for certain now that Gryder was indeed running a scam. But I still didn't know whether Brett was involved.

I paged through the site, stopping on a full-color photo of Michael Gryder complete with his overly gelled hair and shit-eating grin. He wore a gray pin-striped power suit, an elegant navy silk hankie tucked into the breast pocket. The matching tie bore a clip embellished with an American flag. His hands were folded at his waist, his left hand on top, displaying his thick gold wedding band. The photo was clearly intended to portray him as a classy, patriotic family man. He even made reference to his "loving wife of twenty-two years," failing to clarify that she was twenty-two years old, not that the two had been married for twenty-two years.

You might think con artists would be more discreet than to advertise on a Web site. But the truth is there were so many scams the government couldn't keep up. We didn't have time to go looking for trouble. Normally, it wasn't

until after we received a tip from an irate investor that the
government began an investigation. Besides, these guys
were savvy enough to use temporary addresses, untraceable phones, sometimes even multiple aliases.

The page encouraged sophisticated investors to apply
for membership in XChange Investments' exclusive investment program through an online application system.
Only those deemed qualified to participate would receive
a personal invitation to a seminar at a local hotel where
they would meet "world-renowned investor Michael Gryder" in person.

World-renowned, my ass. But he might soon be noto-
rious.

Conveniently, the Web site offered no physical address
for the business, only an e-mail address and a toll-free
phone number. Asking for a wiretap on the phone number
was an option, but with all the flack the government was
taking for the Patriot Act, an agent had to jump through
flaming hoops before a wire would be approved. It would
be easier to obtain information in person.

According to the site, to be considered as a potential
investor, those interested must first attend one of Gryder's
in-person seminars. Hmm . . .

I sent Eddie an e-mail containing a link to the XChange
Investments Web site, asking him to check it out and give
me his opinion later that afternoon when we'd meet for a
workout at the YMCA. Then I called Christina on her
cell. "Want to help me out?"

"Nope."

"I'll buy lunch."

"All right, then. What is it?"

"Come to my office when you get to the building."

I took all of the information I'd printed out down to Lu's
office and showed it to her. Once she'd read through it all,

she handed it back to me with nothing more than a nod. But it was enough. With that small gesture, she'd given me the okay to officially open a new case on XChange Investments and Michael Gryder.

Christina arrived at my office around noon. She flopped into my swivel chair and, at my direction, completed the online application on the Xchange Investments Web site, claiming to be a nail technician who'd recently inherited four thousand dollars from an uncle who died of a "microbial infarction."

Christina looked up at me, her brow furrowed. "That's not a real thing."

"My point exactly. This guy claims to deal only with wealthy, sophisticated investors, but my hunch is he'll take anyone's money."

She pushed the enter button to send the application. Since Gryder had already met me, Christina would have to attend the seminar. I had no doubt she'd receive one of his exclusive invitations. Sure enough, not two minutes later, a return e-mail, likely an automated response, popped up in my personal e-mail in-box, addressed to Redneckgirl1963. Who would've thought there were 962 others like me?

I read the e-mail. "Wednesday at 7:00, the Sam Houston Salon at the Adolphus Hotel. You're in." And with any luck, I'd soon be taking Gryder out—of business, that is.

When we arrived at the crack house, Christina had a surprise for me. "I brought you a present." She held up a thin, black yoga mat wrapped in plastic.

Thinking back on my quivering, achy muscles, I asked, "Am I supposed to thank you for that?"

She bonked me on the head with the mat and shoved it into my hands. "You may not thank me now, but you will later when your ass looks as good as mine."

"My ass already looks as good as yours."

She glanced down at my backside. "Debatable."

I save her from a rabid raccoon and this is the thanks I get?

We opened the windows to let in the fresh spring air. Given that most of the windows lacked screens, a few flies and a speckled gecko came in with the air. We'd hunt down tax cheats and drug dealers, no problem, but neither of us wanted to handle a slimy little reptile. The lizard ran unfettered down the wall, across the floor, and into a bedroom.

Christina pulled out her yoga mat and slid an exercise DVD into her laptop. I ripped the plastic off my new mat and rolled the mat out on the floor next to hers. Within minutes, we each had our arms and legs tangled around ourselves as if we were playing solitary games of Twister. While we exercised, we discussed our weekend plans.

"I'm going home to Nacogdoches for a gun show," I told Christina, "but I can stay here tonight and head out in the morning." Of course I couldn't come back to the house tonight until after I'd met with Dave Edwards at the coffeehouse, got the inside scoop on the goings-on at First Dallas. But that shouldn't take too long.

"Ajay's taking me out tonight," Christina said. "I'll have him bring me here after. We'll have ourselves a regular slumber party."

"I'll bring snacks."

"Now you're talking."

When my stomach growled, I sat back on my mat and picked up my cell phone and the tattered phone book. "What sounds good for lunch?"

"How about pizza?" Christina said from behind her awkwardly crooked knee. "Order a vegetarian so we can at least pretend it's healthy."

I dialed the first major pizza chain on the list. After placing my order, I gave them the address for the house.

"Sorry," said the girl on the other end of the phone. "We don't deliver to that neighborhood. Four of our drivers got rolled there last year."

I tried the next chain. Same response. After placing six more calls, I'd heard it all. Delivery drivers robbed of their cash and jewelry, delivery drivers carjacked, delivery drivers stripped naked and dumped on the outskirts of town.

"I've got a gun and pepper spray," I told the last person to turn me down. "Does that help?"

The woman hung up on me.

The final listing in the Yellow Pages pizza section was "Wong-Fu's Eggroll Express and Pizza."

"Do we dare?" I asked Christina.

She shrugged. "Why not? We're brave girls."

While we waited for lunch to arrive, Christina showed me more yoga moves. She stuck one leg out straight behind her, the other bent to her side. "This pose is called the 'King Pigeon.'"

"And this is called the 'Funky Chicken.'" I flapped my arms and walked knock-kneed in a circle.

"Grow up."

"What fun would that be?"

A half hour later, a silver Honda Civic hatchback pulled up to the curb, two young Asian men inside. The guy in the passenger seat ducked low, his eyes darting around the area for a few seconds before he threw open his door. He leaped out, lugging a metal baseball bat, and grabbed our pizza out of the hatchback the driver had just popped open. He dashed to our door, taking our three front steps in one long stride, banging hard and fast on the door.

When I opened the door, he all but threw the pizza and a handful of fortune cookies at me. I handed the guy a twenty, told him to keep the change, and watched him barrel across the front yard and dive into the open door of the car. Tires screeching, the two took off at warp speed, leaving tread marks and a small exhaust cloud at the curb.

Christina stood behind me, sodas in hand. "Wimps."

We brought our food out onto the front porch and dug in, enjoying the unseasonably cool day. The guys who lived across the street weren't outside today, but their dog was lying in his usual place under the tree. The dog sniffed the air, smelled our food and stood, dragging his chain until he'd pulled it taut. I hoped it would hold. With his wide mouth, pointy teeth, and rock-solid muscle, the dog looked scary as hell.

I took a bite of pizza. "At the rate we're going, we won't have Joe busted till Christmas."

"Don't sweat it," Christina said, waving her hand dismissively. "We're wearing him down."

Surely Christina knew what she was talking about, but frankly I was going stir-crazy. Stakeouts aren't as much fun as you'd think. Too much downtime for a girl of action like me.

When I finished my pizza, I cracked open my fortune cookie and pulled out the slip of paper. My fortune read "One cannot find true love without first being true to oneself."

Freaky.

A few minutes later, we heard ice-cream truck music. Joe rolled slowly up the street, stopping at our curb. The two guys from across the street walked over, casting glances at me and Christina.

Christina put a hand on my arm, stopping me as I began to stand. "Wait," she said in a low voice.

One of the guys took a quick glimpse back at us as Joe handed a small paper bag through the window to the other. They made no attempt to hide their transaction this time. Looked like we'd successfully pulled off our cover, convinced them we were nothing more than trashy slackers.

I wasn't sure whether to be proud or ashamed that I made such a convincing skank.

After the two guys returned to their house, Joe looked over at us. "Ice cream?" he called through the open service window.

Christina shook her head.

I didn't exactly understand the dynamics here, but figured Christina knew what she was doing. She looked away from Joe, ignoring him now, cracking open a fortune cookie.

Joe watched her for a minute. "Come here," he called.

Christina didn't look up, appearing to be talking to the cookie in her hand. "Why should we?"

Joe put his hands on the top of the window, exposing sweat-stained armpits. "Just come here."

Christina slowly stood, and took her time walking to the truck. I followed her lead, stepping slowly through the yard.

Joe glanced nervously up and down the street before bending down to speak to us. "What are you in the market for?"

"What do you got?" Christina asked, raising a brow.

"I can get my hands on just about anything."

Christina jutted out her chin, using it to gesture across the street at the house the two Latino guys lived in. "What did you get for them?"

Joe snorted and cocked his greasy head. "Girl, you couldn't handle something like that."

Whoa. Had he just admitted something? His words were probably too vague for Judge Trumbull to issue a search warrant. They'd communicated, sure, but they'd talked around the subject. We needed some hard evidence or, better yet, probable cause. With probable cause we could search the truck on the spot. But we had to be very careful. One false, premature move and any evidence we seized could be challenged, the case thrown out of court.

Christina crossed her arms under her breasts, forcing them up and out for maximum effect, and stuck out her bottom lip in a sexy pout. "I can handle anything."

Joe watched her for a moment, his eyes flicking from her chest to her face. "You like crank?"

What the heck was crank?

"Hell, yeah, if it's pure," Christina said. "Nothing like it."

"I can hook you up next week," Joe said.

"Promise?" Christina put a hand on Joe's forearm and had a suggestive tone in her voice. "I don't like to be let down."

Joe glanced down at her hand and grinned. "Don't worry, babe. I'll come through for you."

She gave him a sultry smile.

Joe's tone turned businesslike now. "One hundred. Cash."

Christina nodded. "I'll have it."

We bought two ice-cream sandwiches and walked back into the house. Once the door shut behind us, Christina began jumping up and down and clapping her hands. A couple of pom-poms and she'd be right at home on a football field. "We've got him!"

"We're going to get him," I admonished her. "Don't count a chickenshit until you've got him by the nuggets."

Ajay planned to bring Christina to the house later that evening after their date, so I drove Christina back to the DEA office in Pinky, dropped her off, and took the car to the Y. After I'd stripped down to my bra and panties in the ladies' locker room, I stepped onto the scale and slid the register to its usual position. The balance remained fully tilted to the right. Uh-oh.

Slowly, I edged the weight higher until the balance leveled out. Dang. I'd gained four pounds. Had to be all that ice cream. We'd better bust Joe before I busted out of my pants.

I slid into my shorts, thankfully stretchy black spandex, and threw on a wrinkled blue T-shirt. I gathered up my novel and towel and went in search of Eddie. He'd already logged eight minutes on the stationary bike where he sat pedaling and reading the *National Review*. He squirted water into his mouth from a clear plastic bottle.

I climbed onto the bike next to him, adjusted the seat, and cranked the resistance up three levels higher than usual, having to push extra hard on the pedals to get the machine going. I glanced over at Eddie. "You get a chance to look at that link I sent you? The one for XChange Investments?"

He nodded.

"And?"

He put one bent arm out in front of him, the other behind, Egyptian-style. "Pyramid scheme."

"That's what I thought, too."

He put his hands back on the bars. "What's going on with the ice-cream man?"

"We're close to nailing Joe. He's supposed to get us some crystal meth next week." Christina had explained to me earlier that "crank" was the street name for the popular methamphetamine, so called because it was often hidden in a car's crankcase. Once Joe sold us the drugs, Judge Trumbull would have to issue a search warrant for his apartment, bank records, all that stuff. Chances were such a search would turn up more condemning evidence.

After the bike, I dabbed the sweat from my forehead and headed to the elliptical machines. I spent an extra ten minutes on the equipment, cranking the machine up to the most difficult level. Needed to keep in shape so I'd look good for Brett once I'd relieved my suspicions. My suspicions would be relieved, right? God, I hoped so.

My huffing and puffing earned me odd looks from those exercising nearby.

Eddie walked over from the free weights. "Easy, girl. You sound like you're having an orgasm over here."

I didn't break stride. "How would you know what a woman having an orgasm sounds like?"

Eddie put a hand over his chest. "That hurt."

"Sorry." I slowed to a stop and tried to catch my breath. "I'm just a little grumpy. Thanks to all the ice cream I've downed this week, I've put on four pounds." The fact that I'd been battling doubts about Brett didn't help my mood, either.

Eddie gave a knowing nod. "I noticed your tight ass wasn't looking so tight anymore."

I whipped my towel into a twist and snapped it at him, landing a satisfying pop on his butt before he could get away.

An extra four sets on the glute machine rounded out my workout and hopefully took some of the roundness out of my butt.

CHAPTER NINETEEN

Coffee Klatch

I drove home in Pinky, stopping by the grocery store to pick up snacks for later. As I turned into my driveway, I accidentally bumped the curb, distracted by the three-man crew working on my front lawn, one of whom was Brett. From behind the wheel, I took in my town house, hardly recognizing the place. Gone was that stubborn, misshapen evergreen bush. A row of abundant pink rosebushes stood before my living room windows, the ivy underneath thick and lush. The small redbud tree waved its heart-shaped leaves in the breeze, the begonias around the trunk even more vivid against a backdrop of cedar mulch. The multi-colored river stones added yet another dimension to the landscaping. The shepherd's hooks and hanging baskets framed my entryway perfectly.

What a transformation.

Brett raised a hand, indicating I should wait a moment.

He trotted to the curb where he'd parked his Navigator, opened the hatch, and pulled out a pink plastic flamingo. He plunked the tacky bird into the grass next to the driveway, then spread his arms wide, the yard now complete.

I climbed out of the car. "Wow!"

Brett wiped a smudge of dirt from his face with a gloved hand. He was sweaty and filthy, yet still somehow managed to look sexy. "You like it?"

"I love it!" I grabbed his face in my hands and planted a big kiss on his mouth.

Brett smiled and dismissed his crew.

"Thanks, guys!" I called as they loaded their tools into the back of a green king cab pickup. They waved and headed off.

I walked over to the bushes and fingered the fragrant roses.

Brett followed me. "You weren't kidding about that crazy evergreen bush. I thought we'd never get all the roots out."

"I'm so glad you did." I looked up at him. "The yard looks absolutely beautiful now. I can't thank you enough." Of course, there were ways I'd be willing to show my gratitude, none of them involving clothing and at least one involving whipped cream.

He removed his gloves and tucked them into the pocket of his shorts. "Ready for your trip home tonight?"

"Pretty much." I wasn't actually leaving town until the next morning since I'd be meeting with Dave Edwards shortly then spending the night at the crack shack, but I couldn't get into that right now.

"Have a safe trip. I'll miss you, Tara."

"I'll miss you, too." My heart felt as if it were being squeezed in a juicer. I should be ashamed of myself, keeping secrets from a sweet guy like Brett. After all, he'd just spent a small fortune landscaping my front yard. I'd never dated someone so thoughtful and generous. But what he didn't know, he couldn't worry about, right? Besides, he was keeping secrets from me, too. Even if he wasn't involved in Gryder's scam, he had yet to tell me about the business venture reported on his tax return. Then again, the business was apparently a start-up and had produced a small loss. Maybe he wasn't even running the business anymore. Maybe that's why he hadn't said anything about it. But I couldn't very well ask him about it. If I did he'd know I'd been snooping through his tax files and he'd want to know why. Admitting I'd questioned his integrity would put an immediate end to our relationship.

After Brett left, I went inside, showered, and threw on a pair of jeans and a sweatshirt. I applied minimal makeup, just enough so I wouldn't scare small children. No sense spending a lot of time on my face if I'd just be hanging around the 'hood all evening. I tossed a few things in an overnight bag and grabbed some snacks for later. Checking the map I'd printed out from the Internet, I aimed Pinky toward Mesquite.

Half an hour later, I sat across a small circular table from Dave Edwards, the bank employee who'd ratted to the OCC. Dave was a squarely built guy with a blondish flattop and meticulously groomed goatee. He wore standard bank attire—navy pants with black loafers, a white button-down shirt, and basic red and navy striped tie. He chewed his thick bottom lip, his right knee jerking up and down like a jackhammer. As jittery as Dave was already, I hoped he'd ordered a decaf.

I wasn't sure what I wanted to hear tonight. Part of me hoped he'd hand me the smoking gun to nail Shelton and Gryder, but another part hoped he'd found nothing. Because if he found nothing to implicate Shelton and Gryder, there'd be nothing to implicate Brett, either.

I took a sip of my latte and a bite of pumpkin scone before pulling a small notepad out of my purse. I kept my voice low so as not to be overheard, probably not necessary given that most of the people at the surrounding tables were too busy yakking on their cell phones or listening to their iPods to give us a second thought. "Got anything for me?"

Dave nodded, his fingers drumming nervously on the sides of his tall paper cup. He glanced around the room and leaned closer to me over the table. "When things get busy at the bank, my boss makes me help with paperwork, including regulatory reports. Last week I prepared a cash transaction report for the banking department on a large wire transfer to a foreign bank. I ended up working late that night to catch up on a few things and I found Stan Shelton feeding my report into the shredder. When I asked Stan what he was doing he claimed he'd made a mistake, picked up the wrong stack of documents, but I have a hard time believing he screwed up accidentally."

I nodded, my mind working to process the information. I jotted a few notes on my pad.

> *Bank department report.*
> *Wire transfer to foreign bank.*
> *Scone is stale—next time try cinnamon bun.*

Dave reached down into a hard-sided black briefcase he'd stashed under the table and pulled out a manila envelope. He slid the envelope across the table to me. "These are copies of the cash transaction reports I prepared and others I found in the backup files. They'd been deleted from the bank's active network, but our computer security system would have prevented Stan from deleting the forms from the archives. If you run the reports against the government's records, you'll see none of them were ever filed."

"Sounds like a potential money-laundering situation." I opened the envelope and pulled out the forms. Each form documented a wire transfer of a large sum of cash, the smallest for thirty grand. A number of the transfers went directly into an account in the name of XChange Investments at Banco Primero de San Jose in Costa Rica.

Gryder.

My instincts had been right. I knew there was something sleazy about that guy the second I laid eyes on him. I just wished my instincts would be clear where Brett was—or was not—concerned.

The documentation included transfers in and out of a number of other accounts, some in the name of Michael Gryder, others in the name of Chelsea Reynolds, and more in the names of various businesses and trusts. Euro Investors Incorporated. Petroleum Partners Ltd. The MG Family Trust. Several of the more recent transfers went into an account at First Dallas Bank held in the name of Banco Primero, no doubt a correspondent account established and held by the Costa Rican bank to help its clients avoid reporting requirements and thus thwart U.S. law enforcement.

Dave had included statements for the various accounts as well, many of which showed transfers in amounts just under the $10,000 threshold, structured to avoid the cash transaction reporting requirements and hopefully avoid catching the government's eye. This type of money-laundering process was often referred to as "Smurfing." It was unclear who'd coined the term. Some sources attributed it to a defense attorney, others to a federal law enforcement officer. At any rate, the term referred to breaking down large transfers into a series of small transactions, like the numerous teeny blue Smurfs milling about on the children's cartoon.

I shuffled through the papers, mentally calculating. "Whoa. There's over four million in transfers here." Big-time stuff. This case could be much bigger than I'd thought. I looked up at Edwards. "Do you know anything more about this XChange Investments?"

He shook his flat head. "I asked Stan but all he'd tell me was that it's a private investment firm for the filthy rich. The guy who runs it has been in the bank several times."

"Plastic hair? Shit-eating grin?"

"That's the guy. His head looks like it belongs on a Pez dispenser. Name's Michael Gryder. You know him?"

"Met him last night at the Rangers game."

"You sat in the bank's skybox?"

I picked a corner off my too-dry scone. "Yep."

Dave snorted. "Then I guess you met Stan's wife, Britney, too. She's a piece of work, huh? Stan's first wife was much nicer and a hell of a lot classier. He was an idiot to divorce her."

"Midlife crisis?"

"That would be my guess." Dave swallowed a gulp of his coffee. "Stan's never offered to take me to a game. He only invites the bigwigs and major clients. How'd you get to sit in the box?"

I brushed a crumb from my blouse. "My boyfriend is doing a landscaping project for the Sheltons' lake house."

"Lake house?" Dave slammed his coffee cup down on the table. Good thing the cup was made of paper or it would've shattered. "No wonder Stan's been busting our balls. He's made the salaried staff put in all kinds of overtime. With as many hours as I've put in, I've barely earned minimum wage. All so we can pay for a lake house. Unbelievable."

While he stewed, I continued to riffle through the paperwork. An illegible signature purporting to be that of Michael Gryder appeared on many of the documents, while a signature allegedly belonging to Chelsea Reynolds appeared on others.

"Ever seen Gryder's wife in the bank?"

Edwards shook his head.

Sheez. Gryder had been forging Chelsea's signature, implicating her in his scheme. Poor girl. Her white knight was not what he seemed. "I have to ask," I said. "What's in this for you?"

Dave tossed back the dregs of his coffee, set his cup back on the table, and leaned toward me, jamming his index finger on the table to emphasize his points. "I've worked my ass off for Shelton for ten years—ten freaking years!—trying to make something of myself, and he treats me like shit. If you've got a nice pair of tits you can move up the corporate ladder at warp speed, but if you're a guy? Forget it."

A disgruntled employee. Could he be trusted? What kind of witness would he make if this case went to trial? Oh, well, I'd let Ross O'Donnell, our attorney, worry about that. It was unlikely Edwards would risk making false accusations against his boss even if he was pissed off at him. "So your coming forward is a revenge thing?"

Dave spun the now-empty cup with his fingertips. "I wouldn't call it revenge. I'd call it justice."

"That does sound much nicer." I swallowed hard, afraid to ask my next question, but knowing I had to. Once again I felt sick to my stomach. "Is there anyone else who may be involved?"

"You mean another bank employee?"

I nodded. "Or anyone else associated with Gryder or Shelton outside the bank?" Like my boyfriend? *Oh, please, please, please! Tell me no!*

He paused a moment, chewing his thumb knuckle as

he thought. "Maybe. There's another guy who's come in
the bank a few times. I don't know his name, but he's got
light brown hair, average height. Saw him in the parking
lot once. Drives a black Navigator."

Brett.

Aw, hell.

CHAPTER TWENTY

Party Pooper

My heart raged against my ribs like a rabid monkey in a too-small cage. I took a deep breath to try to calm myself. Dave had jumped to conclusions. Brett was probably in the bank to talk about the landscaping project, not to play a part in the investment scam. But at this point, with the landscaping project already under way, couldn't any of the landscaping business be handled by phone or e-mail? What need would there be to meet in person?

"The guy came in with Gryder several times to meet with Stan," Dave continued. "They usually come late in the day, at closing time. They always go right into Stan's office and shut the door."

After-hours, closed-door meetings. This didn't sound good. In fact, it sounded bad. Real bad. A hollow feeling shot through me.

I pulled one of my business cards out of my wallet and

slid it across the table to Dave. "I'll see what I can do from
here. If anything else comes up, let me know."

The two of us walked out to the parking lot together.
When I stopped next to Pinky, Dave scrunched up his face.
"You sell makeup, too?"

"Not exactly." Though maybe I should consider it. My
job as a special agent had proved to be riskier than I'd
imagined, as evidenced by the fading scar on my forearm. The biggest risk I'd face hawking cosmetics would
be poking myself in the eye with a mascara wand.

I drove back to the 'hood, having to stop for a tank of gas
on the way. Pinky sucked down gas like Britney sucked
down tequila shots. I tried not to think about what Dave
had said about Brett meeting with Gryder and Stan at the
bank. Surely Brett couldn't be involved. He seemed sincerely in the dark when I'd questioned him about Gryder's
investment scheme. There had to be another explanation
why Brett would meet privately with both of them. But
what?

I couldn't come up with anything. Damn.

Damn.

Damn.

Damn.

The night began to grow dark and I paid extra attention
as I wound my way through the 'hood. Cars seemed to be
everywhere, lining the curbs, parked on lawns, cruising
slowly down the roads. Friday night and no place to go.

I pulled into the driveway and lugged my snacks and
overnight bag inside. Ignoring the police sirens that seemed
to be constant background noise, I watched a little TV,
enjoying a rerun of *Reba*. That Reba McEntire had spunk.
I hoped I looked half as good at her age. Heck, I wished I
looked half as good at *my* age.

When the show ended, I read for an hour, finishing the

novel I'd been reading. I even spent a few minutes twisting myself into knots on my new yoga mat. I rolled onto my back with my legs up in the air, spread wide. "This pose is called 'the drunken cheerleader,'" I said, talking to myself to break the quiet. I shifted onto my knees, head hung forward, arms stretched out in a circle in front of me. "This pose is called 'praying to the porcelain god.'" After a few minutes, even the yoga grew tiresome.

"I'm bored," I told the housefly resting on the windowsill. Apparently he didn't find me all that interesting either and flew off, leaving a speck on the paint. Eventually, I decided to take a nap until Christina arrived, although going to sleep alone in this neighborhood seemed a risky proposition. I slid my holster around my waist, pushed it down into position, and stuck my gun in the sheath. After switching off the bare bulb that lit the room, I plumped up my pillow and stretched out on the sofa for a snooze.

Around ten-thirty, a key jingled in the door lock and Christina and Ajay bounded through the front door, both dressed in jeans and T-shirts. Christina yanked on the light, giggling and shoving Ajay's hands away as he tickled her with his free hand. In his other hand he held a large paper grocery bag.

I raised my head off the pillow and rubbed my eyes.

"Wake up, sleepyhead," Christina said, nudging me with her toe. "It's party time."

Ajay looked around the room. Not much to see other than the grungy sofa, the yoga mats, and the portable television. "I love what you haven't done with the place." He set the bag down on the floor and unloaded the contents—a bottle of butterscotch schnapps, a bottle of Irish cream liqueur, a box of disposable paper cups, and a deck of red and white playing cards.

I raided the fridge and, using my cooler as a makeshift coffee table, set out a plastic tub of hummus with sesame

crackers, a small wheel of brie, crudités with creamy arti-
choke dip, and garlic-stuffed olives. A pretty fancy spread
given the surroundings. I took a seat on the couch next to
Christina while Ajay played bartender, mixing the schnapps
and liqueur in the paper cups and handing a creamy cocktail to each of us.

Christina raised her cup. "To Friday night."

We tapped our paper cups carefully to avoid crushing
them and took a sip of our drinks. The concoction was
delicious, creamy, and sweet.

"Yum." I turned to Ajay, who'd taken a seat on the floor
on top of a yoga mat. "What do you call this?"

"Buttery Nipple."

Hmm.

Ajay bounced on the mat and cocked his head at Christina. "I'd love to see some of your yoga moves."

He stood as she made her way to the mat. She knelt on
the mat, then pushed herself up on her forearms, her back
arched, her legs bent backward, her feet nearly touching
her head. Ajay's mouth gaped, his eyes glimmering with
unfettered lust.

I had to admit, Christina was impressively strong and
limber. "What's that position called?"

"The Scorpion."

"What a coincidence," Ajay said, looking down at her
and waggling his eyebrows. "That's also a position from
the Kama Sutra."

Christina looked up at him from under her dark bangs.
"Don't get your hopes up. I can only hold it for ten seconds."

Ajay's lips spread in a grin. "That's long enough."

"*This conversation* has gone on long enough." I shoved
a hummus-covered cracker at each of them, hoping to put
an end to their exchange.

Ajay resumed his seat on the mat and shuffled the deck
of cards. "Texas hold 'em?"

"Sure," I said. "I'd be glad to take your money."

"You wish," Christina hissed. "Poker's my game."

The three of us emptied our wallets. I had only eight dollars and fifty-three cents. I'd better get lucky fast. Ajay slid on a pair of sunglasses and dealt the first hand.

Several hands into the game, I was up by twenty bucks. Ajay's glasses hadn't helped him any. The guy couldn't bluff if his life depended on it and, besides, the mirrored lenses reflected his hand. Christina and I hadn't bothered to point that out to him. Naughty girls.

A knock sounded on the door.

Ajay glanced at the door. "Expecting someone?"

We shook our heads.

I stood and walked to the door. No peephole. I walked to the window and snuck a peek through the blinds. The porch light was burned out and I couldn't see anything but a dark shadow. Should've bought light bulbs. I pulled my gun from my holster and stepped back to the door. "Who is it?"

"Joe," came a muffled voice through the door. My eyes met Christina's.

"Joe, the ice-cream guy?"

"Yeah."

Christina sat bolt upright and frantically scooped up the fancy snacks. "Say as little as possible," she whispered to Ajay. "Follow my lead. And pretend you're with Tara."

She dashed off to the kitchen with the food clutched in her arms.

I shoved my gun back into the holster and fluffed out my top to make sure the weapon was sufficiently hidden. Glancing quickly around the room, I spotted nothing else that might give away the fact that we didn't actually live in this dump. I went to the front door and opened it.

Joe stood on the porch wearing a dingy blue T-shirt and hideously tight jeans, a bulge against his left thigh showing

us what little boys were made of. A six-pack of Milwau-
kee's Best hung from his fingers. If he was trying to impress Christina, he should've brought something better
than that cheap swill. But the rules of Southern etiquette
dictate that anyone bearing beer is guaranteed entry to
any venue, so I had no choice but to invite Joe in.

"Hey, Joe," Christina said, returning from the kitchen
and plopping down on one end of the couch. She draped
one leg over the armrest and leaned back in a sexy pose.
If the DEA ever made a calendar, that crotch shot would
earn her a spot as Miss January.

Joe's eyes went from Christina's face to her crotch, then
to Ajay, who sat scowling up at him from the yoga mat,
having removed his mirrored sunglasses.

"That's Ajay," I said, gesturing.

Joe pulled a beer from the six-pack for himself and
handed another to Ajay. Good thing he'd brought cans.
Ajay looked as if he'd like nothing better than to slit Joe's
throat with the jagged edge of a broken bottle.

Christina tilted her head and eyed Joe. "Got anything
else to make this a real party?"

Joe shook his head. "Can't get my hands on anything
until Monday."

"Promises, promises."

Joe smiled his gap-toothed grin. "I'll come through for
you. Don't you worry."

He was the one who ought to be worrying. Idiot.

Joe slid onto the couch next to Christina. He looked
down, noting the cards on the cooler. "Texas hold 'em?"

"Uh-huh." Ajay picked up the deck and tapped it in his
palm.

Joe stood and dug through his front pocket for coins,
having a hard time getting a finger into his skintight jeans.
He turned to Christina, his genitals at her eye level. "Little help?"

Christina looked away, faking a giggle, but making a gagging face at me behind the drape of her long hair.

I snuggled up next to Ajay on the mat. He put an arm around my shoulders and nuzzled my neck, probably trying to get back at Christina for flashing her crotch at Joe.

"Maybe you two should get a room." Joe laughed. Alone.

Maybe he should get a haircut that's not two decades out of style.

Ajay dealt another round of cards.

Joe eyed Ajay. "That your car outside?"

Ajay dipped his head. "Yeah."

"That Viper's a sweet ride, man," Joe said. "You a pimp or something?"

Ajay peered out from under his thick, dark eyebrows. "You could say I make a living off other people's bodies."

Good improvising, Ajay. I shot him a surreptitious wink.

We played another round, Christina winning. With her elbow, she nudged Joe. "Winning back some of my ice-cream money."

Every few minutes, Joe eased himself a few inches closer to Christina on the sofa. She'd scrunched herself into a tight ball in the corner, her arms wrapped defensively around her curled-up legs. Eventually, Joe's thigh made contact with hers and Christina leaped off the couch.

"'Nother beer?"

Joe chugged the dregs of his drink and set the can on the floor, crushing it with his dirty sneaker and kicking it aside. He emitted a beer-scented belch. Classy.

Christina darted to the kitchen before Joe could get to the fridge and see the bottle of wine and the swanky spread we'd stashed there. Joe's eyes didn't leave Christina's denim-covered butt until she rounded the corner. Ajay put a hand on my knee and squeezed out his frustrations.

"Ouch!" I shoved his hand away this time.

Joe flashed another grin at us. "Y'all want to get it on, don't mind me. I'll just watch."

I fought the urge to punch those crooked teeth right down his throat.

A few hands later, both my luck and my money had run out. I raised my hands in surrender. "I'm out."

"Me, too," Christina said. She walked to the bedroom and returned with a manicure kit and a couple bottles of nail polish. She waved them at me. "How about I give you a French manicure?"

Joe grinned. "How about you give her a French kiss?"

My hand instinctively went to the handle of my gun, hidden under my shirt. One more perverse comment and this guy was losing his nuts. In those tight jeans, they'd be easy to target. Christina faked a giggle and shoved him off the couch. Joe looked a little confused when his ass hit the floor.

Christina knelt down next to me and the two of us gave each other French manicures while the guys played a few more rounds of poker. When Christina finished, I held up my nails and took a look. Not as good as a professional nail tech, but Christina hadn't done too bad for an amateur.

Joe nudged Christina's thigh with his toe. "Why don't you and me go somewhere, get a drink or something?"

I didn't even want to think what the "or something" could be.

Christina glanced up at him. "You bring me something Monday, we'll talk."

Joe somehow looked both frustrated and hopeful, but he seemed to realize he'd get nowhere with Christina tonight. "I'm gonna go meet some friends."

This loser had friends?

Christina stood and walked him to the door. "See ya Monday." She shot Joe a wink.

Joe gave Christina one last, longing glance before walking out the door and tripping down the front steps in the dark.

CHAPTER TWENTY-ONE

$\mathcal{M}$y Redneck Roots

The next morning, I quietly packed my things and slipped outside to Pinky, noting Ajay's expensive spinners were gone. Hoped he had a low insurance deductible.

Fighting sleep, I headed east on Interstate 20, making my way home in the Caddie. Mom and Dad would get a kick out of the tacky car.

The landscape slowly evolved from flat grasslands to the tall piney woods of east Texas. I exited the freeway, heading south down Highway 259 to Nacogdoches. I drove past the dense, lush woods, looking forward to being home again and spending some time with my family. Maybe getting some distance from Brett for the weekend would help me gain some perspective, see things more clearly.

The confusion and uncertainty were killing me. I wanted to get to know Brett better, to be closer to him. He had all the qualities I'd been looking for in a man. But I couldn't simply ignore the facts. Whether knowingly or not, Brett had already played a role in the XChange Investments scheme by shuttling the funds from the lake house to the bank. Without more, that minimal role wasn't likely to support an indictment against him. But there was more, wasn't there? Huddling with Gryder and Shelton at the Rangers game, the covert meetings at the bank. Was I dating a criminal? Or was there some other explanation?

Unfortunately, even if I resolved my uncertainties about Brett, our relationship wouldn't be totally problem-free. There was still the issue of my job, his feelings about my special agent position. If anything, as my career progressed, I'd be assigned bigger, more dangerous cases. How would he deal with that? But I wouldn't—couldn't—change who I was for him. He'd either have to find a way to deal with the situation or . . .

I sighed. I didn't want to think about the *or*.

People could have differences and still make a good couple, couldn't they? Sure. My parents were proof of that. Dad came from a blue-collar family and didn't need much in the way of material things to be happy. My mother's aspirations were somewhat higher, though she'd found my father's gray-blue eyes, easygoing demeanor, and broad, rock-hard shoulders irresistible. The two had compromised. In return for being permitted to dip snuff in the barn and watch every Dallas Cowboys game without interruption, my father indulged my mother, wearing the monogrammed shirts she bought him, forcing down the occasional escargot, spending his weekends on the never-ending projects required to keep up the ancient Victorian farmhouse my mother insisted on buying just days before it was to be condemned.

My clever mother had named the house Holloway Manor and obtained an economic development grant to finance a large part of the renovations. The house was painted a soft blue, with ivory trim and shutters and a shiny tin roof. A large floral wreath graced the wide front door, while white curtains of Battenburg lace adorned each window. A half-dozen mismatched wooden rockers lined the front porch, giving the house a folksy, homey feel. My mother earned a tidy sum renting out the downstairs for bridal showers, wedding receptions, and Red Hat Society teas. The old house had even been featured once in *Southern Living* magazine, a good part of the article focusing on Dad's antique gun collection, displayed in a glass case in the study. A framed clipping of the article now hung in the foyer.

Dad looked over from his perch on the riding lawn mower as I pulled into the long gravel drive, the rocks *plink-plinking* against the car's undercarriage. Dad wore his standard canvas work pants and worn leather boots, along with a loose blue cotton shirt and a straw cowboy hat to keep the sun out of his eyes. He did a double take when he realized it was me driving the pink monstrosity, a welcoming grin spreading across his weathered face as he waved to me.

Mom was out front, kneeling on a folded blue tarp in the flower bed. Beside her sat a rusty Radio Flyer wagon filled with yellow lantana, red salvia, and purple-flowered Mexican heather, the staples of Texas landscaping. Like me, Mom was petite with brown hair. She sported a pair of pale green Capri pants, a short-sleeved yellow shirt, and a red bandanna on her head to hold her shoulder-length hair out of her face. She stood, smiling, sliding her feet into a pair of waterproof gardening clogs. She walked over to the car to give me a hug and kiss, careful to avoid touching me with her dirty garden gloves.

She gestured toward the car. "What in the world is this?"

"I'm on a stakeout," I said. "The car is part of our cover."

Dad pulled up on the mower, cut the engine, and climbed off, giving me a big bear hug. He smelled like hard work and fresh-cut grass. While Dad fanned himself with his hat, I gave him and Mom the scoop on our impending bust. Forcing a smile, Mom tried to hide her concern.

Dad shook his head and put his hat back on. "Well, don't that beat all. If you can't trust the ice-cream man, who can you trust?"

After Dad carried my bags inside, I grabbed a spare pair of white garden gloves and a red-handled trowel from the barn and knelt down next to my mom in the flower bed. I'd always enjoyed gardening with her, the satisfying physical work of digging and planting, the fresh, raw smell of the earth.

After a few minutes of digging, I came across a fat grub in the dirt. I tossed the offender into the grass, sat back on my heels, and looked over at my mother. She turned my way, her expression expectant.

"I don't know what to do, Mom." Tears welled up in my eyes. "Brett may be involved with a con artist." I told her everything I knew, all of which was circumstantial, but still enough to raise reasonable doubts.

Her face appeared thoughtful for a moment, then she gave a small shrug. "Believe none of what you hear, hon, and only half that you see."

I wasn't sure where that left me. "Got anything better'n that?"

"Wish I did, hon. I hate to see you upset." She patted my knee. "Time will tell, Tara."

But what would time tell me about Brett?

Mom stood and held out a hand to help me up. "Let's go have a praline."

Mom and I spent the rest of the afternoon cleaning the house and preparing for a rehearsal dinner that was to be held in the main dining room later that evening. The caterers arrived at four and took over the kitchen and downstairs. Mom and I slid into our boots—mine old, worn ropers and hers new, oiled English riding boots despite our lack of horses—and headed out to the barn behind the house.

We'd never raised livestock, but the barn had provided shelter for a dozen or so cats and dogs, all strays we'd collected one way or another over the years, as well as three goats we'd inherited when the farmer next door had passed away. A family member had asked if we might care for the goats temporarily until they could figure something out. We'd had those sweet, coarse-haired, round-bellied goats going on eleven years now, and weren't about to cut them loose even on the slim chance the family ever did come back for them. I fed each of the goats a handful of raw peanuts, their soft lips tickling the palm of my hand, and scratched them in their favorite spot at the base of their horns.

It felt good to be home. The feel of my old worn boots, the smell of fresh hay in the barn, the taste of Mom's tea, so sweet your glucose levels skyrocketed after just one glass.

When Dad finished mowing our ten acres, he grabbed a quick shower and the two of us climbed into his pickup, heading out to the county expo center for the gun show. Dad had searched high and low for an M1860 Army revolver to add to his Civil War collection and he'd tracked down a dealer who'd promised to bring one to the show. Last Christmas I'd surprised him with an M1851 Navy revolver I'd found in a pawn shop in Fort Worth. The octagonal barrel had been scratched some, but Dad didn't seem to mind. "A gun in mint condition lacks history," he'd said. The M1860 was the last gun he needed to complete the set.

We wandered up and down the makeshift aisles spread throughout the expansive metal building, admiring the ornate styling of some antique rifles, as well as the sleek sophistication of the latest handgun designs, some so small they'd fit in the palm of your hand.

Though I'd been raised around guns and wasn't intimidated by firearms, I was admittedly a bit disturbed by how easily and readily guns changed hands at these shows. Thanks to what was known as "the gun show loophole," private individuals who sold guns on an occasional basis only in their home state were exempt from the record-keeping requirements imposed on interstate gun dealers. Nor were these sellers required to perform background checks on their customers. Criminals could easily pick up guns at these shows with law enforcement being none the wiser. Given that I was now a member of law enforcement, the loophole rankled. But with the NRA being the powerful lobby that it is, it was unlikely the loophole would be closed any time soon.

"There he is." Dad lifted his chin to gesture two booths down at an older man with a thin beard of gray stubble and a faded red and black western-cut shirt. A yellow nylon banner hung behind him, advertising Civil War–era guns, replicas, and memorabilia. We made our way through the crowd to the booth. Dad stuck out his hand. "Harlan Holloway."

The man shook Dad's hand, then reached under the counter and pulled out a small black case. "Gotcher gun right here." He unsnapped the locks and opened the lid, revealing a shiny revolver with a polished wood grip, blued barrel, and shiny brass frame. "Not many of this model left these days."

Dad maintained a poker face, but I knew on the inside he was as giddy as a kid on a Tilt-A-Whirl. He carefully picked up the gun and inspected it closely for several moments before laying it back in its case. "How much you askin'?"

"Sixteen hundred."

Dad paused as if considering, though I knew he'd pay the asking price if he had to. "Would you take fourteen?"

After a minute or two spent dickering over the price, the men eventually agreed on fifteen hundred. Dad wrote the man a check and his collection was now complete.

We rounded out the day with a little father-daughter bonding activity, spending half an hour on the improvised firing range at the back of the expo center. As usual, each of my shots landed precisely in the center of the paper target.

My dad beamed. "You haven't lost your touch."

"What can I say?" I winked at Dad, took aim again, and landed my final shot. "I learned from the best."

Mom, Dad, and I holed up upstairs while a rehearsal dinner went on downstairs. We watched some television, then I went to my room, which hadn't changed since I'd left for college almost a decade ago. Silk mum corsages from high school homecoming games still hung from the posts of my rice bed, their royal-blue streamers dangling down the posts. A thick crocheted afghan in hues of green and gold covered the bed. My sizable collection of Breyer horses posed proudly atop the pine bookcase my father had built for me.

A multicolored braided rug covered the original wood floor, left unrefinished at my request. The scratches, gouges, and scuffs implied a fantastic history had taken place right there in my bedroom. In high school, I used to sit on the floor and examine the scars in the wood, wondering how they'd gotten there, dreaming up romantic stories of a winsome country girl swept up into the arms of a rugged, handsome cowboy, the passionate lovers oblivious to the scratches his spurs made on the wood floor as he carried the young woman to bed for a night of raw passion. Yep, my hormones were pretty much raging back then.

The showpiece of my room was an enormous, intricately carved cherry wardrobe that stood imposingly in the corner. I remembered when Mom brought the piece home in the back of Dad's pickup. The armoire had been coated with dirt and cobwebs. One of the doors had split and hung precariously off to one side. Most of the wooden knobs were missing and the few that remained were cracked.

I'd stood at the end of the truck's bed, wondering if my mother had lost her mind. "Where'd you get this piece of junk?"

Mom lowered the tailgate. "Yard sale."

"How much did you pay for it?"

"Forty bucks."

"You got ripped off."

Mom shot me one of her looks, the one that said I'd soon be eating my words. The look also said to meet her in the barn in ten minutes ready to work my butt off for the rest of the afternoon. We spent five hours cleaning, stripping, sanding, gluing, and staining the piece, then removing the broken knobs and replacing them with a set of ivory porcelain pulls.

When we were done the piece was gorgeous, the crack in the wood visible only on intimate inspection. In fact, my mom was later offered two grand for the armoire by a woman who'd rented the house for a bridal shower. But she'd refused to sell it, knowing I'd fallen in love with the piece, not only because it was so beautiful, but because Mom and I had made it beautiful together. At one point, I'd considered moving the armoire to my town house in Dallas, but it belonged here, and seeing it when I came home was like visiting an old friend.

My collection of nineties-vintage country music CDs,

everything from Alan Jackson to George Strait, lay stacked in the CD rack on my dresser next to my CD player. I slipped some classic Garth Brooks into the stereo and grabbed my photo album from the shelf. Inside were photos of me and friends from high school, an inordinate number of them showing us in the back of pickups with cans of beer in our hands. But, heck, it isn't like there's a lot to do in east Texas.

I spent a lot of time in the back of pickups back then. I'd even lost my virginity in the bed of a pickup truck, my high-school sweetheart and I just about wearing out the shocks on his dad's Silverado. My boyfriend had been a lot of fun, but all he'd wanted to do after high school was stay in town and work in the oil fields. I knew I could never be fully satisfied with that kind of life. We'd grown apart when I went off to college and eventually he'd married another local girl better suited for him. I hoped he still thought of me occasionally, though, perhaps in the middle of a really rocking orgasm. Selfish, I know. What can I say?

I put the photo album back on the shelf and picked up a Rubik's Cube I'd been working on for almost twenty years, the multicolored blocks on each side of the cube betraying my lack of success. I lay back on the bed, staring at my ceiling and twisting the blocks on the puzzle cube. I probably should have worked on my tax return, but my mind was too occupied with thoughts of Brett to concentrate, plagued with nagging doubts I'd tried so hard to ignore.

Was Brett the man he appeared to be, an honest, hardworking, though somewhat naïve guy? Or was he a willing participant in Gryder and Shelton's scheme?

I fell asleep with these questions echoing in my mind.

CHAPTER TWENTY-TWO

The Bust
Goes Bust

The questions remained unanswered when I awoke the next morning to the ruckus of my brothers and their families arriving for church. My brothers chose to return to east Texas after college. Though they could have made more money in larger cities, they held my father's belief that more money didn't necessarily translate into better living. Staying in Nacogdoches wouldn't have worked for me, but I respected their decisions.

My bedroom door banged open and onto my bed leaped my favorite niece, five-year-old Jesse. Maybe it wasn't right to have a favorite, but I couldn't help it. She was so much like me it was scary. I grabbed her in a big hug and gave her a noisy kiss on the forehead. She smiled up at me. "Hi, Aunt Tara."

I released her and ruffled the bangs of her long, dark

hair, the length pulled back into a single, thick braid. "How ya doing, cutie?"

She hiked her thumbs in the front pockets of her tiny, elastic-waist blue jeans, "Never been better."

Oh, to be five years old, life having yet to kick you in the ass. "Glad to hear it."

After an enormous breakfast of scrambled eggs, sausage, and home fries, we all drove to church and sat together in the same Baptist church I'd grown up in, our expanding family now taking up an entire pew. My square-jawed brothers and dad were virtual clones in their starched, creased jeans, button-down shirts, and straw cowboy hats, my mother the epitome of country chic in a chartreuse prairie skirt and matching blouse. Jess sat next to me, swinging her legs, her pointy-toed pink cowgirl boots not quite reaching the floor. There was no denying my family were country folk, upper-crust rednecks. They were also extremely kind, generous, and loving.

Would Brett fit in with them? I bet he'd never been to a gun show, never partied in a cow pasture, never driven a tractor to the grocery store because the truck battery was dead. Poor guy. He'd missed out by growing up in the big city.

Afterward, everyone drove back over to Mom and Dad's for lunch.

"Boy howdy, that's one butt-ugly car," my oldest brother said as he walked past Pinky in the driveway.

Mom prepared chicken-fried steak, fried okra, and fried pies for dessert, her artery-clogger special. After we'd stuffed ourselves silly, Jesse and I headed out back with my old BB gun. I made a pyramid of empty root beer cans on the picnic table and knelt down next to her to help her take aim.

"A little higher, Jess," I suggested. "And don't forget, the gun's going to kick a little."

Jesse closed her left eye, sighting the gun, her tongue sticking out the side of her mouth as she focused on her target. She pulled the trigger. *Ping!* The BB hit the bottom middle can square in the center, sending the pyramid tumbling to the ground.

"A girl after my own heart." I held up my palm and she gave me her best high five.

Back at my town house Sunday night, I chowed down on a bowl of Fruity Pebbles for dinner. Brett called as I was rinsing out my cereal bowl.

"How about dinner tomorrow night?" he asked. "We could cook out."

I wasn't sure a private dinner at his house was a good idea. After all, his house contained a bedroom and, doubts or no doubts, I wasn't sure I'd be able to resist giving in to the desires Brett sparked in me. It had been all I could do to put a stop to things at the lakeside resort. His kisses, nuzzles, and caresses would surely wear down my resistance, turn my brain to mush, make the suspicions—and any other conscious, coherent thought—fade away, at least temporarily. Besides, rejecting him, refusing his advances, could seem strange, prudish, and further complicate things.

But so would turning down his dinner invitation. He hadn't seemed to buy the bad bratwurst excuse I'd offered on Thursday. Any further excuses for avoiding sex would likely cause him to back off, question my commitment to our relationship, make him wonder about my motives. In fact, refusing to sleep with him could jeopardize my ability to investigate his involvement in XChange Investments. Yep, sleeping with Brett was the only thing a dedicated special agent could do. I'd do it for all those honest taxpayers out there, for my country, for Uncle Sam. Then again, maybe I was just horny and trying to justify sleeping with a potential criminal by making it sound like my patriotic duty.

"I'd love to have dinner at your place." I wondered if I could buy some truth serum somewhere, slip a few drops in Brett's drink, find out what he really knew about XChange Investments, Stan Shelton, and Michael Gryder. But where would truth serum be sold? I didn't recall seeing it on the pharmacy's herbal supplement aisle with the echinacea and Saint John's wort. Probably it was regulated, available only with a court order. Damn FDA.

Monday morning dawned bright and warm. The perfect day to bust a drug-dealing ice-cream man. Also the perfect day to finally sleep with my hot, sexy, surely innocent boyfriend.

After my shower, I strapped my holster over my polka-dot panties. I slid into a pair of cutoffs, the frayed ends of the denim tickling my thighs. I threw on a loose-fitting dark blue T-shirt that would conceal both the gun at my waist and the handcuffs crammed into the front pocket of my shorts. Tennis shoes were the best thing to wear on a takedown, where traction could become an issue if a target bolted or resisted arrest, so I pulled my running shoes out of my gym bag and put them on.

I checked myself out in my full-length mirror. "Joe Cool, watch out," I said to my reflection, forming pretend guns with both hands and aiming them at the glass. "Today, you're going down."

A half hour later at the office, Josh sneaked up behind me and peeked over my shoulder as I searched online for the cute bikini Christina and I had seen the other day in *Cosmo*.

"Busted," he said, adding *chink-chink* as he pretended to snap handcuffs on my wrists. "You're not supposed to use government equipment for personal purposes. If I know of an offense, I'm duty-bound to report it."

Busybody. The Lobo wouldn't give a rat's ass. My on-line shopping wasn't costing the government a cent. I was debating my response when I noticed a cheap ballpoint pen sticking out of the breast pocket of Josh's shirt.

I pulled the pen out of his pocket and read the logo inscribed on it. "Bryson and Associates, CPAs, hmm? Weren't you investigating them for preparer fraud?" I faked a gasp and put a hand to my heart. "Josh, did you take this pen as a bribe?"

Josh rolled his eyes. "I must have picked that up by accident."

He reached for the pen, but I jerked it back away from him. "I think I need to turn this in to the Lobo. Like you said, we're duty-bound to report offenses."

Josh paused for a moment and our eyes seared holes into each other. "Reporting these minor infractions would be a waste of Lu's time," he said finally.

I slid the pen back into his pocket, finished my swimsuit search, and ordered one in my size. I still hadn't finished my tax return yet, but I was hoping for a refund big enough to cover the purchase. I was also hoping the swimsuit would cover my ass. Still had those extra ice-cream pounds loading me down. Maybe I should order the matching cover-up, too, just in case.

As I was on my way out, Eddie caught me in the hall and handed me a heavy cardboard box filled with the last of Chisholm's paperwork. "We're almost done."

"You still owe me," I said, hefting the box onto my shoulder. "Big."

"Don't worry," Eddie assured me. "I'll pay up."

"You can start by giving Josh some hell today."

Eddie grinned. "It would be my pleasure."

* * *

When I pulled up to DEA headquarters, Christina hopped into Pinky. She wore cargo shorts along with a colorful Hawaiian-print cotton top and an equally bright grin on her face. "Today's the day! Joe's last ice-cream round."

"It'll be an awful disappointment to our neighbors."

Christina lifted her shoulders. "I never liked them anyway."

At the crack shack, I reviewed a stack of invoices from Chisholm's meat supplier while Christina paced back and forth. I might have been able to ignore her if it weren't for her dangly charm bracelet constantly tinkling. "Would you be still? You're making it hard for me to concentrate on this paperwork."

"I can't," Christina said. "I'm too excited. I've got that prebust buzz."

I felt the same way. A special kind of excitement preceded a takedown, the adrenaline already beginning to flow in anticipation. My nerves were on edge, as if I'd shaved over goose bumps. I couldn't wait to take down that mullet-topped tax cheat. Still, another part of me was terrified. This was my first bust since Battaglia had attacked me. What if Joe fought back? What if he had a weapon? What if I got cut again, or worse?

"Christina?" I said, unsure whether I should ask the next question, but needing to know I wasn't alone. "Are you ever . . . scared?"

She turned and looked me in the eye. Her eyes were hard, but her voice was soft. "All the time, Tara."

"Why do we do this?"

She closed her eyes then, as if looking inside for the answer. "Because it's who we are."

Around one, Christina and I began preparing for Joe's arrest, each of us hiding a small canister of pepper spray in the front pocket of our shorts. After loading clips into our guns, we slid them into our holsters and put on our ballistic vests. Neither the weapons nor the vests would likely be needed, but procedures required we wear them. After all, you never knew what criminals were capable of, especially when surprised and cornered.

Two o'clock came and went with no sign of Joe. We opened the windows wider to make sure we'd hear his music the minute he entered the neighborhood. We took turns peeking out the blinds. By two-thirty, we'd grown antsy and moved outside onto the porch. My back began to perspire in my vest, my skin sticky with sweat. Kevlar doesn't exactly breathe. Ick.

The guys across the street came out to sit on their stoop, too. Their dog lay in the shade under their porch, chewing on the bottom step. He'd probably have the whole house eaten before long.

I went inside, grabbed a couple of Diet Cokes from the fridge, and ventured back out on the front porch. We drank our sodas and waited, Christina anxiously chewing her lower lip, constantly checking her watch. I relieved my anxiety by wiggling my toes and clenching my buttocks, working my glutes. I wasn't just nervous about arresting Joe. I was also feeling anxious about my date with Brett that evening. Had I really tried to convince myself earlier that it was my patriotic duty to sleep with my boyfriend?

The chunky blonde from next door came outside to retrieve her mail from the dented mailbox at the curb. She extended no greeting to us, just thumbed through her mail, tearing open an envelope. She read the contents and muttered to herself, an unflattering and expletive-ridden diatribe about the electric company and where it could put its bill.

After waiting another long, anxiety-filled hour, I said, "Joe's always come before four o'clock. Something's up."

Christina's only response was to bite her lip harder.

Joe never came, but five o'clock did. "No way he'd be this late," Christina said.

I whispered, "Do you think he figured out who we are?" We'd put on a pretty convincing act. But had Joe caught on? Did he notice something Friday night that clued him in to the fact we weren't the skanky slackers we pretended to be?

Christina blew out a breath. "I hope Joe isn't on to us. The last agent who blew his cover got transferred to Bismarck." She gestured at her torso. "A body like this wasn't made to be covered up with a parka."

CHAPTER TWENTY-THREE

$\mathscr{H}$owdy, Neighbors

Christina and I went back inside. She stood at the window, her hand in her hair, worried. The dog across the street barked once, and Christina's eyes narrowed. She turned to me. "Just so the day isn't a total waste, how about we go bust our neighbors?"

I hadn't signed on for that, but what the hell. At that point we had no idea whether we'd ever see Joe again. I couldn't bear the thought that I'd spent the last three weeks in this hellhole for nothing. At least if we could bust those two, we'd have something to show for our efforts. Or at least Christina would. The IRS wasn't interested in drug users, only in dealers who failed to report and pay taxes on their profits. But no way would I leave Christina to handle their arrest on her own.

"I'm in. What's the plan?"

A sly smile spread across Christina's mouth. *"Puta."* She quickly ran through her proposed strategy.

"Seriously?" I asked.

"Seriously," she said. "I'm telling you, it works every time. You offer sex to a man and his mind stops working. They'll be putty in our hands."

Not a strategy I could ever use in a tax investigation, but it would be a learning experience.

"I don't know what they bought from Joe, so we've got to be ready for anything." She retrieved her purse and pulled out a syringe, a roach clip, a lighter, and a small brass tube with a mouthpiece.

"What's that?" I asked. "A kazoo?"

She snorted. "This is for smoking crack, not playing 'Jimmy Crack Corn.'" She tossed it to me. "Put it in your pocket."

I slid the pipe into the back pocket of my shorts.

She pulled one final thing from her purse, her field test kit. She stuck it in the oversized side pocket of her cargo shorts. "Let's roll."

I followed Christina out the door and across the street. When the guys realized we were headed their way, they stood from their spots on the steps. Their expressions were both interested and wary. The dog wore the exact same expression.

Christina stepped right up to them. I wasn't sure exactly what she said next since she spoke in Spanish, but since a lecherous sneer spread across both of their faces, the men were clearly interested in what she was offering. The guys turned to go inside. Christina gestured for me to follow them.

We stepped into the living room, furnished only with a lumpy metal-framed futon, a battered army trunk that served as a coffee table, and a big-screen television, all of which bore a coating of dust.

"What do you got?" Christina asked, pulling out her syringe and roach clip.

I followed suit, removing the crack pipe from my back pocket. Apparently, we were drug whores, willing to try anything these guys might have.

"First things first," the taller guy said, a perverse smile on his face as he began to unbuckle his belt. The other did the same.

"Oh, hell no," Christina said, making a slash through the air with her index finger. "You're not getting any until we see the goods."

The two men exchanged glances and the taller one left the room, returning a moment later with a Baggie. Inside was a dark powdery substance that looked like brown sugar. I had no idea what it might be or how it might be taken. I let Christina take the lead.

She snatched the Baggie from his hand and opened it, releasing a faint vinegar-like smell. She grinned, resealed the Baggie, and dropped it on the trunk.

"Okay, let's go," she said. "Which bedroom is yours?"

This must be the "divide and conquer" part of the plan.

Christina followed her prey into his bedroom, closing the door behind her. The shorter guy jerked his head toward another door. I followed him in, my heart pounding so hard I was sure he'd hear it.

The bedroom was a pigsty, the floor covered with dirty, discarded clothing. The space smelled like dirty socks and sweat. Not exactly a romantic love nest. The guy stopped next to the unmade bed and began to unzip his pants.

I'd never been so nervous. I was supposed to act like I'd done this before, but casual sex didn't come naturally to me. "If we're going to do this," I said, "I should at least know your name."

"Shit, girl. I'm not your prom date. Just get naked." The guy unzipped his pants and shamelessly dropped trou.

He wasn't hard. I wasn't sure whether to be grateful or insulted. But, what the heck? It looked like his thingy was wearing a turtleneck.

"Ew!"

The guy looked down at his crotch, then back up at me, frowning. "What the fuck is your problem?"

"Sorry. I've never seen an uncircumcised . . ." I gestured in the general direction of his nether regions. "You know."

He gave me a lewd grin. "Want to take a closer look?"

He laughed when I involuntarily grimaced. He sat on the edge of the dingy, unmade bed and looked at me expectantly.

This situation had not been covered in my training at the IRS. But it was too late to turn back now.

"What are you waiting for?" the guy demanded.

Okay, now I was mad. Which was good. Anger worked for me. I knelt down in front of him. He emitted a nasty chuckle. Before he could figure out what was happening, I slid my cuffs out of my pocket and clasped one around each of his ankles.

"What the fuck?" He leaped to his feet. Big mistake. The momentum carried him forward. I scurried out of the way while he toppled forward across the room, unable to get his balance. He crashed into the door and fell to the ground, shouting something in Spanish that I could only guess was a warning to his roommate.

The guy struggled to get to his feet, but couldn't. When he realized the futility of his efforts to stand, he began grabbing anything within reach. He hurled a shoe at me first. Then a lamp. I easily evaded both, then batted away a barrage of dirty sweat socks. When he reached for a crumpled pair of underwear, I yanked my pepper spray from my pocket. "Freeze!" I commanded. "IRS!"

The guy stopped moving. "IRS? What the hell?"

I couldn't blame him for being confused.

The door swung open behind him with brute force, knocking the guy in the head. He cried out and wriggled out of the way.

Christina stood in the doorway. "You okay?" she asked me.

"I'm fine." Thoroughly disgusted, but unharmed.

She looked down at the guy at her feet. "I'm with the DEA," she said. "You're gonna be a good little boy and let her cuff your hands, too. Got it?"

The guy glared up at her. He said nothing, but gave one quick nod.

Christina tossed me another pair of handcuffs and I quickly secured his hands behind him. Christina stood in the hallway between the bedrooms and barked instructions to the men. The two squirmed and inched their way into the hall where we could keep an eye on them and they wouldn't be able to access any hidden weapons. The taller guy had a harder time moving around. Christina had somehow shackled his left hand to his right ankle and vice versa.

"Nice work."

"It's my signature restraint," she said. "With their arms crossed over like that, it hides their junk."

"Wish you'd shared that sooner."

I stood guard over the guys, gun in one hand, pepper spray in the other, while Christina retrieved their pants and removed their wallets. According to their IDs, the taller one was Gustavo, the shorter one was Hector.

Christina searched the place. In addition to the bag of brown powder they'd brought out earlier, she found a small stash of marijuana tucked inside a boot in Gustavo's closet. Christina tested the drugs and called her office to request two plainclothes officers to come pick up our neighbors. "No uniforms," she said into the phone. "Don't want the

other neighbors getting wind of this and blowing our
cover. We haven't hit our main target yet."

While we waited for the agents to arrive, I read the
guys their rights. That part I was comfortable with. Rights
are the same regardless of the crime. When I finished, I
turned to my partner and pointed to the bag of brown powder on the trunk. "What is that stuff?"

"Mexican brown heroin," Christina said.

Heroin. Whoa.

She eyed the men. "You bought this from the ice-
cream man, didn't you?"

Gustavo glared at her. "We don't have to tell you shit."

Hector tried a different tack. "It's all his!" He jerked his
head at Gustavo. "I never bought nothin'."

"Fuck you, man!" Gustavo twisted on the floor in a vain
attempt to land a punch on or kick his roommate.

Hector kicked his shackled feet at Gustavo. "Fuck you
right back!"

"Boys!" Christina hollered. "Settle down or we'll shoot
you with pepper spray."

Her threat worked. The two men grew still, though
they continued to shoot daggers at each other with their
eyes.

A half hour later, a white SUV pulled up in front of the
house. The dog barked and strained at his chain. Two
agents climbed out and came to the door. One was white,
skinny, and scruffy, the other was black and beefy.

"Hey, guys." Christina let them into the house.

The skinny guy cringed when he noticed both Gustavo's and Hector's pants around their ankles. "Should've
known," he said. "Every time Christina busts a guy, he
comes in with his pants down."

"What can I say?" Christina raised her palms. "It always works."

The black agent bent down in front of Gustavo and

Hector. "I'm going to uncuff you now. Any funny business and I'll bust a cap in you. Got it?"

They both nodded.

He removed the cuffs from Hector's wrists and hauled him to his feet. "Keep your hands up," he commanded.

Hector raised his hands, causing his shirt to ride up, exposing his turtleneck-wearing genitals. The agent turned his head. "Dude. Put your hands behind your back instead." The agent uncuffed his ankles next, and allowed Hector to secure his pants. Once he'd finished with Hector, he did the same for Gustavo.

In minutes, the agents had hauled the guys off to jail. Our bust was complete.

Christina and I stepped onto the porch.

"That was easy," she said.

"Easy?" I said. "That was revolting. I can't believe you do this kind of thing on a regular basis."

"At least these guys showered recently. Sometimes I run into guys who haven't showered in weeks."

"Ick." I cringed at the thought. "Ick, ick, ick."

We'd made our way down the steps and halfway across the yard when we heard the jangle of a chain behind us. We turned to find the big dog standing in the yard, his black brow furrowed in confusion.

"Crap," Christina said. "We forgot about the dog."

We eyed him for a moment. He barked again, but at least he wasn't growling.

That was a good sign, wasn't it?

Christina pulled out her cell phone and called the agents who'd picked up Gustavo and Hector. "Ask them what they want us to do with the dog."

She listened for a moment and rolled her eyes.

"What did they say?"

"That he's our problem now."

We looked at the dog again. He looked back at us,

his nose twitching as he smelled the air, assessing our scent.

"I bet it costs a fortune to feed him," Christina said.

No way the IRS would pay for dog food. But I didn't have the heart to call animal control. The poor beast wasn't a puppy and he wasn't cute. Add those factors to his size and his chances of adoption were slim to none. I couldn't bear the thought of the alternative. "Are you friendly?" I asked him.

He began to wag his tail, the movement causing his enormous pendulous testicles to swing back and forth. I hoped he wasn't too attached to the pair. As soon as possible, he'd be taken to the vet to be neutered.

I eased toward him.

"Careful, Red Riding Hood," Christina said. "He may be trying to lure you in so he can eat you."

I reached the dog and tentatively held out my hand. He sniffed it for a few seconds, then gave it a solid lick! Apparently he was all bark and no bite. "Okay, boy. You're with us now."

CHAPTER TWENTY-FOUR

Spoil Me

As I stood in the shower at home that evening, my stomach knotted up. Would tonight be my last date with Brett? I stuck my head under the spray as if I could wash away my doubts. If nothing else, at least I wouldn't have to wait much longer to find out for sure whether Brett was a criminal. Christina was scheduled to attend Gryder's seminar in just two days. I'd use the information she gathered, along with the documents Dave Edwards gave me, to seek a search warrant and launch a full-scale investigation of XChange Investments. If Brett were involved, damning evidence would surely turn up then.

And if it did? What then?

I slipped into a pair of jeans, a silky tunic-style top, and black flats. I was ready half an hour early, plenty of time to prepare my simple tax return, but I was too restless to concentrate. Once again, I set the papers aside for later.

The doorbell rang promptly at seven-thirty. Brett stood in the doorway, dressed in navy pants, a striped button-down, and the scuffed boots. Apparently he'd only been supervising projects today. He bent down and gave me a slow, lingering kiss. *Mmm.* He pulled me to him. "I missed you last weekend."

I looked up at him.

He looked exceptionally handsome.

Undeniably sexy.

And totally innocent.

Sheez. What a doofus I was. Surely there was a logical explanation for why he met with Gryder and Shelton at the bank behind closed doors. Probably it had something to do with the landscaping project. A project that large had likely been financed. Maybe they were discussing the payment schedule. I wished I could ask him, but there was no way I could pry for details without giving away that I'd received inside information from someone at the bank.

"I missed you, too." I locked my door and we headed out to his car.

While Brett drove, he talked about a new project he'd been hired for, a rooftop garden at a residential high-rise downtown. I stared out the window. I wanted to tell him about my job, too. About last Friday's impromptu poker party with the ice-cream man. How Christina and I had waited in vain to buy crystal meth from Joe today. How Joe hadn't showed so we'd offered sexual favors to our neighbors and busted them instead. But, despite the fact that the arrests went down without a hitch, Brett might freak out if I unloaded all of this on him.

Or would he see how capable I was? And how a strong and adventurous woman like me could bring an element of excitement and fun to his otherwise conventional world? Really, that was part of the reason he was attracted to me, wasn't it?

I hoped he'd learn to accept what I did for a living. I wouldn't quit my job for anyone, and I needed a stable, calm guy like him in my crazy and tumultuous life. But I also needed someone I could be completely honest with, and who was completely honest with me.

Brett lived in Upper Greenville, an older area of northeast Dallas that had once flourished, suffered decline, then been reclaimed and renewed by yuppies looking for both home ownership and a convenient commute to their jobs downtown. He pulled into the driveway of his house, a white brick ranch home with glossy black shutters.

As expected, the front yard was manicured within an inch of its life, the edges crisp, not a brown spot or weed anywhere. A white brick path wove its way from the street past a magnificent magnolia tree. Soon the tree would be covered with dozens of ivory, teacup-shaped blossoms. The base of the magnolia was home to a bed of large-leafed caladiums, no doubt grown in a greenhouse and just recently transplanted here once the risk of a late-spring frost had passed. The beds running along the front of his house were home to reddish flowering azaleas, which presided over bedding flowers ranging from white vinca to purple hostas.

Brett put a warm hand on my back as he guided me up the three steps to his front porch. After unlocking the door, he stepped back to allow me to enter first.

His den was decorated in typical bachelor style, spare with furniture chosen for comfort rather than fashion, including an overstuffed tan couch and matching recliner situated around a sturdy coffee table. The floors were dark hardwood, crisscrossed with the telltale scratches of dog claws. A flat-screen television was mounted on the wall next to the fireplace, a short bookcase below it. On top of the bookcase sat the close-up photo of me that Brett had snapped at the Sheltons' lake house. The orange-hued wood

frame perfectly matched the auburn highlights in my
hair, letting me know it had been carefully and thought-
fully selected. Brett definitely had an artist's eye for color.
Clearly one of the many reasons why his landscape designs were so breathtaking and his services in such high
demand.

I picked up the wood frame, flattered he'd taken such
pains in its presentation. My surprised smile, my tossed
head, my hair blowing slightly in the breeze, all combined
to show off my fun, natural, free-spirited side.

Brett's dog, a male Scotty mix with dark eyes and long
black hair, scrambled down the hall toward us, his nails
clicking happily on the floor.

"Hello, Napster." Napoleon put his front paws on Brett's
leg, wagging his shaggy tail as Brett greeted him with a
two-handed scratch behind the ears.

I bent down. "Hey, there, boy. Nice to meet you."

Napoleon abandoned Brett and turned to me. I ran my
hand down his furry back. The dog emitted one quick,
shrill bark. *Arf.*

Brett smiled down at us. "That means he likes you."

I gave the dog another pat. "I like you, too, boy."

Brett let Napoleon into the backyard to relieve himself.
Seconds later, the hairy little beast popped back in through
the flap in the doggie door. We walked to the kitchen,
where Brett grabbed a handful of T-bone-shaped treats
from a box in the kitchen pantry and tossed them to the dog,
who caught them in midair. Apparently the treats served as
hors d'oeuvres, tiding the dog over momentarily until Brett
could empty a small can of dog food into a bowl, warm it
in the microwave, and set it down before his spoiled, but
not at all rotten, pet.

Brett uncorked a bottle of wine and poured us each a
glass. He searched through his fridge, coming up with a
jar of maraschino cherries that hadn't yet been opened,

clearly purchased just for me. He used a spoon to fish a cherry out of the jar, dropped it into my glass, and held it out to me. "As you like it, milady."

I gave him a smile as I took the glass from him. Apparently his dog wasn't the only creature he was prepared to spoil.

He picked up his wineglass and took my hand, leading me out the French doors from the dining area to the backyard. Napoleon scampered after us, following us outside into the cool, moist evening air. Goose bumps spread across my arms momentarily until my skin adjusted to the outside temperature.

The evening had grown dark, but Brett's backyard was well lit by the back porch light and the solar lights outlining the flower beds. His back fence was covered in trumpet vine, a few early blooms in bright orange dotting the green background. The rest of the backyard was a lush garden, featuring a white Victorian gazebo surrounded by redbuds in full pink bloom. A small koi pond with a gurgling fountain in the center flanked the gazebo. An opalescent gazing ball rested on a carved stone pedestal. I made my way over to the ball and waved my hands over it. "I'm going to get you, my pretty," I said in my best Wicked Witch of the West voice.

Brett ducked and looked up at the sky in mock terror. "Don't summon the flying monkeys!"

Too bad the thing wasn't truly a crystal ball. Then I could look into it and have the answers to all those questions that had been nagging me for days.

Brett fired up his propane grill and slapped a couple of chicken breasts on it. While our dinner cooked, we sat on the white wooden porch swing that hung inside the gazebo. The jasmine climbing on the latticework enveloped us in its soft, pretty scent. Kicking off my shoes, I nestled against the back of the swing, the boards giving off a soft

creak with my movements. Brett scooted closer to me and
draped an arm along the back of the swing behind my
shoulders, the warmth of his body taking the edge off the
slight evening chill. I took a sip of my wine, savoring the
flavorful liquid on my tongue.

Napoleon nosed around in the flower beds and, finding
his bright yellow tennis ball, bounded into the gazebo
bearing the ball between his teeth. The dog hurled himself
into Brett's lap, causing the swing to rock back at an angle.
"Whoa, boy!" Brett held his wineglass up over his head,
trying to prevent the liquid from sloshing over the rim. He
pointed a scolding finger at the adorable beast. "Napoleon,
mind your manners."

Napoleon jumped down from the swing, dropped the
ball at our feet, and issued a demanding bark.

"Yes, sir." I gave the dog a firm salute, picked up the
ball, and tossed it underhand into the yard. Napoleon
darted after the ball at warp speed. In an instant, he was
back with the ball, dropping it at my feet again. Bending
over, I picked up the ball, now coated in gooey Scotty slob-
ber, and tossed it across the yard again. Once again, Napoleon darted after it.

"He's such a sweetie. Where'd you get him?"

"I found him on a country road outside the city. The
folks out there said he'd been dumped a few days earlier.
Poor thing was half starved."

The dog was lucky he'd survived. He could've been hit
by a car or bitten by a rattlesnake. But Brett had rescued
this mischievous little mutt, showing once again what a
sweet, caring guy he was. And sweet, caring guys aren't
con artists. Right?

CHAPTER TWENTY-FIVE

Things Heat Up

Napoleon bounded back with the ball yet again, pressing it against my leg. He was panting, winded from the play-time. I threw it one last time, all the way to the far fence where it bounced off the wood and landed in the ivy. The dog nosed around, searching under the greenery. This time when he found it he lay down in the ivy and simply chewed the ball.

Brett checked on the chicken, slathering the pieces with barbecue sauce and flipping them over so they'd cook evenly. In the kitchen, I set the table while Brett removed a tub of potato salad and another of cole slaw from the fridge. When the chicken was ready, we sat down to our meal. Brett poured us each another glass of wine.

"How are things going at the Sheltons' lake house?" I asked, taking a bite of the chicken.

"We're almost done with the decks and gazebo. We're

still waiting on the ground cover and bushes, but the live oaks finally arrived. In a couple days we'll be ready to put them in. That'll be a big job since we ordered mature trees."

"The project seems to be moving along quickly," I noted.

"Stan wants the landscaping completed by May." Brett picked up his fork and poked at his potato salad. "He even paid a premium so we'd make the project our top priority. But things would go faster if Chelsea Gryder would stay out of our hair."

That comment got my attention. "Chelsea?" I asked, taking another sip of my wine, trying to appear casual. "How is she getting in the way?"

"She and Michael are staying at Stan's lake house. Michael is usually gone all day, but Chelsea just hangs around, drinking and sleeping, watching television. The minute the crew starts up the equipment in the morning, she comes out half dressed and hungover and complains the equipment is too loud. I've explained to her several times that the only way we can meet Stan's deadline is for the crew to start at eight each morning. I suggested she turn on a box fan in the room or try earplugs, but she just gets snitty."

It was easy to visualize Chelsea with bloodshot eyes, her oversized breasts hanging out of a robe as she lambasted the crew. At least now I knew for certain Gryder was residing at the lake house. That information could come in handy.

"You said Michael is usually gone all day?" I tried to sound nonchalant. "Any idea where he goes?"

Brett shrugged. "Not sure. Probably out taking care of his investments." Brett passed me a basket of rolls.

I took a piece from the basket and tore off a small bite. "Has Michael told you any more about his business?"

Brett shook his head. "No, but he and Stan seem to be

at odds with each other right now. Michael apparently recruited an investor who is a major client of First Dallas
Bank and Stan was none too happy about that."

No wonder. Stan was probably trying to keep his hands
clean. Or at least to make it look like his hands were clean.
By distancing himself as much as possible from Gryder's
business dealings, Stan could feign ignorance of Gryder's
pyramid scheme, at least to any of Gryder's clients who
might come to the bank, demanding to know where their
hard-earned money had gone. But if an important client
of First Dallas Bank got wind that Shelton had wired his
money out of the country, the client might demand a thorough investigation into the bank's practices. If it was discovered that Shelton failed to properly document the wire
transfers, he could be in deep doo-doo.

Since Brett had raised the issue, I could dig for details
now without seeming obvious. "Do you see Stan and
Michael a lot?"

"Here and there," Brett said, noncommittal.

I wondered if "here and there" included private meetings at the bank. I chose my words carefully, wanting more
details but not wanting to tip my hand, either. "I've heard
some bad things about these foreign currency exchange
programs. Apparently some are nothing more than pyramid schemes. Outright scams."

Brett's face flashed shock and alarm. His brows drew
together as he looked at me. "Really?"

I nodded, continuing to watch him intently for a few
seconds. His expression was pensive, as if he were mentally sorting through facts, trying to determine if what I'd
just told him had any relevance to his client and his client's
houseguest. But when Napoleon trotted in and pawed at
Brett's leg, insisting on a bite of chicken, Brett's attention
shifted to his pet.

Brett seemed genuinely in the dark about Gryder and

Shelton's illegal activities. But how could I know for sure? Many criminals feigned ignorance in an attempt to keep their sorry asses out of jail. If Brett were merely on the fringes as a gopher he might not even be aware the program was a scam. Many a sap had been duped into unwittingly helping con artists.

But Brett was too smart to let himself be used, wasn't he? Then again, he'd already played courier for Shelton and Gryder. That alone could implicate him in their scheme, though it was not likely to be enough for any charges to stick. More likely, Brett would become a witness for the prosecution, feeding the government facts that could be used to nail Stan and Michael—assuming his involvement only went so far as unknowingly shuttling deposits, that is.

We finished dinner and for dessert enjoyed a scrumptiously creamy chocolate cheesecake Brett had picked up from a local bakery.

"Mmm, that cheesecake was incredible." I ran my finger over the rim of my plate, capturing the last bit of whipped cream my fork had missed. I was about to stick my finger in my mouth when Brett grabbed my hand and brought it to his lips, licking the cream from my finger. He eyed me with a devilish, sexy grin as he sucked gently on my fingertip, the same effective foreplay technique that had sent me for a sensual loop at the lake resort.

Gulp. "Whoa." His manipulations created exciting sensations, forcing all thoughts of currency scams to the far recesses of my mind. I tilted my head and eyed Brett. "Is that a promise of things to come?"

He released my finger from his mouth, enveloping it in his warm fist. "Count on it."

As our dinner settled in our stomachs, we settled on the sofa, Napoleon curled up on the cushion beside us. Wasting no time, Brett dimmed the lamp and began to nuzzle my neck, applying his lips lightly to those sensitive sweet spots, igniting my need. My eyes closed involuntarily, his warm, gentle ministrations hypnotizing me.

Moving faster today, as if fueled by lingering, pent-up desire, Brett put his arms around me and pulled my body to his, one hand cupping my rear as he pressed himself against me. I wanted him. And clearly, he wanted me. My body began to buzz with anticipation, virtually vibrating with sexual energy. No, wait. Something was vibrating. But it wasn't me.

"Damn." Brett pulled away and stuck his hand into the front pocket of his pants to retrieve his cell phone. He consulted the readout and groaned. "I've got to take this. It's my boss." He said hello into his phone, holding up one finger to let me know he'd make it quick.

Napoleon rolled over onto his back beside me, his legs in the air, wriggling around and begging to have his belly rubbed. "You and me both, buddy." The dog's eyes closed in pure bliss as I scratched his chest.

Brett sat up straight, his brows lifted in surprise. "They did?" A short pause. "That's fantastic news. Thanks for calling." He snapped his phone shut, leaped off the couch, and threw his fists in the air. "Yes!"

Brett executed a happy dance across his living room floor, an odd mix of hip-hop gyrations and the Texas two-step we'd all been taught in sixth-grade gym class. He rushed over to me and pulled me up from the couch, in the process upsetting Napoleon, who complained with a half-hearted growl. Brett clutched me to his chest, my feet no longer touching the ground, and twirled around the room with me. As fast as he was spinning me, I was afraid I might lose my dinner if he didn't stop soon.

Finally, he set me down, his arms around my waist. His eyes shone bright with excitement. "The American Society of Landscape Architects chose me for this year's Landmark Award. For my work at city hall. They'll present the award to me at the annual meeting in Fort Lauderdale next month."

"Brett, that's wonderful!" Recognition by his professional peers was certainly something to celebrate. I was happy for him, proud of him, as if he were . . . mine.

Brett gave me another hug, then stepped back, taking my hands in his and meeting my gaze, his face serious and expectant. "Come with me, Tara. It'll mean even more if you're there with me."

My heart twirled with joy in my chest. Unfortunately, five inches lower, a stab of guilt sliced through my stomach. This man—this sweet, smart, sexy man!—wanted me to share in his big moment, and I'd been harboring doubts about him for days. He'd be absolutely crushed if he knew. I opened my mouth, intending to say "Brett, we've got to talk," but instead the words "I'd love to" came out.

Uh-oh. I was in way over my head now.

Before I knew what was happening, Brett swept me up in his arms. In my heart, I knew I should protest, tell him we couldn't make love until we knew each other completely, had no secrets, no suspicions between us. But I couldn't resist. I wanted him. I was the only one with secrets and suspicions, and I was just a rookie agent with too much imagination and too little experience. Brett would prove to be innocent, and everything would work out. Right?

Of course.

I melted against him as he carried me to his bedroom.

Brett didn't turn on the bedroom light, the space lit only by the moonlight streaming through the wooden window blinds. He wasted no time sliding my shirt up over my head, undressing me quickly as if not wanting to give me time to think, to change my mind, to say no. But I wouldn't say no this time. I wouldn't put a stop to things. Hell, I wasn't sure I could even if I wanted to. My entire body pulsed with an accumulation of raw, hot desire, and if I didn't allow Brett to quench this burning flame I'd self-combust.

I took off my jeans while he draped my shirt over one of the posts at the foot of his four-poster bed. He emitted a lustful groan of approval when he turned and took in my red lace bra and thong. He threw back the plush navy comforter. I slid out of my shoes and onto the fresh white sheets. The thought of him planning for this moment, preparing to make love to me, wanting the experience to be perfect, made me feel wanted, desired, feminine. And now, I'd show him that he was wanted, desired, and oh, so masculine.

Brett shed his clothes in record time, flinging his socks, pants, and shirt aside and climbing into bed with me, now wearing nothing but a pair of blue boxer briefs that hugged his lean, muscular thighs and buttocks and emphasized his manly bulge. In one swift, smooth motion, he slid a hand behind my neck and covered my mouth with his, my body with his warm body. The coarse hairs of his chest met the lace of my bra, the textures creating pleasurable sensations against my skin. He ran a hand down my side, then back up again, seeking the apex of my breast and finding it, his fingers encircling my breast while his rough, callused thumb played back and forth across the sensitive, swollen tip.

Brett's skillful ministrations removed, once and for all, any reservations I might have about him. In fact, they removed any conscious thought whatsoever. Even if someone had presented me with incontrovertible proof that Brett was a con artist, I wouldn't have been able to stop then, to deny myself the pleasure promised by his firm flesh pressed against my inner thigh.

Seconds later, my bra was gone, and Brett's chest was pressed directly to mine, skin to skin, man to woman, lover to lover. He wrapped his arms around me and turned us as one to the other side of the bed, positioning me on top of him, still kissing me deeply as he cupped my buttocks and ran a finger inside the line drawn across my backside by the strap of my thong panties. He twirled his index finger, wrapping the thin lace strap around it, drawing his hand, and my panties, down. I wriggled out of them and he tossed them aside.

Completely naked now, I straddled Brett, the warmth and wetness of my womanhood pressed into his abdomen. I leaned forward, the tips of my nipples just touching the flesh of his chest. I brushed them back and forth across his skin, teasing, titillating. His eyes flashed darker in the soft moonlight, and his chest vibrated as his heart pounded within. It was my turn to put my lips to his, to breathe warm breaths against him, and ask, "You like that, don't you?"

Brett emitted a primal sound, half groan, half growl. In a split second, he rolled me onto my back and stood to remove his briefs and retrieve a condom from his night table, sliding it quickly over his erection. Back on the bed, he knelt over me, putting a hand on my inner thigh and pushing my legs farther apart so I could better receive him. His fingers sought his target, finding it ready, willing, waiting. Then, with one mind-blowing thrust, Brett plunged himself into me.

CHAPTER TWENTY-SIX

That Morning-After Glow

The next morning I woke in Brett's arms, sweetly sore and with a satisfied smile. Brett proved to be an incredible lover, giving me just what I needed precisely when I needed it, taking me to that tantalizing edge of oblivion, then carrying me over it, time and time again.

I climbed out of bed and sneaked into Brett's bathroom, examining my face in the mirror. My cheeks shone with a morning-after glow. If I could bottle this radiance, I'd make a killing in the cosmetics market.

But now the qualms kicked in. Had making love with Brett been a colossal mistake? Had I made love with a criminal, slept with the enemy? Had the pleasure Brett gave me been a guilty pleasure? Was I no better than Gustavo and Hector, stupidly giving in to my carnal needs?

No. I refused to believe any of that. At worst, Brett had

been an unwitting delivery boy for Shelton and Gryder. Nothing more. Surely a criminal wouldn't have been such a generous, giving lover. And give he had. He'd given me not one, not two, but *three* orgasms. A new record and a testament to the depth of my feelings for Brett. Any distrust or doubts I'd ever had were nothing more than the result of an overactive imagination, an overdeveloped sense of skepticism by an overzealous, rookie federal agent. And Gustavo and Hector were no more than horny men looking for a quick lay. What I had with Brett was so much more than that.

While Brett got ready for work, I whipped up some scrambled eggs and toast. It was the least I could do after the dinner he'd made the night before. One of these days I should learn how to cook.

Brett drove me home after breakfast. I took a quick shower and dressed in my running shoes, lightweight pink sweatpants, and a short-sleeved white hoodie, a comfy, easy-to-move-in outfit. I needed to be ready in case Joe showed today. Packing up my long-neglected tax records and forms, I headed out to meet Christina.

When Christina pulled up in front of the IRS office, I hopped into the pink Cadillac. Today she wore a teal baby-doll top that was tight at the bust and loose at the waist, perfect both for distracting Joe and concealing a hip holster. She'd pulled her long hair up into a ponytail where it couldn't get in her way during the bust. Her scarf was tied around the ponytail.

The dog stood on the backseat, wagging his tail. I gave him a good-morning pat on the head.

I fastened my seat belt. *Click.* The car didn't move. I glanced over at Christina to find her focus locked on my face.

Her eyes narrowed and she tilted her head, a questioning look on her face. "You look different today."

I shrugged. "Don't know what you're talking about."

A sly grin spread across her face. "You got some last night."

Was it that obvious? "Did not."

"Did, too. You've got that satisfied, morning-after sparkle."

No wonder she was such a good agent. She had incredible intuition.

"You're right!" I cried, unable to contain my joy. "Brett and I did it. Three times."

She rolled her eyes, but continued to smile. "Well, I don't have to ask how it was."

Definitely obvious.

She slid the car into gear. "I just hope you saved some energy for Joe's bust."

"No need to worry. The way I'm feeling today, I could take down ten men with both hands tied behind my back."

She eased away from the curb. "Were your hands tied behind your back last night?"

I crossed my arms over my chest, feigning outrage. "That's none of your business."

She chuckled. "You're right. Besides, nobody ever does the kinky stuff the first time."

The tax deadline was fast approaching, but I only got as far as line thirteen on my tax return before I was forced to stop, distracted by my partner. Christina paced the floor of the crack shack in her sneakers, watching the clock and chewing on the white tips of her nails.

"Stop that," I said. "You're destroying the manicure I gave you."

"Can't help it," she said, shoving her hands into the

front pockets of her jeans to try to control her nail-biting. "I've got the prebust jitters again."

I did, too, feeling tingly all over with a raw, nervous energy.

For lunch we nuked a frozen pasta primavera, light enough so the food wouldn't weigh us down when we'd need to be fast on our feet yet loaded with carbs for the quick energy we might require later. Joe wasn't likely to resist arrest, especially when he wouldn't see it coming, but it never hurt to be prepared. Even if Joe did resist, a scrawny guy like him wouldn't pose much of a challenge for two well-trained, armed federal agents. With everything I'd faced on the job, that mullet-topped doofus didn't scare me a bit. Or at least that's what I told myself.

After lunch, Christina and I performed stretches and jogged in circles around the living room a few times to get our blood flowing and our bodies warmed up. The huge dog lay on the floor, happily gnawing the bone-shaped chew toy we'd bought at the pet store that morning.

Like she had the day before, Christina opened every window in the house so we'd be sure to hear the ice-cream truck music as soon as Joe entered the neighborhood.

A faint stench drifted through the windows. Ew. Garbage day. I'd noticed bags at the curbs on our way in.

Christina sat on the dusty windowsill and stared out the grimy window. "Joe better show today. The guys back at the office gave me all kinds of crap this morning. Guess I shouldn't have bragged that we'd be bagging Joe yesterday."

"I told you not to count your chickens—"

Christina put up a hand to silence me and cocked her head toward the open window. Sure enough, the faint warbling bars of ice-cream music came through.

We slid our loaded guns into our holsters. Christina scrambled to spread the pieces of her field test kit on the kitchen counter where she'd be able to access them quickly after we bought the drugs. We stepped out on the front porch and sat down on the steps, trying to rein in our adrenaline, act nonchalant. It wasn't easy.

The minutes crept by like a bad date as we waited for our pimple-faced prey. The ice-cream music grew gradually louder and, finally, Joe's orange truck turned onto our street a few blocks down. It eased slowly toward us, stopping twice for women with small children. Eventually Joe rolled to a stop in front of our house.

We made our way to the truck. Christina leaned in close, resting her arms on the window ledge, and looked up at Joe. "Where were you yesterday?"

Joe's gaze darted to the blouse drawn taut across Christina's chest. "Fucking health department," he said to her breasts. "Damn inspector chased me down yesterday morning and issued me a citation for an expired permit."

Another government employee taking crap from an asshole for doing his job. Been there, done that.

Joe emitted an irritated huff and finally looked up at Christina's face. "I spent all day in line downtown getting the permit renewed."

If he didn't like standing in line all day, he certainly wouldn't like what we had in store for him—five to ten in the state pen.

Christina drummed her fingers on the window ledge. "Got something special for me today?"

Joe bent down, putting his face close to hers. "Got some cash for me?"

Christina reached into the neck of her shirt, pulling a folded, and marked, hundred-dollar bill from between her breasts. She handed it to Joe.

His eyes flashed. "It's warm."

Sheez. Joe Cool needed to cool off.

We watched through the window as Joe went to the

front of the truck and pulled a large metal toolbox from under the driver's seat. He retrieved a set of keys from the glove compartment, unlocked the box, and removed a small paper bag. He handed the bag through the window to Christina. "It's good stuff."

"It better be."

I could feel Joe's eyes on us as we walked up the steps and back into the house, forcing ourselves not to run. We heard Joe put his truck in gear behind us and pull away from the curb.

In rapid motion, Christina dashed to the kitchen and dumped the contents of the paper bag onto the countertop. A small plastic bag slid out. Inside was a substance that looked like tiny shards of ice. I could see where crystal meth got its name.

Christina ripped the clear bag open and dropped a small sample of the substance into one of the tubes from her field test kit. She shook the vial and the water turned from clear to orange. "Bingo. Let's roll."

CHAPTER TWENTY-SEVEN

*H*ot Pursuit of Joe Cool

We dashed out the door and down the street after Joe's truck, walking fast but not running, not wanting to alert him to the fact that his minutes as a free man were numbered.

Joe's brake lights flashed red as he eased around a turn a block ahead, the tinny music still blaring through the neighborhood.

With Joe now out of sight, Christina sped up and I followed suit, the two of us now bolting after Joe like overzealous contenders in the fifty-yard dash on field day. With her long legs, Christina easily hurdled a pile of garbage bags in a front yard, gaining a small advantage since I had to maneuver around a shopping cart, assorted lawnmower parts, and a chipped lawn jockey.

We continued our pursuit and were only a dozen feet behind Joe's truck when he spied us in his side mirror. He stuck his head out the window and looked back at us. "What the fuck?"

"DEA!" Christina hollered, running up to the side of his van, her gun now drawn. "Come out of your truck with your hands up!"

He hesitated for a split second, a dumbfounded look on his face. He pulled his head back inside, the van's tires screeching as he floored the gas pedal and roared off, leaving us in his dust.

"Shit!" Christina spat.

The two of us took off after Joe again.

Joe careened down the street, one eye on the road, the other on his side mirror, narrowly missing a chubby black teenage boy who'd stepped into the street wearing nothing but a faded pair of teddy-bear-print pajama bottoms and waving a dollar bill. "Get your ass back here, ice-cream man!"

When we passed the kid he joined in, running after us as fast as he could in his bare feet, his boy-boobs and Buddha belly jiggling with the effort.

Christina hollered back at the kid. "Shouldn't you be in school?"

"Missed the bus."

"Go home, kid," I shouted. "This could get ugly."

"I seen that ice-cream man," the kid called back. "It's already gotten ugly." The footsteps behind us slowed as the boy ran out of steam. That's what happens when you skip too many gym classes.

Joe turned another corner, taking the turn much too fast, jumping the curb. His tires kicked up a spray of dust and pebbles from the yard. He floored the gas pedal, banging down off the curb and roaring out of sight.

"He's getting away!" I yelled. I was tempted to pull out my gun and shoot out his tires, but then I'd have to fill out another firearm discharge report and face another internal investigation. I'd managed to keep my job last time, but I wasn't sure I'd be so lucky if I fired my gun again.

We were losing ground when an enormous green garbage truck rumbled into the street ahead, spewing black smoke and looming over the intersection, blocking Joe's escape. Joe swerved to miss the garbage truck, his van tilting first to one side then the other, tires squealing as he overcorrected. He hit the curb. The van bounced up into a yard and—*POOM!*—crashed into a tree stump, the back tires of the vehicle leaving the ground as momentum caused it to rock forward. The van slammed down and bounced to a cockeyed stop straddling the curb, half in and half out of the street.

Christina bounded up the right side of the truck, while I took the left, approaching the driver's window with my gun clasped at the ready in case he tried to escape out the driver's door. Joe was no longer in his seat. I reached out and yanked the side mirror inward until it gave me a view inside Joe's van. I saw him standing hunched over in the middle of the van, hands in his mullet, turning one way then another, trying to figure out what the hell to do. Thank goodness he wasn't holding a weapon.

Christina stepped up to the open window on the other side and peered through it, both of our Glocks trained on Joe.

"Don't move," Christina ordered, "or we'll blow that greasy mullet right off your head."

Her threat was a lie, for two reasons. One, Joe had yet to use deadly force and all federal agent manuals prohibited the use of deadly force unless faced with the same. Second, with agents on both sides of the truck, if either of us shot at him there was a risk we'd end up taking out each other. Nothing like shooting your partner to ruin a perfectly good working relationship.

Joe probably wasn't savvy enough to make this logical

connection, but the guy still wasn't willing to go down without a fight. "Fuck that shit!" Joe jerked the freezer door open and ducked behind it to shield himself from Christina's view. "And fuck you, too!"

I could still see Joe plainly from my side, but apparently he hadn't noticed me. Moron.

"Hey, Joe," I called through the driver's side window. "What she said."

His head spun around so fast he risked whiplash. He spotted my face in his window and banged his fists on the rim of the freezer. "Fuck!"

That was Joe's third "fuck" in less than fifteen seconds. "You really need to expand your vocabulary."

Desperate, Joe reached into the open freezer, grabbing armfuls of frozen treats and hurling them at the windows, raining a hailstorm of ice cream down on me and Christina. I ducked, but not before I took a Drumstick to the forehead. Damn! Who would've thought a frozen ice-cream cone would make such an effective weapon?

When I stood back up and looked through the window, Christina had Joe by the hair, and was attempting to yank him out the service window by his mullet. Bent over, he slapped at her hands, trying to free himself from her grip. Sheez. He fought like a girl. But we girls didn't.

I ran around to the other side of the truck, grabbing him by his shirt and the seat of his jeans to help Christina drag him from the window to the ground. He twisted as he fell, and I felt the fingernail on my index finger rip. Another manicure biting the dust. Dang.

While I checked my nail, Christina wrangled with Joe on the asphalt. For such a runt, he was putting up a pretty good fight now. They rolled over a couple of melting fudge bars, the ice cream leaving wet, brown stains on the back of Christina's top.

I watched the two of them grapple, looking for an op-

portunity to jump in and help my partner. Just when I'd
decided to try grabbing Joe's arm, the two of them rolled
over again and his arm disappeared into the mix of
wriggling bodies. Should I try grabbing his ankle? When
Joe bucked under Christina, tossing her a foot in the air, I
saw an opportunity I simply couldn't pass up. Christina
now lay sideways across Joe's chest, her hands wrapped
around his wrists, trying to pin him to the ground. But
Joe's lower body, including his groin, was exposed, accessible. Heck, the guy was practically begging to be kicked
in the nuts.

A swift punt to the crotch was all it took to put an end
to Joe's resistance. Christina climbed off him and he
pulled his legs up, rolling onto his side in a fetal position,
his hands on his groin, retching. We gave him a few seconds to finish writhing in agony before Christina rolled
him onto his stomach, sat on his lower back, and pulled
his arms up behind him. Under other circumstances, Joe
probably would've loved this.

She held out her hand and I handed her my cuffs. Once
he was properly cuffed, she ruffled Joe's hair playfully
and climbed off him. "You made this fun, Joe. Thanks."

Joe turned to look up at us, his face red and spotty with
road rash. "Bitches!"

Christina knelt down then, putting her face in Joe's
and—dear Lord—the guy still couldn't resist looking at
her breasts. "You have the right to remain silent," she began. "Anything you say can be held against you in a court
of law. You have the right to a decent haircut."

She continued on. By the time she finished reading Joe
his rights, local police had arrived, alerted by a concerned
resident who'd reported "two skanky hos trying to rob the
ice-cream man." Officers shoved Joe into the backseat of a
cruiser and kept onlookers at bay as we explained the situation to the sergeant in charge.

As the cruiser pulled away, Joe looked back at us through the rear window, eyes narrowed in fury, his mouth forming unheard curses behind the glass.

"He never saw this coming," I said. "Part of me almost feels sorry for him."

Christina sighed. "Me, too." And with that, she lifted her blouse and bra, giving Joe a glimpse of the last set of boobs he'd see for years to come.

CHAPTER TWENTY-EIGHT

Pride and Procedures

Once the dust had settled, I looked over at Christina. She'd acquired a few abrasions in the melee, as well as a dark spot on her cheekbone certain to turn into a sizable bruise. That had to hurt. I retrieved a Popsicle from the ground and handed it to her, gesturing to her face. The cold would help numb the pain.

She held the still-wrapped frozen treat to her cheek. "Thanks."

We searched Joe's truck, which turned out to be a veritable pharmacy on wheels. There was cocaine in the glove compartment, more crystal meth in the toolbox, a dozen prerolled joints tucked inside a folded map under the seat.

I lay on my tummy to search under the freezer. "Holy shit." Reaching a hand underneath, I pulled out a double-barreled, sawed-off shotgun. I sat cross-legged on the floor and checked the chamber. Loaded. Whoa. I looked up at Christina.

Her eyes were wide. "Yikes."

"Yeah," I said. "Yikes."

"He must've panicked and forgot he had the gun."

"Thank God." I was a good shot, sure, but my Glock would have been no match for a shotgun at point-blank range.

Once we'd secured the evidence and had Joe's ice-cream truck towed to the federal impound lot, the two of us headed back to the stakeout house on foot.

We'd need to obtain a search warrant to look through Joe's apartment, but it couldn't hurt to get Christina some medical attention before heading to the courthouse. I felt a little guilty that I'd escaped unscathed this time—other than my fingernail, that is.

"Let's make a quick stop by the doc-in-a-box," I suggested. "Ajay'll fix you up."

We left the dog in the backyard with a bowl of water, piled into Pinky, and headed to the clinic. You might have expected us to be jovial then, celebrating our victory. But everything was still too fresh, the adrenaline not yet gone from our systems. I felt myself begin to shake and glanced over at Christina. She, too, was quivering, as the adrenaline drained from her bloodstream. We drove the entire way to the medical clinic in silence.

Kelsey spied us as we came in the door. "Back again?"

I nodded, hiking a thumb at Christina. "Her turn this time."

Kelsey pushed away from the counter, rolling back in her chair. "I'll make a new file."

Once Christina had completed the same reams of paperwork I'd filled out not so long ago, a nurse led us to a exam room to wait.

A moment later Dr. Maju entered the room. His T-shirt

today sported a picture of Bart Simpson with the words DON'T HAVE A COW, MAN printed below. When he noticed that the patient sitting on the table was Christina, he bolted across the room. He brushed back her bangs, tilting his head as he eyed her bruise and abrasions. "What the hell happened?" He retrieved his flashlight from his pocket and shone his light in her left eye.

"Stop that." She pushed his arm away. "That's annoying. I'm fine."

Christina told Ajay about the takedown.

Ajay's face clouded when he learned that Joe had been the one to hurt his woman, his mouth dropping when she told him about the loaded shotgun I'd found under the freezer. Ajay's eyes narrowed. "That asswipe. I should've offed him last Friday night. I could've cut him into pieces and had him hauled away with the other biohazards. No one would have been the wiser."

I filed that tidbit of information away for future reference. It might come in handy someday.

Ajay cleaned Christina's superficial wounds, applying antibiotic ointment and covering them with small circular Band-Aids, then giving her a kiss on the cheek.

When he finished with Christina, he took a look at my forearm. "The cream seems to be working."

A slightly raised, uneven line crossed my skin, the surrounding flesh still pink, but it looked much better than it had initially. It was my battle scar. A wound that would serve as a constant reminder of the dangers of my job. But hell, it was nothing compared to the hole Joe's shotgun could've put in me and Christina.

I would never have faced dangers like this if I'd stayed with Martin and McGee. Was that where I belonged? What would I have done if Joe had pulled the shotgun on us? Was I just fooling myself that I had what it took to be a special agent?

Then again, Christina and I had taken Joe down today with little effort, despite his hidden weapon and his attempts to resist arrest. We'd stopped a tax cheat and taken a drug dealer off the streets, saving untold numbers of children from a life of drug addiction. We had a lot to be proud of. This feeling, this sense of accomplishment, duty, purpose, and—why not admit it?—heroism, was precisely why I loved my job.

I'd never felt like a hero at the CPA firm. It simply wasn't the same. Even though it was an auditor's job to search for internal-control issues, clients weren't too happy when you discovered their CFO had embezzled hundreds of thousands of dollars or that their accounting staff had overstated earnings by a few million or so. Telling a client they'd have to reissue that glowing earnings report to show the company had actually incurred a net loss was awkward, especially when you followed it up with a hefty bill for your services. Yep, Martin and McGee could keep their 401(k) matching, their cushy corner office, their six-figure salary, safety, and security. Tara Holloway was born to be a special agent.

Once we'd finished at the medical clinic, we made a brief detour by the courthouse. Ross O'Donnell met us there, arguing to get us a search warrant for Joe's apartment.

One glance at the wounds dotting Christina's skin and Judge Trumbull granted our request without so much as a question. She might be a bleeding heart, but a bleeding federal agent was something even a liberal judge like Alice Trumbull couldn't ignore. Besides, once we mentioned the loaded shotgun, her bleeding heart had been stanched.

Joe's apartment was in a rundown gray stucco complex located a few miles from the crack shack. We parked Pinky next to a graffiti-covered Dumpster and picked our way among cigarette butts, broken beer bottles, and trash to

Joe's building. The water in the pool was green and cloudy, the bottom not even visible through the murk. I hung on to the rickety iron rail as Christina led the way up cracked concrete steps to the third-floor apartment. She fumbled with the key ring we'd confiscated from Joe's truck, eventually finding a key that fit the lock. She pushed the door open and looked inside. "Wow."

I stepped up behind her and took a look. Mounted on the wall opposite a cheap metal-frame futon was an enormous state-of-the-art high-definition flat-screen TV, one of the items Joe had foolishly purchased with cash, resulting in the electronics store reporting the sale to the feds. An Xbox game system and a DVR were hooked up to the TV. Off to the left stood a cabinet filled with top-of-the-line stereo equipment, every video game known to man, and a CD rack full of the latest music. Despite the high-dollar electronics, the place was filthy and unkempt, a thick layer of dust coating the equipment, the blue carpet stained, unopened mail littering the Formica breakfast bar. A faint smell of stale beer and cooking grease permeated the air.

I riffled through the mail, confiscating an invoice from Joe's ice-cream supplier, his bank and credit card statements, and his bills. The supplier could provide us with information detailing how much ice cream Joe had purchased. All we'd have to do was tack on the standard markup and we'd be able to compute his profits and the taxes owed on his ice-cream business. The bank statement would show any cash Joe had run through his account that might not have been accounted for on his tax return. The credit card statement and other bills would enable us to estimate how much money Joe had spent. Any spending in excess of his ice-cream profits would presumably be funded by income from drug sales. Then, of course, we'd adjust for cash on hand. Not an exact method, but the best we could do. And hey, if Joe didn't like the numbers we came up with, he was welcome to provide reliable financial records to support an adjustment.

In Joe's bedroom, we found a pricey laptop computer on his unmade bed. When I hit the space bar, the screensaver disappeared, replaced by a photo of a blond woman with enormous breasts lying spread-eagled on a hammock, pleasuring herself with what appeared to be either a zucchini or cucumber. I didn't look long enough to figure out for sure. "Ew." I drew my hand back in disgust and slammed the screen closed.

As happy as I was to have helped put an end to Joe's career in illegal pharmaceuticals, drugs were Christina's domain. Cold hard cash was what I was after. As an IRS special agent, I served as Uncle Sam's bill collector. After a thorough search, we found a thick wad of hundred-dollar bills in a Ziploc bag floating in Joe's toilet tank, a sizable stash of marijuana in his bottom dresser drawer, and a box of tissues and an extra-large jar of Vaseline—lid off and half empty—on his night table. Urk.

Christina sat next to me as I counted out the bills on the kitchen table. "There's over seventeen grand here." I dialed the Lobo to give her the good news.

"Good job, girl. I don't care what those asses up the line say, hiring you was no mistake."

"Um . . . thanks?"

Our next stop was the nail salon. The technician filed my jagged nail and repaired my French tip. For kicks, Christina and I had her paint tiny pink-topped ice-cream cones on our thumbs.

Alicia met us for dinner and celebratory margaritas at a Mexican restaurant in the West End. After dinner, Christina and I bade each other farewell, knowing we'd meet again at Joe's trial if the guy was stupid enough to plead not guilty. At this point he'd racked up an extensive array of charges. Not only would he face drug, weapon, and tax violations, but he'd also face charges for resisting arrest and assaulting a federal agent. Still, his worst crime was his mullet. They say fashions come back around every twenty years or so. Joe wouldn't see the light of day until his haircut was in style again. In the meantime, it would give his boyfriends in prison something to run their fingers through.

I ran back by the crack house and picked up the dog. Christina's apartments didn't allow pets, so it looked like he was mine now, at least until I could figure out what to do with him. When I finally arrived home, I was exhausted to the core. I'd planned on finishing my tax return, but my body wasn't in agreement. My muscles ached and I had a major tension headache.

I led the dog through the service door that opened from my garage to my tiny back patio. He immediately made himself at home, jumping onto the padded wicker patio chair and settling in for the night. I filled his bowl with water and gave him a pat on the head. "Good night, boy."

As I stepped into my town house, Annie ran up and rubbed against my ankles. I picked her up carefully and nuzzled her, her white fur sticking to my lashes, wet with fresh tears I could no longer keep in check. Sheez. I was losing it. The bust had gone well today, for the most part, but if Joe had gone for his shotgun . . .

I let the cat go, plopped down on my couch, and closed my eyes.

Things could have easily turned out different today. I could've ended up with much worse injuries than a chipped fingernail. If Joe had gotten to his gun, Christina and I could've lost our lives. I found myself wondering who would have delivered my eulogy.

Eddie.

Maybe talking things through would help. I called Eddie's home number. Thankfully he was on my speed dial so I only had to manage one key on the cordless phone. I couldn't see much through the tears I was fighting. When he answered, I gave him the rundown on Joe's bust.

"A shotgun?" Eddie said when I finished. "No shit?"

"No shit."

Eddie paused a moment, then exhaled loudly. "Shit."

"Yeah," I agreed. "Shit."

There was silence for a moment, a silence that communicated things better left unsaid, fears better left buried. How many times could we expect to cheat death? We were well trained, sure, but there was no denying that sheer luck played a large part in our coming out of these busts alive.

"Look on the bright side," Eddie said. "With Joe's bust over, you get to come back to work with me. The Lobo sent me a new case today. I've got twenty boxes full of financial records you can help me sort through."

"Ugh. Now I wish Joe had killed me." As usual, Eddie had cheered me up in his own warped way.

After we said good-bye, I went upstairs to the bathroom to run a bubble bath. Henry had kicked most of the cat litter out of his box, but I didn't have the energy to sweep it up just then. I soaked in the lavender-scented water until it went cold. I'd just finished patting myself dry when the phone rang. I wrapped the towel around me and grabbed the receiver in the bedroom.

"I've been thinking about you all day," Brett said, a sexy, teasing tone in his voice. "Some parts of you more than others."

Despite my wretched state, even I had to laugh at that. "I've been thinking about you, too."

"When can I see you again?"

As much as I'd love to experience another dozen or so Brett-induced orgasms, it would have to wait at least a couple more days. Tomorrow night Christina and I were heading to the Adolphus Hotel to get the goods on Michael Gryder and XChange Investments. "I'll be tied up with work tomorrow night. Why don't you come over for dinner on Thursday?"

By then, my investigation into Gryder's scheme would be well under way, and I'd know once and for all whether Brett was a willing player in the scam. If he was involved, I'd ply him with a few glasses of wine, get him naked, then slip my handcuffs on him as he lay there, unsuspecting. And if he wasn't involved, I'd ply him with a few glasses of wine, get him naked, then slip my handcuffs on him as he lay there, unsuspecting. Either way, only one plan to remember. That kept things simple.

If Brett proved innocent, I'd also come clean with him about what had happened today. About Joe. The drugs. The loaded shotgun. Brett had a right to know, didn't he? Of course he did.

"Dinner sounds great." Brett paused for a minute. "You sound tired. Everything okay?" The concern in his voice wrapped around me like a warm blanket, my reservations temporarily set aside.

I sat down on the edge of my bed. Should I tell him? At least tell him as much of the story as I could without giving everything away? "It was a . . . tough day." My voice quavered.

Brett was quiet for a moment, waiting for me to say more. When I didn't, he said, "What happened, Tara?"

I desperately wanted to talk about it. I wanted Brett to hold me in his arms again, make me feel safe and feminine and protected, make the bad guys, and their bad hair, melt away. But that couldn't happen until I could be totally honest with him. And I couldn't be totally honest with him until I knew whether he was willingly involved in the Forex scheme.

"Tara? What's wrong?" His voice was firm now, insistent. "Tell me. I want to know what's going on."

"I'd rather discuss it in person."

"Okay, then. I'm on my way."

"No," I said. "Not tonight. We can talk about it on Thursday."

"Tara, please," Brett's tone was pleading now. "I'm worried about you. I'm your boyfriend, for Christ's sake. Talk to me."

"I will," I said. "I promise. I'll tell you everything. On Thursday."

I wondered how that would go. Because despite the emotional breakdown I was experiencing at the moment, there was no way in hell I'd leave my job. Every job had a downside, and an occasional crying jag was a small price to pay.

I ended the call, sighed, and snuggled up in my soft bed for some well-deserved rest. But rest didn't come. Instead came fears of losing my life. And fears of losing Brett.

I wasn't sure which scared me more.

CHAPTER TWENTY-NINE

*S*cammed

Wednesday morning, I arrived at the office dressed in a silky gray tank and basic black linen pantsuit, one that would fit in with the crowd at the hotel's bar where I planned to hang out while Christina attended the XChange Investments seminar.

The Lobo walked up then, today sporting a one-piece melon-hued jumpsuit intersected by a shiny white belt. Her eyes locked on mine. "Eddie told me about the shotgun." She grabbed me in a tight, menthol-scented hug. "Glad you're okay, Holloway."

So the Lobo had a soft side. Who knew?

She released me and took a few steps toward her office before she turned back around. "By the way, Eddie's located another hundred and fifty grand we can collect from Chisholm's owners. Just a million left to go and I'm out of here." She flashed a pleased grin.

I headed straight for Eddie's office. "The Lobo says you'll bring in another one-fifty from Chisholm's?"

Eddie grinned. "Froze the accounts this morning."

I gave him a thumbs-up. "Way to go."

"I couldn't have done it without your help. I'd still be going through that paperwork if you hadn't taken some of that on."

"True," I said. "And you still owe me. What's on your agenda for tomorrow?"

He picked up his leather-bound planner and flipped through it. "No appointments. Why?"

"Pack a lunch," I said. "And your water wings. We're going to the lake."

At five-thirty, Christina arrived at the Treasury Department in her Volvo, Pinky having been returned to the DEA's impound lot. She wore tight, low-slung blue jeans, high-heeled black sandals, and a low-cut black satin blouse, dressed to play the part of the ditzy nail technician–heiress she'd purported to be when she filled out Gryder's online seminar registration form. She'd layered on the makeup, the bruise and scrapes on her face visible only on very close inspection. She'd applied concealer over the bags under her eyes. Apparently she hadn't slept well last night, either. Despite these minor shortcomings, she still managed to look gorgeous. I might hate her if I didn't know what a good person she was at heart. Few supermodels would risk their lives to clean up the streets.

On the drive to the hotel, I jotted down a list of questions for Christina to ask Gryder during the seminar, inquiries that would pin him down and prove his investment scheme was nothing more than an elaborate scam.

Ironically, the Adolphus Hotel was located on Commerce Street, only two blocks from the federal building that housed the Treasury offices. The fact that Gryder had chosen to host his seminar in a location so close to the Treasury's turf rankled me. Clearly, he had no fear that he'd be caught. I knew I shouldn't take it personally, but it felt as if he were thumbing his nose at me.

Christina pulled into the parking garage, circling around and around as we descended to the lowest level. Other than a few vehicles parked in the designated employee section, the bottom floor was empty. Good. We wouldn't be spotted together.

Christina pulled out her cell phone and dialed mine. I slipped on my earbud, turning up the volume as loud as possible, sliding the phone into the inside pocket of my jacket. Christina slipped her phone into the outer pocket of her purse, where the seminar would be transmitted to me. I muted my phone so I wouldn't transmit any noise, then handed Christina a tiny digital tape recorder, giving her a quick lesson in how to use it.

With Christina's help, I disguised myself behind a pair of plastic reading glasses and my black pashmina, wrapped strategically over my head and around my neck.

She reached out, tucking a stray strand of my hair under the fabric. "Heck, I don't even recognize you now."

Good. The disguise worked.

"You look like a nerdy grim reaper."

"Gee. Thanks."

I slipped out of the car and rode the elevator up to the lobby.

The ostentatious, baroque-style Adolphus Hotel had been built nearly a century ago by Missouri beer baron Adolphus Busch, who'd found none of the other accommodations in Dallas acceptable to his elegant taste. The hotel's tapestries were imported, the banisters gilded, the European furniture hand-carved. Such snobbery from a man who made his fortune selling alcohol to beer-bellied, butt-scratching rednecks. Go figure.

I crossed the marble foyer, thankful the interior lighting was dim, and quickly took a table at the back of the bar, situated in an open atrium across from the Sam Houston Salon where the seminar was to be held. A leafy, ornamental ficus tree obscured any view Gryder might have of me.

A young waiter stepped up to my table, subtly eyeing my getup, not sure if I was a poor imitation of Jackie O or if the head scarf were a religious statement. "What can I get you?"

"Latte, please."

Once he'd gone for my drink, I pulled my tax return out of my briefcase, figuring I could finish it while I waited for the seminar to start. I'd made my way down to line twenty-two on my Form 1040 before accidentally spilling my drink on my W-2. I gave up and stuffed the paperwork back into my briefcase. I should probably just take the damn return to H & R Block.

A half hour before the seminar was scheduled to begin, a hotel employee pushed a beverage cart loaded with water pitchers, a large metal coffee urn, glasses, and mugs into the meeting room. No appetizers, finger sandwiches, or petit fours. Gryder had cheaped out, too chintzy to even treat his victims to a snack before he stole their money.

Not long after, the hotel's double glass doors slid open and Gryder walked through rolling a luggage cart loaded with three cardboard boxes. Along with his hair gel, he wore a light gray double-breasted suit, a stiff white shirt, and a shiny black tie, looking every bit the sophisticated, successful financial genius he purported to be. He stopped and pulled a folding display easel out of the top box on his cart, placing a large sign that read XCHANGE INVESTMENTS—CHANGE YOUR LIFE SEMINAR just outside the door to the Sam Houston Salon. He took hold of the cart again and disappeared into the room.

I pulled my phone from my pocket and temporarily disabled the mute feature. "The eagle has landed," I whispered.

"Could you be any more melodramatic?" Christina asked.

I huffed. "Just get your ass in here."

A minute later, Christina wandered through the revolving door, looking around the expansive lobby for the meeting room. After she spotted the sign for the seminar, she stopped and pulled a compact and lipstick out of her purse. "That you behind the potted plant?" she asked as she gazed into her mirrored compact, applying the lipstick.

I grabbed a leafy branch and waved it in reply.

Christina dropped her makeup back in her purse and walked into the seminar room.

"Hi," Christina's voice cooed through my earbud a few seconds later. "I'm Chrissie."

"Michael Gryder," he said. "I'm so pleased you're here."

Amazing. I could *hear* his shit-eating grin.

"Guess I'm a little early," Christina said.

"Glad you are," Gryder said. "It'll give us a chance to speak one-on-one." He paused a moment and a rustling noise came through the phone. "Your online application says you've recently come into some money and you're looking for income potential."

"Right," Christina said. "It would be great if I could earn enough return on my inheritance so I could attend school full-time. I'm studying to become a massage therapist."

"Massage therapy?" Gryder said. "Bet you'd be great at it. You have beautiful hands."

Through my earbud, Christina giggled. "Maybe you can be my first client."

"Count on it."

I gagged on my latte.

"What's this painted on your thumb?" he asked. "An ice-cream cone?"

An elderly couple in clothes two decades out of date shuffled up to the door, the woman holding on to the man's arm to keep him steady the same way my grandmother had supported my grandfather as he neared the end of his life. These people had fixed income written all over them. Gryder would no doubt be more than happy to relieve them of their paltry Social Security checks. Luckily for them, Tara Holloway was on the case now.

Others began to trickle in. A pudgy middle-aged man. A young clean-cut techie type. A few more older couples. I had no idea what I'd do if Brett showed up here tonight. I'd probably shoot him, then turn the gun on myself for being stupid enough to fall in love with a con artist.

I pulled a pen and notepad out of my purse to take notes. Through my earpiece, I heard Gryder ask everyone to take a seat so he could begin his presentation. He started by introducing himself and detailing his investment experience, telling his potential clients he had decades of experience in the investment arena, working with both public and private investments ranging from stocks and bonds to venture capitalism.

"Those few of you who qualify to participate in the unique opportunity offered by XChange Investments will enjoy a thirty percent annual return on your investment, guaranteed." He went on to explain their invested funds would be used in Forex transactions involving the purchase and sale of foreign currency. Gryder told the attendees that the old adage about risk being inversely proportional to reward was merely an old wives' tale, that in today's modern financial world a substantial return could be achieved absolutely risk free if an investor only knew how. And, of course, he knew how.

Then the fast-talking began, Gryder tossing out confusing concepts in rapid-fire motion as he shot through a slide-show presentation. He shoveled bullshit like the cleanup crew at a rodeo, perplexing the potential investors with terms like "corporate loan guarantees," "interbank transfers," and "timing differentials."

"Yes, Chrissie?" Gryder said.

"I'm not sure I understand. How is this guaranteed?" Christina asked, the first on my list of questions.

Gryder offered a convoluted response in which he claimed that because the value of any particular foreign currency fluctuates relative to other currencies, some currencies are always up while others are down, enabling an investor to take advantage of relative price differentials. He claimed there was no way to lose money as long as the investment is spread among counterbalancing currencies.

What a load of crap.

Although money could be made, a crystal ball would be required to know which currencies would increase in relative value and, if an investor had diversified, his portfolio would also contain currency that had decreased in relative value. Moreover, Gryder never explained how a full thirty-percent return could be generated with his proposed investment method.

The waiter stepped up to my table and took my empty cup. "Another latte?"

I nodded. "Thanks."

"Where is XChange Investment's headquarters located?" I heard Christina ask through the phone.

"As you'll note from our brochure," Gryder said, "we're based in Belize. Fantastic business climate there. The expansive international banking market and low tax rates make Belize the perfect place to base a Forex business. If you perform some research, you'll learn that many companies involved in Forex transactions are located in South America."

A young male voice, most likely the techie's, asked the next question. "Is XChange Investments registered in the U.S.?"

"Smart question. Because we are a private investment club domiciled in a foreign country and because all transactions take place outside of the U.S., XChange Investments is not required to register here. The good news is that none of your profits will be subject to reporting or taxation in the U.S."

Bald-faced lies.

Virtually every investment company doing business with American investors was required to register with either the SEC or a state securities board and, with very limited exceptions, the IRS taxes all the income of a U.S. resident, no matter if it's earned in Kalamazoo or Timbuktu. I looked forward to bringing this lying, cheating son of a bitch down.

When the seminar wrapped up, Gryder said he would contact the attendees individually to let them know if they qualified for the program. Each attendee was encouraged to write out a check—now—for the amount they wanted to invest, which he would deposit only if they passed muster. Gryder promised that those deemed unqualified would have their checks returned.

Yeah, right. The guy was simply playing on their emotions, going for the snob appeal. I had no doubt he'd cash every one of those checks.

I heard Gryder thank several attendees for their checks, telling them to let their friends and relatives in on this great, secure investment opportunity. It was all I could do not to run across the lobby, grab the trusting suckers, and try to shake some sense into them. Didn't they realize his investment scheme was too good to be true? Didn't they watch the news? Hadn't they heard of Bernie Madoff and his Ponzi scheme?

With any luck, I'd have Gryder in handcuffs before he could transfer their funds out of the country. Of course I'd have to get a search warrant first and collect enough evidence to sustain a case against him. But it wouldn't be too hard to get a preliminary order freezing his accounts, not with the evidence currently being collected on that little chip inside the tape recorder.

One man said he wanted to consult his financial adviser first.

"Don't blame you one bit," Gryder said. "But be aware that this type of investment is not your run-of-the mill, everyday investment vehicle. This is an extremely sophisticated arrangement that only a very experienced adviser would be able to fully comprehend. Don't be surprised if your adviser doesn't understand it or tries to steer you into stocks or bonds so he can generate a commission. A small initial setup fee is all that investing with me will cost you."

As if.

I'd instructed Christina to request a copy of anything she signed, but when she asked Gryder for a copy of her new account form he sidestepped.

"There's no public copy machine available here. But I'd be happy to mail a copy to you."

"How about you give me another form and I'll just fill it out like I did the first one?"

Quick thinking. How could he refuse?

Gryder paused a moment, then acquiesced.

A stream of people flowed out of the room, their murmurs traveling across the open foyer. Christina was the last to leave. She and Gryder stood in the doorway. I downed the last of my third latte and watched through the ficus leaves.

"This sounds like a great opportunity," Christina said, handing over a check she'd already instructed her bank to

stop payment on. "I can't wait until the money starts rolling in."

"Remember," Gryder said, "international transactions
involve a bit of red tape up front. It'll take a few months
for the accounts to be set up and the currency purchased."

The only thing that would take a few months was for
Gryder to figure out where he'd run off to with their money.

Gryder stepped a little closer to Christina. "I was thinking of heading over to the bar for a nightcap. Any chance
you'd like to join me?"

Hello? Had the guy forgotten he had a wife? Heck, he'd
even mentioned her on his Web site.

Christina picked up his left hand and pointed at the
ring. "Aren't you married?"

Gryder didn't hesitate a second before shaking his
head. "Lost my wife a few months ago. Cancer took her.
I can't bring myself to take the ring off yet." He looked
down at his hand, then back up at Christina. "Maybe if I
met someone new I'd feel differently."

This guy just didn't quit. I actually found myself feeling a bit of pity for Chelsea.

Christina checked her watch. "I'd love to have a drink
some other time. I promised a friend I'd pick her up at the
airport tonight and I'm already about ten minutes late."

"You've got my card," Gryder said, running his hand
down her arm. "Call me."

First the guy screws her out of her supposed inheritance, then he wants to screw her. He had some screws
loose if he thought that was going to happen.

Gryder headed back into the room to pack up.

Christina walked out through the hotel's front door
and headed into the parking lot. "That guy's so slimy,"
she said directly into the phone now. "I feel like I need a
shower."

I left a twenty on the table, giving the waiter a thirty

percent tip, but I didn't want to wait for my change and
risk running into Gryder. I didn't bother getting a receipt,
either. If I filed an expense report, those tight-asses in the
accounting department would say I could've had water
free.

When I met Christina at the car, she handed me the
thin brochure Gryder had distributed and a copy of the new
account form he'd asked her to complete. Although both
contained language claiming only qualified investors with
a high net worth could participate, the documents simply
gave lip service to SEC regulations Gryder clearly had no
intention of following. Christina had noted on the application that her net worth was only five hundred bucks once
her credit card debt was deducted. If a five-hundred-dollar
net worth was high, so was Gryder. Nowhere in the documents did he disclose his previous brushes with the law,
which was itself a violation of securities regulations.

I slipped the documents into my briefcase. They'd
serve as evidence tomorrow when I'd ask Judge Trumbull
to issue a search warrant for the lake house where Gryder
was staying. "That stuff about his wife dying of cancer
was total crap," I told Christina. "He's married to a skank
half his age."

"What a sleazeball." Christina put her car in gear and
backed out of the space.

"Thanks for helping me out," I said. "I owe you one."

"That creep touched me," she said, shuddering. "You
owe me *two*."

Just in case Gryder had finished packing up, I kept my
scarf on and my head down as we circled our way back
up through the parking garage. Fortunately, there was no
sign of him. When Christina stopped to pay the attendant
at the booth, I sat up and handed her a ten from my purse.
She returned the change and receipt to me, waited for the

attendant to raise the arm, then pulled out onto Commerce Street.

The night was dark now, the flashing lights of the Re-union Arena Tower, the enormous concrete phallic symbol of the Dallas skyline, playing over the car's hood. As we drove through the sparse evening traffic, I felt sad realizing my escapades with Christina were at an end. Sure, we'd see each other as we prepared for Joe's trial, but the girl talk, manicures, and contorting our bodies into bizarre yoga poses were over for now. We'd known each other little more than a week, but spending days cooped up together, sharing a common purpose, each of us knowing her life might depend on the other, brought us close fast.

"I'm going to miss working with you," I said. "It's been fun."

Christina glanced over at me. "Me, too. I usually get stuck with some guy who became a federal agent so he could play cops and robbers and reeks of testosterone. It was refreshing to smell Chanel No. 5 for a change."

When she dropped me at my car in the now dark and empty IRS parking lot, we gave each other a quick hug. Before I realized what she was doing, she'd pulled me down into a half nelson again and rubbed her fist on the top of my head, treating me to a good old-fashioned noogie. She released me, climbed back into the car, and rolled down the window. "If things work out with Brett, give me a call. Maybe we can double-date."

If.

Ugh.

I stood next to my car, watching wistfully as she drove off down the street, her car's taillights fading in the distance.

CHAPTER THIRTY

$\mathscr{S}$earch and Destroy

Three lattes in an hour hadn't been a good idea. My whole body buzzed, every nerve ending on high voltage. It had been a busy day, and under normal circumstances I'd be ready for bed. It was nearly ten o'clock, after all. But with all the caffeine in my system, I'd be lucky to fall asleep before midnight.

I considered swinging by Alicia's, but Daniel's trial had just ended and the two of them were probably fornicating like rabbits, making up for lost time. Instead, I figured I'd drive around for a while, see if the drone of my car engine and the gentle vibration would lull me to sleep. Hey, it worked for overstimulated, colicky infants. Maybe it would work for an overcaffeinated, jittery Treasury agent, too. But where to go?

In my briefcase were copies of the reports I'd printed out on the Gryders and the ones Eddie'd run on Stan

Shelton, including the property tax report on the Sheltons'
principal residence. Their house was valued at a cool $1.3
million. The property taxes alone amounted to more than
my annual mortgage payments.

Curious, I turned on my car's dome light, retrieved
the report from my briefcase, and riffled around in the
glove compartment for my city map. I spread the map
across the passenger seat and located Shelton's street. He
and Britney lived in Highland Park, one of the most exclusive areas in Dallas, the same neighborhood Brett had
grown up in. I made a mental note of the route I'd need to
take, stuck the map back in the glove box, and set my
course.

With my radio tuned to a country station, I sang along
to a rowdy drinking song as I maneuvered through the
freeway traffic, still fairly busy despite the late hour. New
York may be the city that never sleeps, but Dallas is the city
where people stay up late. Can't keep up with the Joneses
without putting in lots of overtime.

A few miles north of downtown, I exited from Central
Expressway onto Mockingbird, the main thoroughfare
through Highland Park. I aimed my car west, driving past
the large Southern Methodist University football stadium,
a red mustang situated on the back of the enormous score-
board at the end of the field. Two coeds made their way
down the sidewalk, returning to their dormitory or sorority house, heavy backpacks slung over their shoulders. A
few more turns and I was cruising slowly down Shelton's
street, searching in the dark for house numbers, trying to
locate his address.

The homes in Highland Park were traditional and taste-
ful, expensive but not excessive. The inhabitants were
primarily well-educated, cultured, old-money families
who didn't flaunt their wealth like the dot-com million-

aires in their gaudy suburban McMansions. Still, the impeccable manners and precise etiquette of the Dallas elite gave the city a reputation for pretension.

Finally, near the end of a block, I spotted the Sheltons' address. I pulled to a stop across the street from their house and cut my lights and engine.

Stan and Britney Shelton lived in a two-story red-brick Colonial with dark shutters and white trim, the conventional style at odds with the unconventional couple who lived inside. Brass coach lights flanked the front door, as well as the doors of the three-car detached garage, set behind a wrought-iron gate to the side of the home. The downstairs lights were on, as well as the lights in one window upstairs, probably the couple's bedroom.

I stared at the house for a minute or two. I didn't know what I'd expected to learn by coming here, but there wasn't much to glean other than the fact that one of the Sheltons appeared to be a night owl while the other was getting ready for bed. Big whoop.

It was then that a pair of headlights became visible, heading up the street. As the car approached and slowed, I reflexively ducked in my seat, avoiding the blinding light, staying out of view. I heard the car pull to a stop nearby, followed shortly thereafter by the sound of a parking brake being set. A door opened then slammed shut. Footsteps, the clack of men's dress shoes.

I eased myself up until I could just see over the windowsill. A late-model silver Lexus sedan sat in the Sheltons' driveway now, the engine giving off clicks and creaks as it cooled in the night air. On the back of the car was an Arizona license plate. My eyes moved to the man making his way across the porch to the front door, a large manila envelope clutched in his hand.

Gryder.

He knocked only once. A short, soft knock, the knock
of someone whose arrival was expected. The door opened
and Stan appeared in the doorway, dressed in nightclothes.
Gryder disappeared inside with the envelope, presumably
filled with the night's take, a stack of checks from the hopeful yet hapless investors who'd attended his seminar.

I glanced at my watch, making a note of the time. It
was 10:08. Five minutes later, the door opened again and
Gryder emerged, his hands now empty. As I watched from
my slouched position in my car, Gryder returned to his
Lexus, backed out of the driveway, and drove off in the
direction from which he'd come.

Where was he going now? Back to the lake house?
Given the late hour, he may have secured a hotel room in
Dallas instead. Better follow him to make sure. I'd need to
know where he was in the morning in order to serve my
search warrant and arrest his sorry, scheming ass.

I gave Gryder a one-block lead before starting my engine and easing back into the street with my headlights
off for now so he wouldn't notice me. Unfortunately, my
car was aimed in the wrong direction. I'd have to pull into
the driveway next door so I could turn my car around.

"What the crap!"

Reflexively, I slammed on my brakes, my seat belt jerking against my shoulder. I'd been so focused on watching
Shelton's house before that I'd paid no attention to the vehicle parked in the street. But there at the curb, halfway
between the Sheltons' house and the one next door, sat a
black Lincoln Navigator.

My heart beat so fast I could hear my pulse in my ears.
Was that Brett's car? Or did it belong to someone else?
Navigators weren't that uncommon. But what were the
odds that one would be parked here? I glanced at the license plate, desperately trying to dredge up information
from my memory banks. What was Brett's license plate

number? I couldn't remember. Dang! I banged my fist on the steering wheel.

I glanced in my rearview mirror. Gryder's taillights disappeared as he turned. I'd have to move now if I planned to follow him.

I knew I should.

But I couldn't.

Failing to follow Gryder was a dereliction of my duties as a Treasury agent, but at the moment I had to follow my heart. And my heart told me to find out whether this was Brett's car parked at the curb.

There was one way to tell for sure. If the passenger door bore the telltale dent from an errant golf ball, the car had to be Brett's. The passenger door faced the house, not visible from the street. I drove past the Navigator and two more houses, parking on the nearest side street just in case Brett or one of the Sheltons came out of the house while I was on the sidewalk. It wouldn't be hard to slip off into the darkness on foot, but it would be much harder to jump into my car and drive off undetected.

I draped my pashmina over my head once again and crept down the street, doing my best to stay in the shadows. Finally, I reached the front of the car. I took a deep breath and sneaked forward.

I took one look at the door and covered my mouth to squelch my involuntary cry. Clearly visible on the passenger door was a round, white, golf-ball-sized dent. Damn.

Damn. Damn. Damn!

Back at my town house, I fed the dog and the cats, then poured myself a glass of wine to counteract the caffeine and calm my nerves. I stood at my kitchen sink and chugged it down, staring at my warped reflection in the chrome faucet for a few moments while giving the alcohol time to take effect. Annie hopped up onto the countertop and made her way to me. I set my glass in the sink and picked up the cat. Cradling her in my arms, I ran my hand again and again down her back, as much to soothe myself as to show affection for her.

I tried to think. Brett was parked in front of Stan Shelton's house, late in the evening, at the same time Gryder had come by to drop off an envelope. Why was Brett there? What did it mean? "What's going on, Annie?"

My cat looked up at me, momentarily halting her purr as if she'd clued in to the urgency and angst in my voice. Acid churned in my stomach. As much as I wanted to, I couldn't pretend anymore that the odd circumstances were mere coincidences, that the facts didn't implicate Brett. Not only had he transported a hefty deposit of cash and checks from the lake house to the bank, he'd engaged in meetings with Gryder and Shelton at the bank and, now, he'd been parked at the Sheltons' house late in the evening when Gryder had delivered another deposit.

But there had to be some other explanation, didn't there? Maybe they were engaging in nothing more than a friendly poker game, or watching the Mavericks on television. But it took more than two people to play poker and there'd been no other cars parked near Shelton's house to indicate a crowd inside. Besides, Brett had never mentioned spending any time with Shelton on a friendly basis.

I simply didn't want to believe that Brett could be involved in anything illegal and was trying, yet again, to fool myself. I had refused to face facts because that would mean the end of my relationship with Brett, the man who had seemed so perfect, so right for me. Regardless, I had to admit now that the likelihood of Brett's innocence seemed smaller than ever, infinitesimal even.

Still, the only thing I knew for certain was that tomorrow would be a busy day and I had to be at my professional best. I was a special agent for the Treasury, dammit, and, despite my feelings for Brett, I had a job to do.

Thanks to the overdose of caffeine and emotional distress, I hardly slept Wednesday night. It was all I could do not to hurl my alarm clock against the wall when it buzzed Thursday morning. I felt emotionally wrung out. But I couldn't let my feelings cloud my judgment today.

After I arrived at the office, I called the Adolphus Hotel, figuring it was the most likely place Gryder would have stayed last night if he'd remained in the city. But when I asked for Michael Gryder's room, the hotel operator told me there was no registered guest by that name. I tried several of the more exclusive hotels in the Highland Park and downtown areas, but none showed a Michael Gryder on their guest lists. It was possible he'd stayed at one of the less extravagant hotels, but somehow I just didn't see him doing that. He was a man who enjoyed the finer things in life, and paid for those finer things with other people's hard-earned money.

I ran a quick computer search to determine which county the Sheltons' lake house was located in, then telephoned the Henderson County sheriff's department. Fortunately, they had a deputy in the area who agreed to swing by the place. The deputy reported back that a silver Lexus with Arizona plates was parked in the driveway. Looked like Gryder had made the long drive out to the lake last night, after all. I crossed my fingers he'd still be at the lake house when we arrived a couple hours from now. Didn't want to risk alerting him too quickly and giving him a chance to hide evidence or flee.

After spending several unsuccessful minutes on the Internet, I was forced to form an unholy alliance, asking Josh to help me track down information on the address in Belize where the headquarters of XChange Investments was allegedly located. With his computer skills, Josh could locate information ten times faster than I could. And with Gryder surely poised to leave the area soon, time was in short supply. After I promised he could share in the glory when we brought Gryder down, Josh agreed to help me.

He spent a few minutes on his computer and handed me a printout. "That address in Belize isn't for an office building. It's for one of those storefront mail centers where you can rent a post office box."

A phony address. That clinched it.

Armed with this additional information, Eddie and I headed over to the courthouse. We were dressed as virtual twins today, both in navy blue pants and white shirts, forgoing our usual suits since we'd be putting on our Kevlar vests and raid jackets later. The only difference was our shoes. While I'd worn my cherry-red steel-toed Dr. Martens, Eddie'd worn brown loafers.

We met up with Ross O'Donnell in the courtroom and waited for the bailiff to call our case. Fortunately, it didn't take long.

As we stepped up to the bench, Judge Trumbull looked down at me over her glasses. "You? Again? I'm not giving out green stamps, you know."

I forced a nervous smile at her. "It's been a busy week, your honor."

Ross stated our request for a search warrant, and I handed the judge the tape recorder, the paperwork Gryder had given Christina at yesterday's seminar, the printouts from the XChange Investments' Web site, and the computer printout showing that the address in Belize was phony. Judge Trumbull leaned back in her chair and took a few minutes to read the documents over. When she finished, she glanced down at me. "You sure this is a scam?" She held up the brochure. "Says here this Gryder's a 'Certified Senior Investment Manager.'"

"That's a mail-order title," I said. "Anyone who pays the fee gets the designation. There's no training or test to qualify." I explained how the arrangement was nothing more than a pyramid scheme, how Gryder's guarantees were bullshit, how Gryder had violated numerous banking, securities, and tax laws.

She listened to the tape next, shaking her head. "Fools and their money." Trumbull gathered up the documents and the recorder and handed them back to me. "Some con artist like this took off with fifty grand of my dad's retirement funds. He was long gone before anyone caught on. Never found the guy. Pop couldn't afford his rent and moved in with me. It's been prunes for breakfast ever since. Pure hell."

She signed the warrant and handed it to me.

We'd received our marching orders.

Time to march.

In addition to the search warrant, Ross had obtained an injunction—an order prohibiting Stan Shelton from transferring any further funds out of the country on behalf of Gryder or any entity with which he was associated. The injunction also prohibited Shelton from contacting Gryder regarding the order. Didn't want him to tip our hand and give Gryder time to hide evidence, or himself. We returned to the office and handed the order off to Josh. He grabbed his raid jacket and headed out immediately. Josh loved serving warrants and injunctions. Bossing other people around made the sniveling little weenie feel like a big shot.

Since his minivan would be more comfortable for the long drive ahead of us, Eddie and I decided to take his car for our drive to the lake. After he negotiated his vehicle out of downtown Dallas and onto the eastbound interstate, he turned on the radio, which was tuned to an easy listening station. I reached for the button but he slapped my hand away. "My car, my music."

He had me there.

The buds on the trees had opened now, new green leaves beginning to fill out the branches. The weather was perfect, low seventies, not a cloud in the sky. About a dozen miles past the outer Dallas suburbs, we reached our exit and turned off the highway.

Josh rang my cell then, letting me know he'd been able to intercept the checks written at last night's seminar before they'd been cashed and the money sent off to South America. "Good job." Part of me wished I could have been at the bank to see Stan Shelton's reaction when the order had been handed to him. According to Josh, he'd shit a brick.

Eddie and I made our way past farmland and ranches dotted with grazing cattle, slowing down as we drove through several small towns boasting a Dairy Queen as their focal point. We made small talk along the way. His girls' soccer team was having a good season. Six wins, no losses. He'd been nominated for coach of the year by the youth league. His wife, Sandra, had put new curtains in their bedroom. Eddie hated them. Too frilly. His mother-in-law was coming for a visit next week. "Too bad we'll be on mandatory overtime."

I glanced over at him. "I didn't hear anything about OT."

Eddie put a finger to his lips and shot me a wink.

"Oh, right," I said. "The mandatory overtime." I slapped my forehead. "How could I have forgotten?"

The two of us exchanged conspiratorial chuckles.

He glanced over at me. "You're not going to shoot anyone today, are you?"

I narrowed my eyes at him. "Ha-ha," I huffed.

A grin tugged at his lips. "Jus' messing with you."

"Gee, thanks, partner." The edge in my mind-set was apparent in my voice.

He eyed me, his face serious now. "Relax, Tara. White-collar types usually give themselves up easily. We shouldn't have any problems."

Eddie thought I was anxious about the bust. In truth, my anxiety stemmed from my concerns about Brett. I'd opened up to Christina about my suspicions, but as close as Eddie and I had become, I hadn't yet had an opportunity to discuss my doubts about my boyfriend. But now was as good a time as any, I supposed.

I stared straight ahead, my eyes locked on the highway. "I may be dating a criminal."

"What the hell?" The car swerved slightly as Eddie looked over at me.

I laid my head back on the headrest, closed my eyes, and spilled my guts, telling Eddie everything I knew. When I was done, I opened my eyes and looked over at him. "What do you think?"

Eddie cocked his head, his expression wary. "I think you need to have a long, hard talk with your boyfriend," he said. "And I think you need to have your handcuffs ready when you do it."

CHAPTER THIRTY-ONE

𝒦nock-Knock

An hour later, we reached the lake and turned into the exclusive waterfront development.

"These are some huge-ass houses," Eddie said, taking in the English Tudor flanked by topiary horses. He rolled down his window and sniffed the moist lake air. "This place reeks of pomposity."

"Nah," I said. "I think that's a dead fish."

He pulled up behind a mud-encrusted pickup at the curb in front of the Sheltons' imposing stone house and parked. Various other trucks and inexpensive commuter cars, probably belonging to the landscaping crew, were parked along the curb, including Brett's Navigator. I wondered if he was working on the landscaping outside or was inside the house with Gryder conspiring to defraud investors.

The front yard was still bare dirt, but the scrap wood and scrawny trees had been removed from the property.

An assortment of large live oak trees, all more than a dozen feet tall, leaned against the front of the house, waiting to be planted, their roots balled up in burlap. The rumble of heavy equipment grew suddenly louder as a green John Deere tractor emerged from behind the house about forty yards away, sending up a low, dense cloud of dust. The tractor dragged a wide, triangular apparatus that broke up the dirt and raked it smooth.

Brett sat at the wheel. That was convenient. After I arrested Gryder, I could bring Brett in right away, too, for double bonus points. The thought made my stomach queasy again. The tractor made a U-turn at the edge of the lot and headed back behind the house. He hadn't noticed me. Good. I'd rather deal with him later. We had bigger fish to fry at the moment.

Before Eddie and I headed to the door, we donned our raid jackets and ballistic vests. Not that we were likely to need the vests, but IRS procedures require an agent to wear the vest any time a warrant is served, just in case. My raid jacket bore an irregular line of stitching across the right sleeve where Jack Battaglia had sliced it with the box cutter. My tailor had done his best to fix the gaping hole, but it hadn't been an easy job. The patch job on my jacket mirrored the battle scar on my forearm. Ajay'd done his best, too, but that thin, raised scar would likely be with me the rest of my life. Years from now, my grandchildren would sit on my lap, begging me again and again to tell them the story of the hairy man with the box cutter and how their gunslinger granny had shot the blade right out of his hand.

Eddie and I slid our guns into our hip holsters, zipping our jackets halfway up to conceal the weapons. Our handcuffs and pepper spray went into our briefcases, and our briefcases went into our hands.

Now properly prepared, we picked our way across the

edge of the yard to the sidewalk, avoiding the dried dirt clods and a man driving a small orange and white Bobcat excavator. Gryder's Lexus sat in the driveway next to a banana-yellow Camaro, presumably Chelsea's, parked at a sloppy angle, the right front tire resting in the dirt off the edge of the driveway. The paint on both cars was dull with dust generated by the landscaping crew.

We stepped up to the oversized door and Eddie pushed the doorbell. Tones rang out inside playing the notes to "The Yellow Rose of Texas," the quintessential song of Texas pride.

When there was no response, Eddie rang the bell again, twice. Still no response. Eddie added a few persistent knocks on the door. No answer.

I cupped my left hand around my eyes and peeked into one of the narrow glass windows flanking the door. "No sign of life."

"Maybe Gryder's in the shower," Eddie suggested.

The search warrant technically gave us the right to storm the place if need be, but without a battering ram or assistance from the Dallas Cowboys' offensive line, we weren't likely to have much luck getting into the stone fortress.

I stepped back from the window. "Gryder gave Christina a business card last night. Maybe it's got a phone number on it."

Setting my briefcase down on the porch, I knelt down, snapped open the clasps, and rummaged through the paperwork. I found Gryder's business card tucked into a pocket and looked it over. Sure enough, the card included a toll-free phone number, one that, more than likely, was programmed to forward all calls to Gryder's unlisted, untraceable cell number. I stood and dialed the 800 number on my cell phone.

On the fifth ring, Gryder answered. "XChange Investments, Michael Gryder."

"Hello, Mr. Gryder. This is Tara Holloway. We met at the Rangers game?"

He hesitated a moment. "Right. I remember. Brett's girlfriend. What can I do for you?"

"For starters, you can let me in the front door," I said. "I'm on the porch."

Several seconds of silence followed, Gryder no doubt trying to figure out what the heck I was doing at the lake house. But I knew better than to tip my hand too soon, lest he rev up his shredder or take a hammer to his laptop's hard drive.

"Mr. Gryder?"

"Uh . . . yeah, I'll be right down."

Gryder answered the door a moment later, cracking it just enough for us to see he was wearing moccasin-style slippers and a bathrobe, a silky paisley-print number that seemed a little fruity, even for him. Though he wasn't yet dressed, he'd already shellacked his hair with gel. He gave off a faint smell of deodorant soap and pomade that clashed with the earthy smell outside. His grin today was half-hearted at best. I handed the search warrant to him through the small open gap.

"I'm here on official IRS business," I said. "This is my partner, Eddie Bardin. We need to search the place."

"IRS?" Gryder looked from the document in his hand to me, his face contorting in anger and disgust. "Brett said you were a CPA."

"I am. I'm also a special agent with the IRS Criminal Investigations Division." As in kicking ass and taking names. And today the name was Michael Gryder.

He handed the warrant back to me. "Why are you interested in me?"

"We have reason to believe there may be some issues with your investment business."

"Issues." Gryder enunciated the word as if it left a foul taste in his mouth. "What makes you think that?"

I wasn't about to divulge that Dave Edwards, the bank employee, had spilled the beans. Shelton would fire the guy if he knew. "We received a report of suspicious activity."

"From who?"

"I'm not at liberty to discuss that at the moment."

Gryder's eyes narrowed. "It was your boyfriend, Brett, wasn't it?"

Funny. I'd been suspicious Brett was involved with Gryder and now Gryder was suspicious Brett was involved with the IRS. I shook my head. "Brett doesn't know anything about our investigation."

Gryder stood a little straighter. "I'll need to call my attorney before I allow you in. I'm sure you understand." Right on cue, there was the shit-eating grin.

Gryder's lawyer would tell him what all lawyers do in this situation. Gryder had no choice but to comply unless he wanted to find his ass in jail for contempt of court. If the search were improper, the best he could hope for was that the court would throw the evidence out.

"Sure. Call your lawyer," I said. "No problem."

Gryder went to shut the door but found himself unable to do so with my steel-toed Dr. Martens lodged between the door and the frame. I hadn't been around long, but I'd learned never to let a tax evader shut a door on me. I'd also learned—the hard way—not to stick my foot in a door if I wasn't wearing steel-toed shoes. "We'll wait inside."

Gryder reluctantly stepped back and allowed Eddie and me into the foyer, eyeing the words IRS CRIMINAL INVESTIGATIONS on the back of Eddie's raid jacket.

"Don't touch anything other than the phone," Eddie warned.

Gryder's eyes met Eddie's. "Certainly." His tone was falsely cordial.

While Gryder stepped away to call his lawyer, Eddie and I kept our ears pricked, listening for any suspicious sounds—shredders activating, toilets flushing repeatedly, garbage disposals grinding flash drives—not easy with all the noise emanating from the tractor and landscaping equipment outside.

A minute later, Gryder returned, his cell phone still at his ear. "My attorney says that since I don't own the house you don't have the authority to search it."

"Our lawyer already discussed that issue with the judge," Eddie said. "Tell your lawyer to call our lawyer. Ross O'Donnell will confirm what I've told you." Eddie rattled off Ross's phone number and Gryder repeated it into his phone.

The three of us waited in awkward silence while Gryder's lawyer called Ross.

A few minutes later, Ross called my cell phone. "The search warrant stands," Ross said. "Gryder's lawyer insisted we teleconference with Judge Trumbull. She upheld it. Gryder must have a lot to hide if he's fighting this hard to keep you out of there."

"The same thought crossed my mind." I glanced over at Gryder, who glared back at me and Eddie. If looks could kill, Eddie and I would be laid out at a joint funeral and closed caskets would be in order.

"His lawyer's heading out there," Ross continued, "so I'm coming, too. I'll be there in an hour or so."

Gryder's cell phone rang then. "Gryder," he spat. "Yeah? . . . Yeah?" His jaw flexed. "Make it quick. I've got plans later." He snapped his phone closed.

I hiked my purse up on my shoulder. "Since you've got a busy schedule today, why don't you show us where you keep the records for XChange Investments and we'll get started?"

Gryder crossed his arms over his chest. "You're not touching anything until my lawyer gets here."

"That's fine with us," Eddie said, "but you're not leaving our sight, either."

"Of course not," Gryder said, as if the concept were his idea. "I wouldn't leave you two unsupervised and un-attended."

I plopped down on the steps in the foyer and pulled a legal pad out of my briefcase. "Hangman?" I asked Eddie.

"Why not?" He took a seat next to me.

Eddie guessed various letters, but only got two *s*'s and an *e* before he was hung.

"The word was 'shyster.'" I glanced over at Gryder.

Eddie went next. I quickly guessed the words he'd chosen. "Tax evasion."

When we grew bored of hangman, we played games on our cell phones. I placed a call to my insider at Neiman's, a sharp salesgirl whose clever shopping strategies helped me achieve four seasons of high fashion on a limited budget. "Hi, it's Tara. Any chance that blue Donna Karan suit's been marked down?"

"Not yet, sorry. But there's an adorable cranberry-colored sweater in your size on the clearance rack for eighty percent off. A new associate spilled her chai tea on the matching pants. Ruined 'em. Want me to hold the top for you?"

"Definitely."

A loud knock sounded on the door behind us. Gryder opened the door for his attorney, a wide, square-jawed older man with close-cropped white hair and an expensive, custom-tailored gray suit.

On the doorstep behind Gryder's lawyer stood Ross, also dressed in a gray suit though his was clearly off the rack. "Let's get this party started."

Gryder led our entourage upstairs, past a half-open bedroom door through which we heard snoring and saw Chelsea lying facedown and topless on the plush bed, her blond hair tangled and tousled, black satin sheets bunched around her waist. Gryder opened the door to an adjacent room and walked in ahead of us. "All of the records are in here. Keep them in order."

Eddie and I exchanged knowing glances. The more guilty people were, the more they pretended we were simply a pesky nuisance rather than a real threat.

The only furniture in the room was a large computer desk with an open laptop resting on it. In the corner sat the three boxes Gryder had lugged into the hotel the night before, still strapped to the luggage cart. A half-dozen larger boxes were stacked between the two uncovered plate-glass windows overlooking the back of the property and the lake.

Ross slid out of his suit jacket and draped it across his arm as he stepped up to one of the tall windows. He gazed out at the lake. "What a spectacular view."

Gryder's attorney retrieved three metal folding chairs from the table in the kitchen and Gryder and the attorneys sat near the windows. The attorneys focused on me and Eddie, while Gryder stared out through the glass, watching the landscaping crew, his arms folded tightly across his chest, his robe riding up to reveal blindingly white legs. Guess he didn't spend much time in shorts while he was in Costa Rica.

"I'll start with the boxes," Eddie told me, gesturing toward the desk. "You try the computer."

I settled into the chair at the desk while Eddie knelt on the floor and began sorting through the first of the larger boxes. I pushed the button to boot up Gryder's computer. The machine beeped and a few seconds later a log-in screen popped up, requesting a password. I turned to Gryder. "What's your password?"

Gryder's attorney bent over, whispered in his client's ear, then looked up at me. "Mr. Gryder won't be answering that question."

Ross turned to the other attorney. "On what grounds?"

"Fifth amendment."

Eddie and I exchanged glances again. Gryder was refusing to answer on the grounds of self-incrimination. Typical. Refusing to give us the password wouldn't stop us. It would only serve to delay our investigation a few hours.

I turned the computer off and closed it. "We'll have to take the laptop back to the office with us then." With his hacking skills, Josh could have the password for us in less time than it took Gryder to apply his hair gel.

Gryder leaped from his chair, his robe momentarily flapping open to reveal black bikini briefs. "You can't take my computer. It has personal information on it."

Before I could respond, Gryder's attorney put a hand on his client's arm. "They can and they will, Michael. We can challenge the search in court later."

Gryder turned purple, exhaled sharply, then muttered something under his breath.

Neener-neener. I stifled a snicker. I unplugged the computer and slid the laptop into a case I found in the desk drawer before joining Eddie on the floor in the corner.

Eddie had finished searching through the first box, which contained only blank account application forms and stacks of the same brochure Gryder had given to Christina at the seminar the night before. He started on the second box, which contained a stack of labeled file folders. He pulled out each file, looked the contents over briefly, then handed them to me for a second look.

The first folder was marked "El Paso," followed by a date two months prior. The file contained copies of checks the duped investors had made out, as well as a list identifying the names and addresses of those who had attended the seminar. Underneath were similar files which took us on a western trail from Las Cruces, New Mexico, to San Diego, California, and led us back in time from January of this year to the previous July. Gryder might be a cheat and a fraud, but he was a meticulous bookkeeper.

From the bottom of the box, Eddie pulled out a legal-sized document a hundred pages thick, held together with a binder clip. He laid it on top of the box in front of him and flipped through the pages. "Whoa. I found the smoking gun."

I scooted closer to him and looked over his shoulder. The document was a spreadsheet detailing the names and addresses of XChange Investments' investors with the amount invested and the so-called returns paid to them. The summary showed payments made to the first investors, enough to string them along and encourage them to tell their friends what a great investment they'd found and recruit the friends before the house of cards fell. The spreadsheet tracked the funds coming in and the funds going out. But nowhere on the page were any actual foreign currency exchanges accounted for. Clearly, the investors' funds hadn't been used to purchase foreign money. The funds were simply being shuffled around in Gryder's financial shell game.

According to the addresses on the spreadsheet, Gryder'd also recruited investors in Florida, Arizona, and Nevada, all states with warm climates and popular with retirees, before moving on to Texas. How could Gryder live with himself, preying on the elderly, those least able to protect themselves or recover from a financial loss?

Per the records, Gryder had brought in over twenty-three million dollars over the last few years, a large portion of it during the final quarter of the previous year. Yet that income had not been reported on any tax return. No doubt about it, the guy had balls. It would be a pleasure yanking them off.

I handed the spreadsheet to Ross. "Here's Treasury exhibit number one." Okay, so that comment was admittedly a bit snarky. It was Ross, not me, who would determine how to present the case in court, if it got that far. But I couldn't help myself.

While Gryder and his attorney watched, Ross set the paper on his lap and looked the spreadsheet over, running a finger down the columns and across the rows. Still looking down, he shot me a discreet look from under his brows, one that said, "Slam dunk." Gryder's fastidious record-keeping would make our case easier to prove.

We had more than enough evidence to justify his arrest now. I looked over at Gryder. He stared out the window, his eyes squinting against the early afternoon sun. I followed his gaze to the landscaping crew, wrangling a large oak tree into one of several deep holes dug in the backyard. We'd been trained not to unnecessarily antagonize a suspect, but I couldn't help myself. "That's what honest work looks like."

Gryder didn't turn around but his jaw flexed.

Eddie put the paperwork back in the boxes and stood. "Let's take these boxes out to my van."

Sounded good to me. My legs had grown stiff from kneeling on the floor. Eddie stuck the laptop in one of the boxes and he and Ross grabbed the others to carry them out to the car.

Since I was the primary agent assigned to the case, it was understood that I'd have the honor of reading Gryder his rights. I picked up my purse and pulled out my Miranda cheat sheet. I had the litany of rights memorized by now, but best not to take any chances. The last thing I wanted was for Gryder's case to be dismissed on a legal technicality and all of our hard work to go to waste.

"You have the right to remain silent," I began.

Gryder's eyes narrowed and turned dark, but below them a smirk quirked his lips. He'd been through this routine before, several times, and come out virtually unscathed. If he thought he'd skate through another investigation, he was dead wrong. I vowed the XChange Investments scam would be his last. With his accumulation of transgressions and the public's increasing awareness of financial fraud, no jury would let him slide again. Barring any unexpected events, Gryder would serve time.

When I finished reading Gryder his rights, I slid the cheat sheet back into my purse. "I'll take a quick look around," I told Eddie and Ross, "to make sure we haven't missed anything." I turned to Gryder's attorney then. "I'm assuming your client would prefer to change clothes before we take him in?" Gryder wouldn't last a second in jail in his paisley robe and black bikini briefs.

Gryder's attorney nodded. "He'll change after you finish your search."

"Okeydokey."

Gryder and his attorney followed me as I quickly went through the remainder of the upstairs. Since we'd already hit the mother lode, my search was cursory. The upstairs rooms were empty, other than the guest room being used by Michael and Chelsea. I peeked under the bed and in the drawers in the guest room as Chelsea snored. The only thing I noted was that the bottle of Viagra held fewer pills than before. I didn't want to risk waking Chelsea and have to deal with that twit again, so I didn't bother checking under the mattress.

It seemed like a small oversight at the time.

But now, in retrospect, it was the biggest mistake of my career.

CHAPTER THIRTY-TWO

*D*irty Business

As I grasped the railing at the top of the stairs to head down to the first floor, Gryder excused himself to change. Frankly, I was glad to be rid of him, even if for just a few moments. The guy reminded me of the Joker from *Batman*. He gave me the willies with his slick hair and fake grin.

Gryder's attorney followed me down to the first floor where I went from one end to the other, checking closets, cabinets, and the kitchen pantry. Other than the folding table in the breakfast nook, several takeout boxes in the fridge, and a few pots and pans in the cabinets, the downstairs was empty.

After I closed the last cabinet, movement outside the kitchen window caught my eye. Brett stood on the patio with his back to me, pulling pieces from a stack of white plastic lawn sprinkler pipe. He turned and our eyes met through the glass.

His face registered surprise and his mouth formed the word "Tara?" just before a bullet whizzed by me, passing so close to my head it took a few strands of my hair with it. The glass separating Brett and me burst into shards raining down on the patio.

Behind me, Gryder's attorney shrieked, hurling his black leather briefcase at his client in an instinctual act of self-preservation. Gryder stood in the doorway to the kitchen, pistol poised for another shot. The briefcase hit Gryder broadside in the face, knocking him aside, buying his attorney enough time to sprint for the front door and me enough time to scramble onto the countertop and dive out the window.

As I fell to the ground, I instinctively put out my right hand to break my fall. Another mistake. My wrist snapped as it absorbed the weight of my body full force, the bones crunching, crushed by the pressure. I cried out in agony, rolling onto my back and holding my right hand in my left, writhing in pain among the pieces of broken glass.

Brett stood on the patio, looking down at me, his mouth gaping. His years of friendly competition on the golf course hadn't prepared him for this type of violent, life-or-death confrontation. If he'd been involved in Gryder's scheme, he clearly hadn't expected things to end like this.

I needed to get up, get the hell out of there before Gryder could shoot again. I rolled onto my knees, but with only one functioning hand, I had a hard time getting to my feet on the slipping, sliding shards of glass.

Brett grabbed me by the arm and yanked me first to my feet, then off the porch, out of the line of fire. "What's going on?"

"We came for Gryder!" I cried, unable to breathe and gulping for air, my right arm hanging limp and useless at my side. "To arrest him!"

Brett's face registered surprise, then comprehension.

The landscape workers nearby had heard the gunshot, abandoned their equipment and scattered, some running along the lakeshore, others rocketing around the side of the house to the street. Only the guy operating the Bobcat down the hill continued to work, the noise of the machine having drowned out the sound of the gun's blast. One of the other men ran toward him, frantically waving his arms.

Brett and I took off running along the back of the house. We were a dozen feet from the corner when Eddie came around it.

"Go back! Gryder's got a gun!" I motioned with my left arm. The gesture threw me off balance. *Whump.* In my hurry to get the hell out of Dodge, I'd fallen into a four-foot-deep hole, one the crew had dug for the oak trees, and knocked the wind out of me. Brett pulled on my good arm, trying to help me out of the hole, but my feet kept slipping in the loose dirt. I couldn't get enough traction to climb out. Bullets hit the dirt around us, kicking up small poofs of dust. It was only a matter of time before one of those bullets would find its mark.

I yanked my arm out of Brett's grip and rolled onto my back inside the hole, fumbling with my left hand to free my Glock from my hip holster. Shrieking against the pain in my right wrist, I gripped the gun with both hands and fired back at Gryder. My shots went wild, none coming remotely close to the French doors from which he was firing. Gryder ducked back inside, probably to reload.

"Shit!"

Brett tried again to pull me out of the hole. If I had ever doubted his loyalties or his character, I sure as hell had no doubts now. He was risking his life.

For me.

Gryder's face reappeared at the glass doors. He took aim at us again.

"Brett, go! I'll be okay!" At least I had the hole to hide in. Brett was a sitting duck.

"I can't just leave you here!"

A bullet hit the ground just inches from us as Brett continued to try to wrestle me out of the hole. Brett would be killed trying to save me. And I would be killed because I couldn't get myself out of this hole with my broken wrist.

Another bullet hit the loose soil in front of us. I pointed my gun up at Brett's face. "Go or I'll shoot you myself!"

Brett's eyes met mine over the barrel of my gun. He glanced back at Gryder and finally seemed to realize the hopelessness of our situation. "I'll get help!" He turned and ran, a bullet lodging in the dirt where he'd just stood.

I ducked down into the hole and made myself as small as possible as the bullets flew over me. I could have used some of Alice in Wonderland's shrinking potion about then. I heard cars start up and roar off, tires screeching, as the landscape workers fled.

Gryder squeezed off another shot, this one hitting the top edge of the hole, sending a cascade of dirt into my eyes. I blinked hard, trying to clear my vision. When Gryder paused to reload again, I peeked out from the hole and squeezed off another round, taking out a chunk of wood trim two feet to the left of the back door. Dammit! With my shattered wrist, I couldn't aim for shit.

Where the hell was Eddie? Why hadn't he taken Gryder out yet? He wouldn't have run away and left his partner in danger. He was probably crouched nearby, gun drawn, waiting for a clean shot and thinking what a great character-building experience I was having down in this hole with bullets raining down on me.

"I have all the character I need!" I screamed to the cloudless blue sky, all I could see above me.

I hoped someone had called for backup. My cell phone

was in my purse back on the kitchen floor where I'd dropped it.

"Nowhere to run to," Gryder's voice was coming closer. "Nowhere to hide." Another bullet lodged in the dirt just above my head, showering more loose earth down on me.

I stuck my hand up over the edge of the hole and fired off a few rounds toward the voice. I squeezed again but nothing happened.

My clip was empty.

And I didn't have another.

A panicked cry tore from my throat. Ross or Gryder's attorney would surely have called the local cops by now, but out here in this secluded location it would take precious minutes for help to arrive. For a few seconds, everything was quiet. Had I hit him? Was Gryder dead? My breath came in loud gulps and white sparks twirled around my vision.

A dark shadow fell over the hole. I looked up to see Gryder smiling his shit-eating grin down at me. His belt had come undone and the paisley robe hung loose, revealing the too-tight bikini briefs that barely contained his guy parts. I would've been disgusted if I hadn't been so terrified.

The shit-eating grin turned even shittier as Gryder pointed his gun at my face. "They say there are only two sure things in life. Death and taxes. I say there's only one sure thing." The smile morphed into a nasty leer. "Death."

I was going to die. No doubt about it. At least by dying I'd avoid all the paperwork this shootout would generate. With that realization, something in me snapped. Funny how staring death in the face can make a person bold. Really, what have you got to lose at that point?

I eased myself onto my elbows and glared up at Gryder. "You're a scumbag. My partner will have to fill out a bunch of forms after you kill me. He hates filling out forms as much as I do. Your wife's a skank and you've got the second-worst hair I've ever seen." Hey, I only said facing death made me bold, I never said it made me eloquent.

Gryder sniggered down at me. "Forms? Bad hair? You really want those to be your last words?"

"No. She doesn't." Brett stepped into my field of vision. In his left hand he held a Glock. In his right he held an eighteen-inch section of PVC pipe. He swung the pipe and smacked Gryder upside the head with it. *Whack!*

If this had been a movie, Gryder's grin would have melted away, the evil gleam in his eyes would have gone dull, and he would've fallen face-first into the hole. Unfortunately, this wasn't a movie and the plastic pipe to the head only stunned him momentarily. But a moment was all we needed.

Brett flung the pipe aside and held the Glock out to me. "They didn't teach us how to shoot at the country club."

I dropped my empty gun and took the weapon from Brett, wincing as the movement sent shooting pains up my arm. Wait. This was Eddie's gun. What was Brett doing with Eddie's gun?

Putting a hand under each of my armpits, Brett hauled me out of the hole. A few feet away, Gryder staggered to his feet, his robe dusty, his gun still grasped in his hand. With an improvised war cry, I crouched and hurled my entire body against Gryder's legs, knocking the man backward into the dirt. As Gryder fell, he got off one last shot that hit the rooster-shaped weather vane on top of the house, sending the bird spinning with a resounding *ping*.

Brett pounced. Straddling the older man in the dirt, Brett pounded Gryder's face with his fists, bloodying his nose. A string of expletives spewed from Brett's mouth as he wrapped his hands around Gryder's neck, squeezing and banging the older man's Pez Head against the hard-packed earth.

If I hadn't seen it with my own two eyes, I never would've believed Brett was capable of such violence. I scrambled across the dirt, stuck the Glock in my waistband, and picked up Gryder's gun, which he'd dropped when Brett took him down.

I debated letting Brett bang Gryder's head against the ground until his skull caved in, but letting Brett take care of my problems for me would only cause more problems for him. What would the Rotary Club think if they learned Brett had killed someone with his bare hands? He might be forced to resign his membership.

I stepped over to the two men. "Stop, Brett. We've got him. He can't get away now."

Hands still around Gryder's neck, Brett turned to look at me. "Just one more?"

I shrugged. "Sure. Why not." And a pinch to grow an inch.

Brett punched Gryder's swollen purple face one last time then let go, dropping his head back to the ground where it bounced slightly. Gryder turned his head to the side and spit out a bloody bicuspid. "Thit!"

As Brett and I stood, a door above us banged open. Chelsea stepped onto the balcony wearing nothing but a drunken scowl and a pair of pink panties. "Keep it down! Some people are trying to sleep." She turned and staggered back inside.

Sirens wailed out front. A few seconds later, a police officer rounded the corner of the house with his gun drawn. The officer pulled Gryder to his feet and fitted him with handcuffs.

Everything in me wanted to burst into tears right then. Not only was my wrist sending sharp bolts of pain up my arm, but I was emotionally shattered, as well. Still, there was no way I'd let Gryder see me cry. I wouldn't give that bastard the satisfaction.

As Gryder was led to an ambulance in his dirty paisley robe, he glanced back at me, his shit-eating grin now an eat-shit glare.

With the con artist now in custody, my focus shifted to Eddie. Where was he? "Let's go find Eddie," I told Brett. "I've got a bone to pick with him."

Brett's face clouded. He gently grabbed my shoulders, his eyes locking on mine. "Tara," he said, shaking his head as if trying to dislodge a mental image. "Eddie was hit."

Eddie? Hit? "What?" My mind didn't want to go there, refused to go there. "No. No? No!" I ran to the corner of the house where I'd last seen Eddie, frantically looking around for my partner.

I could see Ross crouched in the open hatch of Brett's SUV. I ran to the car to find Eddie lying in the back. Ross had his suit jacket pressed to the side of Eddie's head to stanch the flow of blood from what I feared was a bullet wound. Eddie's eyes were closed, his face slack. A red smear of blood ran along the floor of the cargo bay.

My brain whirled and my hands reflexively went to my face. "Ohmigod!" I struggled into the space. Putting my left hand to Eddie's neck, I felt a slow, weak pulse. "Eddie?" I croaked. "Eddie?"

No response.

Ross met my gaze, his eyes wide. The unflappable attorney was flapped now. I took Eddie's right hand in both of mine and, despite the pain it caused my wrist, squeezed it, holding it to my cheek while I prayed, tears streaming down my face. Brett leaned into the trunk, his hand on my back, the warmth of his touch letting me know he was there for me.

Whup-whup-whup. A medical helicopter appeared overhead, searching for a place to land. The pilot set the chopper down next to the house, kicking up a tornado of dust and pebbles that plinked off the car while we shielded our faces. In minutes, the medics had loaded Eddie's limp form onto the helicopter and flown off.

I collapsed on the tailgate, watching the helicopter disappear into the empty, cloudless sky. Brett sat next to me, his arm wrapped tightly around my shoulders, pulling me to his chest when I broke into uncontrollable sobs.

Ross sat on the other side of me. He ran a trembling hand through his thinning hair and filled in the blanks for me. He said he and Eddie had found the front door locked when they returned from loading the boxes in the van. Gryder must have locked them out of the house. Eddie'd gone to try the back door and was headed around the house when Gryder had fired, hitting Eddie in the head. Eddie'd dragged himself a few feet before he lost consciousness. While I'd been stuck in the hole out back, Brett had pulled Eddie out of the line of fire, possibly—*hopefully*— saving Eddie's life. Brett and Ross carried Eddie to the Navigator. Brett had then grabbed the pipe and returned to rescue me. My God! How brave of him.

I owed him my life.

My wrist had swollen, the skin pulled tight over bones that didn't seem to fit together anymore. The injury hurt like hell, but I endured it as if it were a penance. It was my fault Eddie had been shot. I was the one who'd asked for his help serving the search warrant. I was the one who'd failed to perform a thorough search of the house, failed to find the gun Gryder used against us.

Brett looked down at my arm, noting the swelling in my wrist. "We need to get you to a doctor, Tara. Right away."

No way would I ride in the same ambulance with Gryder, give him the pleasure of seeing my tearstained cheeks. Instead, Brett helped me into the front seat of his car and followed the ambulance to the small local hospital.

Only one doctor was on duty in the ER facility, and once he learned the details of my injury, he made my treatment a priority over Gryder's. I emerged from the hospital a couple of hours later. On my arm was a fresh white cast, a souvenir from a bust sure to go down in the annals of IRS history and proof positive of the dangers of my job.

The helicopter had flown Eddie to Parkland Hospital's trauma center in Dallas. With Ross following close behind, Brett hauled ass back to Dallas, his speedometer not dipping below eighty-five until we hit the city limits. Brett glanced over at me occasionally on the trip, his eyes full of unasked questions I was in no shape to answer right then.

My eyes met his through fresh tears. "Obviously I've got a lot to tell you."

"Ross told me why you were here today," he said. "The rest can wait."

Eddie was still in surgery when we arrived at the hospital. The smell of burned coffee from an empty pot left on too long met us at the door to the ER's waiting room. A television mounted on the wall in the corner played an afternoon talk show, the volume turned down to a virtually inaudible level.

Eddie's wife, Sandra, sat in a chair, dressed in a soccer mom outfit of sneakers, white shorts, and a green and gold striped polo shirt, her black hair pulled back into a ponytail. Her frightened eyes looked up as we entered. Ross stood and helped me to a seat directly across from Sandra.

I reached across the space to pat Sandra's hand, to reassure her, but I only managed to pat once before I grasped her hand in a desperate grip, as if by holding tight enough, I could somehow keep Eddie alive for her, for their daughters . . . for me, too. I lunged across the space and the two of us clung to each other, one of us terrified she'd lose her husband, the other terrified she'd lose her partner and friend.

Poor Sandra. Only in her mid-thirties and she might become a widow. And the girls. Oh, God, the girls! They might never again have their daddy to tuck them in at bedtime. Who would kick a soccer ball around the backyard with them if Eddie didn't make it? Who would accept his coach of the year award? A fresh round of sobs exploded from my chest.

I sat back in my chair, violent tremors replacing my tears. A heavy pall of guilt settled over me. Eddie'd never had any trouble until he'd partnered up with me. Something about me just seemed to bring out the whacko in people. Now, Eddie might pay the ultimate price. This was my case. It should have been me who took the bullet. It should have been me in the operating room right now.

Brett slid into the chair next to me, his arm around my shaking shoulders. I needed him now more than ever. I leaned into him, my head ducked against his chest, taking all the comfort he could give. He ran a hand down my back, trying his best to soothe me.

The Lobo darted into the waiting room then, remarkably quick for a sixty-year-old on four-inch cork platform shoes, the hem of her peasant dress whipping around her meaty calves when she stopped abruptly in front of Ross. The attorney stood and, in hushed tones, gave her a status report. Lu's brows drew together in concern. She nodded at me and Sandra, then stepped back outside the automatic glass doors and lit a cigarette, her hand quivering as she flicked the lighter. Through the glass, I saw her cheeks hollow as she took a deep puff.

Ross, Sandra, Brett, and I sat in somber silence for what seemed like an eternity, the only sound the hum of the fluorescent lights and the soft murmur of voices from beyond the swinging doors. Finally, a heavyset dark-haired nurse in pea-green scrubs stepped into the room, her gaze moving over the crowd before stopping on Sandra. "Mrs. Bardin?"

Sandra looked up, eyeing the nurse warily as if afraid to respond, afraid to hear the news about her husband. Through the glass doors, the Lobo spotted the nurse, tossed her cigarette into the bushes, and dashed inside, smoke wafting in with her.

The nurse walked over and knelt in front of Sandra. "Your husband's still unconscious, but the doctors say he was very lucky. The bullet lodged in his skull, just behind his ear. He's lost a lot of blood and part of his earlobe, but there's no apparent brain damage. The doctors expect he'll make a full recovery."

"Oh, thank God!" Sandra cried, throwing her clenched fists in the air in unbounded relief. Sandra, the Lobo, and I stood, grabbing each other in bear hugs, tears of relief flowing freely down our faces.

CHAPTER THIRTY-THREE

Coming Clean

Brett drove me home from the hospital, a heavy silence hanging between us. He opened the passenger door and helped me out of his car. At my front door, I handed Brett my keys and he unlocked my town house. Inside, I hung my raid jacket on a hook in the coat closet and aimed straight for the kitchen. Henry scrutinized me contemptuously from atop the armoire as I walked past without bothering to give him a pat on the head. Annie ran out from under the couch and trotted after us, apparently feeling brave today.

"I could use a glass of wine." With my left hand, I wrestled a bottle from the wooden wine rack on the counter, nearly dropping the damn thing.

Brett took the bottle from me. "You're not supposed to drink alcohol when you're on painkillers."

"Oh. Right." Damn.

Annie jumped into my lap as I flopped into a seat at the kitchen table. Brett returned the bottle to the wine rack and poured us each a glass of juice instead.

He slid into the chair across from me. He took a drink, then slowly twirled his glass with his fingertips, watching me intently, waiting for me to say something, to explain.

But hell, I didn't even know where to start. All I could think of to say was, "I'm sorry I wasn't totally honest with you, Brett."

Fortunately, he appeared more confused than angry, at least for now. "Why didn't you tell me you were investigating Gryder?"

I looked down at the cat on my lap and ran my hand down Annie's back, trying to build my nerve. I took a deep breath and forced myself to look at Brett. "I wanted to tell you, Brett. Really. But . . ."

"But what?" He continued to peer expectantly into my eyes.

I squirmed under his piercing gaze. I didn't want to tell him that I'd doubted him, that I'd suspected he might be in cahoots with Shelton and Gryder. But he'd saved my life today, saved the life of my partner, too. If I owed him my life, then I owed it to him to be honest, too, didn't I? "Until today I thought you might be involved in Gryder's scam."

Brett's eyes flashed with shock before dimming with hurt, and his usually strong shoulders slumped. "My God, Tara." His voice was soft and sad, with an undertone of indignation. "How could you think that?"

I looked down, unable to meet his wounded gaze any longer. I had been utterly stupid to question his integrity and my distrust hurt him, deeply. He had every right to feel offended, betrayed. I'd feel the same way if someone I cared about had misgivings about me. Still, there had been grounds for suspicion, hadn't there?

I took a deep breath, steeled my nerves, and spilled my guts. "It started with the brochures you took to Gryder at the lake house and the box of checks and cash you brought back to Shelton. It seemed odd that the two of them would trust you with so much money if you weren't involved with them. At the hotel, I heard you arguing with someone on the phone, something about a deal for fifty grand in cash. You seemed pretty cozy with Shelton and Gryder at the ballpark and when I asked you later what you three had been talking about you said it wouldn't interest me, which seemed evasive. You mentioned you had some investments that had paid off recently and I thought those investments might be with Gryder's company."

I stopped to gauge his reaction, but Brett said nothing, just waited for me to continue.

"An informant from First Dallas Bank tipped us off about some suspicious activity relating to Gryder. When I interviewed the informant, he said you came into the bank several times with Michael near closing time and had private meetings with Stan. And then, last night, I saw your car parked in front of Shelton's house."

Brett was quiet for a moment, his expression pensive as he tried to sort through everything I'd just thrown at him. Finally he spoke. "I didn't give much thought to the boxes Stan and Michael asked me to shuttle back and forth. I figured I was simply doing them a favor, saving them some travel between the lake house and Dallas, and that their business wasn't any of mine." He paused a moment, skewering me with a pointed look. "Apparently they trusted me more than you did."

I cringed at the dig, knowing I'd earned it but hating it all the same.

"The phone call at the hotel was with one of my landscape suppliers. The guy made a bunch of promises to me, then tried to jack up the prices after I'd placed a large order. When I was talking with Stan and Michael at the ball game, they spent the whole time trying to outdo each other with their sexual exploits. I would've walked away, but since Stan invited us to the game I didn't want to be rude."

"What about the closed-door meetings at the bank?" I asked. "And the investment?"

"Chelsea's car was towed when she parked illegally at a nightclub in Dallas. Michael left Chelsea his car to use and bummed rides with me to and from the lake property and bank a few times while the car was in hock. Every meeting I had with Stan was about the landscaping project. He and Britney changed their minds about a few things and I had to rework the plans several times. Michael sometimes sat in on our meetings so he could mooch scotch from the minibar in Stan's office. The investment I mentioned was some land northeast of the city that I bought a couple of years ago. An oil and gas company paid me a small fortune to drill a well on the property."

He'd covered all the bases but one. "Why were you at Shelton's last night?"

"I wasn't, Tara. I was at my parents' house. Stan's their next-door neighbor. He's lived there since I was a kid. Hell, I used to mow his lawn."

"Oh." Damn. "Wish I'd known that."

Their relationship as longtime neighbors further explained why Shelton trusted Brett with the checks and cash, and why Brett hadn't considered the arrangement necessarily peculiar. I gave Brett a feeble, contrite smile. His explanations made perfect sense. Which meant I'd made a perfect ass of myself and, quite possibly, ruined a perfect relationship.

He leaned toward me across the table. "Why didn't you just ask me about these things?"

"How could I, Brett? If you had been involved it would've blown the investigation. And how would I have known if you were telling me the truth? I had to find out for myself. It was my only choice." I hesitated a moment before reaching out to him. He let me take his hand. I gave it a firm squeeze. "I'm sorry I ever doubted you, Brett."

Brett stared at me for a moment, his expression confused, disappointed, troubled. But who could blame him for feeling such a mix of emotions? I'd given him a lot to deal with. Hopefully, not too much to deal with.

"You were going to tell me tonight about what happened on Tuesday."

"Right." I remembered our earlier phone conversation, Brett's concern when I had put the discussion off. I'd gotten lucky. After what went down today, a drug-dealing ice-cream man with a shotgun hidden under his freezer would seem like chump change.

After I gave Brett the rundown of Joe's arrest, he emitted an elongated groan, looking down at the table and running his hands through his hair until it stood up in crazy spikes. "How did you feel today, Tara? How did you feel Tuesday when you arrested the ice-cream man?" He looked up at me. "Weren't you scared?"

"Terrified," I admitted. "But once things were over, I felt good. Proud, even." Annie stretched out her nose to sniff my cast as I scratched at the dry, itchy plaster encircling my thumb. I sat up straighter in my chair. "My work means something, Brett. I've taken a drug dealer off the streets and put a con artist out of business. I've kept elderly couples from losing their life savings, protected kids from drugs, maybe even saved lives." I wasn't bragging. I was simply letting him know why I found my job so fulfilling, why I wanted to keep doing it—despite the risks.

Brett's face softened. He looked down, his fingers drumming on the tabletop as he appeared to be thinking things through, attempting to sort out his feelings, make sense of this mess. Finally, his fingers stopped drumming. He shook his head once as if to arrange his thoughts and looked up at me.

My heart seemed to stop beating as I asked the million-dollar question. "What are you thinking?" I hoped he wasn't thinking it was time for me to find a new job or him to find a new girlfriend.

"Three things." He counted on his fingers as he spoke. "First, I'm hurt you would think I'd be involved in a scam, but after everything you've told me I can see how you got that impression. Second, seeing that bastard standing over you with a gun pointed at your head made me more frightened and more furious than I've ever been in my life."

The first and second things weren't so bad. "What's the third thing?"

His cocked his head. "You look hot with a gun in your hand."

"Hot, huh?" I could deal with hot.

He gave me a small, sexy smile. "I've never dated a woman who could handle a gun. On some weird level, it's arousing."

"I've got handcuffs, too, and I'm not afraid to use them."

"Good to know." He relaxed back in his chair. He paused for a long moment, his eyes gazing into mine. "I'm not going to lie to you, Tara. I'll fear for you every day." He took in a long breath and let it out slowly. "More than anything, though, I want you to be happy. Your work is important and it means a lot to you. I'll just have to sack up and deal with it, huh?"

I stood, walked around the table, and grabbed him in a bear hug, my chin on top of his head. "You're a great guy, Brett," I said into his wild hair.

He gently pulled me down onto his lap. "No more secrets?"

"No more secrets. I promise." I gazed back at him and

drew an *X* over my heart with my index finger. "Cross my heart and hope to die."

He put his forehead to mine. "Don't ever hope to die, Tara."

He had a point. In my line of work, it just might happen.

My stomach growled then, reminding me not only that I'd missed lunch but that I'd also invited Brett over for dinner tonight. "Hungry?"

"Starved."

We fixed two bowls of Fruity Pebbles. When we were finished eating, Brett rinsed our bowls and spoons in the sink and stuck them in the dishwasher. Henry wandered in then, loudly demanding his dinner. While I fed the cats, Brett went out back to feed the orphaned dog.

When Brett returned, he pulled me to him and kissed my forehead. Complete and utter exhaustion took over my body and I leaned against him for a moment, barely able to stand on my own. We took our glasses into the living room, plopped side by side on the couch, and drank our juice while unwinding and watching a sitcom on BBC America.

Brett's hand rested on my knee, his thumb rubbing soft circles around my kneecap. A warm heat raced up my leg, stopping at my upper thigh and turning into a warm pulse of desire. Who knew a kneecap was such an erogenous zone?

My earlier exhaustion was now forgotten. I closed my eyes and leaned my head against Brett's shoulder as his circles slowly made their way up my thigh. "Promises, promises," I whispered.

Brett scooped me up and carried me upstairs to my bedroom, leaving the light off. We slid onto my rumpled bed. Brett kissed me gently, caressing my stomach, his hand slowly working its way from my belly up under my shirt, inch by inch, much too slowly for my current state of arousal.

"Brett?"

He nuzzled my ear. "Yeah?"

"Make me forget everything that happened today."

He paused for a moment, moaned, then bit that sensitive spot between my neck and shoulder. I gasped with pleasure.

This time as we made love, cries of passion echoed off the walls. The sex was rough, primitive, and profoundly satisfying. We ended up rolling off the bed, tangled in sweat-soaked sheets, to finish our lovemaking on the floor. Anne watched us from her hiding spot under the dresser. I probably should be ashamed to be doing this in front of her. But I wasn't about to stop.

When we were both spent, Brett rolled onto his back next to me, panting from exertion. When he was finally able to catch his breath, he glanced over at me. "Well?"

"Well what?"

"Did I make you forget?"

I gave him a fully gratified grin. "Forget what?"

The alarm blared at seven A.M. Friday morning. Damn. I'd forgotten to turn the thing off the night before.

Brett snuggled up to my back, spooning me as he spoke softly into my ear. "I want to show you something."

I shot him a sexy smile over my shoulder. "I thought you showed me everything last night. Some things twice."

"Not quite."

We decided we could both use a vacation. We called our offices to let them know we'd be playing hooky today.

"You've earned some time off," the Lobo agreed. "Just be sure to fax Viola your firearm-discharge report."

Ugh. Another form. Another interrogation. Another entry in my personnel file. I hoped the incidents wouldn't affect my chances for promotion later.

Brett and I took a long, leisurely shower together and had two more bowls of Fruity Pebbles for breakfast before heading out with the dog in tow. At my request, Brett stopped by the nail salon, patiently perusing a *People* magazine while the technician trimmed, filed, and painted my nails, repairing the damage caused to my French tips by the preceding day's gunplay.

When I was finished at the salon, we drove to Brett's house. On the way, I called Alicia from my cell and updated her on recent events.

"I used to wonder whether you were brave or crazy," Alicia said when I'd finished. "I've decided now you're both."

Napoleon yapped happily and jumped on us as we came in, overjoyed to see his master who'd been AWOL and to receive his overdue breakfast. While I stood by, ready to break up a fight if necessary, Napoleon sniffed the bigger dog, who sniffed him back. Both tails wagged. A good sign. Brett had offered to take the dog off my hands. I knew the orphaned beast would be happier here. Not only would he have Napoleon to keep him company—and vice versa—but Brett worked a more regular schedule than I did and had more time to devote to his pets.

Once the dogs had settled down with their bowls, Brett stood, took my hand, and led me down the hall to his home office. A desk situated in the middle of the room was covered with paperwork, everything from tractor warranty information, to landscaping proposals, to invoices for bedding plants. He waved me over to a drafting table situated under the window and spread a blueprint on the surface.

The paper featured what appeared to be a rural property dotted with several dome-shaped buildings and one large square facility. "What's this?"

A broad smile spread across Brett's face. "The design for Ellington Nurseries."

"Ellington Nurseries?" I looked up at him.

"We've had trouble finding reliable nursery suppliers, so I've decided to start a landscaping supply business, grow some of the plants and trees myself."

Having control over the landscaping stock would not only reduce the uncertainty and hassles, but it would also allow him to keep a bigger share of the profits on his projects.

"Wow. I'm impressed." I looked back down at the blueprint.

He pointed to the dome-shaped structures. "These are greenhouses." His finger continued on to the square building. "And this will be the wholesale facility. It's not ready yet. I planned to take you out there once it was all complete, to surprise you."

Aha! The nursery explained the entries on Brett's tax return, the business deductions he'd claimed. The last piece of the puzzle fell into place.

"The gas well I told you about is at the back of the property. It's beautiful out there. Twenty acres with lots of trees and a creek running through it."

"Deep enough to skinny-dip in?"

A smile tugged at his lips. "As soon as your cast comes off, we'll find out."

I stopped by the hospital Saturday morning. Sandra met me in the lobby and led me to Eddie's room. My partner lay in bed, the bright white bandage on the side of his head stark against his dark skin. He was hooked up to an IV and a heart monitor emitting soft, rhythmic beeps. His eyes were closed, his chest rising and falling slowly.

"He still hasn't come to," Sandra said. "But the doctors have assured me it won't be much longer." She took a seat beside the bed. "Eddie?" She rubbed Eddie's arm and caressed his cheek with the back of her hand. "Eddie, can you hear me?"

Eddie moved a little in the bed, emitting soft groans and grunts as he fought to regain consciousness.

I stepped to the head of the bed. "Quit being a wuss, dude," I whispered in Eddie's ear. "A bullet to the head is no big deal. It builds character."

Eddie's eyes remained closed, but his mouth spread in a slow, dopey grin. "I know I'm not dead," he murmured softly in a hoarse, gravelly voice, "because that certainly isn't an angel talking." He opened his eyes, blinking against the harsh overhead lights.

"Eddie! Thank God!" Sandra threw herself on his chest and dissolved into sobs again, this time crying happy tears.

Eddie slid his hand across the sheet, resting it on his wife's back, the clear plastic IV tube draped over her heaving shoulders. He turned his head to me, taking a deep breath before speaking. "Did we get Gryder?"

"Hell, yeah," I said. Thanks to Brett, of course. I gave Eddie the details. "Emptied my entire clip. I can only imagine the paperwork we're going to have to fill out."

Eddie cringed but gave a soft chuckle. "Don't remind me."

Warm tears welled up again in my eyes. I bit my lip. "Eddie, I'm really sorry. This is all my fault."

"Bullshit," Eddie snapped, both his expression and voice firm now. "This isn't your fault, Tara."

"Yes it is. I didn't look under the mattress in the bedroom. I should've found Gryder's gun."

Eddie shook his head, grimacing as the motion apparently hurt his wound. "Who knows where he hid that thing. I'm the one who told you white-collar types go down easy. I let my guard down. I should've known better, been more careful." He paused a moment, his eyes softening now. "You're the best partner I've ever had, Tara. You're smart, tough, and one hell of a shot. I wouldn't want to work with anyone else."

I wiped my tears with my sleeve. "Really?"

"Really."

The nurse glanced into the open door of the room and noticed Eddie was awake. She came in. "How are you feeling, Mr. Bardin?"

"Never better," Eddie said.

The nurse offered Eddie some ice chips.

"No, thanks. Got any Heineken?"

Brett and I decided to spend a couple of days with my family. I had so much to tell them, but big news is best delivered in person. Brett swung by for me Saturday afternoon in his freshly washed SUV, the bloody evidence of Eddie's tragedy rinsed from the cargo bay.

We enjoyed each other's company, the three-hour drive to my parents' house seeming to take no time at all. Brett had never been to my hometown of Nacogdoches. As we drove through town I pointed out some of the sights, including the Old Stone Fort built by the town's founder in the late 1700s and the L. T. Barret Memorial, erected to honor the man who had drilled the first oil well in Texas back in September of 1866, when the earth still sported an intact ozone layer.

I instructed Brett which turns to take and soon we were on the outskirts of town, pulling down the noisy gravel road that led to my parents' house. Brett parked his truck in the shade of a pine, cut the engine, and took in the stately Victorian farmhouse. "Wow. It's beautiful."

"Don't look too closely," I admonished him as I swung open the truck's door and climbed out. "The whole thing's held together with duct tape."

My parents stepped out onto the porch to greet us, Mom wearing a floral-print sundress and Dad in jeans and a blue button-down, sleeves rolled up to just below the elbow.

Dad came down the steps, stopped by the truck, and held out his hand to Brett. "Nice to meet you, Brett."

Brett gave my dad's hand a firm yet friendly shake. "Likewise."

"Tara!" my mother cried when she spotted the cast on my arm. She rushed down the steps. "What happened to you?"

Brett and I exchanged glances.

"It's a long story," I said. "One best told over lunch." I knew my mother would have a fully stocked fridge and, frankly, I was looking forward to being taken care of a little.

Brett reached into his truck to retrieve the gifts he'd brought for my parents. "These are for you."

Mom was impressed by the hanging basket Brett had brought for her, filled with lush blue trailing verbena. She was also impressed by the dessert wine he'd brought for us to enjoy later. She handed the plant and wine to my father, then took both of Brett's hands in hers. "Glad to know you, Brett. Tara's told us a lot about you." She glanced over at me, questions in her eyes.

"There's a lot more to tell," I said.

My mother looked from one of us to the other. "Well, come have some lunch and catch us up."

We sat around the kitchen table, drinking sweet tea and eating fried baloney sandwiches, a down-home delicacy that had been a regular staple of my childhood.

Brett took a bite and groaned in delight. "This is delicious."

"Yeah," I said, "especially when you consider what baloney is made of."

"Tara, you hush," my mother scolded, giving me the evil eye over the top of her tea glass. Some things never change.

When we'd eaten all we could, we pushed back our

plates and updated my parents on the recent developments. My parents gaped when I relayed how Gryder had taken potshots at the two of us and put Eddie in the hospital, my mother reflexively putting a hand over her heart when I told her about being trapped in the hole, out of ammo, waiting to die, until Brett had whacked Gryder with the PVC pipe and brought me Eddie's gun.

Dad's forehead creased with fury. "You should've shot the son of a bitch, Tara."

"Nah." I waved my hand dismissively. "Too much paperwork. It'll be much more fun to take shots at him on the witness stand."

Dad turned to Brett then, giving him a pat on the back. "You've got some mighty big *cojones,* son."

"Harlan," Mom spat, scolding Dad now. "Watch your language." She turned to Brett. "You were extremely brave, hon. I can't tell you how grateful we are for that." She gave each of us a squeeze on the shoulder while she cleared our plates. "I'm glad you two worked things out."

Brett's gaze met mine and we exchanged smiles.

Later that afternoon, Dad set up a paper target on a bale of hay in the backyard and taught Brett how to shoot a handgun, a hunting rifle, and a shotgun. Mom and I sat in lawn chairs to watch. Brett had surprisingly good aim for a beginner. All that time on the golf course, aiming for a tiny flag hundreds of yards away, had given him a good eye. When they finished their shooting lessons, Brett helped my father perform a tune-up on his ancient John Deere tractor. Brett seemed right at home in the barn, a smudge of engine grease on his chin.

My brothers brought their families over for dinner. We put the extra leaf in the dining room table and feasted elbow to elbow on a fried-food fiesta, everything from catfish to okra to jalapeño hush puppies. Brett hit it off with everyone, discussing this spring's rainfall with my father, organic gardening with my mother, and pickup trucks with my brothers. He even entertained my nieces and nephews with recounts of Napoleon's silly antics. When dinner was done, the dessert wine he'd brought served as the perfect complement to Mom's cherry pie.

I'd often wondered how Brett would get along with my parents and brothers. He'd been raised in such a different environment. But he fit in easily, comfortably, like he belonged here. Like one of the family.

Would he become an official member of the family someday? It was too soon to tell. But he was definitely the kind of guy I could see myself filing joint tax returns and creating dependents with.

CHAPTER THIRTY-FOUR

Here We Go Again

Ross O'Donnell called my cell Monday morning to catch me up. Gryder had gone before the judge this morning—with a new attorney, of course—and had been denied bail as a potential flight risk. He faced an assortment of charges. Tax evasion. Criminal fraud. Money laundering. Racketeering. Attempted murder of federal agents. With so many varied counts against him, there was no way he'd skate this time.

Neener-neener.

As for Stan Shelton, we'd given Josh the pleasure of arresting him. The Banking Department had set its sights on him, too. Shelton faced a varied, though slightly shorter, list of charges than Gryder. He'd posted bail and been released, but he'd likely serve some time for his role in the scam. His personal accounts had been frozen until it could be determined how much he'd profited from the Forex con. One of the vice presidents had taken over Shelton's job at the bank and immediately given Dave Edwards, our informant, his long-overdue promotion.

If the rumor mill was right, both Britney and Chelsea had promptly filed for divorce. Looked like Stan and Michael would be filing single next year.

As we headed back to Dallas that afternoon, Brett detoured by his nursery property, situated fifteen miles northeast of Dallas, stopping his truck on the shoulder of the road. Three complete yet empty greenhouses stood near the center of the property, with another under construction next to them. There wasn't much else to see except the nursery's potential, but I had no doubt Brett would make it a success.

Our next stop was Eddie's house. He'd been released from the hospital and was recuperating at home. When Sandra led us into the bedroom, we found Eddie sitting up in bed, plump white pillows stacked behind his back, one adorable pigtailed twin nestled on each side of their daddy, watching cartoons. Eddie was all smiles, the only sign of his near-death experience an oversized bandage on the side of his head.

I plopped myself down on the buttercup-yellow duvet, folded back at the foot of the king-sized bed. "So, lazybones, when are you coming back to work?"

"Next week," Eddie said. "Try not to get yourself into trouble while I'm out."

"I'll do my best."

I introduced Eddie to Brett. "Glad to finally meet you," Eddie said, shaking Brett's hand. "Word is you pulled me out of harm's way." He glanced down at his daughters, then back up at Brett. He choked up, his voice breaking. "Can't thank you enough, man."

Brett gave a quick, modest nod and smiled at the girls.

I glanced around the room. On the windows were yellow curtains that matched the bedcovers. The fabric was sheer and poofy, the sides pulled back in oversized bows.

"See?" Eddie said. "Too frilly."

"I like them."

Eddie snorted. "Should've known. You women always stick together."

"I'm with Eddie on this one," Brett said. "Those curtains are awful."

"Right?" Eddie held out a fisted hand and Brett bumped knuckles with him. Eddie turned back to me. "Josh hacked into Gryder's computer. He had a little trouble getting in until he figured out the password was"—he put a hand over the outer ear of each daughter and pulled their little heads to his chest to block the other ears—"blow job."

I rolled my eyes. "Why am I not surprised?"

The phone rang as Eddie released his squirming girls. He picked up the receiver from his bedside table. "Hello?"

I could only hear his side of the conversation. "Hi, Lu . . . Feeling great . . . Tell me." His voice rose an octave, betraying his excitement. "Two mil? No shit?" The twins looked up at their father and frowned. "I mean, no kidding?" He glanced at me. "She's right here with me. I'll tell her. Bye, Lu." He returned the phone to its cradle and flashed me a grin.

"What's up?"

"The collections division seized over two million in assets from Gryder's bank accounts, plus a ski boat he'd just purchased, his car, and a case of hair gel."

I sat bolt upright. "We did it!"

"The Lobo can retire now."

In all likelihood, the majority of the funds would be returned to the duped investors rather than added to the government's coffers, but Lu would be credited with the take nonetheless.

My partner raised his right hand for a high five. With

the cast on my right arm, I had to use my left to return Eddie's gesture. A bit awkward, but it got the job done.

Reassured Eddie was recovering nicely, Brett and I left him with the gifts we'd brought—a recently released thriller novel, a six-pack of Heineken, and a new straw Stetson cowboy hat that would hide the hard-earned scar on his temple.

A dozen voice-mail messages awaited me when I returned to the office Tuesday morning, mostly fellow agents congratulating me and Eddie for getting the Lobo to the hundred-million mark. I'd brought my tax return to work on and finally completed the darn forms. I was due a four-hundred-dollar refund, enough to pay for the bikini I'd ordered and then some. Woo-hoo!

The Lobo stepped into my doorway, wearing a lemon-colored knit pantsuit with a flared hem and cuffs edged in green rickrack. Groovy.

"Hi, Lu," I said. "We're getting plans in the works for your retirement party. Have you turned in your notice to the DFO yet?"

"About that." She leaned against the door frame and crossed her arms over her ample chest. "I've given it some more thought and I don't think I'd be happy sitting at home all day. I've decided to hang on another year or two."

"After all this talk about retiring you're staying on?"

She shrugged. "Consider it a motivational tool. It worked, didn't it?" She handed me a check for one-third of the ten-grand bonus. The rest would be split evenly between Eddie and Josh. She gestured for me to follow her. "Come on. Got a new case I want to discuss with you."

I grabbed a legal pad and pen from my desk and followed Lu to her office. A man stood at the window inside, looking out onto the dreary, drizzly downtown streets. The April showers had hit town. Next month they'd bring the May flowers. This month, though, the rain brought only fender benders, traffic tie-ups, and the frizzies.

As Lu closed the door behind me, the man turned around. He was fiftyish, with thick, dark gray hair. He wore a stylish gray business suit and a serious, intent expression. Though he wasn't tall, he was stocky and had a commanding, formidable presence.

Wasting no time, he stepped toward me, holding out his hand. "Nice to meet you, Miss Holloway. I'm George Burton."

I went rigid. "*The* George Burton?" As in the name at the top of the organization chart? The big cheese? The grand poobah of IRS Criminal Investigations?

He nodded. "Flew in from Washington last night."

Holy crap! I took his hand and shook it the best I could given the cast on my arm, praying I didn't look like a gaping idiot. I'd hoped to meet him someday, but I'd never expected to have this opportunity so early on in my career. "Nice to meet you, sir. This is an honor."

Lu rolled her eyes and plunked herself into her chair. "Save your flattery. George doesn't like suck-ups any more than I do."

Although Burton gestured for me to take a seat, he didn't take one himself, instead returning to his spot at the window. Though he appeared to be addressing the skyscraper across the street, it was clear he was speaking to me. "Lu tells me you've done some good work in the short time you've been with the IRS."

Did she mention I'd had to fire my gun on two occasions? "Thank you. I love my job."

"We're putting you on a new case. A big one."

A big case? I was flattered. Obviously, they wouldn't assign me to an important investigation if they didn't think I was capable of handling it. My lips spread in an enthusiastic grin. "The bigger the better."

He turned to me now, his narrowed eyes and severe expression instantly chasing the smile from my face. "Not only is this case big," he said, "but it's highly sensitive." He paused a moment, eyeing me as if trying to determine if I was up to the task.

I sat up straighter in my chair and tried my best to look competent, focused, and intelligent.

"You ever heard of Marcos Mendoza?"

I shook my head.

"I'm not surprised," Burton said. "He's very private. Keeps a low profile here in the States."

Lu pulled a photo out of a file folder on her desk and handed it to me. The photo featured an attractive Latino man wearing a tuxedo. A few strands of silver streaked through Mendoza's otherwise dark hair. Mendoza's arm was draped over the shoulders of a pretty teenage girl in a bright purple ball gown. Judging from the matching widow's peaks the two shared, I guessed the girl to be his daughter. A sprawling, Spanish-style mansion appeared behind the two.

"That photo was taken three months ago, at his daughter's *quinceañera* in Mexico. Mendoza is a U.S. citizen. His wife is a Mexican national from a wealthy, well-connected family. Mendoza maintains a home for his family in Monterrey, as well as a penthouse in Crescent Tower here in Dallas."

Not too shabby. The price of downtown penthouses ranged from a few million dollars on up.

"We've been after this guy for years," Burton continued. "We thought we were close a few years ago, had infiltrated his operations, but then one of our own tipped Mendoza off."

I gasped. "That's low."

"That's greed," Burton said. "Mendoza paid the agent a fortune and set him up in a nice place on the beach near

Cancún. Mendoza's got the Mexican judges in his pocket. They won't extradite the agent back to the U.S. for trial."

The traitor now lived in luxury in a virtual paradise. So much for justice.

"Mendoza's one smart bastard," Burton said. "He's insulated himself with layer upon layer of corporations, partnerships, and limited liability companies. His name doesn't appear in any of the paperwork, but it's clear he's the one in charge of the operations, the one reaping the financial rewards. He pays his top brass enough to keep their mouths shut. Of course the fact that one of his associates disappears every so often encourages them to keep mum, too."

A lump formed in my throat. "Disappears?"

"Perhaps that's an overstatement," Burton said. "We did find the last guy. In Houston. San Antonio. Harlingen. His right foot surfaced in a Dumpster in El Paso."

The lump in my throat was forced aside by rising bile. Instinctively I covered my mouth.

Lu chuckled. "Don't get your panties in a wad, Holloway. Once Eddie's back from leave, I'll assign him to work with you on this one. I'm sure you two can handle it."

Burton stepped toward me now, stopping in front of my chair and looking down at me. "Given the nature of this case, you can't tell anyone anything about it. Not your mother. Not your friends. Not your cats." How'd he know I had cats? "You can't even breathe a word of this to your coworkers."

Whoa. Telling Brett was definitely out of the question, then. Damn! Just days ago I'd promised there'd be no more secrets between us. I'd even crossed my heart, hoped to die. Yet here I was, already forced to betray him once again.

But what choice did I have?

Read on for an excerpt from Diane Kelly's next book

Death, Taxes,
and a Skinny No-Whip Latte

Coming soon from St. Martin's Paperbacks

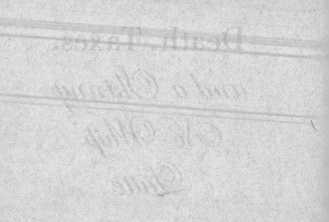

CHAPTER ONE

$\mathscr{I}$t's a Terrifying Job, But Somebody's Gotta Do It

"I'm scared shitless, Eddie."

I looked over at my partner as he pulled his maroon minivan into the parking lot of the downtown Dallas post office. Eddie Bardin was tall and lean, sporting a gray suit and starched white dress shirt with a mint-green silk tie. Though Eddie was African-American, he was more J. Crew than 2 Live Crew, like a dark-chocolate version of President Obama. Not that Eddie'd ever condescend to vote for a Democrat.

Despite the fact that my partner was a conservative married suburban dad and I was a free-thinking single city girl, the two of us got along great and made a kick-ass team. Problem was, the current ass we were aiming to kick was a very frightening one.

A row of cars stretched out in front of us, a solid red line of brake lights illuminating the early-evening drizzle.

Apparently I wasn't the only slacker who waited until April fifteenth to file their tax return.

Eddie pulled to a stop behind one of those newer odd-looking rectangular cars. Cube, was it? Quad? Shoebox? He glanced my way. "Scared? You? C'mon, Holloway. You've been slashed with a box cutter and shot at and lived to brag about it." His scoffing tone might have been more believable if I hadn't noticed his grip tighten on the steering wheel. "We're invincible, you and me. Like Superman. Or toxic waste."

I scrunched my nose. "Ew. Couldn't you have come up with a better metaphor?"

"I'm exhausted, Tara. And besides, it was a simile." He muttered something under his breath about me being the child the education system left behind.

I might have been offended if I thought he truly meant it. You didn't become a member of the Treasury Department's Criminal Investigations team without a stellar academic record, impressive career credentials, and a razor-sharp intellect, not to mention a quick hand on both a calculator and a gun. Not that I'm bragging. But it's true.

I toyed with the edge of the manila envelope in my lap. "Battaglia and Gryder were chump change compared to Marcos Mendoza, and you know it."

Eddie and I had recently put two tax cheats—Jack Battaglia and Michael Gryder—behind bars, but not before Battaglia had sliced my forearm with a box cutter and Gryder had taken pot shots at me with a handgun and pierced Eddie's earlobe with a bullet. Not exactly polite behavior. What's more, neither of those men had a history of violence prior to attacking us. The focus of our current investigation, Marcos Mendoza, was an entirely different matter. Due to a lack of evidence, Mendoza had never been officially accused of any crimes. Yet his business associates had a suspicious history of disappearing.

And resurfacing.

In Dumpsters.

In pieces.

They'd found parts of Andrew Sheffield, a former employee of Mendoza and presumably his most recent victim, spread among garbage receptacles from Harlingen, to Houston, to San Antonio and beyond. The sanitation department of El Paso found Sheffield's right foot, still clad in a pricey Ferragamo loafer, in the trash bin behind the police headquarters. Andrew had yet to be fully accounted for.

Hence my scared shitless state of mind.

We inched forward, the only sound the occasional *swish* of the intermittent wipers as they arced across the windshield.

I knew Eddie well enough to know his lack of response meant he agreed with me. But perhaps some things are better left unsaid.

Think happy thoughts, I told myself. *Fluffy kittens. Colorful rainbows. Big tax refunds.* Of course it would be easier to think happy thoughts if my right arm didn't bear a plaster cast. I'd fractured my wrist diving out a window to evade Gryder. The con artist was rotting in jail now. Hey, now there's a happy thought.

Finally, we reached the bleary-eyed postal worker standing in the parking lot. She wore a dark blue rain slicker and held an umbrella in one hand, a white plastic box bearing the Postal Service eagle logo in the other. I unrolled my window, letting in the dank air, and dropped my return into her nearly full bin. "Thanks. See you next April fifteenth."

A drop of rain rolled off the tip of her nose as she forced a feeble smile.

How much longer would I file single? I wasn't yet ready for diapers, play-dates, and PTA meetings, but the thought

of joint tax returns didn't frighten me as much as it used
to. Maybe because of Brett Ellington, the sweet, brave,
and incredibly sexy landscape architect I'd been dating
the past few months.

I rolled up my window and checked my watch. "6:37
PM. That's a personal best."

Eddie snorted. "I filed my return two months ago. Already got my refund."

I cut my eyes to him. "Oh, yeah? And what did Sandra
and the twins spend the money on?"

He turned away, letting me know my jibe had hit home.

"Ha! You are whipped, dude."

"Better to be whipped than to be a procrastinator."

"Hey, I've been busy." Busy shopping and packing for
my upcoming trip to Fort Lauderdale with Brett. I'd made
no less than three trips to Victoria's Secret before deciding on the red satin teddy with black trim and those little
clip thingies to hold up a pair of old-fashioned fishnet
stockings. I couldn't wait for Brett to see me in it. He was
a perfect gentleman in public, but in the bedroom, well,
let's just say he left his decorum at the door. A new red
chiffon cocktail dress had made its way into my shopping
bag, too. The spaghetti straps and handkerchief edge gave
it a feminine and festive feel. It was the perfect outfit for
the American Society of Landscape Architects' awards
banquet, where the Society would bestow its prestigious
Landmark Award on Brett for his work at City Hall. I'd
scored the dress forty percent off at an after-Easter sale.
Christ may have risen, but Neiman's had lowered its prices.
Hallelujah!

I stifled a yawn. Not surprising I was tired since we'd
been on the job since nine o'clock that morning and at the
office until midnight the last few nights reviewing paperwork. The Mendoza case was so highly sensitive we'd been
forbidden to discuss it with anyone, even our co-workers.

To maintain secrecy, we'd been forced to perform some of our work after hours.

Why the secrecy? Three years ago, a special agent named Nick Pratt had infiltrated Mendoza's operations and purportedly obtained evidence that Mendoza had earned enormous sums of illegal, unreported income. Though the details were sketchy, Mendoza allegedly got wind of the investigation, bought off the agent, and set up the traitor in a luxury beachside condominium in Cancún, Mexico.

Tough life, huh?

Lawyers at the U.S. Department of Justice fought to extradite Pratt back to the U.S. on charges of obstruction of justice and theft of government property, but the Mexican judge refused to cooperate, claiming all Pratt did was quit his job at the IRS, which wasn't illegal. He argued the theft charge wouldn't stick since Pratt's government-issued cell phone and laptop were mailed back to the department. Of course all of the data had been wiped clean, the hard drive erased. Presumably Mendoza had the judge in his pocket.

If only money were at stake, the government might have let the case go. But given the recent increase in body count, the case was reopened. Come hell or high water, Mendoza had to be stopped.

And it was up to Eddie and me to stop him.

We'd been on the case only four days, since Eddie had returned from his medical leave, sans one bullet-damaged earlobe. We'd finally finished our review of the documentation. We'd painstakingly searched through Mendoza's tax filings and those of the businesses linked to him, document by document, page by page, entry by entry. But this guy knew how to cover his tracks.

We'd found no evidence. No leads. *Nada*.

Nada damn thing.

CHAPTER TWO

*C*affeine Fiend

Eddie drove on, pausing at the exit to the parking lot. "Where to?"

I pulled the papers out of the manila envelope and riffled through them until I found the printout listing directions to Pokornys' Korner Kitchen, a small Czech bakery and cafe located in an older section of Garland, one of the many mid-sized cities making up the sprawling Dallas suburbs.

"Central north to Loop Twelve," I instructed.

Eddie gave me a salute. "Aye-aye, Captain."

He took a right turn out of the parking lot and in minutes we were driving north on Interstate 75, known to locals as Central Expressway, one of a dozen freeways that crisscrossed the extensive Dallas metroplex area. We had a 7:30 appointment scheduled with Darina and Jakub Pokorny, the owners of the bakery.

Early last week, the head of the Treasury's Criminal Investigations Department had flown in from Washington D.C. to meet with our boss, Lu "The Lobo" Lobozinksi. George Burton had asked Lu to put her top agents on the Mendoza case. She'd immediately assigned Eddie to the investigation. Eddie was one of the more senior special agents, experienced, clever, and intuitive, the *crème de la crème* of the Dallas team. As a rookie, I hardly qualified as *crème* of any sort yet. I should've been flattered to be put on the case. But I feared it was my skills with weaponry rather than my skills with a calculator that landed me the assignment. If ever there'd been a case that called for an agent adept with a gun, this case was it.

As far as career enhancement, this was definitely the job to be on. As far as my boyfriend Brett, well, if he knew what I was up to he'd shit a brick. Maybe even a cinder block.

Before coming to work for the IRS, I'd spent several years in the tax department of Martin and McGee, a large regional accounting firm. I'd learned a lot at the CPA firm, earned a lot, too. But sitting in a cubicle day after day, week after week, year after year, sorting through paperwork and staring at a computer screen had eaten away at me. I'd felt unsatisfied, caged, trapped. It was a good job, but it wasn't right for me.

Of course I still dealt with a fair share of paperwork and computer screens at the IRS, but I loved the action in Criminal Investigations, hunting down clues, the thrill of the chase, the sense of purpose and justice. My job called for financial savvy, investigation expertise, and weapons proficiency, a unique skill set possessed by very few. This job was made for me.

Still, Brett worried about the risks my job posed. Who could blame him? He'd recently witnessed me cowering in a hole amid a shower of bullets and risked his own life to rescue me from certain death. Of course I'd done my best to convince him that the attack was a fluke, that the vast majority of tax evaders surrendered peacefully, that most special agents went their entire careers without facing real danger.

But I wasn't most special agents. As Eddie'd once pointed out, something about me brought out the homicidal tendencies in people.

Forcing that ugly thought aside, I rubbed my eyes, which were beginning to feel heavy. "I sure could go for a latte."

"Not a bad idea."

Eddie took the next exit and pulled into the drive-thru of a twenty-four-hour coffee house. New York isn't the only city that never sleeps. Dallas doesn't doze either. "The usual?"

"Yep."

The barrista at the drive-thru opened the window, releasing the invigorating aroma of French roast. I closed my eyes and took a deep breath. "Mmm."

Eddie placed our order. "Small coffee. Black." Eddie was a purist. I was anything but. "And a large caramel latte. Extra whipped cream, heavy on the drizzle, sprinkle of cinnamon on top."

Just the way I liked it. Eddie knew me well. I handed Eddie a ten from my wallet. "My treat."

When we received our drinks, I removed a dark-skinned doll from one of the cup holders. "Nice job on Barbie's hair," I said, holding up the doll. One of Eddie's girls had pulled the doll's hair up into a ponytail on the top of her head, and the black locks cascaded down on all sides of the doll's head, making her look like a palm tree.

"That's not Barbie," Eddie said. "That's Christie. Barbie's black BFF."

"Oh, yeah?"

"Yeah. My girls set me straight on that right away."

I tossed the doll into the backseat. "Girls'll do that for ya'." I sipped my hot drink. Yum. I could live on these things.

Eddie stuck his cup in the holder, pulled out of the drive-thru, and headed back onto the freeway.

My thoughts returned to the case, to Mendoza and the earlier agent he'd bought off. What kind of guy would turn like that? Give up his job, his reputation, his life for money? Nick Pratt had to be one sorry-ass son of a bitch. "Hey, Ed. I was wondering. How well did you know Nick Pratt?"

Eddie hesitated a moment, seeming to consider his words. "Nick and I partnered on several big cases, had a beer together after work every now and then. He covered for me when the twins were born."

I snorted. "You make him sound like a nice guy." As if. Nice guys don't sell out.

"You would've liked him. He was a country boy, wore snakeskin cowboy boots with his business suits. Didn't take crap from anybody." Eddie cut his eyes my way. "He was a lot like you, only with—"

"Guy junk?"

"I was going to say more muscle and less mascara. He could handle a gun almost as good as you, too."

I offered a derisive snort. "Nobody handles a gun as good as me." They didn't call me the Annie Oakley of the IRS for nothing.

Eddie rolled his eyes. "I said 'almost.'" He stopped talking for a moment and looked solemnly out his window as if looking for answers to questions that had none. "When Pratt disappeared, Lu told the rest of us he'd turned in his resignation. Claimed the stress of the job got to him."

"Did that seem odd to you?"

"Odd? Yeah. He was smart as they come. Hard-working, too. But he could be a little intense at times, so we bought the story. Figured he'd burned himself out. It happens." Eddie's jaw flexed as he clenched angry teeth. "But I can't believe he turned on us."

"Guess you never can tell, huh?"

Eddie turned back to me then, our eyes locking. "People aren't always who they seem to be."